For Cat

SUMMER OF FEAR

On a bad night here in the canyon, the wind can hit so hard it feels like my house is coming down.

The place is built on stilts, perched high on the steep east slope of Laguna Canyon. From the road below, the stilts look frail as mosquito legs, wholly insufficient for holding up a home. When the wind is strong, it can change course a hundred times a minute, trapped as it is by the canyon walls. With too much gale in too little space, the air doubles back, howls in fierce frustration, then whips around for another bellowing pass. Order breaks down. My home sways, leaning with each crazy reversal. Windowpanes ripple and timbers groan. Within the fury of these moments, I await a nudge from the master's hand. Infinity yawns back.

Some nights, when the wind is at its worst, I sit outside on the deck, feel the deep sway of the structure in which I live, look down through thirty feet of darkness to the sandstone below, and admire the way that nature can go so quickly from order to chaos. The popular notion is that nature's world is ultimately ordered and systematic, that only man's woeful intrusions can ruin that balance and harmony. This is not true. When I sit on my deck in the blackness of a high-wind night— the higher the better—I realize that the natural world isn't neatly ordered, isn't flawless, isn't perfect. Sometimes it is just like our human one: angry and yearning for mayhem. People want to "get back to nature." But she wants to get back to man sometimes, too, to regress to the liberating, transcendent state of violence. On a dark night with a high wind in the canyon, it's obvious.

My wife and I are leaving for Mexico next month. That leaves me thirty days to finish this, then pack our bags and drive to the airport.

My name is Russ Monroe, and I am a crime writer. I was once a cop. I retired from duty ten years ago to write—first newspaper pieces, then books. My first book, *Journey Up River: The Story of a Serial Killer,* was a mild success, well received, and into a second printing before publication. My last two books you've probably never heard of. I find them sometimes at Friends of the Library used-book sales, often inscribed to the original purchaser, who started the book on its journey to the fifty-cent bin. I harbor resentment at this, one of my thousand faults. I still write newspaper stuff because I need the money.

This is the story of the Summer of Fear. *The Summer of Fear.* I coined that phrase myself. Not terribly imaginative, I know, but how much imagination can you get into a headline?

There are a few things you should know about me. I offer them both as background and for the simple reason that for the first time in my life as a crime writer—and I pray the last—I myself play a major part in the story. This is a terrible burden for an author. But it is nothing compared to the burden of that summer, and I was there, centered in the middle of it like 2.6 million other Orange Countians. It changed us all.

◼   ◼   ◼

I am forty years old, tall and dark-haired, of English-Irish extraction. My family has been here in the county since 1952, when the orange groves outnumbered the housing tracts and it was a beautiful place to live. My great-grandfather married a Yukon Territory dance-hall girl during the Alaskan gold rush. His son was an explosives expert who invented a triggering device for dynamite that was patented and is still in use today. He secretly wrote science-fiction stories, which I found in a trunk of his belongings passed down to me by his son—my father. The stories are frightening things, obviously written more as an exorcism of my grandfather's many demons than as entertainments or for serious publication. I used one of his titles for my second book, *Under Scorpio*, which, if you read the critics, should have been locked away in a massive old tool chest, as was grandfather's original text.

My father was ranch manager—Director of Field Operations, Citrus Division—for the SunBlesst Company here in Orange County. SunBlesst, during my father's tenure, made the transition from farming to leasing out land for development. Later, in the sixties, they began selling off the groves outright. My father grew bitter as he watched his kingdom dwindle. At the end of his working days, I remember him as a tall, wiry man who still rode his groves on horseback. He was always tall in the saddle, paramilitary and fierce, to no particular effect. He stated his refusal to let the shrinking of his empire shrink him.

But on the inside, it did. He grew harder and more knotted with each season. He moved way out to one of the remote canyons when he finally retired, five years back. The canyon is called Trabuco, which is Spanish for a crude firearm the settlers brought to the county in the 1700s. My father now lives in a cold little cabin, deep in Trabuco, a place constantly in the shadow of the haunted native oaks.

My mother's side of the family accounts for a certain self-absorption I am prone to, along with an appetite for chaos, and a distrust of authority that runs, I will confess, not very far beneath my generally peaceful surface. (This made my first career in law enforcement difficult.) She was a farm girl who grew up an only child, spent hours alone with her imagination and a pet goat named Archie. To say that she mastered self-reliance is an understatement. To my mother, most things in life were intrusions on her inner world, her secret world, the world she inhabited with Archie for those long years of childhood. She graduated from high school early. One day shortly after, she closed her eyes, put her finger to a map of the United States, and found herself pointing at Denver. At age seventeen, she was living in the YWCA there, working as a secretary and taking an occasional job as a model for Daniels & Fisher department store. My father fell in love while looking at her through a store window one afternoon. Two months later, they were married and moving to California for my father's work. A year after that, Russell Paul Monroe was in the offing.

She lived out in a remote canyon, too—one very much like my father's—until her death three years ago, exactly one year to the day since divorcing my father. She was fifty-five. I thought it was telling that they divorced, left the SunBlesst ranch house where I'd grown up, then each proceeded to his and her own distant canyons, ending up just a few miles apart. They each proclaimed happiness then, a contentment at being apart that they had never admitted when they were together. I want to think they were lonely, but this may be a son's way of believing that his parents still loved each other. She died in her sleep; likely of an aneurism, though I would not allow—because of my father's insistence—an autopsy. The idea of scientists sawing into the head of this intensely private woman seemed to us an atrocity beyond bearing. She had a long history of hypertension.

■   ■   ■

It is winter now, but nothing is the same—not here in my house with my wife, not two miles south of here in the city of Laguna Beach, where so much of it all happened, not anywhere in a county that once prided itself on Disneyland, an airport named John Wayne, a thriving weapons industry (they call it aerospace), and real estate prices among the highest in the nation.

It has all changed because the Summer of Fear taught us that there is something about ourselves—something in us, of us—that breeds a terrible, terrible thing.

The Midnight Eye—I first brought his name into print—was not our first. We have a track record of serial killers here in Orange County. But before, we always let ourselves view them as predators who inflicted themselves on us. You've heard of these monsters. You've read about the break-ins, the strangulations, the knifings, the close-range hollow-points, the knockout drugs hidden in beer offered to hitchhikers, the pentagram on the palm of the drifter, the poisoned, sodomized remains of servicemen quartered like beef, then bagged and dumped beside freeways or far out in the National Forest that makes up the border of our county (near where my father now lives).

You have heard of them—the Freeway Strangler (ten alleged victims); the Nightstalker (fourteen); Randy Kraft (seventeen). Incidentally, they play bridge against one another now, in the maximum-security wing of Vacaville State Correctional

Facility. This has been documented in, of all places, *Vanity Fair* magazine. (Kraft generally wins. He is impatient with the Freeway Strangler and treats him like a crude child. The Nightstalker is vindictive and makes foolish opening moves. Kraft admires his aggressiveness.)

These men we regarded as outsiders. Even Kraft, a mild-mannered computer programmer who grew up in the county, seemed alien. Maybe that was because his victims were all young men, many of whom he had either seduced or raped in one way or another. Kraft's homosexuality seemed to confine him to a subtle, mysterious world. He inhabited a place where few of the county's straight population could imagine themselves. The unspoken rationale went something like this: I'm not gay, so I'm not going to worry. During Kraft's trial I had a number of talks with him, and I was struck by his intelligence, his humility, his apparent forthrightness. I might add that he was found to have in his possession at the time of arrest (1) a dead Marine Corps private in the front seat of his car and (2) an address book with the names and descriptions of several men who had been drugged, buggered, chopped to pieces, and dumped. A great many of the other entries were of men listed by police as "missing." In spite of all that, Kraft never worked his way into the county's subconscious the way that the Midnight Eye did during our Summer of Fear.

The Midnight Eye came from among us. He was created by us, fostered by us. In the end, I think, people believed he *was* us, and in a smaller degree, of course, that we were him.

Now it is winter, and the county can begin to forget.

One thing I will not forget is this: The truth will not always make you free.

2

I can't fully explain why I called Amber Mae Wilson that night, Saturday, the third of July. Yes, I had once been her lover, but that was twenty years ago. Yes, I had thought about her—off and on—for all of those twenty years. Yes, I had been married, happily and without a trace of regret, for the last five.

Maybe it was the dream I had had the night before, in which four-year-old Amber Mae Wilson stood on my porch buck naked and said to me, "My name is Amber Mae. I'm three years old. I live in the white house. Can I have a cookie?"

That was a story—a true one, I believe—Amber had told me about herself back when we were in love. I say I believe it was true because it seemed to capture some of Amber's several essences: her boldness, her innocence, her willingness to change the facts, her nakedness. But as I came to understand in the two brief years we were together, Amber had always been and always remained in the process of inventing herself. She invented herself to make Amber Mae Wilson—I understand now—someone she could stand to be around. For her, the truth was never static or absolute, never irreversible or binding. It was a wardrobe to be changed as she saw fit.

I called her from a bar that night—a moist, sweltering night—and got no answer, just the machine and message. It was twenty minutes past midnight and I believed I had a mission.

So I drove down to her place in the south of town and sat outside in my car, looking at the wrought-iron gate, the palms illuminated by ground lights, the courtyard behind the gate that featured a fountain in the shape of an airborne dolphin with a stream of water coming out of its mouth. The huge home loomed behind, locked in darkness. It was high in the coastal hills and looked down over the Pacific. She had paid $2.8 million for the place and the 3.5 acres it sat on, as reported in a local paper. The neighbors were hundreds of yards away.

This was the third night in a week I'd been there.

Amber had lived in this house for five years—some kind of record for her, I'm sure. I know for a fact that she had changed the landscaping three times. First, brick walkways and copper weathervanes everywhere, lots of wooden flower boxes—Cape Cod run amok. Next, a xeriscape of drought-tolerants, decomposed granite trails, cactus. Finally, this California-Mediterranean theme. I know all this because my work takes me all over the county. Some things, I can't help but notice.

As I said, the night was unforgivingly hot. I rolled down the windows and laid my head back on the rest. I thought of my wife, Isabella, at home. Isabella, the truest love of my life, who not only taught me love but allowed me to learn it. She would be asleep now. She would be wearing the red knit cap to keep her head warm, in spite of the temperature. The wheelchair and quad cane would be close beside the bed. Her medications would be lined up on a low shelf within arm's reach,

each dose contained in a white paper cup, ready to be taken by Isabella in the dark, half-asleep, still stunned by the last ingestion.

Isabella was twenty-eight years old. She had a malignant tumor in her brain. She had been living with it for a little over a year and a half on that night of July 3, when for the third night in a week I sat in my car outside Amber Mae Wilson's home in South Laguna, wondering whether I would find the courage to go up and ring the bell on the gate.

You may say, right here, that this Russell Monroe has some explaining to do.

You can't possibly imagine how much.

I can only tell you that then, on the humid, heated night of July 3, I was deeply unwilling to explain anything, most of all to myself. I refused to. That would have been contrary to my mission, which was this: I was in the process—I hoped—of beginning a secret life.

I opened the glove compartment, took out my flask (slim, silver, engraved to me "With all my love, Isabella"), and drank more whiskey. *Isabella*. I replaced the flask, lighted a cigarette, laid back my head, and looked out to Amber's courtyard. I tried to banish all thoughts from my mind. I replaced them with memories of Amber, of those days from our youth when the world seemed so ripe for our picking, so pleased to have us aboard. Isn't there always a year or two in everyone's twenties that, when remembered, seem as near to perfect as life can get?

That was when I saw Amber's front door open and shut, and someone moving across the courtyard toward the gate.

It was a man. He wiped something off with a handkerchief before letting the gate swing shut behind him. He walked with his head down and his thumbs hooked into the front pockets of his jeans, the handkerchief balled in his right fist. He turned south on the sidewalk without hesitating, took three steps to the curb, then angled off across the street, let himself into a late-model black Firebird, and drove away.

He didn't see me, but I saw him. Oh, did I see him.

His name was Martin Parish. He was the Captain of Detectives, Homicide Division, of the Orange County Sheriff's. He had been an acquaintance, then a friend, then a near friend of mine for twenty years.

Marty Parish was a large man with kind blue eyes and an ardent love of bird hunting.

Marty Parish and I had graduated from the Sheriff's Academy together, winter of 1974.

Marty Parish had introduced me to Amber Mae Wilson at our "commencement" bash.

Marty Parish was the only man that Amber had ever married. It lasted one year, about fifteen years ago. Now he had just left her home after midnight and wiped his fingerprints off the handle of her gate.

I watched the Firebird's taillights disappear in the dark and wondered whether Martin Parish had come to draw from the same well that I had. I always thought Martin was stronger than that. A wave of shame broke over me. For Martin? I wondered—or for myself?

I called Amber's number from my car phone and got the machine again. What an inviting, conspiratorial voice she had!

I took another swig from the flask, set it back in the glove compartment, then rolled up the windows and got out.

Don't do this, said a receding voice inside me—*you have no reasons, only a million excuses*—but I was already walking toward her gate. It was not locked. The house was dark except for a very minor glow coming from what was probably the kitchen. I knocked, rang the bell, knocked again. The door was locked. I followed a pathway of round concrete stepping-stones around to the backyard. The moon was half full, and in the mild light I could make out the rolling lawn, the orange trees huddled in a grove at the far end, a pale island of concrete. Steam leaked up from the edge of a covered hot tub.

The sliding glass door stood open all the way. The screen door was open about two feet. Open! My heart dropped, but I fought to remain thoughtless. Is this how a secret life begins? The drapes were pulled back on their runner. To let in the night air, I guessed: Air conditioning gives Amber headaches. But the screen. Had Marty come in this way? So I pressed against that screen with my fingertip. The slit was six inches long, vertical, just left and slightly above the lock. You could have cut it with a table knife.

Demons began to lift off inside me; I could feel them swirling up through my arteries, coiling along my spine. They felt like sea creatures that live down where there's no light— knife-toothed, blunt-headed, colorless. I could feel the vein in my forehead throbbing.

What I did next went against all my training as a police officer, against my instincts as a writer, against the logic of the situation, even against the emotions I felt boiling up inside. Somehow, I lost it. I panicked. I let out the fear. Maybe it was only a nod of respect for Amber Mae Wilson's well-being—I would like to believe it was just that.

I jumped inside, found a light switch, flipped it on, and yelled her name.

"Amber."

"Amber."

Amber!

No answer. I charged through all the downstairs rooms— empty. I threw on lights willy-nilly. I tripped over my own feet, charging up the stairs, hit my shin on a step, hard. I couldn't get enough breath. The light seemed arbitrary, beveled with the darkness into treacherous edges, planes, drops. Everything was moving. I crashed into a low credenza in what appeared to be her study. Magazines slipped off the top; the lamp tilted and fell over and the bulb burst with a soft pop.

Amber!

Then I was running down a long hallway toward a half-open door. Paintings on the walls streaked past; the ceiling pressed down low. My heart was working so hard, there was hardly a space between beats. I was inside the door. The switch was just where it should have been. The room snapped to attention with light. Nothing could have prepared me for what I saw.

At first, I thought it was blood. My second thought was a correction: Red spray paint. The biggest words were on the mirrored walk-in closet:

SO JAH SEH

Across the wall over the headboard of the bed:

AWAKEN OR DIE IN IGNORACE

On the far wall:

MIDNIGHT EYE IS RETURN

And everywhere the peace symbols, those hideous sixties ankhs or chicken feet or modified crosses or whatever in hell they were—everywhere, trailing around the room in poorly formed, inarticulate red circles.

Amber lay on the floor by the bed, faceup, her arms and legs spread. She wore a blue satin robe. Her hair—thick dark brown waves—spread out against the carpet. Big pieces of white and pink were scattered through that dark hair, strewn from what I could see had once been her head. And her face! Amber's lovely, ageless, beguiling face—somehow lifted back now, flap-like, hinged on only one side, turned almost down, as if contemplating her own hair afloat in that pond of blood.

In ten years of police work, I had never—

In ten years as a crime writer, I had never—

Never. Not once. Not even close.

I can remember standing there, weight back on my heels, thighs quivering, face raised to the ceiling, mouth stretched open to release a howl that I instead choked dead in my throat. The throttled scream came from deep inside, from my very toes, it felt like—a wild discharge that left my eyes throbbing and a terrible pain from my stomach clear up to my jaw. The peace symbols swirled around me.

I went to the side where her face was. I turned toward her and, bending low, looked into her dull gray eyes. They were lifeless and remote as old glass.

Never, in ten years—

Reaching out from the red that had settled over me—everything I saw was red, tinged in red, outlined in red, steeped in it, drenched in it—I touched my fingers to my lips, then stretched my hand toward hers. From my mouth to Amber's, a distance it seemed my hand would never cover, how much farther could it be? And what a cold and trembling arrival, fingertip to cool gray lip!

I stood. In the bathroom, I got a handful of toilet paper, went back to Amber, and for a moment looked around the room again. I noted the packed suitcases—still open—on the floor beside the walk-in. Where had Amber been going? I forced myself to look at her again. Then I knelt, reached out my hand, hesitated, then reached out again, wiping her lips with it. Then the light switch in her bedroom as I turned it off. The other switches, too—all of them, even ones I was sure I hadn't touched. Then the spot where I'd fingered the screen-door flap, the front doorknob, and a few red, dreamlike moments later, *finally*, the same cold brass handle of Amber's gate that Martin Parish had cleansed.

It was roughly ten thousand miles to my car.

■   ■   ■

I drove to Main Beach and waded along the shore, soaking myself to the thighs. I jammed my hands in the sand, threw the seawater against my face. I stood there, knee-deep, and scrubbed my arms with the rough, dripping mud. Now what? I could call the cops—anonymous tip. I could call the cops, tell them who I was, and that Martin Parish had killed his ex-wife. I could do nothing, sit back, wait, and watch them go to work. The one thing, though, that I was not going to do—even with the smell of murder in my nostrils—was to admit that I had been at (inside!) Amber Wilson's home, ever. For Isabella, I told myself. For us.

I had one more thought. And though it seemed as dismal a product as my mind had yet rendered, I will confess also to the sizable thrill that accompanied it down my spine and into the chaos of my heart. As I stood there, earnestly grinding my fingernails into the abrading Pacific sand, I realized I might have just stumbled onto the biggest story of my life. Golden material, pure and mine only. *Play this smart,* I told myself. For here was more than a secret life, more than a diversion. Here upon my platter was the kind of event—*event!*—that, if handled right, could do more for my career than a dozen secondhand crime books. *I knew these people. I'd been there.* I felt a little sick to see finally, in all its hidden rapacity, the true face of my own

14

ambition. But at that moment, with the chill of the ocean working its way up my legs and arms, what shame could find airtime in a soul still writhing with the image of pure horror that was Amber's face?

Finally, I went back across the beach to my car in the light of the half moon. Couples walked arm in arm. Lovers kissed on the boardwalk. A dog trotted by.

So Jah seh.

So God speaks.

Suddenly, it hit me how badly I wanted to be home, in bed beside Isabella. The yearning surged over me as if a dam had been blown. God, take me back. I drove fast out the canyon, up the winding road that ends at our precarious, stilted home.

In the kitchen, I checked my knees for blood. I saw none but sprayed them with a stain lifter, anyway. Stripping down upstairs, I threw everything washable into the hamper.

I showered forever—hot at first, then cold.

Isabella whimpered and placed her arm across my chest when I got in beside her. Her face was next to mine and I could smell the breath of sleep from her.

"Your heart is pounding," she whispered.

"It's because of you."

She "hmmed." I knew what it meant: a small smile, tender and brief, already drifting back toward the sleep from which it had come.

"It's late, R-R-Russ."

"I only had three."

"Hmm . . ."

"I love you, Isabella."

"I love you, too."

"I really, truly love you."

"Hmm. You're my h-h-hero."

The pounding in my chest got louder and faster. I remember it getting so big, it finally just picked me up and carried me, with the sound of boots descending steps, down into the detailed silence of dreams.

3

I spent the next morning at the Laguna police station, waiting
for the call. I was going to get them to take me along. Although
Amber's home stood on unincorporated land, the Laguna force
was contracted to respond to emergencies and felony calls. So
I flattered the chief about a book he wanted to write, but I had
to cut off the conversation and head for the bathroom, where
I threw up, camouflaging it by flushing the toilet. I had never
vomited in revulsion in my entire life, before that day.

My need to talk about what I'd seen—to confess—was
an actual ache, located near the center of my chest, just an inch
right of my heart. I began to understand what a guilty suspect
feels under interrogation. Oh, to *know*. I spoke frankly, with
grave sincerity, to the detectives—the subject was the drought
in California, I believe. I sneaked off to the rest room and threw
up again. I yakked with one of the narcs, the watch commander,
the dispatcher, a couple of meter maids. They all looked at me
with suspicion.

But the call never came. No reported homicide at 1316 Ridgecrest. It was a slow morning, considering it was the Fourth. It made sense, I thought; someone might not find Amber for days.

Besides, the Laguna cop house wasn't where I really wanted to be anyway. Where I wanted to be was in Marty Parish's face—right, straight in it, looking directly at him when he got the news. Finally, by noon, I couldn't stay away from him any longer and I drove up to the county buildings in Santa Ana, where the Sheriff's Department is headquartered.

He was at his desk, clipping his fingernails, when I walked in. I knew he'd work the Fourth of July. Marty always had a thing about holiday pay: He could get almost two days' pay for one day of work, then take off some time during the season and go hunting on the county's nickel.

I put my briefcase on his desk and took out three boxes of new .20-gauge shot shells. My hands felt flighty and cold. "Bought these by accident," I said, which was true. "Thought they were twelves. They're yours for the Browning."

He nodded, set down the fingernail clipper, then stood and shook my hand. His eyes were blue, shot with blood. The left lid hung just slightly lower than the right, giving Martin his usual expression of sleepy calculation. His skin, as always, had the weathered tan of the outdoorsman. He was forty-two years old but looked to be in his upper forties.

Marty was a born predator. He had 20/15 vision, fine hearing, and a heavy, muscular body that he could deploy with surprising speed and agility. He was a superb marksman, one with a seemingly inborn understanding of distance, trajectory, and lead lines. Years ago, in our hunting days, we had made each other gifts of game freezers, along with an annual wager as to whose would be filled with the most birds by end of season. (Marty always won.) Parish had the thick hands and blunt fingers of a carpenter, though I never knew him to be handy with a hammer or saw.

The bags under Marty's bloodshot blue eyes were dark and heavy. He had cut himself shaving, and a little horizontal line was visible directly on top of his Adam's apple. It had bled onto his shirt collar, which was open. Even in the air-conditioned county building, the Fourth of July heat was a presence.

"How's Isabella?"

"Doing well. Strong."

"She's an incredible woman. You don't deserve her."

"People keep telling me that."

"I guess the chemo is about over?"

"One more, then we wait and see."

"I admire you, Russell. You've been good about all this."

"I don't see much choice."

"Some guys would just give up. Take a hike or something."

"No."

Marty was a soft-spoken man, and he seemed to get even quieter when Amber left him those many years ago. But when excited or drunk, he could be loud and demonstrative. At times, he struck people—me included—as almost dull. But if Marty Parish was a little slower on the uptake than some, he never had to be told something twice. Some people were convinced that Marty's brooding, big-jawed silences were the mark of some deeper understanding. I was convinced of that. There was, I had always believed, a certain moral force in Martin Parish.

He had remarried since Amber, to a very pretty woman named JoAnn. They were going on fourteen years together. They had two daughters. Marty was uncommonly devoted to his family, if his well-known humorlessness about womanizing was any indicator. Martin Parish was a private man. He drank too much.

He pointed to the chair and I sat. "So, what's up?"

I had prepared my cover, although my curiosity was real enough. "The Ellisons," I said. What a strange, terrible thing it was to have seen what I saw—and what I knew Marty had seen, too—and not say a word about it.

"It was bad," he said.

"You guys serious about a two-eleven?"

"That's what it was—started as, anyway."

"Hmm."

"Hmm shit, Monroe. A robbery is a robbery no matter how it ends up. Want to see the pictures?"

"Thought you'd never ask."

He threw a manila envelope onto my lap and I opened it.

Mr. and Mrs. Ellison—Cedrick and Shareen—had not strictly parted, even in death. Shareen had gone down in about the middle of her bedroom, one cheek against the hardwood floor. Her husband had come to rest on top of her. They were both naked. Someone had done the same thing to their heads and faces that had been done to Amber Mae Wilson's. I felt a cold wash break out on my face, and that vein in my forehead beating.

There is something even more obscene about CS photographs than the crime scene itself. The scale is reduced, the horror concentrated and depersonalized at the same time. And there's always the sense that you're intruding needlessly into some great, miserable intimacy. At the scene itself—if you're a cop, at least—there's the redeeming belief that you are there to, well, strange as it seems, help. In the case of these pictures was the added mystery of where the blood began and the flesh left off, because the Ellisons were both black, and the photographic contrast is different from that of people with lighter skin. The sprawl of their young, strong bodies was dreadfully graceful.

"You figure one creep, or two?" I asked.

"Two. That's a lot of bashing for one guy to manage—drop them both in their tracks."

"Have any physical yet . . . that shows two and not one?"

Marty glowered at me and picked his fingernail clipper back up. We were approaching a sore spot for him, and we both knew it. One of the consequences of my quitting and getting rich and famous (ha) was that cops like Marty thought they should hold out on me, as a matter of principle. It was a game: If I suspected something that they didn't want to see in the paper (I was taking newspaper work from the *Orange County Journal* then), they tried to steer me away from it. If I *almost* knew something for certain, they'd deny it. If I'd start to look in the right place, they'd point me someplace else. A game.

But this particular point—the one we both knew I was getting to—was not part of a game at all. It was as dead serious as anything can get.

"Hell yes, we've got physical. We don't sit around here and dream things up."

"If it was a robbery, what'd *they* take?"

"I can't release that now."

"No."

"No's right."

"So what about the Fernandez couple?"

"What about them?"

"Can I see the shots?"

If Marty didn't show me the Fernandez pictures, the assistant medical examiner would, and Marty knew this.

The two envelopes passed in midair. I studied the CS shots of Sid and Teresa Fernandez, both age twenty-six, brained while sleeping in their apartment. Neither had even made it out of bed. The sheet was hardly disturbed. Sid was scrunched down under it like any working man might be after a long day

21

in the shop. Fernandez painted cars. His head was broken open and most of what had been inside it was sitting on the pillow beside his face. Teresa was beside him, turned the other way, her face and right arm hanging over the mattress and her dashed skull leaking hugely onto the floor. It looked as if their heads were growing devils, and I thought of Isabella and wondered how big it was now. It was the size of a golf ball thirteen months ago. Was this a better way to go, all at once, or one cell at a time? The clammy wash had come to my face again. I'd showered again that morning but already stank like a man who knew too much.

"And of course, this was one creep," I said. "And you've got physical evidence to prove it."

"We don't prove things. The DA does."

"You're avoiding the point."

"What is the point, Russ?"

"A serial."

"Two incidents don't make a serial. Maybe there's another book in it for you, is what you hope."

"Look at this, Martin. Four bashings in a month. All in the county. All around midnight. Point of entry the same—a sliding glass door left open because of the heat. You say the Ellisons were robbed, but nobody's found out what got taken. I talked to some of the evidence techs last week and they found an eighteen-inch pearl necklace in the bed-stand drawer."

"The evidence techs ought to keep their mouths shut."

"While you tell me it started as a two-eleven? The Fernandez couple goes the same way, but you're not calling *them* a robbery. Look at the Ellisons. How about this? He clubs the mister first, to calm him down. But the woman is faster than he thinks—she gets up and starts across the room. She's clear on the other side of the bed, remember. He catches up halfway and lets her have it. By then, Mr. Ellison is coming at him, but

Mr. Ellison is naked, hit once already, and doesn't have a weapon. Down he goes, with his wife."

I could see Amber on Marty's floor now. She was so close, I could have touched her lips again. My throat got so tight, I had to cough to get it open.

Marty didn't look much better. His eyes had that low-gloss, matte finish that comes from not enough sleep. He was looking at the same spot on the floor that I was. Way out on the edge of my mind, somewhere between thought and fear, I let the idea float by that Martin Albert Parish had killed not only Amber but the Ellisons and Fernandezes, too. It was an ugly construct, one of those notions that start up high in your head, then quiver down into your heart, which then beats harder, trying to get rid of it. The same thing a heart does when it finds out that something horrible is real and true. *Broken Badge, From Cop to Killer,* by Russell Monroe.

Christ.

"You're going to cover this for the *Journal*?"

"Not as yet."

"Maybe they can't afford you."

"And maybe you're right—four unrelated homicides."

"Well, then what do you want?"

"Let me in on some of the physical."

"No can do."

"Because you don't have any?"

"We've got it. If we can link these killings, we'll do it. You'll know; the county will know. But, Monroe, I'm not going to start yelling fire until I'm goddamned sure there is one. Two incidents, Russ. I've got plenty of physical that tells us we're looking at two, maybe three shitheads at the Ellisons and one at the Fernandez place. We're working on it. We've released what we can release, and there isn't more to say. It isn't right to send people into a panic over a coincidence."

"Not right to let them sleep with their screen doors open in a heat wave, if there's a serial out there."

Marty Parish's face went from ruddy tan to sick pink. He looked back down to that place on his floor where Amber had been. He picked up the nail clipper. It clicked, loudly.

"Shit," he said, raising his left thumb to his mouth. "Thanks for the shells, Russ. Maybe we'll go get some quail in October. I'll have a few days off by then."

It was Marty's opening farewell, but I didn't move. "Okay. Keep the physical and thanks for the peep show. But at least come clean with me, Marty. Are we talking common sense here, or is Herr Sheriff leaning on you?"

"Beat it, Russ. You want to know what the cops are doing, you should have stayed with the cops."

"What's your gut say?"

"Where will I read about what my gut says?"

"Nowhere. I've never burned you, Martin—you or anybody else with a badge."

"You burned Erik Wald."

"He doesn't have a badge."

"Neither do you. Look, Community Relations is calling the Ellison and Fernandez shots, but I'll tell you this much. Our evidence isn't matching up—that's the truth. We're looking at two different things, at least two different guys, *not* the same one. To be honest, though, whoever conked them didn't take anything."

The idea formed that Marty was playing with me, fueling my tank with enough bad information to get me down the wrong road, or at least out of his office. It struck me as odd that the CS photos he'd just meted out to me contained no establishing shots, no wide-angles, no walls. Just bodies. Why?

"Give me one thing on him, Marty."

"*Them*, Russ."

"Them."

"You've got what I've got."

"This happens again, how are you going to stomach yourself?"

"See you later, Russ. I read about any of this and it's all she wrote for you here. I don't have to tell you that."

"Don't worry."

I stood to go. Marty was examining the drop of blood on his cut thumb.

"Have you seen Amber lately?" I asked.

Parish shook his head without looking up at me. The phone rang. He reached out, but before he touched it, he wiped his brow with the crook of his elbow, moving his arm across his forehead, blotting up the sweat.

I lingered to see whether the call was Amber's 187.

"Hi, honey," Marty said.

4

I called my editor at the *Journal* from the car phone. Car phones are supposed to be for people who think they're more important than they really are, but they're also for people who don't want to be seen making calls they shouldn't be. Like one to Amber at 12:42 last night. Like this one.

My editor's name was Carla Dance. She is a short, heavy-set woman, fiercely intelligent and unceasingly levelheaded. Over the last ten years, she had a way of dangling assignments just when I needed the money. I like her very much, and I think she likes me. Her father has cancer, and Carla takes care of him, except when she's at work. When Isabella was diagnosed nineteen months ago, Carla and I spent some anguished afternoons together in a bar up by the *Journal* offices. Something about her reasoned outlook helped me. Carla already knew then what I have come to know: When someone you love has a bad cancer, the line between hope and despair is one that you crisscross a thousand times a day. It is a true crazy-maker. I also learned that we are a closed society—we who love and care for someone with cancer. To the outside world, we proffer only optimism. But among ourselves, we can admit without feeling weak or needy or unduly bleak that the one we love may very well not be with us for nearly as long as we'd like. We are a society of helpless helpers. But there is something in our bond of foxhole faith, and something of the cleansing that I used to feel, long ago, in church.

"I may have something for you," I said.

"Sunday magazine would pay best, if it's not too grisly."

"It's too grisly. I'd call this hard news. Real hard."

"Breaking?"

"Yes."

"The Ellisons?"

I didn't mention that Carla Dance is also prescient.

"Yes again."

"What's the angle?"

"That he'll do it again."

"We'd have to be real careful, Russ. The racial overtones are touchy."

"Well, let the story slip and see how touchy it can get."

"I've worried about that, too."

"I need something first—space for another Dina story. It wouldn't have to be front of the section."

"Dina again?"

"The big game starts next week."

Dina was the DNA typing apparatus that the county crime lab bought the year before. It cost $800,000, it hadn't produced a shred of admissible evidence yet, and, worse, defense attorneys were just then getting the hang of demonstrating what "genetic fingerprinting" had been from the very start—complex, unproven, and without agreed-upon standards. There had been two reversals from higher California courts in the last six months, and one acquittal by a jury that believed the defense had put genetic typing well within the shadow of doubt. Dina, needless to say, was supposed to become the county's biggest crime-busting star. But her luster was fading before she had even gotten to trial, and nobody at the crime lab, or the Sheriff's, or the DA's office could seem to talk fast enough to quell the increasingly vocal critics. The first trial in which she would be used—the Ballard rape case—was set to open next week. The defendant was on trial, but so was Dina. A pro-Dina story by Russell Monroe in the *Journal* could help set a more comfortable atmosphere for her tryout. For me, it was a bargaining chip.

"Can the police link the Ellisons and the first couple—what's their name, Fernandez? We ran the story today that says they can't."

"They can, but they don't want to."

"We'd like it first, if and when they do. I'll make space for Dina."

"Thanks."

She told me to take care of myself, then hung up. I knew she wouldn't ask about Isabella, the same way I didn't ask about her father: The subject of cancer was not something you tagged onto the end of a business call, even one about murder. There were other times for that.

Next I called Martin Parish's boss—Sheriff Dan Winters—and pitched him my deal: a good solid Dina piece in trade for pole position on . . . I *almost* said the Midnight Eye.

I explained.

He acted as if I was a fool, which I knew he would, pretended to dismiss my offer, which I also knew he would. But the seed was planted, and that was all that mattered. That, and perhaps the fact that I'd generously volunteered my minor celebrity (and less-than-minor money) to Daniel Winters's reelection campaign two years ago. Now, Dan was knee-deep in bad ink: jail overcrowding, lawsuits, rising crime stats, shrinking budget. My offer of good ink would get under his politician's skin and it wouldn't cost him much. He said he'd think about it.

I kept the police scanner in my car turned up for the 187 at Amber's. I've got a scanner in every room of my house—a questionable luxury I paid for with the movie money from *Journey Up River*. In my early years as a successful news writer, I left the scanners on every minute that I wasn't asleep, and often when I was. Isabella put an end to this shortly after we were married. It wasn't hard for her to do—any man on earth would rather listen to Isabella's dusky smooth voice than a dispatcher droning code numbers.

But the 187 didn't come. It was 5:30 and I was starting to wonder.

So I called Amber's agent in Los Angeles and said I was Erik Wald. Erik Wald, like myself, was a former "companion" to Amber. I had introduced him to her, just as Marty had introduced her to me. That was six years ago, long after Amber and I were over, and I was escorting her socially, occasionally, without romantic interest on her part. It was my own somewhat pathetic way of keeping the possibilities open, but I brought what dignity I could to the job. Shortly thereafter, Amber and Erik were an item. I was briefly jealous, but their affair was short, and I had since fallen deeply in love with Isabella. I tracked the dashing couple in the society column of the *Los Angeles Times*. From my occasional social and professional contact with Erik, I knew that Amber had managed to keep him immersed in the quagmire of her financial affairs as surely as she had managed to keep me immersed in the swamp of my own desire. It seemed to me that Wald had gotten the better terms.

Erik Wald had never been one of my favorite people, though I was a distinct minority in this matter. As do most people in semipublic life, Erik groomed an outward persona that, like the copper casing around the softer lead of a bullet, protected his passage through the perils of media coverage, county politics, and—in Erik's somewhat unique case—the often mercurial world of academia.

He was a professor of criminology at the local state university. He had been tenured twelve years ago, at the age of thirty-one, shortly after applying the principles of his dissertation, "Aspiring to Evil: Transference Identification in the Violent Felon," to help successfully discover the identity of a rapist who had claimed eight victims in the north part of our county in six short months. The gist of Wald's paper was that because certain paranoid types are subject to delusions of grandeur (a fact), these persecuted "geniuses" could act out scenarios in which they willfully play a role totally opposed to the higher behaviors approved by society. In effect, Wald argued, they were providing their own "evil" at which to gaze in their daily lives, while at the same time satisfying their inner needs for superiority/persecution.

What it all boiled down to, he said, was a well-read, middle-class suspect of sterling reputation (possibly a church-goer) who had aspired to a higher station in life than he had achieved, likely because of some profound unsuitability in his character, or perhaps even physiognomy. All eight of the women had been elderly, some enfeebled. While the police and sheriff combined forces to round up the usual suspects, Wald fed his thesis to an ambitious black Sheriff's Department lieutenant named Daniel Winters, who linked two of the victims to a Meals-on-Wheels service provided by a church located in the north county. An investigation of the volunteer drivers revealed nothing, but Wald pressed Winters deeper into the congregation, to find that one of the actual Meals-on-Wheels cooks fit the profile rather neatly. He was thirty-four years old, a bachelor with a law degree from a Catholic (!) university who had failed the

California bar three times and seemingly retreated to a quiet life of Christian service and paralegal work. He lived with his grandmother, who, it turned out, was a friend of three of the other victims. Winters's closing net ended in a stakeout and tail done after hours and without pay, which resulted in observing the suspect—one Cary Clough—driving early one morning to a quiet suburban street, where he sat in his car until daybreak. The same afternoon, Winters established that eighty-two-year-old Madeline Stewart lived alone in the house outside which Clough had parked. Madeline was a recent sign-up for the Meals-on-Wheels program. The following night, Winters waited for Clough in an unmarked station wagon, and when Clough approached the house in the dark morning hours, Winters shook him down for suspicious behavior. Winters's yield was a red ski cap and a pair of latex gloves. He made the collar, took Clough downtown, and after some exemplary work by the crime lab, matched not only fibers from the cap to those found on four of the victims but Clough's teeth prints to those left behind in a decorative wooden apple that Clough had mistakenly tried to eat after raping his third victim!

This story, such a resonant marriage of the biblical and scientific, made great headlines, television fodder, even a "60 Minutes" segment. Wald's entry into the public eye was swift and certain. The state university tenured him a year later. Dan Winters was bumped up to the rank of captain, the youngest one in county history, and the first black. Clough got 150 years.

More interestingly, Wald was made head of the Sheriff's Reserve Units, a position for which he would neither be paid nor deputized. He was given an office on the same floor as the newly sainted Dan Winters, and the two men crusaded to make the Reserve Units into potent allies of the professional deputies. (The public ate up this idea, too: more law enforcement for the same amount of money.) All of this reflected well on Jordan

Clemens, a tough politician whose years as elected sheriff would obviously not last forever.

I watched these events from the uncomfortable position of junior investigator, uncomfortable because I could hardly wait to abandon the department ship in order to write and because my heart was still tender with the tramplings it had received from parting with Amber Mae Wilson. Moreover, I had met Wald on his late-day visits to the office of Dan Winters and had found him—against the sum of all my efforts—both intimidating and likable.

Physically, he was impressive, one of those tall and slender men whose muscles knotted effortlessly with the most casual movements. He was handsome and knew it, but he played off it in an apparently unselfconscious way that the television cameras loved. His face was wide and boyish, with laugh wrinkles parenthesizing a mouth that was quick to smile. His hair was a curly golden mop that he managed to keep rather longish but still trimmed, a perfect compromise between academic eccentricity and Sheriff's Department conservatism. He was rumored to hold a black belt in a particularly difficult Chinese-Philippine martial art and to be a collector of antique weapons. Most impressive of all was his mind, however, which was possessed of a nonchalant sharpness that left most people—myself included—eternally off balance. He could be outrageously charming and mortally offensive, all in the same sentence. One more quality about Wald struck me in those early years—namely, his willingness to offer confidences and to receive them in return. I had never met a man in whom the illusion of trustworthiness had been so deeply and convincingly cultivated. For that specific reason, I did not choose to trust him. So, when Amber Mae began asking me about this "handsome crimebuster type," I was unsurprised, if somewhat angered. I was still not fully adjusted to the idea of being a used person.

What sat most disagreeably upon my opinion of Erik Wald, though, was the simple fact that he had applied to the Sheriff's Academy three times and been rejected each. This was common knowledge in the department and had even been written about in the first feature articles regarding Wald's unconventional help in identifying Cary Clough. Wald suffered from mitral-valve prolapse, a leaking heart valve brought on by fever in his infancy. I was pleased that Wald couldn't make the physical cut, though you certainly wouldn't have known it by looking at him. His powers of compensation were magnificent. More important, however, I was solidly resentful of the fact that he had risen to such prominence with the Sheriff's without ever making the grade to join it. I saw him as some kind of immune diplomat, running stylish circles around myself and the other rank-and-file deputies. And I will confess, too, that the wit and clarity of his dissertation language infuriated me. I envied him. I found ludicrous his intimations of securing, someday, a paid position as undersheriff to Dan Winters. His ego seemed to have no limit. I derived an arid comfort from realizing that his insight into the character of Cary Clough came at least in part from kindred rumblings in his own thrice-rejected soul.

Four years later, when I was working on *Journey Up River,* Wald offered me some astonishing insight into the mind of the killer, who turned out to be a forty-one-year-old part-time butcher (really) named Art Crump. Crump was not yet a suspect at the time of my interviews with Erik. Upon Crump's arrest, most of the "insight" turned out to be misleading, useless, or wildly ass-backward. I used it in the book anyway, much to the embarrassment of Erik. Crump and I had a laugh at this up in Vacaville.

But I knew why Amber had been drawn to Erik Wald: Amber was always drawn to men who could inflict harm. And never since my first meeting of Wald did I doubt that his fury, if unleashed, might prove formidable.

So I called Amber's agent and said I was Erik Wald and asked whether he could tell me if Amber was on a shoot today.

He chuckled in the way that only busy, superior people can do.

"Just one moment," he said.

The next voice that come on was one of the last I expected.

"*This* is Erik Wald. Who the hell are you?"

I told him. Erik laughed, too. It was a low, even baritone that spoke of advantage. I let him laugh some more. I could hear Amber's agent—Reuben Saltz—in the background, joining in. When the hilarity had waned, I asked him whether Amber was on a shoot or not.

"Why?"

"It's about Grace."

I'm a good liar. Grace is Amber's daughter.

"Why not talk to Grace about Grace? She's a big girl now."

"I know that, Erik. Finding her is the hard part. I was hoping Amber could—"

"Finding Amber isn't any easier. She was supposed to work today, a shampoo deal, but she never showed. Nobody knows where she is. With five grand an hour at stake, Reuben here is a quivering mass of anxiety and thwarted greed."

I tried to sound casual. "Maybe she stayed home sick."

"Reuben has called every hour since ten. I imagine you have, too, if you really needed her. Reuben is enterprising, though. He just got back from the Wilson manse in Laguna—nobody home."

The demons starting stirring in my blood again. "Maybe she was sleeping one off."

"Nobody *home* is what I said, Russ. Reuben, the concerned mentor, has a key."

It was one of those moments when the gravity inside your chest seems to multiply. My heart felt as if it were down

34

next to the seat belt. I turned the air conditioner on high and aimed the stream into my eyes. What could possibly have happened? Didn't Reuben go upstairs?

"Well," I said, trying to steady the breath in my throat. "You know Amber."

"We know Amber," said Wald. "If I find her first, I'll tell her you were looking for her. Heh, heh."

"Heh, heh. I'll do the same."

Trying to sound satisfied, I changed the topic. "What's your call on the Ellisons and that Mexican couple?"

"I believe the cops, for right now. Talk to Marty yet?"

"Sure."

"I did, too, last week. The captain doth protest too much. To me, it looks bad. Blunt-force trauma. Quite a ring to it. Bashers are furious, very bold, and poor personal groomers. They sometimes affect beards. They often see themselves as outdoorsmen, lovers of nature. They also have the problem of what to do with their blunt instruments—leave 'em or keep 'em? You know what intrigues me? His marks are all minorities. I sense the offspring of some racist, archconservative, neofascist John Birch Society Orange Countians. So stay on it, Russ—maybe there's another book in it for you. Speaking of which, I saw *Under Scorpio* at Crown for a buck ninety-eight yesterday. Hardcover."

The two-dollar shelf at Crown is a pillory. On the other hand, a book is a book and a lot of hard work goes into one, and some are bound to do better than others.

"It wasn't that bad a book. I took some chances."

"So did Custer. I bought six anyway. Gifts, you know."

"Thanks, Erik. Still enjoying your appointment as Amber Mae's financial czar?"

"Yes. Consulting with Mr. Saltz on any of Amber's many financial messes is a balm to me. Not surprisingly, she only trusts me with the small stuff, the *liquid diet,* she calls it."

This I understood. Amber's parsimony and hypercautiousness regarding money had been clear to me from the beginning, back when she was poor and had good enough reason to act that way. I recalled a caustic remark from Martin Parish, made a few years ago, after Amber had "settled" their divorce with a mere $75,000 for the vastly outearned Marty—something to the effect of her wallet being even tighter than her ass. Could Martin's resentment have festered? I also recalled, oh, quite clearly, how Amber had previously offered me that same amount—$75,000—as enticement to keep me from filing a palimony suit. I had no intention of suing her, nor of accepting the money, and I clearly remember the bitterly comic battles we had over the issue.

What I would have given at that point, some twenty years later, to have $75,000 in the bank!

"I can smell her perfume on the checks," said Erik. "I'd screw them if I could get them to hold still long enough. It's amazing how a person so beautiful and bright can be so stupid. Speaking of beauty, how is Izzy?"

"Isabella is perfect."

"Your insurance doing what it's supposed to?"

"Yes."

"Let me know if there's something I can do for you two. We rejects have to stand together."

"The proud, the many."

"Take care, Russell, and don't try to pass yourself off as me again. You're not nearly smart, handsome, or dangerous enough."

"But I've got the same pain-in-the-ass attitude."

"Mine's better. It comes from the heart."

"When did you get one of those?"

5

That night, distressed and despairing, I made dinner for Isabella. Our dinners were always complex productions because Isabella was once a superlative cook and loves to eat. The steroids she was taking to reduce swelling in her head also gave her a robust appetite. She planned the menu; I followed her directions as best I could. The maid prepared breakfast and lunch, then went home. Dinnertime was strictly for us.

Isabella would sit in her wheelchair and direct. She was rested by then, up from a long afternoon nap that sometimes started after lunch. I would fuss around in the kitchen, trying to do things right, open a bottle of wine, and start in on it. We would talk.

It was a lot like the old days, if anything can be said to be the way it was before you have a massive seizure, are diagnosed with an inoperable tumor, undergo an experimental radiation-implant procedure, and lose most of the use of your legs because of it. No, it was really not very much like the old days at all. In fact, Isabella couldn't even look at pictures of herself from earlier times. The smiling, black-haired woman she saw in them seemed a prior blessing that had since been revoked. Isabella is not a vain person—no more than any of us are—but to see that old, strong, vital self was too much for her. She was a big woman. She had gone from 130 shapely, capable pounds to almost 200. Her coal black hair (Isabella is of Mexican descent; her maiden name is Sandoval) had fallen out with the treatments, every last beautiful, wavy shoulder-length strand. Her legs had shrunken from disuse.

It was all that Isabella—a woman who could once skip along on one ski behind a boat doing forty miles an hour—could do to struggle up from her chair and use the cane to move across a room. The stairs leading up to our bedroom were impossible, so we had an elevator installed. The first time Isabella used it, she put on a pair of angels' wings and a halo that she'd worn to a costume party just a few months before. On her lap, she carried the plastic toy-store harp. She started out smiling and ended up crying. I stood there and watched her descend, filled with that strange combination of love for this woman and fury at what had happened to her.

Isabella's world fluctuated between transcendent humor and bitter despair. So did mine.

One thing that Isabella's disease hadn't threatened was her piano playing, the lovely sounds of which would fill our home each afternoon when she got up from her nap. She played Bach and Mozart; she played the show tunes of the thirties; she played Jerry Lee and Elton John; but most of all she played her own compositions, which had come, over the last year, to be the most achingly longing music I had ever heard. When her chords echoed through our stilt house on late afternoons, it was as if Isabella herself were in the air, vibrating through every particle of the place that we called home. It was her breath, her heart, her life. She no longer taught—travel was too difficult, and she didn't want her students to see the weight she'd gained and the hair she'd lost. No, Isabella's music was no longer a profession, but it was one of the two main things that kept her sane. The other—I realized later—was me.

That night, she had chosen an impossible recipe—roast lamb and a chutney sauce I couldn't get right. The vegetables were slaughtered. The rice was dripping but hard. The meat was overdone. Every time I looked down into my wineglass, I saw the puddled ooze on Amber's carpet. I drank the bottle fast.

We were sitting outside on the deck, next to each other, facing south down the canyon toward the sea. Isabella spent hours there during the day, staring off at the parched hills.

"You drink a lot of wine," she said.

"I'm a lot of man."

"Well," she said finally, "be careful, Russ. It's getting to be every night. More than a little."

"I know."

"It w-w-worries me."

The truth of the matter is that I was drinking an awful lot then. There were two different worlds for me—the regular one and the one I could enter through alcohol. I preferred the latter. It was a place of only the past and the future, no present, a place where action won out over thought, where possibilities seemed to wait. There was no cancer in it. I was drunk when I'd called Amber the night before. I was drunk when I'd gone over there. Sober, I'd have done neither. Sober, my world had begun to be a land of pure obligation and utility. I felt like a post in the ground. But from the bottle called the twin worlds of yesterday and tomorrow—thoughtless acceleration, unrestrained speed. I needed motion. I craved it.

So I opened the second bottle. The sun had gone down, but there was still an orange glow over the hills. A vulture landed on the power pole and looked down at us. I despised it. It was a huge bird, and Izzy had named him Black Death. She named a lot of things in our hillsides. I threw the empty wine bottle at it and it flew away. The bottle vanished into the sagebrush that thrives on our thirsty hillside. Predictably, with all the new development to the south and west behind Laguna, the displaced wildlife has begun to concentrate in our hills. Deer and coyote abound, much to the denigration of local roses and cats. Hawks and vultures fill the air daily, and I have spotted, just recently and for the first time, several bobcats. I killed two five-foot rattlesnakes on my driveway last summer and captured a third that had two heads, which I donated to the Los Angeles Zoo. An older woman on our street was walking her teacup poodle one spring afternoon, only to have the tiny dog swept from the pavement by a vulture (possibly Black Death himself). Since the vulture is, according to ornithologists, strictly a scavenger, the vulture attack was downgraded to a hawk attack by the local press. But I know the old woman—her name is Astrid Kilfoy—and she's lived in this canyon long enough to tell a vulture from a red-tail. As nature is compressed, she metastasizes terrible, aberrant things. Like the tumor in Isabella's skull. Like the Midnight Eye.

I told Isabella about my day—mainly hanging around the cops trying to get the scent for my next book. I came *that* close to telling her about Amber, but *that* close was still a million miles away.

"Do you have your subject y-yet?"

"No. I'm still thinking about fiction."

"I think you'd be a fine fiction writer."

"I'm tempted and worried at the same time. Before, I've always had the story there for me. In fiction, I'd have to make it up."

Isabella thought about this for a long minute. "But that

way, it can end how you want it to. The hero can get the girl and the good guys can shoot the bad guys. And you wouldn't have to visit those terrible men in p-prison."

She asked for seconds. I served them up in the kitchen and started back outside. Around the house, Isabella wore baseball caps to hide the nakedness of her head. I liked her head the way it was—its smoothness and humility, its honesty—but I liked it a whole lot better when it had Isabella's rich black hair. Coming up on her from behind with the plate, I stopped for just a moment, rocked for the millionth time by how it had all changed. She looked like a little man sitting there, a fan perhaps, her cap tilted at a jaunty angle as she looked off into the western hills. I could see the line of her cheek, her fork held midair and not moving. God I love you, I thought. God, help me love her more. God, do something good for her or I'll cut your heart out with a chain saw and feed it to Black Death. *So Jah seh.*

I put down the plate, sat, drank. "Things are starting to scare me," I said. The wine was beginning to talk. "Nonfiction seems like a terrible thing to try to capture. Who wants to? There's no order. Killers prey on people at random. Good people like you get sick."

"Nature is cruel," said Isabella. "I quit trying to figure out why a year ago. But if you wrote f-fiction, you could change all that. The killer could get a brain tumor. The hero's wife could be beautiful and slender and have long black hair and help him solve the crime. She could cook for him. At night, she could take him to bed and love him. She wouldn't be a two-hundred-pound bald whale."

"You're not a whale—"

"I look like one. I look in the mirror and I can't believe it's me."

"You'll lose the weight when you get off the steroids. It's not your fault."

"No wonder you drink so much. I would, too, if I had to look at me."

And there sat Isabella in her wheelchair, a once-beautiful woman racked by medicine and cancer, tears running down her face and off her chin. The neurologist had warned us about mood swings caused by drugs. *Swing* is not the right word.

I knelt down beside her and put my head in her lap. The Fourth of July fireworks show started down on Main Beach and I could see the bright blossoms unfolding in the sky, followed by the distant thud of the launcher. I kept seeing Amber's head in the red explosions.

For a moment, I thought about Amber and Isabella together, about how different they were and how different—opposite, really—were the things that had led me to love each of them. What had drawn me to Amber was her mystery, her odd lack of substance, her absolute aloneness in the world. She rarely spoke of her family, and not once in the years we were together did I ever meet her parents or her sister, who lived, Amber said, in Florida. She told me once, with that natural, unforced arrogance she wore so well, that her sister—Alice, I think it was—was the only woman in the world prettier than she was. There was some feud between them that had ended in estrangement, but Amber's details were not forthcoming. She never called anyone in her family; never wrote; never mentioned missing them even around the holidays. Her family name was actually Fultz, which Amber changed to Wilson as soon as she was old enough. I wanted to protect her. I wanted to give her connection. I always believed that I could fill that huge emptiness surrounding Amber Mae. What I didn't understand until much later was that she never wanted it filled.

Years after that, when I met Isabella's family for the first time, I saw the difference in bold relief. There was a closeness there, a strong sense of interconnectedness, a blurred set of borders where she left off and her parents—Joe and Corrine—began. And where Amber was alone and vague and forever molting one skin for another, Isabella was positioned firmly with her people, forthright, and quietly content with them and with herself. As I fell in love with Isabella, I plunged gratefully into that pool of connection, wondering sometimes why I had been so taken with Amber's solitude and secrecy.

And while I sat there on the deck with my head in Isabella's lap, I was proud of her, and of myself for having had the good sense to marry her.

"When you go downtown at night, do you look at other g-girls?"

"No. I think about you."

"Then why do you go?"

"I need to be away sometimes."

"That hurts me more than anything else. That you need to get away from me. Remember how it used to be when we were always together?"

"It can be that way again. We'll have that again."

"But you need to get away from me and I understand. I know you have to dress me in the morning when you wish you were writing, and you do all the shopping and errands, and you clean up after me. And you do the c-cooking at night and the dishes. And you don't have a social life anymore because I don't want people to see what a pig you have for a wife. And I know I don't like our friends to come over. And I know you wanted babies, Russ—because I wanted them even more than you did. And I know now when you look into the future, all you can see is me getting w-worse. I can't stand the look on your face sometimes. It's so full of regret and hate. It scares me."

I drank more. "It's not you I hate, Iz. It's the sickness. It's not our life I regret. It's all the things we wanted to do."

43

"I wish I could change it. I've tried so better to get hard. I mean—"

"I know. You're doing everything you can, baby."

Her speech was deteriorating more rapidly. She stroked my hair for a long while. The fireworks burst open in colors, lobbed fading comets down toward the hills. Fresh ones wobbled upward through the darkness, leaving smoke trails. Coyotes yipped from some unspecified distance, their cries bouncing madly around the night. I looked out to the hillsides and followed the outline of Our Lady of the Canyon—one of Isabella's favorite formations. At night, two hills running one behind the other became a pregnant woman lying supine against the sky; the sandstone became her hair, the oak stands became her breasts, and the lights of the city spraying up from between her legs became a soft glow in the place her genitals would be. Isabella had named her. You couldn't even see her during the day. Isabella had even named the sound the wind made—or was it the cry of some misplaced animal?—a keening moan that issued from deep in the canyon on some nights. She called him the Man of the Dark.

"Our Lady of the Canyon looks nice tonight," I said. Her sobbing stopped. She drew a deep breath and I felt it shudder back out of her chest. "She's watching the show, too."

It is hard to describe what I felt then, kneeling beside Isabella's chair. Have you ever known helplessness while someone you love is suffering? Have you ever cursed God for what He has done? Have you ever felt your heart throbbing with so much love and rage that they get mixed up and you can't tell one from the other?

Well, let me tell you this: No matter how deep my own despair was, I knew it was nothing compared to hers; knew that I could only follow her so far out on that gangplank she was being forced to walk over deep black water. Isabella was

44

the one it was happening to. Isabella was having this nightmare. Isabella—no matter how I felt or what I said—was in this alone. And she knew it.

"I'm done with my little outburst," she said finally. "What's for d-dessert?"

■   ■   ■

By nine, I had done the dishes, gotten Isabella undressed and into bed, and almost finished the wine. My heart was beginning to beat faster. I could feel the motion coming on. I imagined a breeze blowing against my face, objects racing past. I was an unfettered spirit, rushing with the wind down Laguna Canyon. I was a thing without conscience. I was free.

I kissed Isabella good night.

"Don't stay out too late," she said. "Don't smile at any big-titted blondes."

"No. I'll be good."

6

I drove back down to South Laguna and parked a hundred feet short of Amber's solitary mansion. It looked just as it had the night before, the one faint light coming from deep within. Reuben Saltz had not gone into the bedroom. No, of course not. He had stood in the entryway, called out to her, heard nothing, maybe climbed halfway up the stairs before the creeping dread of being in someone else's home uninvited turned him back.

I took a drink from the flask. *With all my love, Isabella.* A voice inside told me to get out of there, go back home to all that love, preserve myself. But the voice was faint, drowned by alcohol. Yes, I wanted that love, but I wanted more. I wanted that other world now, the world of speed, the world with no history and no conscience. I got my gloves from the trunk and put them on.

Down the sidewalk, through the gate, along the stepping-stone walkway, around the corner of the house and onto the patio. The same half moonlight of the night before, a fractional gradient brighter, maybe.

The glass door was shut and the screen door was pulled tight. I put my finger to the mesh—the flap gave, then closed.

But neither was locked. Because you can't lock them from the outside, I thought, because whoever has been here since last night didn't want to be seen going out the front. Reuben?

I slid open the doors and stepped in. I went to the stairway and climbed. On the landing, I stopped for a moment to receive whatever silent messages the house might be sending. A voice told me again to leave. I crushed that voice by walking straight to Amber's bedroom door. I felt the vein pounding in my forehead. I reached inside and flipped on the light.

The bed was made up.

The walls and mirror were clean.

There was a throw rug where I had last seen Amber.

Amber was gone.

Something from hell welled up inside me, rode along with my blood. I felt a tremendous withering—as if my cells were trying to retreat, shrink, cover themselves. I could smell something strong, and it took me just a second to realize what it was. Fresh paint.

I stood beside the new rug, knelt down, and lifted. A stain, very faint, so faint that it vanished when I stepped away and looked from another angle. Was it just a shadow? I arranged the rug over it—just as it had been.

I realized I was scarcely breathing. In the bathroom, I turned on the light to look in the mirror at my own sweating yellow face. The eyes belonged to someone I'd never met and wouldn't want to.

That was when the door slammed shut behind me and I felt the hard steel of a gun barrel jammed into the base of my skull.

"Turn around. Real slow."

I knew the voice. It went with the face. My forehead felt as if it were ready to explode. I turned very slowly, open hands edging up. "Hello, Marty," I said.

"*Monroe.*"

Martin Parish's face looked worse than mine did. His breath smelled like gin. He was wearing a pair of underpants and that was all.

"Nice outfit," I said.

"You're under arrest for, for, uh . . ."

"For what, Marty? Put down the gun."

"Breaking and . . ."

I reached up and, purely on speculation, cupped the gun barrel away from my face and walked past Marty Parish, back into the bedroom. When I turned to look, Marty was standing in front of the mirror, hands to his side, shoulders slumped, and an expression of absolute bewilderment on his face.

"B and E shit," I said. "If you're going to arrest me for anything, it ought to be for the murder of Amber. But then you'd have to explain what you were doing here tonight—and last night, too. I saw you, Martin."

Parish turned to face me. He had the look of a man whose eyes are only looking about one foot into the world. "This is not what it appears. You don't understand what you're seeing."

I had to smile. "What the fuck *am* I seeing, Marty?"

"I didn't do it. I swear to God, I didn't do it."

"Who did?"

"I swear to God, I don't know." He lifted up his gun—a .44 Magnum with a two-inch barrel, a stupidly big gun, I have always believed—and studied the end of it. In a flash, I thought, He's going to shoot himself. But he let his hand drop to his side again. There are few sights in life as vividly unsettling as a drunk man in his underwear with a gun.

"Where are your clothes, Marty?"

"Under the bed."

"Under the bed."

"Yeah. I was . . ."

The brief silence swirled with implications so bizarre, I could hardly keep up with them. "Put them on and let's get out of here. I think maybe we need to talk."

While Marty got dressed, I checked the shower and tub: No one had used them in the last few hours, unless they'd wiped them out. Amber's peach-colored towels were dry. The sink was dry, too, no moisture under the plug. I went back into the bedroom, pulled a few threads from one tassled end of the new throw rug, and slipped them between two bills in my wallet. I got up close to the walls and saw the fresh paint covering the old writing. Amber's suitcases were still near the walk-in. I looked through them at the unremarkable travel provisions. Where had she been going? Marty, tucking in his shirt, watched me. Overwhelmed by curiosity, I knelt down and looked under the bed. I saw nothing but a small, flat rectangular object just a few inches from my nose. I picked it up by one corner, stood, and took it into the bathroom. It turned out to be just what it felt like: three pull-apart plastic ties, like you get with trash or lawn bags. I put them in my wallet, too. A considerable chill blew through me. Running my hands over the carpet near where Amber had lain, I found by touch something I could never have spotted with my eyes. It was a tiny screw, the kind used by jewelers and watchmakers, half-buried in the Berber mesh. I extracted it with my fingernails, examined its copperish color, and dropped it into the casing of the pen I always carry. There was a collection of them in there because my own glasses are always falling apart and I need spares.

■   ■   ■

I got us down from the hills and into a bar on the beach. The place was right on the sand and you could look out at the white water, the dark horizon, the clear, star-shimmering sky. The white water wasn't white at all, but a faint, luminescent violet.

I'd been drinking, and I'd sobered up the second I parked my car near Amber's. But Marty had been *drinking*, and he didn't want to stop. He ordered a double brandy. I got coffee.

"You first," I said. "How come you were there last night?"

Marty drank half the snifter in one gulp. "I couldn't stop thinking about her," he said. "I think maybe I didn't quite get her out of my system." He looked at me, raising his glass again. He had a Band-Aid on his thumb. The shaving cut was still there, a lateral scab on the tip of his Adam's apple. "So I called her and got nothing, just the machine. Then I drove by just for the hell of it. JoAnn and I aren't real good now. I used to love her, but I don't know anymore. I'm fuckin' sick of worrying about us."

It was good that Marty was drunk, I thought. "Fifteen years since you and Amber," I said.

"Yeah. Twenty for you. I got to admit, I hated you back then, Monroe."

"I know. But she married you, not me."

"One great year, that was. Then she left."

"That was Amber."

Marty drank down the rest of his brandy and pointed to the waitress for more. He waited until she brought it. "So last night, I parked down from her house and sat in my car. There was another car, right in front of the house, a Porsche convertible. Red."

"Get the plate numbers?"

"Don't need plate numbers. It was Grace's."

Grace, I thought. Lovely, uncontrollable, unrepentant

Grace—her mother's daughter, from her perfect olive skin to her errant spirit.

"She came out of the house at about eleven-thirty. Got in her car and drove away."

"Jesus, Marty—then she saw what we saw."

Martin drank again, fumbled for a smoke. I lighted it for him. "She must have. She was in a hurry. She tossed her head back when she came through the gate—that way she always did—then walked straight to the car. She stood there beside it for a second, getting out her keys. I don't want to believe Grace could kill her, but she was there. And she didn't report it."

"So were you, and you didn't."

"And so were you. Maybe you ought to tell *me* why."

So I told him. It paralleled Marty's story in a way that made me sound as if I was mocking him. When I explained myself, the whole thing with Amber seemed so puerile, so sentimental, so treacherous. I was suddenly ashamed of myself, of submitting to my own self-created temptations. For a moment, I saw us from the outside—Marty Parish and me—two former lovers of a beautiful woman, nurturing their little hurts, nursing along their little hopes, fueling the ancient torches, dragging around every lost moment of an idealized time so we could remember how good it felt to be heartbroken by Amber Mae. It was disgusting. In that moment, I hated myself.

"Maybe Amber picked us because she knew we'd miss her like this," said Marty.

"Maybe Amber was just a selfish cunt we should have steered clear of."

Marty nodded drunkenly. "Funny you'd mention that, now that she's dead."

"What in hell is going on here, Marty? Someone moved her."

"Cleaned the carpet and brought in a throw rug."

"Painted the walls."

"Cleaned the mirror."

"Closed the sliding door and the screen."

"Took her away."

In trash bags, I thought. "Made the bed."

"God, Russ—and she was all packed up to leave. What am I gonna do? I've got a marriage I'd like to save. I got a job I'd like to keep. I find my ex-wife dead and I can't say a word or the shit's gonna hit every fan there is. I'm not going to lose everything I've worked for because of Amber Mae. She took it all once already. I paid my dues. Christ, do I need a drink."

"Think I'll join you."

Marty ordered up a couple more doubles. I've known only one man who could drink as much as Martin Parish and still function. I saw Marty make a bet once at a party that he could drink a fifth of Black Label in one sitting, do a hundred push-ups, and not puke. He did all those things but still lost the bet, because I drank a bottle, did 150 push-ups, and held. I also went home that night, after Marty had fallen asleep, with the date that he had brought to the party—Amber Mae Wilson, of course. We were young and stupid then.

Now we're just older. "Marty, can you explain . . . uh . . . why you weren't fully *clothed* when I barged in on you?"

Marty drank more. "I still couldn't believe what I saw last night. It was like if I closed my eyes and got under those covers . . . then I heard someone coming up the stairs."

"It was like if you got under the covers, *what*?"

"That she'd be there."

"That's your answer?"

"That's it."

"You're a sick dog, Martin."

"Yeah, I know."

"Let's take a walk."

I paid up and we walked out onto the beach. I guided us south, toward the rocks. I picked my way around to a little cove that closed us off from the rest of the strand. When Marty was almost beside me, I drove my elbow into him as hard as I could, right below the sternum. He folded in half, head down, and I sent my knee into his forehead, hard. Then I grabbed him by the hair, pulled him out to the water, and pushed him in. I got his hair again and leaned into his backbone with my knee. He was taking big gulps of air when I let him; the rest of the time he got ocean. "Truth time, Marty. You kill her?"

"No..."

"Come on, I'm a friend."

"No..."

So I jammed his face down again and gave him a good drink. For a while, he didn't even struggle. He blew bubbles. When I pulled him up, he was just starting to suck in a big breath. He swilled the air and I asked him again whether he'd killed her.

"No..."

Back under for some more quiet time. The water eased in, lifted us in unison, set us back down on the sand. I yanked up on his hair again. "Then what the *fuck* were you doing in her house last night—and don't tell me because you had to see her."

"I had to see her.... I swear to..."

I leaned harder on his back. "And you went back again tonight? For what, Marty? *For what?*"

"I couldn't figure out why... couldn't figure out why nobody called it in... and maybe..."

"Maybe what, Marty?"

"And maybe I didn't really see what I thought I did. I could hardly remember anything this morning. I was hoping maybe I was blackout drunk and didn't really see her...."

"So then you got naked and wanted to get into her bed."

Martin Parish was groaning now, not a groan of physical pain but one of terrible, terrible inner torment. "I just needed... needed five minutes of what it used to feel like. I loved her. I don't know. It's always... worked. I don't know... see... *I'd done it before.*"

"Gotten into her bed?"

"Only when she wasn't there."

"Oh, Christ."

The shore break rolled in harder now and knocked me off him. I stood, balanced myself, and dragged up Marty by his belt. We staggered out, across a few feet of beach, then he sagged down, coughing and breathing hard. I knelt in front of him and yanked him by his shirt collar right up to me, face-to-face.

"We've got five bashings, Marty. Did this guy paint up the Ellison and Fernandez places, too?"

Martin just shook his head. He was drunk enough to admit crawling naked into bed with a murdered woman who wasn't there. But he wasn't drunk enough to break procedure and leak to the press just exactly what their man had left for them at two—and maybe three—crime scenes. Marty's divisions were more profound than I had ever suspected.

"Maybe Amber just got up and walked away," he said, sobbing. In the moonlight, his face looked like a child's, like a slobbering infant who'd finally come to the end of a crying jag. "Maybe it was a makeup job. She knows all those Hollywood types. It was all a trick."

I shook him hard. "She's dead, Marty. But nobody knows that except you and me and Grace and whoever took that club to her. And nobody's going to know, unless whoever moved Amber put her somewhere we can find her."

Marty was nodding along dutifully now. I let go of him.

He brought up his knees and arms and bowed his head against them. He was rocking back and forth a little. He was pathetic. "We need to talk to Grace," he said. "We need Grace."

We sure as hell do, I thought. "I'll find her."

"You should do that, Russ."

"I'll do it."

"Since she's your daughter."

"Right, since she's my daughter."

Grace's red Porsche was parked in my driveway when I came home, and Grace was leaning against it. A quiet alarm went off inside me. I hadn't seen her in almost a year—an occasional phone call was all she had offered. Even though the night was humid and warm, she stood bundled inside a parka with fur around the collar, her shoulders bunched, her head set down into the fur, her hands in the pockets.

Amber had claimed Grace from the start—seized her, appropriated her, removed her. From before the start, in fact: Amber was five months pregnant before she told me. I had first seen Grace when she was two weeks old, then not again until two years later. Amber had taken her to Paris. Amber had taken her to Rome. To New York, Rio, London, St. Barts, Kitts, and Thomas. Grace said her first words to me when she was four. She said, demurely offering her cheek for a kiss, "How nice to meet you, Russell." It was one of the strangest, strongest moments in my life, stooping to kiss that face so much like mine, turned in profile while her long-lashed brown eyes contemplated the sky with supreme control, supreme boredom. I believed that I felt a little part of my heart die in that moment. She referred to me as Russell, never once as Father or Dad or Pop ever since.

Later that same night—the night when Grace was four— Amber and I had walked up into the hills behind Laguna and had the centerpiece battle of our lives. It was the kind of wildly escalating fight where both parties are truly eager. My position was that Amber had stolen my daughter, and I demanded that she be at least partially returned. How naïve I was, at twenty-six, to think that such a return could come from anyone but Grace herself, if ever, if at all. I had no instruments then to measure the distance she had gone. Amber said that I had no more claim to Grace than a flower had to a bee, that I had only supplied the pollen. She actually used those words: "supplied the pollen." We each drew blood that night, though I will say that Amber struck first. The moon was full and ice-bright over the rocky path, and I can still remember the wet black shine on the stone she used.

I saw neither Amber nor Grace again for almost five years.

"Grace," I said, getting out of my car.

"Russell," she said back. She came toward me across the driveway, her heels resonant on the asphalt. She proffered her cheek as she had done those fourteen years ago. Her skin was cold, and she smelled very strongly—a woman's scent cut with nerves and perfume. Grace was a large woman, nearly five feet ten, with an athletic strength to her body and a lovely face. She had her mother's dark wavy hair.

"Sorry to just appear. I must seem like a ghost."

"Is everything okay?"

"Of course not, Russ."

"Come in."

"Thank you."

I left Grace in my study and went upstairs to check on Isabella. She was deep in sleep. I stood there for a moment and looked at her face buried down in the pillow. The crook of her cane was visible where it stood beside the bed, and I wondered for the millionth time why the Good Shepherd had abandoned it to her. Isabella would not be happy if Grace was to be here in the morning: She believed that both Amber and my daughter were the worst kind of manipulators, and she was always irritated—even during five years of marriage—when I mentioned either of them. I learned it was easier not to.

Grace was looking at my bookcase when I went back into the study. In the clean incandescent light, I could see she was a little pale and clammy. A dew of perspiration marked her temples and upper lip with a very slight shine.

"Be a nice place to open a bar," she said.

"What'll it be?"

"Dry vermouth on the rocks, if you have it. A twist."

I made two and brought them back. She had unzipped her parka but hadn't taken it off. I studied her as she came across the room for her drink, feeling as always the astonishment at seeing a part of me in her. She was a beautiful young woman—eighteen years of age, strong, composed. She had gotten Amber's face—with just a touch of my Monroe width to it. She had Amber's fine jaw and full, relaxed mouth, her straight and narrow nose. But some things in her were mine: the heavy, inexpressive brow, the readable brown eyes that could seem at times so undefended. And these features had kept Grace free of Amber's most powerful characteristic—her guile—the very quality, I might add, that had put Amber's face on so many magazine covers and TV screens. Amber could suggest anything from lust to innocence to betrayal to heartache—and plausibly connect them to a certain shampoo, makeup, bra. But just beneath all these "emotions," there was always the guile, that willingness to conspire, the sense that there were only two people in this world: Amber and whomever she was looking back at. It was a wholly private and exclusive contract. Grace, for all her loveliness, could never fake that arrangement. And Amber, I thought, never would again. The terrible vision of her desecrated face came to me as I looked at our daughter.

"What happened?" I asked.

"Two men, Russell, have been following me. One is fat, with big ears, and the other one is slender, with short hair. I've seen them outside my condo, at my work, in a red pickup truck following me. They seem to be everywhere."

"What do they want?"

"How on earth would I know?"

"Have you called the police?"

"No. I came here instead, hoping for maybe one night of peaceful sleep."

"How long have they been following you?"

"I don't know. I noticed a few days ago."

"They've never approached?"

Grace studied me with a peculiarly lucid expression, as if she'd found something in my face she'd never noticed before. "No. I've spent some time with a boyfriend the last two days, but I don't believe he's capable of . . . protecting me."

"Who?"

"His name is Brent."

"Brent have a last name?"

"Sides. He's a bartender, but he wants to write movies."

"What bar?"

"Sorrento's—up in the Orange hills."

Grace finished her drink, put the glass on the coffee table, and sat on the couch. She looked down at the floor, her loose dark curls falling forward and hiding her face. "He's got a crush on me. But as I said, Russell, he's only a boy. He keeps showering me with gifts."

She looked up at me, her eyes a little wet.

"I hear you were at Amber's last night. I thought you two were still hardly speaking."

Grace blinked, then furrowed the brow that reminded me so much of my own. She studied me for a long, very strange moment, during which I felt as if I were being contemplated by my own eyes. She shook her head slowly and looked away. "I didn't see Mom last night," she said.

"Marty Parish said he saw you there, coming out at eleven-thirty."

"Well, I'm telling you he didn't."

"He was positive—last night. Your red Porsche."

"I don't know what to say, Russ, but I wasn't there. Martin drinks too much to be positive about anything, doesn't he? The last time I saw Martin, he was unconscious on Mom's sofa. That was a long time ago. Last night, I was with Brent."

She studied me again. Her expression wasn't locked, but open—an expression that offered as much as it took in. There was no cunning in it—not to my eyes, at least. But there was confusion and curiosity, and a small amount of what I can only describe as hopefulness. "What's going on, Russ? Have you been seeing Mother again?"

"No. I talked to Marty today. That's when he said he saw you, coming out of Amber's last night."

"Then Marty's been seeing her again."

I nodded.

"I've never understood how she turns you all into such grovelers."

"Brent Sides could probably enlighten you."

Grace's brown eyes steadied on my face. "That was never my intention."

"Amber would say it was never hers, either."

"It's like you crave the heartache. Does it really feel that good?"

"Only when you're young."

"Like me."

"Like you. It's the way of the world. *So Jah seh.*"

She looked up at me again, then stood. If the phrase startled her, she gave no hint that it did. She looked out a window for a moment and shook back her dark hair. "So God says. Russ, look, I'll be honest with you. Can I just stay here one night? I'm tired of being harassed, and I'm exhausted. I know Isabella isn't wild about me, but I'll be out early."

"Sure, the guest bed's made up."

"The couch here would be fine."

"Suit yourself, Grace."

She held up her glass. "Have a nightcap with me? Something a little stronger than vermouth would be nice."

I made two stout whiskeys and brought them back. We sat on the couch, at what seemed a proper distance. I told her about Isabella and my work; she told me about hers. The conversation was oddly formal and tentative, like that of an old friendship held together only by some strained honoring of what used to be. But for us, there was no used to be. Still, I couldn't keep the feelings down, the great, tender, protective urges that a man feels for his daughter. I felt them spreading inside me until they reached some invisible barrier where they eddied, settled, pooled. It was just as it had always been—nothing for them to have, nowhere for them to go. There she was, my girl, sitting on my couch, two proper feet away, telling me about selling clothes, and all I could do was sit there. Of the several injuries that Amber's annexation of Grace had caused me, these were the worst: that she had torn away the object of my love and stolen from my daughter and me the one thing that could never be returned—time.

I placed my hand over hers and looked at her. She ended a sentence without finishing it, glanced at me, then turned her gaze to the floor again. Her hair fell forward and hid her face. "I'm sorry, Russ. I could've just gotten a hotel or something."

"I'm glad you're here."

For a while, we sat there, hand in hand, letting the touch be. Grace's muscles wouldn't relax, though; she kept her hand in mine by an act of will.

"It's strange," she said. "I've spent my entire life with Mom, having *fun*. I've been on every continent, lived in ten countries, learned three languages besides my own—but I still can't understand what went wrong. Something's missing, something that isn't there, but I can feel anyway, like a phantom limb. Sometimes I feel like there's a part of me, a big part, that's just now crawling out of the slime for the first time."

I squeezed her hand gently and smiled at her self-awareness, her self-ignorance, her eighteen-year-old's combination of confusion and clarity. "It'll never change, Grace," I said. "You'll be finding out you weren't quite who you thought you were until the day you die."

"Quite a comfort, Russ."

Suddenly, she stood up. I hated the feeling of her hand slipping away. "I should go."

"Don't."

She went to the window and looked down toward Laguna Canyon Road. "I still hate her."

I let that pass for a moment, waiting her out. "You're just seeing her for the first time."

"No. I really like hate her."

The thought came to me that at this moment in time, Grace believed her mother was alive. Not "I hated her" but "I *hate* her." Marty Parish was lying—Grace had not been inside Amber's house last night. The hair on my arms stood up.

Marty, what could you have done?

"Want to tell me about that?"

"No. Some things you can't elaborate on. I can't say it any clearer than I just did." She turned. "Good night, Russ. Man, am I tired."

I hugged her, but she remained erect and unyielding, unoffering. "There's a blanket in the closet," I said.

■   ■   ■

I lay beside Isabella for a while, holding her close to me, watching over her shoulder as the minutes ticked past on the clock.

At 3:40, I went downstairs with a flashlight, saw my study door shut and the light off, then quietly let myself outside and into the dry stillness of the canyon. The smell of sagebrush settled around me. The canyon road bent far below, twisting out of sight, unoccupied, barely lighted, peaceful.

I let myself into Grace's car and found the light.

Her glove compartment contained a few CDs, a tire-pressure gauge, and the usual registration and insurance documents. It also contained a wallet, in which I found $680 in cash, several credit-card receipts—mostly from Sorrento's in the Orange hills, home of writer, bartender, fool-for-love Brent Sides. The three-pack of condoms, I assumed, was probably for those moments when Grace bestowed upon Mr. Sides that most intimate of gifts. The thought of his eighteen-year-old daughter in coitus sits well with no father.

I popped the trunk release, got my flashlight, and climbed out. Nothing unusual in the trunk, either: jack and spare, two cans of oil, a squeegee, a small tool kit. Pushed up near the dash was a box of glass cleaner, car polish, silicone tire spray, sponges.

Lying flat against the far side was a box of thirty-three-gallon trash bags.

I ran the flashlight beam across the label: EXTRA HEAVY DUTY. I reached into the trunk, brought them out, and checked the price tag for place of purchase, but there was only the bar code. I fished out the ties—plastic, joined together, waiting to be pulled apart—and compared them with the three in my wallet, taken from under Amber's bed.

Same ties.

Same bags?

I finally went to bed just after four. I lay there wondering whether Grace was lying, if so, why, and whether she could possibly have it in her to kill. I did not believe she did. Sometime around five, I drifted into an uneasy sleep, from which I woke in a nonspecific panic less than an hour later.

Downstairs, I found that Grace had gone. She had probably coasted her car down the hill to keep from waking us.

In my study, I found her note:

Thanks, Russ—couldn't sleep much, after all. Find anything juicy in my car? I went to pick up a few things. Be back.

—Grace

8

Sheriff Daniel Winters called at 8:10 that morning and told me he expected the Dina piece to be big, subtly persuasive, well played, and on the stands by Tuesday. From the tone of his voice, I could almost picture the resigned furrows on his deep black face. Dan Winters was a sheriff who understood the impurities contained within the larger concept of getting things done. So I did what any writer does when faced with impossible demands—agreed to everything.

He was quiet for a long moment, then gave me an address in the Orange hills and hung up. So, he had taken my bait.

The house was a magnificent wood-and-glass thing, tucked within a stand of Jelecote pines at the end of a long private road. There were two patrol cars, two unmarkeds, and the Crime Scene van parked in the driveway. When I got out, the air smelled like a mountain resort. It was already hot. There was a nervous buzz in my stomach.

Marty Parish met me at the back door and led me past

two dubious uniforms, down a long hallway, through a living room almost as big as my entire house, then down another hallway toward, I assumed, the bedrooms. He turned once to look at me as we walked but said nothing. I sensed a change in him from the night before, a change that went deeper than the simple fact he wasn't dumb drunk. Marty had a red patch where I'd kneed his forehead, but he also had the level-eyed gaze of a man who's got something on you.

"Sorry about last night," I said.

"You'll get yours." He gave me that look again, as if he'd found out something that put me, himself—everything—in a cold new light.

"Ready when you are," I said.

"I'll wait till you're not."

"How bad is this?"

"Worst I've ever seen. Two children."

"So Winters is ready to go public."

"Should have after the Ellisons. What'd you give him for this, another Dina story?"

"That's right."

Marty's eyes bored into me. "Nothing's right, Monroe."

He stopped at the first room on our left. I could see past his shoulder through the open door to a pale blue wall dripped with dark red.

"Meet the Wynn twins," said Martin, and stood aside.

I went in. My first thought was that an industrial accident had happened here, something involving faulty machinery and human flesh. You could smell the foul scent of innards exposed to air for the first and last time. The blood seemed to have been thrown at one wall—large impact splatters that ran like paint all the way down to the blue carpet. On the opposite wall were great wide smears of it, thick in places, then thinning as a brush might make. But the brush was a small boy—a few years old,

I guessed—who lay doll-like beside the wall where phrases had been crudely written with his blood:

MIDNIGHT EYE CLEANS HIPPOCRITTS
SO JAH SEH

I took a deep breath and squatted down, looking at a cardboard mobile that had once probably hung over a crib. Little military airplanes lay flat on the floor at my feet—a P-51, an F-111, an AWACS jet. I took another deep breath, then looked to the far side of the room, where the crib was tucked into a corner, near a reading nook that extended out toward a garden. The alcove had windows on three sides. There was a hook in the ceiling of it, for the potted fern and macramé hanger that were dumped on the carpet below. From the hook dangled another boy, ankles bound, the binding set on the ceiling hook, his small arms out in front of him. He looked like a tiny diver descending toward a pool. There was, in fact, a pool beneath him. He turned very slightly on the hook; turned back.

I looked down at the cardboard airplanes again and apologized silently to these boys whom I hadn't come here in time to help.

I sensed Marty behind and above me.

"Justin and Jacob," he said. "We're not sure who's who yet."

I took another deep breath. My legs had stopped feeling and my pulse was light and fast. I felt Marty's hand lock onto my arm and yank up.

"There's more," he said.

One foot in front of the other, that choking, meaty, slaughterhouse stink all around me, I followed Marty from the room.

We stood in the hallway, our backs against the wall, and smoked. The ceiling seemed terribly low. It was dark, too, even with the recessed flood lamps bearing down from above. A uniform jangled by, his face averted, crossed himself, and headed into the twins' room.

"You make enough money to get out of this business, then come back for this kind of shit," Marty said. "Does it really pay that well?"

"Go to hell, Martin."

"Wish I could."

"God . . . *damn.*"

"He does, He does. Mom and Dad are in the master. There's a daughter, too, but she must have been gone. Her bed's made up and she isn't anywhere around."

I went in. It looked as if something had fed there perhaps—captured prey, torn it apart, partaken. Or maybe not eaten at all, but simply shredded the room and the people in it, searching for something very small, very hidden, very important. The smell was strong. Both bodies—smallish dark-skinned bodies—were opened and emptied like drawers. Their contents were everywhere, strewn around the floor, hurled against walls, piled on the bed, strung from the blades of the ceiling fan, flung onto the lamp shades, the blinds, the television screen, the dresser, hung from the top fronds of a palm that stood by a window, splattered against that same window and drying now from red to black in the golden summer sunlight of morning. The carcass of Mr. Wynn, on his back, arms out, was spread across the bed. Mrs. Wynn was hanging in the shower stall, tied by her hair to the nozzle fixture. Some of what had been inside her was spilled out in a pile over the drain, which had backed up, making a pool of blood.

The two Crime Scene men were going to work with a video camera and evidence bags when I left and found Martin, still in the hallway.

I heard a muted commotion from the living room, followed by Sheriff Daniel Winters and his entourage coming briskly toward us up the hallway. Their footsteps had a ring of assurance. Winters is a tall, very thin man, bespectacled, a sharp dresser. Gray colors his hair at the temples, and his eyes, behind the glasses, are black, hypervigilant, and consuming. He often stoops, catches himself at it, straightens himself, then slumps back into his characteristic posture again. There were three men besides Dan—two assistant DAs I knew, a uniform I'd never seen—and a pretty red-haired woman named Karen Schultz, the Sheriff's Department Community Relations director. Winters nodded at me on his way past, then took Martin by the arm without a word and led him into the master suite. The prosecutors and deputy followed. I heard Winters's shocked expletive, then heard it again, filled with outrage, disbelief, dread.

Karen Schultz studied me with her always-alert green eyes. "We're going to have to hold back a lot of this, Russell."

"You just say what."

"I need to see your copy before you file."

"You can see it, but I won't change it. Tell me what to sit on, and I'll sit on it."

"We'll admit the possibility of a link to Ellison and Fernandez."

"That's why I'm here."

"But nothing positive until the ME's done and all the labs are complete. You will use the words *possibly linked* and say we are attempting to establish a definite connection. You are not encouraged to use the term *serial killer.*"

"Repeat offender sounds a little trivial."

She sighed, glanced toward the door of the master suite, then looked back at me. Karen Schultz's hair was straight and luxurious, her skin pale, her nose freckled. She never smiled.

"Go ahead with it for the *Journal* if you want, but if we can't connect the scenes, you're the one who'll be wearing the ass ears."

"What time is the press conference?"

"Four tomorrow. That vets out to a two-day scoop on all the other print. Spin Dina well."

"I will. Thanks."

She looked again at the door to the master. "God, I hate this," she said.

All I could think of to say back was, "I'm sorry."

■   ■   ■

I loitered, taking notes, getting the basics, sneaking off to a little laundry room with a door that opened to the backyard, so I could smoke, breath fresh air, and have a drink from my flask.

The detectives quickly determined that Mr. Tran Wynn had been forty-one years old, a physician. Maia was thirty-six and had worked for a local aerospace firm.

The twins—Jacob and Justin—were two.

The daughter, Kim, was blessedly gone. Where? I looked into her room. The bed was made, and the cops had found the door open, whereas the doors to the twins' room and the master suite were both closed. Karen Schultz demanded another search of the house for Kim, which proved fruitless. Winters ordered a door-to-door canvass of the neighborhood for the girl, after Martin and DA assistants all impressed on him that for the killer to take the girl alive would be "out of profile." APB pending. Bloodhounds considered.

"No story until we find the girl," said Karen. Her face was so pale, her freckles showed even darker.

They didn't want Kim reading about the death of her entire

family—her entire universe—in the evening *Journal*. I didn't, either.

"Don't worry," I said. "The Wynns are Vietnamese, aren't they?"

Karen nodded. "The last name is an anglicized version of Nguyen—pronunciation is similar. Jacob, Justin, and Kim? I'd say Tran and Maia were trying hard to fit in as Americans."

"A lot of Catholics came down from the North," I said.

"I guess the Wynns should have stayed put. Least they could have been buried in their own ground."

Half an hour later, Martin found me in the laundry nook and waved me back to the living room. I'd already filled ten pages in my notebook. "You'll like this," he said. Winters, the two assistant DAs, both CS men, and Karen all stood in a loose semicircle facing the Wynn's impressive stereo system. One of the uniforms hit a button and the loud hiss of a tape came through the speakers. It continued for ten seconds or so, and I realized it wasn't all hiss—it was also the sound of ocean water on sand, or maybe cars on a highway, or both.

The voice that came on next was a man's—slow, deliberate, almost pleasant. The words were spaced out and carefully enunciated, as if for a student to hear and repeat:

"*Coming . . . Seeing . . . Having . . . Willing
Cleaning . . . Taking . . . Jah . . .*"

Then more waves, tiny voices in the far background, and a long inhalation, followed by silence. What came next was the same ocean-heavy background, the same voice, but now it was slurred, badly garbled, as if the man was in a drug stupor or falling off to sleep:

"Ice-a h-h-homing gen spoon. O-o-ouch treble t-t-tings. A-a-ax is cute me. G-gren duffel m-m-m'back. G-gren duffel m-m-m'back. M-m-make m-m-m'do tings. C-c-cun seed brat cun wormin from he . . ."

Then the end of sound, just the near silence of the Wynn's speakers.

We listened to it again, then a third time.

"Green duffel," said Assistant DA Peter Haight.

"Green duffel on my back," said Winters.

"Green *devil* on my back," said Marty. "Makes me do things."

"Execute me," I said.

Parish stared at me.

"That's what I heard, too," said Karen.

The most pressured of silences came over us. Winters looked around, studying each face in the group. Heads shook. Karen asked to hear it again. We listened.

Suddenly, a cold wave of astonishment rose up and broke over me.

Something was very wrong here.

This I could not believe.

Not only what we were hearing but the fact that the dicks had found it so quickly. A houseful of death and blood, latents, footprints probably, hair and fiber almost assuredly, and *these guys turn on the goddamned stereo*? Winters must have read the amazed doubt on my face. He looked at the two assistant DAs and the two CS investigators and told them to beat it.

Then it hit me. Of course.

"Nothing about the recordings," said Winters.

"Nothing about the writing on the walls," said Schultz.

"And nothing about you guys finding the same things at

the Ellison and Fernandez places," I said. "What have you done?"

"We'll expect you to omit that question in the *Journal*," said Karen. "Or we'll omit *you* from everything that happens in this county from now until the day you die."

"*Why?*"

Winters locked eyes with me. "We made a judgment call, and it turned out to be the wrong one. It was a mistake. We hoped we could get him before he did this again. It's that simple, Russell. We're giving you this story. Don't burn us. Help us. And don't forget that splashing blood all over page one never saved anybody's life. Not in my opinion, anyway."

In the ensuing silence, Parish glared at me; Karen Schultz looked at the floor and bit her lip; Winters sighed and stared stubbornly ahead through space.

I was almost too stunned to think. The only thing I could come up with was to pursue my temporary advantage through this silence.

"Let me hear the other tapes," I said. "Let me see the CS photos of the walls."

"No deal," said Karen. "Never."

"Fine," said Winters. "Okay."

"Monroe is a *reporter*, sir," said Karen.

"That's why he'll sell us his conscience for a story," said Winters, a true master of the art of accommodation. "Right, Russ?"

No reporter on earth would have said anything but yes. If I didn't, I could burn them big-time—once. But the same pages on which I flushed away my access to the Sheriff's Department and prosecutors for the rest of my life would be used two days later to soak up pee in a thousand litter boxes throughout the county. And I'd be out in the cold. And whatever damage Winters's silence had done was certainly, clearly, done forever. I was a little surprised at how Winters had changed since I'd worked for him. He was a harried political animal now, thinking ahead, watching out for himself, but not taking care of business. He'd made a terrible call, a call he wouldn't have made five years ago, and he knew it. He also knew he could hide it. Karen and I would do it for him.

"I'll rent it out for a while," I said.

"And I'll get you a front-row seat when we send this guy to the gas," said Winters. "Until then, you owe us."

He turned and walked out.

■   ■   ■

I stood in the laundry room again, leaning against the washer and looking out the open door to the eucalyptus tree in the yard.

That was when I first heard the faint, shallow breathing very close to me.

It took me a second to realize what it was. I didn't move. I figured a dog sleeping behind the hamper, maybe, or a cat up on the shelf. For some reason, it scared me. I didn't blink. It was coming from just below me, just in front of me, still barely audible.

It stopped, then it started again.

Very slowly, I reached out to the dryer and pulled the door toward me. *God, please,* I thought. . . . The light inside went on and two eyes came into view. I knelt and held out my hands, palms up.

"It's over," I said. "I won't hurt you. You can come out now, Kim."

She climbed out and into my arms. I guessed she was four or five. She began whimpering and her breathing deepened. I walked us out into the sunshine. She dug her face into the crook of my neck. "Mommy screamed and I heard a bang. Mommy screamed and then she didn't scream."

"Did you see him, Kim?"

I felt her forehead nodding yes against my neck.

"He was big and hairy and had a red bat."

"Like a baseball bat?"

"When he came out of Mommy's and Daddy's. I want Mommy and Daddy now."

I rocked her and patted her back and let the sun hit her hair. It was matted with the vomit she'd given up in terror. "Did you see his face?"

"He was a hairy giant and had a green robe. I want Mommy and Daddy now."

I carried her back into the house, down the hallway, and into her living room. Martin and Karen were still there, standing by the stereo.

"Oh God," said Karen. She walked toward us with an officious stride that dissolved about halfway across the room when she broke into a run. She unwrapped Kim from my shoulders, hefted the girl onto her own, and carried her toward the front door.

Martin and I stood alone. The piercing flatness of his eyes unsettled me.

"Was there a tape at Amber's?" I asked.

He nodded. And his expression softened.

"You listen to it?"

"Once. Same garbled shit as this one. Same voice."

"Were there beach sounds, cars in the background?"

"Yeah. Same shit. He left it rewound and ready in her tape player. I found it because the power light was on and that seemed strange."

I considered. "Did the Eye do Amber, Marty?"

"Someone wanted us to think so."

"The Eye doesn't cart his victims off in plastic bags."

"The Eye doesn't make beds and cover stains, either, I'd imagine."

"Then what the hell is going on?"

The smile that Marty offered next was positively bizarre. "It's not that complicated, Russ."

I let the statement go because I didn't quite understand it yet; I hadn't looked at me from Martin Parish's point of view. Now I began to, and a little spasm of fear fluttered in my heart. "Where is it now—the tape from Amber's?"

"The second night, when I found *you* there, it was gone. Just like Amber was."

Then it hit me, clearly and suddenly as a fist in the stomach. Marty was prepared to believe I'd killed Amber. I could see the conviction in his eyes, unalterable as faith.

"Grace told me she wasn't there that night," I said.

"Then one of us is a liar."

"Maybe a killer, too, Marty?"

Marty was actually smiling again when he said, "I confess, Monroe. I did them all. I can't stop because it feels so good. Excuse me now while I go find some evidence so I can arrest myself."

When I returned home, Grace and Isabella were sitting on the porch—Izzy in her wheelchair and Grace on the step. My heart made a minor leap at the sight of them together, apparently at peace. For a brief moment, visions of the Wynns receded and all that mattered was on my porch. We were a family.

Hugging Izzy, I noted her smart outfit—a gewgaw-spangled T-shirt with matching hat and earrings, outrageous surfer pants with an explosive red-black-orange pattern, and her usual tennis shoes with the glitter ties. She was freshly made up and smelled wonderfully of perfume.

Grace allowed me to hug her, too.

"You look beautiful today," I said to Isabella.

"G-G-Grace helped me. She has better taste than y-y-you."

"And probably more patience, too," I said.

"She's got totally great clothes," said Grace.

Grace regarded me with unspoken pride. How she had

found her way into Izzy's heart in so short a time, I could not immediately understand, but I sensed that some workable truce had been struck between them. After that, the exigencies of appearance and fashion had obviously taken over.

Isabella looked up at me with her great dark eyes. "I don't want to be I-I-late."

"I promise we won't be late," I said. "But I need one hour to write an article. Can you two behave yourselves for that long?"

"We definitely cannot," said Grace.

Isabella nodded.

One hour later, I was driving Isabella up to the UC Irvine Medical Center for the reading of her second PET scan. Her doctors were afraid the tumor was growing. We were terrified the tumor was growing. The scan results would help us know whether it was, and, if so, how fast and in what direction. I had written and faxed my first article on the Midnight Eye to Carla Dance at the *Journal,* and a courtesy copy to Karen Schultz. I used his self-given name. Death seemed everywhere, common as air.

These drives from our home in the arid tan hills of the canyon into the smoggy industrial sprawl of the medical center always seemed like a combination of the Bataan death march and a scene from *Alice in Wonderland.* There was a surreal overlay to these dismal journeys, along with a shaken faith that any minute the nightmare would be broken and we would be just another expectant couple heading up to the hospital for a chatty visit with our obstetrician. In fact, we had made just such a trip once, two months before Isabella was diagnosed, after a drug-store pregnancy test went bright pink. But an ultrasound showed no heartbeat. A day later, she miscarried. It was her second loss in six months. Eight weeks later, when the tumor was discovered, we understood that her body had refused to begin another life because it was already in a secret battle for its own.

Isabella sat beside me, staring out the window, lost behind her sunglasses. The spire of Angel Stadium protruded from the haze in the east. The wide parched bed of the Santa Ana River wound beneath us, testimony to five years of drought, a reminder of still another blessing that God seemed to have plucked from our tables. There was a wreck on I-5, as there always seemed to be each afternoon. We came to a stop, funneled over to the middle lane, and looked at the lights flashing up ahead.

"What if it's big-bigger?"

"It isn't."

"It really isn't, is it?"

"No way. The implants killed it all."

"And half of m-me."

"That's right."

"I deserve some good news for a charge-charge . . . change—don't I?"

"You deserve the best news in the world."

We crept around the bang-up. Three cars were off on the shoulder. A woman sat on the asphalt, her back up against the freeway divider, her face in her hands.

"Why do p-people always slow watch and down?"

"It lets them be thankful it's not them."

"Is that why my friends call me?"

"That's not fair, Izzy. Your friends call because they love you. They don't know what else to do."

"My peach-peach . . . speech is getting worse, isn't it?"

"I think so, baby."

"I can see the word but I c-can't say it."

"You're doing well enough for me."

"It's worse than last week, though. But it m-m-might be the drugs."

"It might be," I said.

Isabella stared at the wreck as we moved past, edged into the newly vacant "fast" lane, and sped up.

She was quiet for a while. "I heard a woman's house in the voice last night. Was I d-dreaming?"

I told her it was Grace.

"Why didn't she j-j-just stay with her m-m-mother?"

"Out of town, I guess," I said.

"Do you want her to stay?"

I told her about Grace's trouble.

Isabella thought for a moment. "She might have turned out all right, if she jaw . . . *just* had a mother nother. I mean another mother."

I let that pass. Isabella had always derived comfort from slamming Amber, and it wasn't my duty to deny her that pleasure. The thought came to me again how fundamentally different they were, how opposite.

"Have you seen her re-re-recently?"

"No."

"What about the Fourth of July? You h-had that Amber look at dinner on the d-deck that night."

"No, Izzy. I haven't seen her in months."

"Does Grace want to live with us?"

"No, she just—"

"I don't want her in the house!" Isabella breathed very deeply and her chin shook. A tear flattened under the frame of her sunglasses and smeared her cheek. "I'm sorry," she said.

"It's okay."

"I'm r-r-really afraid they're going to find new growth."

"No. No new growth, Is. Not today."

"We see some new growth," said Paul Nesson, pointing out the dark tumor on the PET scan. "It hasn't been particularly fast. It's about what we expected. Part of it might be mass effect."

Dr. Paul Nesson was Isabella's neurosurgeon, a young, soft-spoken man who managed to be grave, humorless, and warm, all at the same time. Of all the surgeons we consulted, Nesson was the only one who said that Isabella's was not a hopeless situation. He also said there was no cure. He also was the only one who advised against surgery. Instead, he implanted ten radioactive "seeds" into the tumor on a Monday, and by Friday, Isabella's legs had lost 60 percent of their function. He had sat with us for many of those long hours on the neuro floor while the movement in Isabella's legs ebbed away—starting at her toes and continuing up. Paul Nesson had told us then that the function loss was "probably not irreversible," but by now, a year later, we all saw that he'd been wrong. I will never forget the sight of Isabella Monroe, age twenty-seven, lying in that cheerless room, her head wrapped in a lead-lined cap to keep the radiation from damaging anyone but her, trying to move her toes, then her ankles, then her knees. "Well," she said, "I always thought those wheelchairs with motors were nice. Can you get me one in a hot pink, Dr. Nesson?"

"We'll get one in any color you want," he said quietly.

We settled on black, motorless. When it came time to actually get a wheelchair, the concept of hot pink had lost its charm.

Isabella looked at him now, then back at the colorized PET scan pictures. The tumor was a dark mass outlined in red and yellow. It was no longer round: The powerful radioactive implants had contorted it into a lumpy asymmetrical mess.

"What do we do?" Isabella asked.

"How's your leg function?"

"Pretty bad."

"More weakness?"

"Yes."

"Speech?"

"It's g-g-getting worse. Want to see my tricks now?"

Nesson did his usual neurological exam: reflex in the leg (almost none), nystagmus in the eyes (plenty), facial symmetry (good). He asked to see her walk. Isabella labored out of her chair, took the handle of a quad cane in each hand, and picked her way across the room with excruciating slowness, patience, and concentration. Nesson and I followed on each side of her, ready. She made a turn, came back to her chair, and slumped into it.

"Why don't I feel any better, doctor?"

Nesson said nothing, looked up at the scan pictures again, his hands deep in the pockets of his white coat, his head cocked a little to the left. For a moment, he stood there without moving.

"I think it's time to go in and debulk the tumor, clean out the necrosed tissue," he said.

"Cut my head open?"

"That would be necessary, yes."

"If you d-d-didn't want to operate a year ago, why now?"

"It's a different situation, Isabella. I believe that now we have more to gain."

"You mean less to l-lose."

"I suppose you can look at it that way."

Nesson outlined the procedure, its risks and possible benefits, what we might gain and what we might lose.

"What are my chances of waking up a spat-spat-*spit*-dribbling vegetable?"

Nesson said that 90 percent of these procedures were done without that kind of damage.

"Well, my chances of getting a brain tumor in the first place were one in about two hundred thousand. Your odds are one in t-t-ten. Not g-good, if you're me."

"I'd like you to think about it. Any surgical procedure has its risks. This is not urgent. Yet."

I rolled Isabella back to the car in silence. When we were inside, she turned to me. "Does the insurance cover it?"

"Of course."

"But I don't *want* them in my head."

"No. That's okay."

"It terrifies me, Russ, worse than anything in the world. I don't think I'd ever out come of it."

"Then I won't let them take you in."

We spilled from the dark parking structure into the dazzling sunshine of early July.

"Will you do me a favor, R-R-Russ? Take us to the grove? We could get some sandwiches, okay?"

"My pleasure," I said, smiling, heart heavy, hands tight on the steering wheel. I wanted to crush things and cry and curse the Maker at the top of my lungs, but this was not the time. It was never the time.

■   ■   ■

The grove was an orange grove—Valencias, in fact—one of the last still owned by the SunBlesst Company, once operated under the hard scrutiny of my father, Theodore Francis Monroe.

What made the grove important to Isabella and me was a Sunday evening six Septembers ago, after a day I had spent making the ranch rounds on horseback with my father—checking the irrigation, the fruit sugar levels, the poacher and pest damage.

It had been a typical day for me and my father: polite, given mostly to the exchange of professional complaints, which for him always meant the shrinking acreage of SunBlesst Ranch. The day was, on my part at least, less than fully felt. I loved him, but there was a cynicism in my father that he cultivated as carefully as he did his citrus crop, a hardness that left him somehow both unlikable and untouchable. He had tried to pass along those things to me, as if they were gifts, and I accepted them—especially when I was with him. I always felt stronger when I left him, though a little smaller, too. But like most men who protect themselves with toughness, my father revealed his tenderness inadvertently, unbeknownst to himself. There were three things I never saw him handle with anything but deference and care: my mother, Suzanne; the oranges on his trees; and the men—mostly Mexicans—who worked for him. Looking back at him now, I will say that he was, and still is, the most fiercely paternal man I've known, paternal in the atavistic sense of protecting his mate, guarding his cave, commanding his pack of underlings, and treating outsiders with extreme suspicion—particularly males, especially, of course, those most like himself. I will say, too, that despite my efforts to rise above him in the way that all sons try to better their fathers, his imprint is upon me with all its faults and blessings. I am truly my father's son. It was that fact, more than anything, that left me mystified by Amber Mae Wilson's peremptory employment of my "pollen" and my subsequent dismissal, and that left me blindly, numbly, stupidly infuriated by the way that Grace had been removed from my life before ever really becoming a part of it. My father, needless to say, had been horrified by everything about Amber Mae, except for her astonishing beauty. They came to hate each other.

Toward evening, my father and I shook hands outside the ranch house and I left. My mother sent me off with a boxful of food—Russell the bachelor, even at thirty-four still spoiled by his mom. But rather than heading home, I drove down one of the dirt roads that ran along the crest of a hill, wound along the edge of an emerald green grove, then ended in a place that had always been my favorite piece of ground in the entire SunBlesst Ranch. This corner of the grove was originally where the laborers would gather for lunch and, on Friday evenings, dinner. At first— years ago, my father said—there had been just a table that the workers had made of old upturned cable spools. The chairs were orange crates borrowed from the packing house. But as time went on and—I found out later—with my father's help, a few trees had been relocated, a large *palapa* had been built, eight long picnic tables were set up around a square of raked and packed earth, and an impressive ceramic fountain featuring a creature-laden St. Francis of Assisi was placed near the road at the entrance of the "cantina." My father had T'd off of an irrigation pipe to divert enough water to keep the fountain full and flowing.

As a boy, I had spent many hours there, some with the laborers, some on the weekends, when I could be alone to sit in the shade, listen to the water spill around St. Francis's sandaled feet, and look out at the green continent of citrus to the south or to the dry, tormented hillsides to the west. I danced with my first girl there, on the packed ground between the tables, on a Friday night some thirty years ago. I got drunk for the first time in my life there at that "cantina," the same night as my first dance, I believe. When my heart was broken in the fourth grade by a girl named Cathy, I'd spent weekends for two whole months in the shade of the *palapa,* writing her letters that I never mailed, feeling profoundly sorry for myself. You can leave me, I remember thinking, but I'll always have *this*. Boo-hoo.

Of course, this corner of the grove had changed by the time I arrived that Sunday evening in September, after spending the day with my father. The shrinking SunBlesst Ranch meant fewer workers, and fewer workers meant less life. No one worked Sundays anymore.

I'd parked and walked toward the now-tilting, algae-stained fountain and looked at the aging *palapa*.

And to my surprise, someone sat at one of the tables in the shade, looking back.

What struck me first was the whiteness of her blouse against the green background of trees behind her. The rest of her seemed to blend with those trees, as if she were a part of them and they had allowed her to stray just far enough to use the table, as if they could snatch her back at any second. As I walked closer, she came into relief: a young woman, her hair pinned up in a haphazard knot, an open book lying on the table in front of her, regarding me with calm, very dark brown eyes.

"Sorry to bother you," I said.

"No bother at all, unless you've got some planned."

"Just a visit to one of my favorite places on earth."

"Mine, too. Sundays are the best."

I took my eyes off her, looked quickly around the "cantina," then at her again. She wore simple silver hoops in her ears, which shone subtly against her black hair and toffee-colored skin.

"What are you reading?" I asked, strictly as an excuse to keep looking at her.

"Wallace Stevens." She picked up the book, looked at me, then down at the page. I noted her ringless left hand with a thrillingly inappropriate satisfaction. She read:

> Slowly the ivy on the stones
> Becomes the stones. Women become

The cities, children become the fields
And men in waves become the sea.

" 'The Man with the Blue Guitar,' " I said. I'd never been so thankful to have known a poem in my whole life, and probably never will be again.

She smiled for the first time, a small smile with something pleased in it. "I'm reading it with John Rowe out at the university."

"I read it with Bob Peters. Same school. That was a long time ago."

She set down the book. "Do you work here?"

"My father is the manager."

"Mine's one of the supers—Joe Sandoval."

"I've met him. Russell Monroe," I said.

"Isabella Sandoval."

Then a silence pried its way between us, and I couldn't think of anything to say. She smiled at me again, then reached down to the bench and hauled up a rather large canvas tote bag. Out came two beers.

"I'd offer you a bite to eat, but all I brought was this," she said.

"I'd offer you a drink, but all I have is about twenty pounds of food. I'll get some, okay? It's right there in the car. My mom made it. It's always real good."

She suddenly pulled a serious face, then nodded. By the time I came back with Mom's generous box of provisions, Isabella Sandoval was laughing directly and undisguisedly at me.

In that moment, I saw myself as she did: a big thirty-four-year-old dope carrying around a picnic box packed by his loving mother, offering to share it with a pretty girl he'd met two minutes ago. I laughed at myself with her—red in the face, she told me later—and it came out strongly, that laughter, up from a place I kept hidden from my father's cynicism and from my own dull convictions about what it meant to be a man.

I fell in love with Isabella's laugh then, and a few hours later, I had begun to fall in love with the rest of her. I, quite literally, could not take my eyes off of her. It was the purest, widest, most simple emotion I had ever felt, and I've never experienced anything close to it since. I believed then that it was enough to last a lifetime. But all that seemed—as we drove there from the hospital six years later—much, much more than a lifetime ago.

I eased the car up to the grove and swung it around so Isabella's walk would be as short as possible. Her cane tips left two perfect rows of circles in the soil on each side of her. It seemed to take hours to go a few yards. She started to fall and I caught her.

When we got her settled at one of the tables under the *palapa,* Isabella took off her baseball cap and I set out the food. She gave me an inquiring look when I brought my flask from the car and stood it on the old redwood table.

"You forgot the beer," I said, smiling.

Isabella smiled back. I drank.

We ate as the sun drew itself together over the western hills and started its slow summertime descent. The whiskey went straight to my center, then spread outward, suggesting velocity. Neither of us spoke. Few things are as agonizing in this life as a magical place bereft of its magic. The trees and hills around us assumed a fierce specificity in the evening light; each clod of earth and grain of soil seemed isolated, blindingly singular. *Whiskey,* I thought, *blur this moment.*

"Are you okay?" Isabella asked.

"I'm okay."

"I don't need s-s-surgery, do I?"

"No." I drank. A pair of doves split the sky above us with the squeak of dry wheels—tight wings, diminishing shapes, gone. What speed, what motion!

"I wouldn't blame you if you went away for a wall," she said. "For a *while*."

"I don't want to be away."

"If I were you, I would."

"I'd still be with you, even if I was gone."

"Anchored to be. To *me*."

"No," I said quietly, while a voice inside me screamed, Yes! Yes! Anchored! Buried! Chained! *Drink!*

"Do you remember what you said the last time we talked about the . . . the . . . this?"

I didn't.

"You said that tay—taying, *staying* with me was the noble thing to do."

"I didn't mean that in a bad way."

"And I don't want it to be noble for you to stay with me. I w-w-wanted to take care of you. Because you're a hard man and I know you need somebody. I want it to be me."

"It is you, Isabella—only you." Liar! Cheat! Fool! *Drink!*

"I wish we could make love again."

"It's my fault."

"You could close your eyes."

"I know."

"I don't want you going somewhere else for it."

"Never. I want you." I drank deeply. The sun inched down in the sky. I looked for a moment at my hands, how dry and tough and veined they were.

"You know what the w-w-worst thing is?"

I shook my head. There seemed like so many to choose from.

"Losing you."

I stood up and, taking my flask, walked to the edge of the clearing, behind Isabella.

"I won't let that happen," I said. "It cannot happen. It's the one thing they can't take away."

Then my eyes were suddenly burning and I closed them, but the tears came scalding out. I lifted the flask and drained it. There was never enough.

"Oh," I heard her say from behind me. "Oh, Russ . . . *shit.*"

When I turned to look, her head was tilted sharply to the right, her face twitching, and her right shoulder was drawn up, convulsing. Her eyes were wide. I could see her arm jerking as if wired straight into high voltage.

It was the biggest seizure she'd had—bigger even than the first, a year and a half ago. I ran and stood behind her, wrapping her quaking body in my arms, pressing my face against her violent cheek. She felt, to me, as if she were possessed by some alien force. Her words were slow, scrambled beyond comprehension, "Sose oreo d-d-do tis to you . . . nebber won d-d-dis happt . . ."

I timed it on my watch, as always: one minute and forty-five seconds. You cannot believe how long a minute and forty-five seconds can be.

Then she slumped a little, settled down in her chair, the demons departing. He heart was beating hard. She inhaled deeply and let the breath out slowly.

"Am gin hab doot."

"Going to have to do what, Is?"

"Operation. I'm g-g-going to have them do it."

On the way home, she seemed to become clearer. She asked me whether I'd understood what she'd said during the seizure. I told her I didn't.

"It made p-p-perfect sense to me. I said I was so sorry to do this to you. That I never wanted this to happen."

I put my arm around her and brought her close to me. "I know, baby. I know."

10

That night, after Isabella was asleep, I went into my study and took out the stack of unpaid medical bills. It was a couple of inches thick, with plenty of red-edged envelopes and ATTENTION: OVERDUE stamps on the pages. Our insurance had been sufficient until the radiation-transplant procedure, which was not yet considered an approved treatment. I had paid out about ten grand, but the well was almost dry. Try as I did to ignore these debts, I was still aware that some eighty thousand was still outstanding, and my attempts to stall had been intercepted by a case manager, one Tina Sharp, whose telephone calls I routinely failed to answer. A sudden fury shot through me as I held this stack of demands, so I got out my lighter, set the corner of one on fire, and watched it burn upward. So what? I thought. Even if you burn them, you still owe, and what does a roomful of smoke get you? It would be harder to explain *that* to Izzy than it would be to just keep on lying about the insurance. I dropped the flaming paper to the carpet, mashed it out with my foot, and threw the rest of the stack back into the wastebasket.

I turned on the news. There were Midnight Eye segments on two of the three networks and on three local stations. Stunned neighbors of the Wynns were interviewed, impaled on the cameras for close-ups to show their worry and fear. Karen Schultz, looking amazingly composed and fresh for Channel 7, said that they were "investigating the possibility that the Wynn, Ellison, and Fernandez murders are related." But Karen's reluctance to connect the three events was ignored heartily by the reporter, who mentioned everyone from Richard Ramirez (the Nightstalker) to Hannibal Lecter, exhuming whatever past terrors might magnify the present one. Assuming this was the work of a serial killer, he asked Karen how long it would be until they caught him.

"We're working on the evidence right now," she said. "The investigation is going very well, and that's all I can say."

This segment was followed by a short feature piece on a Huntington Beach indoor gun range already besieged by customers—mostly women—wanting to learn how to shoot large handguns. The instructor displayed in his beefy hand a nickel-plated .357 and said it would "stop any intruder in his tracks—*if* it's used right." His business was up 65 percent in one day.

I went out on our deck in the dark heat and drank. I tried to pray, but the prayer turned into a tirade. I could feel the motion calling me, the world of speed and movement. I went to the woodpile, took the ax, and split stumps until my hands bled. I could see the outline of Grace through a window, watching me. Yes, I thought, your father has the seed of madness in him. I grunted the blade into one last log and trudged up the trail that leads from my driveway all the way to the crest of the hills. I did not forget my bottle. I stopped halfway up to continue my challenge to the powers that be. I nearly fell. I picked my way down a narrow trail to the Indian caves where Isabella and I used to picnic—and sometimes sleep—on hot summer nights like this one. The sandstone walls were illuminated by moonlight, and the cave mouths yawned invitations I was tempted to accept. I finished the bottle, threw it into a cave, then climbed back to the main trail. When I made the top, I broke into a run through the low, fragrant sage, snapping through the dry branches until I hit the fire road. I ran faster, toward town. All I could hear, way up there above the city, was the leaden pounding of my shoes in the dust and the sharp rhythmic pattern of my breath. My legs began to ache, so I pressed harder. My lungs seemed too small, so I ran faster. The sage and manzanita took on bright red outlines—the same dire red that had come to me in Amber's bedroom two nights ago—a vibrant, scintillating red. The landscape throbbed with it. I rounded the highest point and the Pacific spread out below, a twinkling prairie of water and light. I made my way down toward town, running, skidding, braking until I hit the first paved streets and ran downhill now past the big walled houses and the peaceful aromatic eucalyptus, down into the quiet streets that feed into Coast Highway, finally to the highway itself—even at this hour a steady river of streaking, moaning cars. I could feel my heartbeat in my fingertips. I turned north on Coast Highway, tripped and fell flat in a crosswalk, labored upright, and continued.

I stopped at Ron's bar for a drink, but they wouldn't let me in. At Adolfo's, they did, and I downed two quick beers. Another one at the Sports Tavern, another at the Saloon, which left me downtown at 1:00 A.M., sweating, stinking, exhausted, drunk, and without immediate prospects for a ride back out the canyon to my house. I called Isabella, got Grace instead, told her breathlessly that I loved Izzy and everything would work out. "Tell her that," I demanded. Grace asked me where I was and I gave her my approximate whereabouts.

At the intersection of Coast Highway and Forest Avenue—the main corner of our little hamlet by the sea—I just stood and watched the cars go by. They all had slowed to that deliberate, negotiable speed perceived as actual by the drunken. The sound of their tires—just a few feet away from me—was of rubber swooshing through water. I wondered whether it had rained while I was in the phone booth.

I put out my thumb and watched the cars pass. I was close enough to the highway to make eye contact with any driver who looked my way. A streetlight beside me cast each passing interior into cool, stark visibility, from which the faces stared back as from a stage. What their eyes offered me was smug refusal, nascent fear, and the overriding desire that I would go away.

I did not. I stood my ground, thumb out, challenging every windshield face that passed by me.

And that was exactly where I was standing a minute or two later when the gray Chrysler K car—a body style so bland as to be noticeable—rolled up and made the right turn onto Forest, directly in front of my outstretched thumb. I was vaguely aware of a yellow rental-company sticker on the right bumper. But what I was most aware of was the driver's face, staring at me in that moment of perfect enlightenment as the car slowed for the turn.

In a heartbeat, I made a positive identification. It was not difficult, not even a little. The driver was—undoubtedly, assuredly, without any shred of doubt at all in my mind—no other person on earth than Amber Mae Wilson.

She looked afraid.

I stepped in the direction of her disappearing car,

misjudged the curb height, and lost my balance again. I was clever enough to make it look as if I was just trying to sit on the curb. So I sat on the curb. People parted around me, muttered, passed on. Amber's car vanished into a left turn on Third. I rubbed my eyes, watched a manhole cover levitate, and listened to the sharp slap of waves mixed with the hissing of car tires on pavement.

A moment later, Grace's red Porsche appeared in front of me and I felt my daughter's strong arms lifting me up to stand on my own two, only slightly functional, feet.

"Get in, Russell."

I felt the transmission engage beneath me, heard the roar of the exhaust, watched the shops of Forest Avenue blink past us. I could hear myself talking. I was telling Grace everything that had happened on the nights of July 3 and 4. I was back in Amber's room, somehow, reliving every detail of those dismal nights, confessing my obsession with Amber, my run-in with Martin Parish, trying to explain to my daughter that her mother's body had disappeared and that truly, truly I loved Isabella more than any living creature and all we'd wanted was a normal life and maybe a child. . . . "*And I swear, Grace, I just saw Amber driving a car not five minutes ago right down this . . .*"

My daughter's hand pressed against my mouth.

"Shut up, Russell, you're embarrassing yourself."

I shut up, melting into the g force of Grace's turn onto Broadway. She glanced at me.

"Look," she said, "Amber's alive, no matter what you think you saw. It's totally in keeping with the way she is. *You,* of anyone, should know that. Were you as drunk that night as you are now? How in hell do you know what you saw? As for you and your pitiful *obsession* with Amber, well, you're just another one of a million men made stupid by her. Maybe the only man made even stupider than you is Marty. *He's* so fucked up, he thinks he saw *me* there that night, when I was watching a goddamned movie with Brent Sides."

"You can prove that?"

"When and if I choose to," she snapped. "I'll tell you something, Russell. My mother is so full of deceit and manipulation, I wouldn't doubt it if she'd played a great big joke on all of you. I know her. Nobody in this world has gotten more of her hatred than I have."

"I wouldn't know."

"You sure wouldn't. While you were slogging away on the Sheriff's Department, Mom and I were galavanting around the world, having *fun*."

Grace turned onto Coast Highway and headed north. She ground the car into second and shot past a tourist trying to make it across the asphalt, flipping him off through the window as we whipped by his wide-eyed face.

"I tried to find you," I said.

"That's not the point. You did, or you didn't. You couldn't have found us, anyway. Those postcards I sent you from Rome? I wrote them from a boarding school not twenty miles from your home, sent them to Amber, who mailed them to you from Italy. By the time you got them, she was in Paris, anyway. We used that trick a lot on you. Amber didn't want you to see me, and she saw to it. It's the way she works. Funny, though, because you were one of the few men in the world she didn't want me to see."

"I don't understand."

"Did you know she tried to turn me out when I was ten? Not like a whore, I mean, but like a ... woman. She had me in nylons and makeup and heels and pranced me around this party like some kind of show pony. She encouraged me to keep the company of men three times my age. And when I wouldn't do what she wanted, when I'd dress the way a girl wants to and mouth off to her big beautiful friends and just get up and leave when I felt like it—*that's* when she started to despise me. Every inch I carved out for myself was a point of betrayal for her. She suffocated me. Later, she became delusional."

"What delusions?"

"That I was trying to take away her men. That I was stealing her money. She accused me five years ago of stealing this stupid netsuke and inro that John and Yoko had given her when we were in New York one year. She loved the ugly little thing because *they'd* given it to her, right? I didn't take it, but she's been obsessing over it for five years now, demanding I give it back, claiming I stole it just to hurt her. I never even wanted the goddamned trinket, though it's worth about twenty grand. But she's convinced I've got it stashed in a safe-deposit box somewhere. For that, she's threatened to write me completely out of her will."

"And your response?"

"I told her to fuck herself, keep her money, and leave me alone. I can work. I've got a job. Or at least I had one until those creeps Amber sent started hanging around the store. They truly scared me. They *really* scared me."

"Amber sent the men?"

"Of course she did. It's all a way to get me frightened back into her fold. She doesn't want to write me out of her will. She just wants me to lick her boots."

Grace jacked a right turn onto Cliff and headed down toward the Canyon Road. "Look, Russell. I've got my problems, but they're not your problems. I appreciate you putting me up for a few days. Take care of Isabella—she needs you. And quit thinking about Mom. She's a waste of time. Believe me."

I thought about these words, and they seemed to be full of great wisdom. From the mouths of babes. "Drive faster," I said.

My head snapped back against the rest and the engine howled from behind us. "I want to see Izzy. I want to love my wife."

"Good thinking, Russell."

Before lying down with Isabella, I had the presence of mind to retrieve the unpaid bills from the wastebasket in my study and replace them in the drawer. The act felt like a step in the right direction. It was something positive, actual, redolent of hope.

Grace had just taken Isabella her breakfast and I had just taken my second handful of aspirin in six hours when the telephone rang. It was seven in the morning, eighty degrees already, and too early for business as usual. I half-expected to hear Amber's voice on the phone. I'd replayed the vision of her in my mind a thousand times that night, even in my dreams, so many times that, by an inexplicable trick of memory, it began to seem unreal. Had I or hadn't I? It was impossible. It was true. I was outraged. I was mystified.

I had read and reread my *Journal* article on the Midnight Eye—front page, above the fold—and it was good. The courthouse and crime-beat reporters would be gnashing their teeth and screaming at Karen Schultz by now. The general public would be buying even more handguns.

I made it to the phone and said hello, my head thundering.

There was a long silence, but I could hear breathing. "Speak up," I said. "Life is short."

"It certainly is. Russell?"

"Yep."

"I am the Midnight Eye."

I entertained the notion, very briefly, that this was a joke. I would not have put it past Martin Parish or Erik Wald or even Art Crump to call so early and with so idiotic a sense of humor.

But something in the pause that followed, something in the firm timbre of the voice, something I remembered from the tape left in the stereo at the site of the Wynn slaughter, something in the center of my soul suggested that I was talking to the real thing.

"Fuck you, Jack," I said, and hung up.

He called back immediately. The voice was even, unhurried, perhaps just slightly lower than average. To my ear, he had no accent, which means a California accent.

"The Wynn wife was still alive when I tied her to the shower nozzle. I wouldn't have tried it with anyone who weighed over a hundred pounds. Blood drains clockwise above the equator, just like water, unless you reverse the flow. I did not. It clogged early, anyway. Cedrick Ellison had a dangling left testicle and a much smaller penis than legend gives the Negro. The picture of Jesus over Sid and Teresa's bed actually brought tears of laughter to my eyes, which, incidentally, are blue. There, Russell, a clue—even though you were rude enough to hang up on me. Convinced?"

It was my turn to breathe wordlessly. No one on earth but a good person of the Sheriff's/Coroner's office could have known what the voice had just told me, except for the man who'd committed the acts. There is no way he could have extrapolated that information from my article that morning, even with the strongest and most intuitive of imaginations.

"No," I said.

"What is your IQ?"

"Higher than yours."

"Mine is one thirty-six, according to the Stanford-Binet they gave us in high school. Junior year. I think I'd have done better, but I was preoccupied that day with a fantasy about the neighbor's cat. I was d-d-distracted. Are you really not convinced?"

"No, I am not."

The line was quiet for a moment. His stuttering *d* reminded me of the garbled, cryptic tape left behind. But this voice, live on the phone, had none of the rambling, slurring delivery that handicapped the maker of that tape.

"Then ask me."

"What do you have on your back?"

"A green devil."

"What does the Midnight Eye see?"

"Hypocrites."

"Spell it."

"You know, this may be the last time we'll get to have a long conversation, Russell, because I know you'll report this call to the Sheriff's, Winters will install an electronic call tracer I will allegedly not be able to hear, and you and I will have to have short talks. Right now, this feels like a luxury. Let's not turn it into a spelling bee."

The line on which we talked was dead quiet in the background, not so much as a hum, no static, clear. He could have been calling from the depths of a tomb.

"What do you want?"

"I liked the article. Thank you for using my name."

"What is your real name?"

He laughed for the first time then, a strange, muted *sh-sh-sh* that sounded wet, compressed between teeth or lips to draw force from both the inhale and the exhale. It sounded like something with scales escaping from a cage.

"How is Isabella?"

Again, it was my turn for silence. I could find no words for the protective fury inside me.

"What do you want?" I finally said again.

"The county should understand my quest."

"Which is what?"

"Cleansing."

"The races?"

"Absolutely. I can remember when the orange groves spread for miles and every face was a white, healthy, brave face."

"So what?" I said. "Places change."

"And change again, Russell. I am doing my part, signaling the change. Tell me, what has Erik Wald given you in terms of profile?"

"Nothing, yet."

"The usual bludgeon stuff, beards and size and neo-Nazi survivalist nonsense?"

"That's not Wald. That's the common wisdom."

"Sh-sh-sh. Wisdom. I'll tie Wald and his ilk in knots. Their arrogance astounds me."

"Where are you?"

"Russell, you are a belly laugh."

"In the county, I mean? Out of? In the state still?"

"Very much where I belong. I was born here. There, clue number two."

"Here, in the county?"

"Yes, Russell, here in the county. You still think like the cop you used to be. It must be hard to write entire books when your mind is so . . . flat-footed. *Journey Up River* was good, though. I think Crump is a terrible self-aggrandizer—a clown. It would be a temptation, with you there to report all of his silly posturing. But Art Crump had no purpose other than his own

103

sex. That's why he was so sloppy. It's hard to think clearly in the middle of a sex act, even when there's killing to be done."

"You manage."

"You can't say that. There have been no traces of semen left at any scene. The bodies have not been penetrated, so far as your medical examiner can tell."

He was right, of course. An idea roamed my head, but I said nothing.

"This is not about a man's desire," he said. "This is about the restoration of place, the dignity of an age that we cannot afford to let slip by. I'm pleased that you'll be writing my story for the county, Russell. You need me. It will be, actually, the greatest story you'll ever tell."

"I still don't know what you want," I said.

"One: Don't let Winters put a tracer on your phone. Record the calls if you'd like—accuracy in reporting is important, isn't it? It will allow me freedom to contact you without worry and you'll learn much more from a leisurely chat than a quick one. Two: I want you to keep Erik Wald informed of everything we say. I am interested in his . . . mind. Alleged mind. Three: I will make a dramatic statement very soon. I would inform the public if I were you—but that's not really your call, is it?"

"No. What kind of dramatic statement?"

"Russell, what do you think? Lobby on my behalf."

I thought for a moment. "I need something from you."

"I wonder what."

"Someone took out a woman named Amber Mae Wilson on July the third. The club, the writing on the walls, the recorded message on tape. Then he tried to cover it all up. He removed her. Why did you do Amber Wilson?"

I heard the sharp intake of his breath. "N-n-no!"

"Yes."

"Her h-head?"

"Just like the others."

"M-my voice, m-my writing?"

"Identical."

He groaned—a long, low, heartsick sound. "Then . . . you say the body . . . disappeared?"

"Where did you take her?"

"Was she white?"

"Where did you take her?"

His voice suddenly accelerated into one long run-on sentence, a stuttering river of syllables. "I didn't d-d-d-do her I've got no i-i-idea who would kill a w-white w-woman my q-q-quest is not for that I have been c-c-copied and m-m-mocked and I forbid you to w-w-write this in the papers I *do not kill white!*"

I listened to his rapid breathing.

"I believe you," I said.

"Ohhh . . ." He sighed, relief draining out of his voice and into my ear. "*Ohhh . . .*"

"Let me give you my number for the car phone."

"I have it," he said almost meekly.

"Where will your 'dramatic statement' take place?"

A long pause ensued. I could hear him breathing more slowly now.

"You need me," he whispered, and hung up.

12

I had never in my life seen more activity or confusion at the Sheriff's Department than I did an hour and a half later, just before nine that morning, when I was finally admitted to the inner sanctum of Sheriff Dan Winters's office, in which loomed the sweating, nervous figures of Winters, Martin Parish, and Erik Wald.

Of course, in the middle of our heat wave, the county building's air conditioning had overloaded and failed. Being a modern building, it had few windows that would even open. Outside, the smog lingered like smoke. Inside, the air was already stale and hot.

Waiting, I heard the phones ringing constantly, saw the double-time scurry of deputies and clerical workers, studied the drawn, tight-lipped faces on the officers who came and went in a steady stream from Winters's lair. The mayor of the city of Orange and one of our county supervisors made what appeared to be abrupt and pointless appearances, then marched straight for the pressroom. I followed, to find Karen Schultz besieged, and took for myself a dozen angry stares from the media and print people who had been treated, just a few hours earlier, to my rather major scoop. Channel 5 tried to interview me, but I walked away when the reporter excused herself to the ladies' room for a quick makeup check. Karen brushed me with an icy glance as I closed the door behind me.

But inside the sheriff's office, Winters, Parish, and Wald had the aura of the chosen. I could feel the energy in the hot room, the energy of organization and execution, of order, method, purpose. And beneath that energy lay another: that of the chaos and mayhem which had brought these men together, the silent and permeating force of their antagonist, the Midnight Eye.

Winters slammed down the telephone and looked at me. "We don't have much time. First, forget Dina. The story now is, we're deputizing the entire county, calling on every citizen to watch out for each other and report back to us anything they might see, hear, smell, or dream that will help us get this guy. We've called it the Citizens' Task Force, and Wald is in charge as sheriff-adjutant. We're setting up phone banks, printing up shirts and caps, trying to get everybody involved. Interview Wald about it. If you can't make it interesting and get us good play, we'll find someone who can. Second, you can get the ME's stuff through Karen but not without Karen. She'll edit out what we need for ourselves. Third, we've already got a goddamned miracle—Wynn's next-door neighbor was shooting video of her family the day before they bought it, and we've got a suspect right there on the fucking tape. Kimmy Wynn ID'd him as positively as a kid half in shock can ID anybody, but it's a damn good start. Documents is isolating a still we'll have within the hour, and every paper and TV station that wants one will get it. Your part is to get this Task Force idea off the ground. Your part is to make us look good. We're asking for help, Russell. We're begging for it."

Wald, standing by a window, looked at me.

"Think you can handle that?" asked Parish.

"You forgot point number four," I said to Winters, ignoring Marty.

"Four what? What the hell are you—"

"He called. The Midnight Eye. I just talked to him."

A pressured silence fell over the room, as if a gun had just been cocked.

"I'm liking this," said Wald evenly.

Parish regarded me with his slightly droop-lidded stare.

"Yes!" shouted Winters, driving a fist into the air. "What'd the son of a bitch say? Are you sure it was him? Any idea at all where he's calling from?"

I told them everything we said, except our exchange about the murder of Amber.

"Dramatic statement," muttered Winters. "Goddamned animal. Erik, you're the psychobabbler here—what's your call?"

Wald crossed the room and stood in front of Winters. "Look at it this way, what would you do if you wanted twenty bucks from me?"

"I'd say, 'Give me a twenty,'" Winters snapped.

"And I'd say, 'Sure,'" said Wald, slipping out his wallet, which he dangled before Winters, showing him the Sheriff's Department Volunteer badge lodged inside. "You're busted, Dan. That's how we play him. Give him what he wants. Play along. Give him enough rope to hang himself."

"Horseshit," said Parish. His face had reddened. "We can dink around with this guy all we want and not get any closer. I say put a CNI intercept on Russell's phone, keep SWAT ready, and hope for the best. When the picture hits the papers, we'll have the whole county waiting for him to show his face. I wouldn't negotiate squat with this scumsucker, or give him one inch of ink. We'll look like idiots."

Winters smiled and nodded, then looked at me. "Monroe, you're his dial-a-date, what do you think?"

"Play him," I said. "I'm with Wald. The intercept is a bad idea—he assumes we'll do it. Why not build up some trust, keep him comfortable, talking? If he wants to know what Erik is doing, we might be able to work that. He wants me as a mouthpiece. I can stall him, question him, maybe even guide him."

"Yeah, right," said Parish.

"He is right," said Wald. "As long as he wants something from us, we should listen."

"Goddamn classroom bullshit again, Erik."

Wald smiled. "I didn't see *you* getting any closer to Cary Clough. If I remember right, you were trying to make latents left by a maid while Clough was sitting outside Madeline Stewart's house with a ski cap, a pair of latex gloves, and hard-on. Get real, Marty. The twentieth century has actually arrived."

The phone rang. Winters said, "Yeah," "No," and "Get your butt up here," then punched the intercom button and told his secretary to hold all calls for ten minutes. "This is the deal," he said. "We go with the CNI intercept, but we keep the communication open. Carfax can rig one he won't be able to hear—he's a magician. We'll work him like Wald says. Erik, you'll need to coach Russell here on what to say—the last thing we want to do is set him off. Keep him hungry for what we can give him. Don't give him too much. *Racial fucking cleansing.* Man, I came to Orange County to get away from that shit. Martin, I know you'd trade a thousand words for one good fingerprint, and Chet Singer's working his ass off on the physical right now. We'll have a picture of him in the papers by this afternoon. Keep your leashes on."

Winters's eyes went to the knock on his door. "Get in here!"

A disheveled Karen Schultz burst in with a large envelope, from which she pulled a stack of eight-by-ten glossies. "Lopez in Documents says it's the best he can get," she said.

The photographs, mined from the neighbor's home video, depicted varying enlargements of a bearded Caucasian man behind the wheel of a Ford Taurus. In three of the shots he was looking at the camera; the others had him in profile, face to the road. The color was poor, but the car was clearly white, the man's shirt almost certainly red flannel rolled at the sleeves, and his hair and beard—which met and blended with the interior shadows of the car—were a chaotic mass of red-brown. Sunglasses hid his eyes. His left arm, dangling from the open window, was thick. His stubby fingers, ringless, were spread against the side panel.

"Exactly what Kimmy Wynn described," said Wald. "Exactly what the general profile indicates."

I stared for a moment at this man, this image. He looked like some demonic visage pressing in from the darkened background of a Caravaggio canvas. Was it his bearded heft that made him so totemic, or our assumptions regarding what he had done? It didn't matter. But I could feel the hair on the backs of my hands rise and a quick shiver wobble down my back as I contemplated the imprecise rendering of his face. Was it good enough for anyone to ID? That was the question that really mattered.

"Copies ready?" asked Winters.

"One hour," said Karen.

"Stay on it, choose the best and load up the press with them. Get a separate phone-bank number for the public, for anyone with information *on the photo*. Everything okay out there?"

"The phone lines are overloaded, so the bank isn't happening yet, the air conditioning is broken, and everybody's pissed off at me because Russell here has the inside track."

"He owes us," said Winters, fixing me with his black eyes. "Karen, get down to the dungeon and wait for Russell. You know what to hold and what to release. Marty, roll that dub for Monroe."

Parish lumbered to one of the three TV monitors lined up to the right of Winters's huge desk, pushed a tape into the VCR that sat below the middle set, and pushed a button.

"What you're about to see is the first Citizens' Task Force evidence we can really use," said Winters. "Pure accident. Pure gold. The neighbor—Lisa Nolan—brought it to Wald."

The screen flickered to life, a front-yard scene, daytime. The date and time appeared in the upper right: July 3, 4:26 P.M. Three kids—two blond girls and a plump red-haired boy—raced on the grass of a suburban lawn, chasing each other into a new red four-wheel-drive Jeep. A panting golden retriever followed them in. The camera moved to the front of the truck, holding for a still on the shiny bumper and winch, the dealer advertisement on the plate holder, the entire gleaming front end. A smiling woman of perhaps forty sat on the passenger's side. While she waved, a similar vehicle (but this one was white) tracked past slowly on the street, stopped, and the driver—a pleasant-looking Asian man in his early forties—leaned out the window and said, "*Rick, you like to trade?*"

"*Lisa would kill me, Tran!*" yelled the camera operator. The lens dipped as he answered and chuckled. Lisa nodded and pointed a finger at the camera in mock warning. The driver in the white Jeep admired the new red one. A woman was visible beside him, leaning forward so she could see. Three children had their faces pressed to the glass of the rear windows—two small boys and a girl.

"Recognize the girl in the white Jeep?" asked Parish.

"Kimmy Wynn," I said.

"Affirmative," said Wald. "Now take a look at her shadow."

A white Taurus came into the picture from behind the white Jeep, the driver pulling the car to his left around the stationary Nolans. When the Taurus came around, the driver looked briefly at the camera, then quickly away. He had just turned to profile when his vehicle disappeared offscreen.

Parish stepped forward and rewound the tape for another look. On the second pass, I saw him more clearly: the bulk of his huge body stuffed behind the wheel, his red plaid shirt, his thick tangle of red-brown beard and matted hair, his apparently sunburned face, black sunglasses, and his arm and hand—broad and strong as a peasant's in a Rivera painting—hanging from the window, fingers spread in perfect relief against the white body of the car. Marty played it again. The focus was excellent, and the Taurus passed by about fifty feet from Rick, the cameraman. For almost a full second, this man—very possibly the Midnight Eye—was center screen, a star.

Winters shook his head at the now-blank screen. "Russell, play up in your Citizens' Task Force article the fact that a citizen—Lisa Nolan—was bright enough to bring this evidence to our Task Force sheriff-adjutant, Erik Wald. We can't stress the need for public input enough. I'm praying somebody can ID this ape from a picture. If not, Chet has some physical that will help. Karen's waiting for you in Autopsy. After that, talk to Chet. After *that*, get to work and find a way to keep that county out there from going ballistic."

■   ■   ■

"He's big, heavy, and strong," said Karen, taking a deep breath and leading me into the autopsy room—the dungeon.

It smelled as it always did—a sweet putrescence of formaldehyde, blood, flesh. The overhead lights are bright but give no warmth. A chilly draft stays down low, clinging to your knees, easing into your joints. I hated this place, not for what it made me see but for the dreamlike unreality it forced upon me. To work the dungeon was always, for me, a matter of trying to chase detail through the silent, obscuring fog that surrounds the dead. The second I walked in, the ceiling dropped, the lights lowered, the walls crept in a few yards. The longer you stay, the worse it gets.

"Six foot two, two ten," she continued once we were inside. "Right-handed is our guess, but it's still just a guess. Yee told me he struck Mr. Wynn too many times to count. There were parts of his gums and a molar stuck to the ceiling."

I asked her how they got height and weight.

"Size twelve foot from the blood tracks, a very wide foot, deep imprint. The spray painting was done from a six-two height. Give or take some, Russell. You know that."

"Blood type?"

"None, but we've got his hair."

"Latents?"

"Dream on. We've found bits of black acrylic material where we might expect prints."

"Gloves."

"Gloves."

"Semen?"

"He's kept that to himself, so far. Or put it where we haven't found it."

We stopped short of a stainless-steel table where examiner Glen Yee was working on Mrs. Wynn. The light seemed to dim again. I breathed deeply the sickening chemical-flesh air. You think it's never going to wash out of your nose hairs. My throat felt sudsy.

Yee, elbow-deep, looked up at me and actually smiled. "All B-I-T," he said. "Except for Mr. Wynn."

I nodded. B-I-T—blunt-instrument trauma. It struck me that it shouldn't take a doctor to figure out that much. But I had been wondering how the Eye had managed two adults and two children with nothing but a club.

I looked at Karen, but she was staring at her own feet, arms crossed, hands clenching and unclenching.

Yee reached into a plastic basin that stood at the head of the table and held up something with his fingers. Between them was the instantly recognizable shape of a .22 long rifle bullet, slightly mushroomed, lopsided, bent from the middle.

"One in the head for Mr. Wynn," said Karen without looking up.

"He didn't really have much of a head left," I said. It wasn't supposed to sound like it did: It was just a numb observation.

"Oh, he did," said Karen. "It was just spread around the room. The techs brought it back in bags. Dr. Yee used all his skills to put it back togther. *Shit.*"

Karen, blanched and sweating, hustled across the autopsy room to a big stainless sink, into which she vomited. Yee watched her go by, looked at me, and shrugged, giving a small embarrassed smile. He carefully put the bullet back. The air conditioner—which can run by generator in case of power outage—blew a death-heavy breeze by me. The ceiling came down another foot.

Yee sighed. "I've never seen anything this traumatic in seventeen years, except the car accidents."

Karen, her back still to us, shook her head, coughed, spat.

"Did you get a shell to go with that bullet?"

"CS brought in no shell. Revolver, maybe, or a single shot. He used a knife to disembowel."

I nodded, staring stupidly into the open carcass of Maia Wynn. "I'm done in here if you are, Karen."

"Take your time," she said. "Don't rush a good thing."

"I said, I was done."

We passed through the sliding doors and down the hallway, the residual sweetness of formaldehyde lessening in my nostrils. Karen Schultz's heels hit the linoleum with a hurried resolve.

"The bullet we don't release," she said. "We don't want him ditching the gun. The knife we don't release—same reason. Don't talk about the wall writing or the tapes—we don't want to put any ideas into any other sick heads. We're trying to get a better description from Kim, but she won't tell us anything at all. She gave me what she gave you back at the house, then went mute. I've never in my life felt sorrier for another human being. All she does is stare."

"Where is she now?"

"*No.*"

"I won't talk to her unless you say I can."

"Damn straight you won't. Kim's going to live with what happened last night for the rest of her life. She's not here for you to draw quotes from. And leave her out of the *Journal.* That's the least you can do."

"Maybe I could—"

Karen stopped, drove a finger straight at my face, and glared at me with her fatigued green eyes. "No. No. *No.* You don't talk to Kim. End of discussion. Besides, I've got more for you in Hair and Fiber."

I put up my hands in mock surrender. "Okay. I'm sorry about all this, Karen."

"Your sorrow doesn't do the Wynns any good."

"You're not the only one who feels bad here."

"Stop, Russ. I know. I *know*. Please, just stop."

Karen's eyes were filled with neither rage nor sadness, but with a churning, undisguisable fear. "We should have put together the first two sooner. Maybe this wouldn't have happened."

■   ■   ■

The Hair and Fiber section of county Forensic Science Services was presided over by an aging, overweight man named Chester Fairfax Singer—Chet for short. He wore suspenders, white shirts, and bow ties and affected a professorial deliberateness that seemed at first a mark of either arrogance or dullness. He was unhurried, quiet.

As I had learned over the years, Chet's bearing wasn't born of arrogance, academic overtraining, or stupidity, but of a broad and genuine gentleness. He was a lifelong bachelor, never mentioned family, seemed to spend virtually all of his free time alone, and though he'd never to my knowledge intimated such a thing to anyone at the county, there was an almost unanimous decision that he was homosexual. But Chet had never been the butt of those secret jokes that follow homosexual men around, especially in the flagrantly hetero world of law enforcement. I think this had less to do with Chester's spotless reputation than with the sense of vulnerability he projected. Chet was a man who'd cried openly when the Challenger went down. Chet was a man who remembered the birthdays of every female who worked in Forensic Services, and honored each with a single white rose—grown himself—in a simple white vase. Chet was a man who arranged to be escorted to his car each night rather than negotiate the dark county-employee parking lot alone. Chet was a man who, despite his sizable quirks, commanded respect.

Chet was a man, I came to understand, who had a secret life. I never got to know him well enough even to guess what it was.

He was sitting on a stool at his light table when Karen and I came in, staring through a swing-out magnifier at something in an evidence bag. He set the bag on the glass and rotated his bulk on the stool, offering me his hand. Chet looked pale and nonvigorous as always, though I knew from my days on the Sheriff's that twelve-hour days were standard for him.

"One of my favorite fellow students," he said, smiling. It was part of a phrase he'd mumbled once to me years ago while working on a perplexing rape case, and I'd reminded him of it often: "We are students of the incomplete." The other statement of Chet Singer's that I will never forget, he made drunkenly to me over the punch bowl at a department Christmas party back in 1982: "Violence is the secret language of the race, and we are its translators."

Chester and Karen exchanged wary looks, and Karen nodded. "Winters says we can talk to him," she said. "I tell him what to leave out."

"Of course. Well . . . where to begin?"

Chet folded his hands over his ball-like midriff and beheld me through the thick lenses of his glasses. "Let me describe a picture for you, and you can tell me what you see."

Chester's "picture" of the Midnight Eye was of a tall, right-handed Caucasian male, age thirty-five to forty, with long, straight red-brown hair and a full beard of a slightly darker shade.

"If we use the 'all hairy' description that Kim gave you, we can say his hair is unkempt—wild-looking," said Chet. "Three of the five hair samples are nearly eight inches long. They contain some polymers I suspect are a fixative of some kind. Very thick in places."

"Hairspray?" I asked

"Apparently."

"A genuine sweetheart," said Karen. Karen was still uncharacteristically pale, the freckles on her nose still standing out in relief against the white skin.

Chet nodded. "Dina can't match the genetic print of the hair with a blood sample from a suspect unless there's root tissue connected to the follicle. So far, I've found none. I don't feel that we're in a strong position right now for typing."

"And we've got no suspect," I said.

"I remain an optimist," said Chester. "Though at times, I don't know why."

According to footprints left in the Ellisons' vegetable garden—through which the Eye had walked—the man would have been wearing size twelve shoes.

"Now, the soils."

The soil was a mixture of decomposed granite and beach sand, and the CS techs had found it in various locations in all three scenes—the Fernandez apartment, the Ellisons' suburban home, the Wynn's big custom house. An alert CSI had checked the blood smears on the walls at the Wynns' and found the sand granules mixed with the blood, along with acrylic fibers most likely originating from the Eye's gloves. A small mound of the granite/sand mix had been found on the floor next to Shareen Ellison's side of the bed. The word *mound* told me how it got there.

"Why a mound?" Chet asked me.

"He knelt down to look at Mrs. Ellison before he attacked—one knee up, one down. The sand came out when his cuff emptied."

"How did it get into his cuff to begin with?"

"The beach. It's beach sand, right?"

"Correct."

Chester's next finding was contrary to what Kim had described, though her mistake was understandable. The murder weapon was not a baseball bat at all, but a heavy length of relatively soft steel alloy, commonly used to make standard irrigation pipe. Yee had found microscopic shards of the metal in the skulls of Mr. Ellison, both Wynn adults, and Sid Fernandez. He found no wood or aluminum that would indicate a sporting bat. From the relatively controlled fury that the Eye had employed on his first three victims—the Fernandezes and Cedrick Ellison—Yee had been able to establish that one end of the pipe was fitted with what was probably a standard threaded cap, giving the weapon a rounded rather than a sharp edge.

"I suspect that the other end is capped also," said Chet, "Or at least drilled."

I waited, as did Karen. Chet had the same smug, almost flirtatious look that he always got when he'd made a tough leap and landed squarely.

"Picture this," Chet continued. "He must find a way into the homes. In the Fernandez apartment, he was lucky and used an open door. At the Ellisons', he climbed through a window. At the Wynns', he cut a five-foot slot through the screen-door mesh and slipped through it. We must assume he arrived at all three scenes by car or motorcycle—surely he can't cover so much of the county by foot and not be noticed—so in each case he must've walked from the vehicle to the home."

I waited again.

"Where does he keep a two- to three-foot-long, one-and-a-half-inch-diameter—I would guess—club? Does he waste a free hand on it? Does he risk being seen *holding* it as he approaches the scene? No. He fits one end with a loop. Leather, or maybe thick twine, even a strip of cloth. He cinches the knot up against the cap, or maybe he's drilled a hole for it—remember, this pipe is manufactured to be relatively soft and rust-resistant because it's often buried. The loop goes over his left shoulder, leaving the weapon to lie against his side. It's hidden, out of the way, but quickly accessible."

"Raskolnikov's MO," I said.

Karen frowned.

"Yes," said Chet. "He's taken the page from Dostoyevski, although I doubt he's read *Crime and Punishment*."

"How do you know what he *reads?*" Karen asked.

"Nobody who misspells *hypocrite* or *ignorance* reads the masters," I said maybe a little snottily. I was hoping to buy Karen's kindness with forensic competence, but the tone of voice came out wrong. She colored and looked away from me.

Chet gave me a very odd look at that moment but nodded, first to me, then to Karen, then studied me again. "Yes."

"Nice, Chet, but a yard-long pipe dangling from a man's shoulder isn't exactly hidden," Karen said.

"That is correct. And that is why, as Kim told Russell, the Midnight Eye wears the green robe."

The green robe turned out to be a blanket—an inexpensive acrylic blanket, fibers from which Chester had already placed at all three scenes. It was likely old. It was very dirty. Fibers of it were found at the Wynns', mixed with decomposed granite and beach sand just inside and to the left of the master suite's door.

"Holding a blanket around you still takes a free hand," I said. "If you're going to keep it over your shoulders."

"He takes it off once he's inside—the CS team found the fibers tightly grouped in all three scenes. He has set down the blanket, in each case, just inside the bedroom door, always on the left, using his freer right hand to slip it down and off."

"Like taking off his warm-up jacket," said Karen. "I wonder if he uses pine tar on his club, for a better grip."

"No evidence of pine tar, Karen. But I had Evidence send up the Wynns' screen door this afternoon, for a closer look at the cut. The jagged ends of the mesh were rich with green acrylic fiber—the top, where his shoulders went through, and the bottom, too, where the blanket dragged across."

Karen looked at me a little wearily. "Nothing on the blanket, Russ. It's too easy to ditch and get another. Winters said okay on physical description and method of entry *only*."

Chester coughed quietly. "I would not release information on his facial hair, for roughly the same reason, Karen. A man with a full beard is much easier to spot than one who is clean-shaven."

"Too late, Chet. We're going with the picture."

Chester shrugged.

Karen hesitated for a moment. A flutter of confusion crossed her eyes. It was then that I realized she was truly making the calls for me, that for all her carping about Winters this and Dan that, Karen Schultz herself was in charge of me and what I wrote. That's why she'd been sitting on me so hard. Any mistake was hers and hers alone.

Chet coughed again, cupping his hand to his mouth. He struck me as a little nervous. I assumed he was plugged into Karen's distress at my presence.

"We know he carries a knife—short-bladed, and I would guess a substantial handle for . . . leverage. It is likely a hunting knife, or one for skinning. So," he said. "That is the picture I've drawn for you. What do you see?"

I gathered my thoughts for a long moment, drawing in Chester's images and information, extrapolating what I could, trying to let a coherent whole emerge. "A beach bum. One of the homeless you find in beach cities. He's got long hair and a beard because he can't afford to have them cut. He wears a blanket for warmth, and to hide the club. He spends his time at the beach because it's free, he can panhandle, use the public rest rooms, check the dumpsters for edible trash, steal from the tourists. On the tapes he made, I heard waves in the background, and voices. He hangs out at a place where the cops are halfway lenient, where other homeless people congregate—no use standing out, and at six two he's not exactly inconspicuous to start with. Venice Beach is a possibility, but it's too far north. The cops would run him out of Huntington or Newport, so Laguna is the best bet. I'd look for him in Laguna. He steals cars to get around because he's too poor to afford one of his own. He gets them in Laguna, leaves them there when he's done. You'd find beach sand in the floor mats, green acrylic fiber on the upholstery, and if you were lucky, Chet's mystery polymer on the headrests. He's a Rastafarian—or thinks he is—from all the Jah shit he paints all over the walls. Rastas smoke a lot of dope—it's part of their religion—so I'd expect him to be around the smoke. Again, he can't buy it, not much of it, so he hangs with people who supply him. We know he's got access to a tape recorder, so I'd guess he stole it from a tourist who was out in the water, not looking after his things. He's either got a speech impediment or he's heavily under the influence when he makes the tapes—maybe both. Epilepsy is possible. We could figure out only half of what he said, and that didn't make a lot of sense. Last, I'd say he's pretty smart. He wears gloves, hides a three-foot steel club under his blanket. He's brave and he's getting braver. First, two people alone in an unlocked apartment, then a couple in a locked house, then a family of four. He won't stop because the more he kills, the hungrier he is for more. There's no sexual turn-on for him in it; he does it because he thinks he has to. Probably hears God—Jah—telling him he has to do this shit. Maybe that's who's talking on the tapes. That's what I see."

Chet said nothing for a moment, then finally looked to Karen. She had her back to us, staring out the vertical slot of window that constituted—twelve hours a day—Chet Singer's view of the outside world.

"Good," said Chet. "I understand you have actually talked to him."

"News travels fast around here," I noted.

"Are you *done*?" asked Karen.

"I'm done. Thanks, Chet. I'll be careful with this."

"Good of you to visit," he said. "I'm sorry we lost you."

Karen had already pushed through the door ahead of me when Chet quietly called me back inside. He gave me that odd look again, as if I were a specimen under his microscope. "That was perceptive of you to remember the Eye misspells simple words, and to mention the similarity to Dostoyevski."

I waited, wheels turning inside my head, wondering what I'd done. "Thanks."

"But nowhere, in any of our crime scenes, did he write the word *ignorance*—correctly or not."

I could see IGNORACE on Amber's wall, clearly, as my mind streaked for the nearest plausible excuse. Even as I stood there, slack-jawed, probably, I saw a way to employ my befuddlement. It was a superb lie, delivered with humility and aplomb. "I write and edit hours a day," I said with a minor smile. "I must have mistaken my ignorace for his."

Chester continued to study me hard for a moment, then smiled. "Well," he said, "we all certainly have enough of that to go around."

For the next hour, I interviewed Erik Wald and Dan Winters to get Citizens' Task Force's information. The formulation of this force, I saw, was clearly a promotional move on Winters's part, a way of enlisting not only public support for the case but of enlisting votes in the next election—still two years away. I tried to remain uncynical. It was also, I understood, some kind of atonement—overatonement perhaps—for the fact that the department had taken so long to connect the Fernandez and Ellison killings. Still, the task force was theoretically a good idea, if it brought results. I personally thought the T-shirts and caps a bit much. Wald seemed almost to glow in his moment; he was sincere, glib, earnest, arrogant. I was reminded again that Erik was an outsider here and that no amount of infiltration of this department would ever render him a sworn officer. But for now, Wald would have heavy coverage, and his Task Force had already produced a potentially huge piece of evidence—the video and resultant photograph. Carla Dance dispatched a photographer who shot Wald during the last few minutes of our conversation. Before the shoot started, Erik brushed his hand through his curly hair and loosened his necktie.

"Hurry up," he told the photographer. "I need to get to work."

■   ■   ■

The last thing I did before heading home to write the article was make a quick stop by Sorrento's up in the Orange hills.

Brent Sides was indeed tending bar. He was tall and tanned, with a swatch of thick blond hair, and eyebrows sun-bleached to white, which hovered over his blue eyes like frosted comets. But in spite of his tan, he blushed deeply when I introduced myself as Grace Wilson's father.

"I like your books," he managed. "And the article today about the killings. The waitresses here are all freaking out."

I watched him drying glasses with a clean white towel before I spoke again. When I did, it was to tell him that Grace was in some very deep trouble with some very unfriendly men. He did not seem surprised by this.

I asked him about his whereabouts on the night of July 3, and he said he had been with Grace—first dinner, then the movies, then drinks. He took her back to her place, late.

"How old are you?"

"Twenty-three."

He blushed again and looked away.

"Do you love her?"

He nodded. "We've never been to bed, if that's what you mean, but I love her."

A cocktail waitress ordered a round of drinks, and Sides was relieved to be away from my prying eyes while he made them, set them on the counter, and recorded his action onto a keyboard. He eased back my way when the waitress swung away from the service bar, tray loaded.

"Have you seen these men?" he asked. "The ones who are after her?"

"No. You?"

"Yeah. They look heavy. I've got some friends, though."

"That's not the point, Brent. Describe them."

He did, and his portraits were very close to those of Grace: one fat man with big ears and one slender young man with close-cropped hair and sunglasses.

I was quiet while he wiped the counter, apparently deep in thought.

"I'd never hurt her," he said finally.

"You'd do just about anything for her."

He nodded.

"Would you lie?"

"Probably. If she asked me to."

I suddenly liked Brent Sides for his guilelessness, his boy's shyness regarding my daughter, his obvious affection for her.

"Please ask her to call me," he said.

"I'll do that."

I paid up, shook Sides's cool, moist bartender's hand, and stepped back out into the heat of the afternoon.

13

Neither Isabella nor Grace was at home when I got there. Instead, there was a note on my pillow:

> Dear Russ,
> I'm sorry but I can't be here alone. I fell in the bathroom
> after the maid left. Not hurt, but it scared me. Grace was
> gone. Mom and Dad came and got me up and are
> taking me to their place. I wanted so badly to be your
> baby, not your infant. I miss you already.
>
> Love, Your Isabella

For a while, I stood there in our upstairs bedroom, listening to the roar of Isabella's absence. The sun was lowering over the hills, and through the picture window came a clear, fierce light that splashed across the carpet, hung against the far wall, angled over the lower corner of our bed. So much was missing: Isabella's wheelchair—a contraption that I'd despised at first, then grown to regard with some sort of odd affection as it came to be more and more a part of her; the bottles of pills that always cluttered her nightstand; the cane, upright on its four-toed foot, always waiting nearby for her; Isabella's journal, catalogs, cookbooks, novels, and travel books that were always strewn across the bed; even her favorite blanket. Now they were gone and the place—our place—was as forbiddingly neat as a motel room. A terrifying, urgent loneliness hit me then as I had a vision—not my first—of what this house and this life would be like without Isabella in them. A voice inside reminded me that the liquor cabinet was just downstairs. But I didn't move. I stood there in that unmerciful sunlight, drenched in a world without my wife.

I looked around the room, wondering whether the truest and simplest measure of a person is in what they love, whether a life is, most basically, a time to discover what those things and who those people are. And here was so much of what Isabella had found to love: the crystal hummingbird dangling on a string just inside the window; the cheap cut-glass figure of an Aztec warrior we'd gotten in Mexico and that now stood guard on the TV; her piano, which sat against the far wall in all its burnished, pampered beauty; her books of Neruda and Stevens and Moore; her hundreds of music tapes—everything from Handel to the sound track of "Twin Peaks." There it all was, illuminated by the sun but enlightened and made precious by Isabella's love.

And as I stood in front of her piano—her deafeningly silent instrument—and looked at the pictures framed and displayed there, I realized for the first time that of everything Isabella loved in this life, she loved me the most. There were pictures as we said our vows, as we climbed into the limo, cut the cake, waltzed the first dance. I'd looked at all these in passing a thousand times—every day, probably—and they'd always struck me as nice but common, charming in a ritual, almost institutionalized way. After all, didn't every married couple have a bunch of shots like these? But then, that day, standing in our room alone, I saw and really understood with absolute chilling clarity that I, Russell Monroe, was the prize of Isabella's life.

I, Russell, who had stumbled upon her reading poetry in the orange grove, five million years ago.

I, who had sworn to love and honor her.

I, who had sat outside Amber Mae Wilson's home not once, but four times, wondering whether I should go in, *knowing* that one night I would.

I, who carried a flask so as never to be too far from my beloved whiskey.

I, who had left her alone to fall in her own bathroom; I, who was now not even the first person she would call to help her get her suffering, besieged body off the floor.

I was her greatest prize.

The sunlight continued burning the room, bearing down into my eyes. I felt singled out by it, revealed, exposed. When I looked to the mirrored closet doors, there was no Russell Monroe to be seen, only the bright outline of something manlike and hollow—a glare. I wondered whether that was what Isabella saw when she looked at me: just the shape of a man where the substance used to be.

I walked down the stairs, acutely tuned to the sound of my shoes on the steps of our empty house.

■   ■   ■

Joe Sandoval, broad-faced and barrel-chested, was doing something to his front door when I parked in front of his house half an hour later. He and Corrine lived in San Juan Capistrano, a quiet inland town south of Laguna, known mainly for its mission, to which the migration of swallows in March of each year is both a local legend and a tourist event. Isabella and I were married in that mission on a scorching Saturday in September, a day that felt much like this one in the sheer overwhelming presence of its heat. I read the inscription on the silver flask again—"With all my love, Isabella"—after taking a slug of the whiskey inside.

Joe stopped his labor and studied me as I came up the walkway. Years of work for SunBlesst Ranch had left his face lined and dark, his black eyes in a perpetual, dubious squint that contradicted his general good nature. His thick gray-black hair was combed straight back as always, tied in a short ponytail. He transferred a screwdriver and offered me a heavy, gentle hand. "She's okay," he said.

"Was the fall bad?"

"Just a bruise, but it scared her. Come in."

He guided me into the house, one hand on my shoulder, the other on the door. I noted that he had been installing a second dead bolt, courtesy, no doubt, of the Midnight Eye. "Corrine is upset," he said quietly as we went in. "You know."

The living room was small but comfortable, furnished in the affordable Sears version of American colonial. There was a braided oval rug on the hardwood floor, pictures of family on one wall, and a simple shrine to the Virgin Mary tucked into the corner by the TV. Corrine's handmade afghans were draped generously over the sofa and chairs. A Bible lay on the coffee table. A window-mounted air conditioner hummed loudly. Beside it stood a .30-06 deer gun.

Corrine sat in the rocker, but she stood when I came in. I hugged her with the genuine affection tempered by dread that many men feel for their mothers-in-law. She had accepted me unconditionally as a husband for her daughter, but slowly over the last year I had sensed her respect eroding, based on the care I was—or wasn't—giving Isabella. She had never said one word to me about it, but I had decided that in Corrine's eyes I was not tending her daughter as well as I could. I began to resent this judgment. The thought had crossed my mind, of course, that in my own eyes I was failing, and what I truly resented was myself. By design, a man's conscience is eager to betray him.

Corrine is a tall woman, especially for one of Mexican blood. She was fifty years old then, the same age as her husband and only ten years older than I. Corrine is graceful in her height, always immaculately groomed, and she is conspicuously beautiful when she smiles. It is a smile to die for. In fact, Joe has a white knife scar across his belly, evidence of only one of the battles he fought in the dusty back streets of Los Mochis to win her hand and protect her honor. They had come north together just after they were married, in the summer of 1964, one year before Isabella—who would be their only child—was born.

She hugged me generously, then sat. "She is sleeping. Please, sit down."

I remained standing and looked toward the hallway. Joe sat down on the sofa and glanced at his wife, then at me. A minor point was about to be won or lost here. It was a matter of honor—or maybe only of pride—that I win it.

So I walked past the sofa, went down the hallway, and opened the door of Isabella's room. She lay on her back, deeply asleep, the breeze of a ceiling fan riffling the bedsheet at her neck. The room was cool, shadowed by an immense pepper tree in the backyard. From the wall directly above her head, an agonized plastic Christ stared, it seemed, straight down at Isabella. His cheapness angered me, his unconcern for the tumor cells growing unchecked and with His blessing, I assumed, in Isabella's lovely body. To ask Him for help seemed to grovel—the very worst of bad faith. I shut the door quietly and went back to the living room, where I sat on the couch and looked out the window to the street.

"Would you like for Isabella to stay with us for a while?" Corrine asked.

"I definitely would not."

"Why, Russell?"

"Because she's my wife and it's my job to take care of her."

Corrine's accusing silence blended with the hum of the air conditioner. Joe got up, went into the kitchen, and came back with a pitcher of iced coffee, three glasses. Joe and I never talked over anything but cold Bohemia. So, I thought, Isabella has mentioned my drinking. Were the beers and the whiskey still on my breath?

"If it is a job, Russ, then couldn't her staying here be a vacation—for you?"

"I don't want a vacation. I miss her already."

"Sometimes it's good to miss someone," said Corrine.

"This isn't one of those times."

Joe poured the coffee and handed me a glass. Corrine ignored him as he gave one to her, though I caught Joe's inquiring glance. He was torn here, I saw, between his unquestioned conviction that a man lives with his wife and his own wife's powerful maternal instincts. Joe was going to sit this one out for a while.

"It would give you more time," she said. "To work, to do the things you need to do."

"I'm working when the maid's there."

Corrine was nodding preemptively: Isabella had already told her this, too. "I know how hard it must be."

Clearly, she suspected that I hadn't actually been writing. One year, two months, and eleven days, I thought. But Isabella would never tell her this, out of her respect for the strange, sometimes misplaced sense of sacredness that many writers attach to their work. I was one of them. Isabella would tell no one that the work was dead, that nothing was happening, because anything sacred—even inappropriately sacred—is diminished by talk.

"Isabella told me you haven't written in over a year," Corrine said flatly. "She told me that in the hope we—she and Joe and I—might be able to help you. Of all the things that are painful to her, this is the worst—that she's made you not able to write."

Well, fuck me, I thought. Was I going to hear about this on CNN next, Charles Jaco live from my study in the stilt house? The fact that our money was almost gone came rushing in from another part of my brain, on a collision course with the fact that I'd written nothing but articles for so long. I resolved, then and there, to check the balances in all our accounts, if there were indeed balances to check. I had been filing bank statements, unopened, for six months now, on the theory that what you can't see can't hurt you. Of late, I'd noted bank correspondence coming in white, rather than tan, envelopes. I wanted my flask.

"I'm working," I said. I could feel the anger boiling over into shame, which was certainly running red into my face by now. I hated the petulance in my voice.

"I told you he was writing up something," said Joe, a mercy pitch that Corrine ignored. "And the insurance covers the operation, right?"

"*Yes.*"

Corrine breathed deeply and leveled her lovely dark eyes at me. "Russ, I worry not so much about your work as about my daughter."

Joe stared down at the glass in his lap. Corrine's eyes remained trained on mine.

"The fall today shouldn't have happened," I said. "But no one can be beside her twenty-four hours a day."

"We can, Russ. Joe and I. Let her stay. You can stay, too. She is our daughter, and you our son."

She turned now to Joe, who, still staring down, must have felt her gaze.

He nodded. "It's better for everyone," he said. "You been taking care of Izzy over a year now. You need a break. You need to make some money. After that operation, well, who knows?"

The air conditioner hummed. I felt like I was being robbed by thieves packing kindness instead of guns. In my heart, I knew they were right.

Why, then, was it so hard for me to agree? It took me a while to understand. When I did, all I could do was look back out the window, avoiding the imploring stares of these good, humble people. I didn't want to agree to leaving Isabella with them because I didn't want them—and myself and Isabella— to know how inviting the idea really sounded.

Contradictory emotions rose up inside me, slamming against one another, tearing at one another, contesting ownership of my heart. I had never felt so divided, so hugely at odds with myself, as if I'd been cut into pieces and put back together wrong. Or was I put back together at all? I felt the motion calling, the velocity and the freedom of velocity. But I felt the same yawning emptiness I'd known as I stood in the sunlight of our bedroom just an hour earlier. I felt the liberty of not being responsible, of not having to listen with at least one ear for the sound of Isabella upstairs needing me to perform a simple task such as putting on her shoes or helping her into the shower or emptying the bedside commode or pushing her wheelchair over a bump in the floor or any of the other thousand tasks a person does each day for themselves, not thinking, not appreciating how *easy* it is to clip toenails when your legs are not paralyzed, how *easy* it is to make it to the toilet when you can walk, how *easy* it is to stand in your closet and pick out something to wear without worrying whether it's big enough to fit over the leg braces you need in order even to stand up without falling to the floor. What liberation, to be free of that! But I also felt at the same time that dismal longing for her when she was out of my life—even for a few minutes! I could see our big bed without her in it. I could hear the silence that she had left behind. I could feel that vast, horizonless sadness of being without her in a world that existed only because Isabella was in it.

My stomach was locked and aching; I could not feel the beating of my own heart.

Finally, I began to swim straight through these opposing, powerful rivers, looking for one thing that I could hold on to without question. And I found it. I reached for it, sunk my fingers into it, and clutched it tightly against my chest. What I wanted, finally and without condition, was what was best for Isabella. Not for me. Not for Corrine and Joe. For Isabella.

"She twisted her knee pretty good today," said Joe.

"Enough," I said. I closed my eyes and rested my head on the sofa back. The clammy breeze from the air conditioner landed on one side of my face. I heard Corrine get up, and a moment later her hand settled against my cheek, fingers patting approval of my surrender.

"Maybe you should go be with her for a while," she said. "I'm going to make dinner."

■   ■   ■

I lay down next to Isabella in the small room. She stirred when I settled in beside her, smiled as I reached out and took her hand.

"So, you ran out on me," I said.

"I'll never run out on you. But this is b-b-better for a while."

"I know. I was only making another bad joke."

"Everything's going to be kay-o, isn't it?"

"Yes."

I kissed her and she moved a hand into my hair and pulled me closer. The kiss lasted a long time. When I moved my face down to her breasts, she spread her hand against the front of my pants and pressed gently. I slipped my arm under the sheets and traced her warm, dry center with my fingers. We lay there for a while, searching very slowly for what used to come so eagerly. Then she moved her hand back up to my face. I took it in mine.

"Maybe after the op-op-operation, every work will thing again," she said.

"Yes. Everything will."

"I love you, Russ."

I lay there with her for almost an hour, stroking her smooth round head while she slept with her face against my chest. I looked out the window at the pepper tree and watched a mockingbird flitting from one branch to another. I became that bird. I was nimble, feathered, capable of flight. I left the tree. I shot upward, piercing the hot blue sky. I streaked through the stars of some as-yet-unarrived night. I careened past the sun, out of the galaxy, deep into gaping, widening, limitless space, tears peeling from my eyes, beak sparking against the resistant atmosphere, feathers aflame, feet melting. I shot forward as a skeleton, a shard of vertebrae, a quivering atom of calcium. Motion. Speed. Velocity. Freedom.

When Corrine called us for dinner, I helped Izzy get dressed and into her chair.

Then I left.

At home, I poured myself a disciplined whiskey, roamed the outside deck for a while, then listened to a rather curt message from case manager Tina Sharp on the machine. I did not return the call. Rather, I sat in a patio chair where Isabella loved most to sit, facing southwest toward town. Our Lady of the Canyon lay atop the hills, the lights of Laguna flowing upward from between her legs, her pregnant belly protruding against the skyline. I went inside to answer the phone, but the caller hung up after I said hello. Cute.

In my study, I set up the computer and went to work on the Citizens' Task Force story.

First, I outlined the thing, thinking of the best way to make the readers feel included in the Task Force, not just reading about it. Basically, it was a flak job.

I drank more because I didn't like the manipulative aspects of this piece, and because I kept seeing Isabella lying on that narrow bed in her parents' house, and because newspaper-story structure is rigid enough to make it undentable by whiskey, resulting, I would guess, in the high rate of alcoholism among journalists. After all, I thought, I could slant the piece only so far before Carla Dance threw it back at me. After all, it wasn't the *Journal* but, rather, a terrified public that would decide what to make of the Citizens' Task Force.

The phone rang again, and again the caller hung up as soon as I answered.

Just like Amber used to do, I thought, twenty-odd years ago, when she was sneaking away from Martin Parish to meet me on the sly. Except our code was usually three hang-ups. That meant Amber was actually with Marty, scheming to be with me. She would tell Marty she was getting busy signals from a girlfriend. Three meant she would meet me that night. Nights with even-numbered dates were the bar atop the Towers Restaurant in Laguna. Odd-numbered nights were the back room of the Mandarin Chinese. Later, two hang-ups—oh, how I lived for two-hang-up nights!—meant she would come to my place. I always felt bad that it was Marty, but back in those days, when we were young, the cost of being with Amber was always worth paying. Always.

The phone rang again, and to my astonishment, the caller hung up. Three calls. I checked the date, purely out of curiosity: an even night, the sixth, the Towers bar.

I stared at the computer screen, searching for my lead. That first sentence is 50 percent of the work. Once the first sentence is right, the rest falls into place. I thought. I finally wrote:

What if she's really at the Towers bar?

No. I erased it. The image of Amber's ruined skull came back to me: the blood, the tangled mass of dark hair, the dead gray eyes. Then I saw her in the rented K car, looking at me fearfully from behind the windshield, illuminated briefly by the Coast Highway streetlight. Haunting me from the grave, wherever that may be. I thought of Isabella again. I wanted so much to love her.

I wrote again:

A drink or two at the Towers bar might be nice. You've earned it. You deserve it.

No. I deleted that, too. I sat for a while, then churned out the first three pages of the story.

I took a break, stared for a while into the refrigerator, although I wasn't hungry. I sat on the deck again. I sat on our bed, missing Isabella in a crazy, grateful way.

I went back into the study, finished the piece, and faxed it out.

Then I went downstairs, got in my car, and drove to the Towers bar.

■   ■   ■

The mirrors and windows of the Towers are bewildering at night, and they keep the place dark. The ocean spreads to infinity eleven stories below, behind a wall of smoked glass. Mirrors throw the Pacific back at you from anyplace in the room, dizzyingly reversed, even along the ceiling, which is mostly glass, too. You can't be sure what you're really seeing. The tables are beveled glass—rectangles of ocean reflected from the ceiling, which picks them up from the windows—the furnishings all Deco: lamps supported by robed ladies, wall lights mounted behind mirrored shells, ornate brass ashtray stands. There is a black baby grand in the middle of the bar, and it was staffed that night by a young man with a nice touch and a voice just like whoever's song he was covering. He did not play as well as Isabella. The place was crowded, but I got a chair in a far corner. To my left was an eleven-story drop to black ocean; to my right, the room; in front of me, a couple kind enough to let me share their drink table. The crowd was eclectic, as one expects in a hotel bar: middle-aged American tourists, perplexed foreigners, a few local dandies and not-so-young-as-they-looked women scavenging for the usual kinds of excitement. A couple kissed rather passionately in a corner. Two men, gay, tried to look at ease. A woman sat alone in the opposite corner from me, smoking a cigarette in, of all things, about a foot-long holder. She had shiny straight blond hair and a truly silly pillbox hat—playing her Deco part with style.

The couple right in front of me looked midwestern, middle-aged, middle management, and, as it turned out, they were. They were gabbing away, obviously a skosh drunk. The black glittering sea stretched out through the windows beside them.

The man smiled at me when we reached for our drinks at the same time. "You a Lagunatic?" he asked, referring to our unfortunate nickname.

"I am."

"Nice little town."

"It's a good place to live."

"What do you do?"

"Word processing. You?"

"Structural engineer, back in Des Moines. Came for Disneyland, and some whale watching."

He'd missed the whales by six months, but it was a little late to point that out. His wife smiled at me and picked up her drink. She was slender, sandy-haired, cute when she smiled. We talked a while, then the conversation dribbled off.

A moment later, they were both looking at me rather pointedly. "*Tell* him, Mike," she said, nudging her husband.

"You tell him, Janice," he said back, not unkindly. "*You* tell him."

"Okay, I'll tell him." She leaned a little closer. "This is the worst place we've ever gone. By the time we book a new flight out and pay for a week's worth of a hotel room we won't use, it will have cost us over two thousand dollars. You've got sunshine, Disneyland, and a person slaughtering people while they sleep. I just felt like, since you lived here and this is a tourist town, you should know."

140

I was in no mood to hear about tarnished vacation plans. "Tough luck. We all have our disappointments."

Mike chuckled uneasily. "You could be a little more polite about it, guy."

"And you could get yourself thrown out this window," I said. "So why don't you give it a rest?"

"I'll be damned," said Janice, slapping her drink glass on the table and standing. "Mike, let's just get the hell out of here. Killers and drunks like this guy. This is a rotten place, and *you* can have it."

"Thank you," I said.

"Hope he gets you."

"Who's that?"

"The *Midnight Eye*."

When Mike and Janice had left, I studied the crowd, observed a bearded man who wore a trim Italian jacket and a pair of expensive round glasses. He was roughly the Eye's size. He had the hair and beard. But I had him for a university type or a shrink. He was with a redhead who pouted, looking out the window.

I smiled, kind of, then turned and watched the black Pacific. The Midnight Eye as a tourism deterrent, I thought, hurting Disneyland and the California gray whale. And what if he goes out again tonight?

It got late and the crowd thinned. Amber, of course, did not show. I was relieved, exhausted, and deeply, furiously, sad when I thought about Isabella, which was every other second or two. Would the operation work? Would it be a disaster? One chance in ten . . .

The piano player did a good job on "The Way It Is." Ponytail seemed to be pleading with the still-dour redhead.

I paid my bill, went into the men's room, and threw some water on my face. Drying off with a paper towel, I regarded myself in the mirror and saw with some alarm the weight that had settled behind my jaws, under my chin. My nose was plumper—maybe a little pink—and my eyes seemed smaller. I look like a fucking manatee, I thought. Booze. Must cut that out. I straightened my back, inflated my chest, shoulders relaxed, head erect. Better. On my way out, the blonde in the corner motioned me over. She had taken her cigarette from its ridiculous holder and now placed it between her lips, aiming it at me for a light. Sure. I bent over, instrument poised.

When my thumb went down and the flame appeared and I set the fire close to her mouth, I saw that I was looking into the eyes of someone I used to know very well.

My heart stalled. I stared into those unmistakable gray eyes, making sure.

By the time my thumb released the lighter and Amber's face returned to the bar darkness, I had already begun—tentatively, very hesitantly—to piece together what had happened.

14

I drove south through the hot darkness. Amber slumped against the far door in her utterly convincing blond wig and a pair of sunglasses across which the city lights inched like rain on a windshield. The breeze whipped through her hair as she stared out the open window. Her face was pale and the shine of tears lay on her cheeks. The air smelled of ocean and exhaust and the opiate scent of nightshade—one of several sweet, poisonous beauties that blossom on our coast.

We went in silence all the way to Dana Point. I locked and unlocked my fingers on the wheel; they were governed by alternating currents of dread and hope that I could hardly identify, let alone control. I felt as if I were falling, twisting untethered through the air, careening toward an impact that promised both death and clarity. I kept glancing across at Amber.

She was crying without sound, a talent that had always amazed me. The only giveaways were the running tears and the sound of her congested inhalations.

When she finally spoke, her voice was thin and tight, stretched to cover the words.

"I . . . *God.*" She produced from her purse a cigarette and lighter. She leaned forward to miss the wind. From behind the blond perimeter of her head, I saw a glow, then a small cloud of smoke. She sat back up, and for the first time since we had gotten into my car, she looked directly at my face. "I was planning to be home on the Fourth—two or three o'clock. Reuben had a morning session set up in Malibu. It was a sunblock ad, and they wanted the holiday crowds for backdrop. At first, I said fine. I doubled my rate for the holiday, so I was getting about twenty thousand for the morning. I went up the day before, got a hotel in Beverly Hills. On my way to Malibu the next day, I changed my mind. It was too pretty and hot for work, so I called Reuben, argued, and headed up the coast to Santa Barbara. I left him believing I'd make the shoot, but Reuben believes what he wants to, no matter what someone tells him. I got a room on the beach in Santa Barbara and spent most of the Fourth. There was a man involved—a friend—someone I'm just starting to know. Don't ask me his name, because I won't tell you."

"The room on the beach was at his place," I said. "It was too late to get a hotel in Santa Barbara on the Fourth of July."

"Yes. I left about eleven that night, made it home at two. I walked into my house, but Alice was gone. Oh God, Russell— *Alice.* Oh God." Amber broke down finally, burying her face in her hands, tears rolling forth over her fingers, smoke from her cigarette wobbling up and out the window.

"Amber," I asked, "what in hell are you talking about?"

"You remember Alice, don't you?"

"Why would I remember Alice? I never *met* Alice. You mentioned Alice maybe twice in the two years we lived together. You said she was the only woman in the world prettier than you."

She looked at me again—face pale, lights creeping along the lenses of her sunglasses. "I said that?"

"You said that."

"God, what a terrible person I used to be. *She was my big sister, Russ. My only big sister, ever.*"

I waited, saying nothing, while Amber turned away to stare out the open window. She pulled off her glasses, wiped her eyes with a balled fist, choked back a sob, and exhaled a long, fluttering breath. "I know you were in my house, Russ. Martin told me. Now you're angry. Is it because I made you mourn me?"

In the two years I had been with Amber, her uncovering of my sundry angers had never done anything but multiply them. Amber had flown to my furies like lightning to the rod. It had not taken me much time with her to realize that she *enjoyed* this, that she craved the flash point. I learned that my rage—exposed and unleashed—was Amber's prize: It proved her power. And it wasn't until much later, when I came to know Isabella, in fact, that I discovered my furies were often little more than the unanswered brayings of a heart greedy for affection. Isabella exploded me safely within her strong confines, as gingerly as might a bomb squad handling some crude amateur device. I would never try to describe the desire that arises when anger collides with understanding. I can only say that into Isabella flowed the most heated and uncontrolled angers, transformed by the genius of her heart into the simple fuels of love. It had been so long since I had allowed them out in the presence of another person.

But now they tried to come again, unchecked and snarling, swirling around like ghosts inside my car. I would have lowered my window to flush them out, but it was already down. I turned up the vent fan all the way. I would not be baited.

"It's because you made me mourn you falsely," I said.

"Does that mean you feel cheated? Yes, I think it does. It means that you were happier believing I was dead. You can admit that, Russ. God, what a vicious, shallow man you are."

I ignored her provocations. I stayed on track. "When were you expecting Alice?"

"How patient you've become. We sure could have used some of that when we were together."

"When were you expecting Alice?"

"On the fifth, originally. But she left a message on the third saying she'd hit Laguna two days early. I was already in Beverly Hills, like I said, so I got a hold of her at her hotel, told her to go straight to my place, get comfortable, and I'd be home the next day. The maid was staying with family down in San Diego for the week, so she hadn't made up the guest room. So I told Alice to take the master. I wanted her to feel welcome. She and I had just started . . . we were trying to . . . well, *I* was trying to connect with her. It was part of my new, well, *self*. God, it sounds so fucking trite."

Amber sniffed and ran her fingers under one eye, then the other.

Amber's new *self*, I thought. My anger slid out of the car, whipping away in the slipstream. I began the long circle around the Dana Point Marina. The harbor sprouted thousands of yacht masts; the dark water shone with wedges of light that flickered on the swells, then vanished.

"But I enjoyed my friend in Santa Barbara, and it was late before I knew it. By eleven, I was on the road. When I got home, she was gone. Her bags were there. I saw a new throw rug beside my bed. There was a stain under it. There was fresh paint on the walls. In my study, someone had knocked over a lamp and some magazines. My heart was racing. The only thing I could think of was to call someone I trusted, someone who might know about these . . . these kinds of things."

"Marty," I said. It explained his abrupt change in attitude that day at the Wynns.

"Yes."

"And it took Marty a long time on the phone to believe you were really you. He didn't believe it at first. He insisted on seeing you that night—morning by then. Drunk or not."

Amber drew lightly on her cigarette, an action so fraught with distaste, I wondered, as I had always wondered, why she bothered smoking in the first place. It was so much like Amber to be able to flirt with a such a strong addiction and never really surrender to it. I'd seen her go for days without one.

"I'd never seen Martin so upset," she said. "Never. And he'd been married to *me* for a whole year, the poor man. He told me that Alice had been murdered, and that someone had obviously cleaned up the . . . my room."

Amber puffed again on the cigarette, staring out the window at the marina. The breeze blew through her platinum blond wig, and in the harsh violet light of the harbor lamps, her face looked like one freshly prepared for burial. For a moment, all the death of the last few days paraded through my mind: the Fernandezes; the Ellisons; the Wynns; their once-perfect twin boys, Jacob and Justin; Alice Fultz, Amber's sister. Then I could actually see the tumor cells raging unchecked in the brain of my Isabella—tiny black star-shaped little fuckers programmed to multiply themselves out of existence, aiming at nothing but the final annihilation of their host. For a moment, I saw those monstrous vultures circling with hideous ease outside our windows. I saw Black Death sitting atop our telephone pole, lazily assured, patient, stinking.

My car was veering off the narrow drive.

I lighted a cigarette and took a pull from my flask, packing my visions down deeper inside with all the efficiency of a Lexington patriot tamping the ball into his musket.

"You smell funny," said Amber, not unkindly.

"I don't feel very funny. What then, after Marty told you what he'd seen?"

"I could only focus on one idea. Something that Martin kept saying again and again: '*Whoever killed Alice was trying to kill you.*' I was terrified, Russ. You know me well enough to understand that I wouldn't react . . . *well* to this kind of thing. So I agreed to do what Martin told me."

"Disappear."

"Yes. And wait for him to handle who had killed Alice."

"That being me."

"You and Grace."

"Does he still believe that?"

Amber studied me for a long while, then turned away. "Yes."

"How much did Alice look like you?"

"A lot. Especially to someone in a dark bedroom, someone assuming I was sleeping in my own bed."

I thought. We circled the marina again, slowly. "So why in hell," I asked, "did you come to me?"

She was watching me again. Amber always had a way of not being there, the capacity simply to exit, leaving only her body behind. She had often done this when under duress. She had sometimes done this when I made love to her—a form of punishment and a way of experimenting with a martyrdom that, like her smoking, she rarely took beyond the casual. I sensed her absence now. Slowly, almost visibly, she repopulated herself.

"Because of Martin. I began to wonder. He told me he was at my house that night because a call came over his police radio, and he was in the area, so he answered it. I believed him at first—he kept saying *we*, like it was he and his partner and everything was official. When he told me what he'd found, I was too afraid to see what a strange story it was—that he just happened to be in my neighborhood. I mean, how long since Martin has been on patrol? How long since he drove around with a partner? So I pressed him. It didn't take much. He kind of broke down—all two hundred pounds of rock Martin always was— he made this, this . . . *confession* that he'd been in my room on his own, that he'd been there before, always when he knew I'd be gone. That he'd lie in my bed and think about *us*. Russ, that scared me almost as much as what he'd found, or said he'd found. So I came to you."

"But you knew I was inside your house, too."

She looked at me through the dark glasses. "I believe what you told Martin. That you'd seen him come out, then found my sliding glass door open. Russ, I understand what you were doing parked outside my house that night. I think of you sometimes and I dream of you, and I know you think and dream of me. It's all about the way we were, the way we won't ever be again with anyone else. But you're not capable of true obsession, Russ—the same way I'm not. You're harmless. That's another way of saying that I trust you. Right now, I think you're one of the few men in this world I can truly trust."

"What about Erik?"

"Erik is still upset about our breakup. I don't think he should see me now."

"A decade of panting after you, and poor Erik only gets one thin year to bathe in the glow."

I simply couldn't resist the opportunity to hurt Amber, if only because I knew that my weapons had always been too dull to dent her shining, perfect surface.

"Russell?" she said, "Why don't you just fucking grow up?"

Not grown-up, harmless and incapable of true obsession, I guided the car back up to Coast Highway and north toward

149

Laguna. The anger I thought Amber's words would bring to me did not come. For a long time, all I could think about was Izzy, asleep in the small bed in her father's house. I tried to send her the most peaceful and hopeful of dreams. And I was aware of Amber as of someone in a dream, too—she was nearby but intangible, present but unavailable. Then, a new emotion began to gather inside me, though at first I couldn't identify it. But as it started to fill the space left by my diminishing confusion and shock at seeing Amber again, I realized what it was: I was pleased that this woman was alive. In fact, I was more than pleased; I was happy, grateful. And deeper down, beneath these understandable and approvable truths, grinned a simple, unsanctioned, forbidden concept that I tried to ignore but could not: I was thrilled by her nearness. Secretly, wildly, insanely thrilled.

"Can I trust you?" she asked.

"Yes."

"What should I do?"

"Did Marty kill her?"

"It could only have been Martin. That's why I didn't go to the cops, Russ. That's why I came to you. He killed her because he came in, thinking the house was empty. She panicked. He panicked. He tried to make it look like that Midnight Eye, but later he got scared and figured he should just hide it all—everything—even Alice. The second night, when you found him there, he'd just finished cleaning. He made up the story about seeing Grace come out the night before. If he has to, if anyone presses him, if he loses that crazy mind of his, he's going to pin it on you and her. What other explanation can there be?"

"I'm working on that."

"*You don't think he did it?*"

I pulled into the Towers lot, waved off the valet, and

parked next to Amber's gray rental K car. "Where were you going last night when I saw you on Coast Highway?"

"Back to Las Brisas Hotel. That's where Martin told me to stay. He forbade me to leave the room, but I was getting suite fever. I was leaving the White House when you saw me. I'd had a table up front, by the band."

I listened to her explanation while staring out the windshield. A pale coastal haze had settled over the city, light dew that would vanish at first sunlight. The cars and streets seemed to sweat now, giving up their heat to the moisture.

"How long since you've seen our daughter?"

"Two months. Three. I've written. Imagine me writing letters, Russ. I've called. She ignores me."

Amber said nothing, sighed quietly—how strange, how compelling it was to hear in her even a hint of surrender—then folded her hands in her lap and looked down at them. "I know I've made some mistakes, Russ, and I'm doing what I can to correct them. I was trying...I've *been* trying to connect. With my family. My old friends. My daughter. I burned so many bridges, it's hard finding my way back. Follow the smoke, I guess. And now...Alice. Poor, poor, lovely girl."

So there it was, the first time in the twenty years I'd known Amber Mae that she had shown anything like doubt, fallibility, regret—and meant it. I discount her thousand well-acted scenes. I was dumbfounded.

"What do you want me to do?" she asked.

"Have you talked to your agent?"

"Reuben is my *manager*. Yes. He knows I'm okay, but not working, not taking calls, not gettable. I swore him to secrecy, and Reuben is good to his word. He's the only one I've talked to. He and Marty, that is."

Amber actually shuddered then, though the night was hot

and damp. A smell came off her that reminded me of the odor of Grace, the night she had come to me: woman, perfume, fear. But most of all, fear. "Where should I go?"

"You checked out of the hotel?"

"No. I didn't want to alert anyone that I was leaving. Martin is probably calling every five minutes. Or waiting. He insisted on having a key. But everything I've been living on is in that car. I've got an eight-thousand-square-foot mansion two miles from here, and I'm living out of a Chrysler. Ugly little thing, isn't it?"

"Marty's idea?"

She nodded, then looked at me again. "How's Isabella?"

"Great."

"I'm so sorry, Russ. If it was in my power to change things, I would."

I said nothing for a long moment, then, idly, "She's strong."

"She must be terribly strong. I don't suppose she would let me stay for a few days? I could cook and clean and stay out of the—"

"No."

It was only then, with the outrageousness of that plea, that I fully realized the depth of Amber's fear.

"No," she said. "That would really not be right. I'm sorry. That was presumptuous."

I thought for a moment. Marty Parish—or anyone else who wanted to find her—would check the local hotels first, then keep working outward from town. Cash payment and a false name would give her a head start, but she couldn't stay hidden for very long, not with a rental car, not being Amber Mae Wilson. Who would think to look for her in my world? Marty, maybe. But I knew someone who could handle Martin Parish. The trouble was, he disliked Amber, and Amber had years ago tired of wasting her charms on him. I turned over a dozen other possibilities but kept coming back to Theodore Francis Monroe, and his little house nestled darkly under the oaks of Trabuco Canyon.

"I'll tell you something, Russell. I'm not going to let Marty get away with this. I'm going to make sure he pays for Alice. I don't know how or when, but I'm going to live to see it happen."

"Follow me," I said.

■   ■   ■

My father was standing on the porch of his cabin before I even shut off the engine of my car. He was centered in the halo of yellow light cast by a bulb above the door, wearing only a pair of jeans, his old Remington 870 cradled in his arms. In the rearview mirror, I watched the Chrysler roll up the driveway behind me. I stepped out, motioned for Amber to stay put, then crunched across the driveway gravel toward my father. A thousand crickets made a continuous, strangely sourceless buzz. The horses shuffled from the darkness of the corral. The stair boards were damp and soft as I climbed.

I studied him as I came across the porch—his large, hard body; the black hair graying only slightly; the eyes made wary and strong by years of ranch work; the downturned, unforgiving mouth of a man familiar with disappointment. Bathed in the yellow bug light, he looked alien, otherworldly.

"Dad."

"Russ."

"Got kind of a problem."

"I can see that."

He set the gun against the house, shook my hand, then hugged me. He smelled like a man's sleep. Looking past his shoulder, I could see the K car reflected in a window.

"What's with the scattergun, Pop?"

"This Midnight Eye's got me spooked. Maybe I'm getting old. What's with *you* being here at this hour? It isn't something with Izzy, is it?"

"She's with Corrine and Joe. She's okay."

"Is that who I think it is in the car?"

"Someone tried to kill her. They got her sister instead. She's scared out of her mind and needs a place to stay."

He looked out at the car, then back at me. "Because they're going to try again."

"Maybe."

"Well, then get that goddamned Chrysler into the shed and bring her inside."

"Thanks, Pop."

"I don't see a great deal of choice."

He gave me a very silent, very assessing stare.

"This isn't what it looks like," I said.

■　　　　　　■　　　　　　■

We sat in the pine-paneled living room as I told my father the story. I did not tell him everything, and I omitted any hint of my own presence outside Amber's home on that hot night of July 3. I could not admit that to him. He listened almost silently, sensing, I am sure, that his was an edited version. Amber sat off to one side of the couch, her hands and ankles crossed contritely, her platinum blond wig rendered suddenly ridiculous by the rustic interior of the cabin. She said little.

By one o'clock, when the night seemed its most private, my father had brewed up a pot of coffee to sustain him through the morning. We agreed that one of them should always be awake. He showed Amber the second bedroom, then I walked her out to get some of her things from the car.

Inside, the shed smelled of wood rot and mildew and

motor oil. It was neat because all of my father's things were neat.

Amber opened the K car's trunk and looked at me. "I took everything Marty collected from . . . Alice. All the Baggies and fingerprints and pictures—all his notes. There's some stuff in here; I don't even know *what* it is. I thought you might want it."

"Jesus, Amber."

"Did I do wrong?"

I prodded through the cardboard box containing fingerprint cards; a dozen or more bags containing hair and fiber, paint chips, soil samples; a tape recorder he'd probably used to catalog and walk himself through the scene; one loose audiotape; a pile of Polaroids; a neat stack of enlarged 35-mm prints. There was even a notebook, with entries matched to the "exhibits." There were several folders of the type the county uses for its criminal files—some empty, some containing the basic rap sheets. I opened one: County Sheriff's employment history of Russell Monroe—1976 to 1983.

"Nice work, Amber, I think."

"He was carrying all that around in his car," she said. "Please take it. He said he found that audiocassette in my stereo, the night that Alice . . . died."

I slipped the tape into my coat pocket.

On the way back to the house, I put the box into the trunk of my car. My father was sitting at the kitchen table, dressed now, drinking his coffee. I walked Amber into the small bedroom. A lamp on the bed stand cast a warm light against the knotty-pine walls.

"Can I ask you a question?" she said.

"Sure."

"Did you like me better when you thought I was dead?"

It was half surprise at the question and half uncertainty

of my answer that left me quiet. All the deep silence of the night outside seemed to enter that small room and encircle us.

"No," I said.

Amber looked at me while she reached up, pulled off her wig, and shook out the great brown waves of her hair. They lengthened as they loosened, down past her shoulders. And I was struck then, as I had been struck before—but never, *never* so hard—by how much Amber looked like Isabella. In the burnished lamplight of the cabin, Amber was, at the moment her hair settled, radiant.

"Thank you," she said. Then she gave me that look, the one that had launched a hundred products into a billion households, that look half virginal and half carnal, inviting—no, imploring you—to partake in what was being offered, reassuring you that this transaction, no matter how publicly tendered, was and would forever remain a conspiracy of only two.

What she saw in my face, I do not know.

"You're welcome," I said. "Good night."

"Good night, Russell."

15

I went to the Marine Room, had two shots and two beers, sat on a stool at the window, and watched the people walk by. The early-morning fog began to settle over the coast. I watched it claim the shoreline, the beach, the boardwalk, then ease across Coast Highway, lap against the buildings, feel its way up Ocean Avenue, bury the streetlights, enfold the men and women and babies in strollers, the bums and dogs, the pigeons and gulls, the cats in the shadows, the eucalyptus and bougainvillea, the parking meters, Hennesey's Tavern, the art gallery, the sunglasses shop, the patrol car turning right on the highway, the sidewalk and the cracks in the sidewalk and the weeds growing from the cracks. With the fog came a hush I was not the only one aware of; it was a collective involuntary pause, a hiatus in the minds of everyone on that busy summer sidewalk. It crossed their faces with the fog, and they slowed just a beat, like film decelerating to almost slow motion, responding as if to a great invisible psychic speed bump that everyone hit at once and no one knew was there. Something rippled across their faces at that moment, a question. Husband glanced to wife; wife looked to husband; lovers cuddled closer; those alone turned to look over their shoulders, crossed the street suddenly, stopped to look around them, all faces asking, What was that, me, someone, who, *me*? And at that precise second, the band in the back room ended its song on the downbeat, and the hush asserted itself through the bar in one of those rare moments during which all conversation waits and silence rushes in to remind us that there was silence in the beginning and there will be silence at the end and silence runs through everything like a secret no one wants to hear. A flicker of fear crossed every face in that bar. Our dread was one dread. Every expression confessed the superfluity of our pretensions, the sheer effrontery of assuming that life in the next heartbeat will be the same jolly thing we pretend it is now. Deep in that silence, I heard a voice—a groan, a low-frequency command—but I couldn't understand what it was saying. I have no idea whether anyone else heard it, too. Then a great gust of laughter—forced, counterfeit, desperately applied—rose up to claim the quiet and deny the truths the silence carried. The band kicked in. I left.

I sat in my car for a few minutes without running the engine and listened to the tape that Amber had stolen from Martin Parish. It was the Midnight Eye. He stuttered and mumbled his way through more unintelligible phrases:

"C-c-cun seed brat cun wormin from he . . .
Mustery move s-s-slime . . . "

I could make no sense of it. Surely, I thought, if Amber was right and Martin was trying to blame the murder of Alice on me, this tape should have been destroyed by now. When I had listened to it twice, I placed the tape carefully beneath the floor mat of the car, where I wouldn't step on it.

■   ■   ■

Traffic slowed to a crawl in the canyon, just out of town, and it took me twenty minutes to inch along far enough to find out why. The Highway Patrol had set up one of its Sobriety Checkpoints to find drunken drivers. I could see the lights flashing, the orange pylons cutting down the outgoing lanes to one, the CHP officers shining lights into drivers' faces. I was secretly rooting for the ACLU when it challenged the legality of these spot checks, but the courts upheld the CHP's contention that they are necessary and constitutional. More of my distrust of authority, more of my rankle at the long arm of control. The thought came to me that I might be better suited to a career in bank robbery than law enforcement, but this was neither a new nor very probing idea. Writing seemed a good way to split the difference.

I rolled down my windows, lighted a smoke, waited.

Up ahead, flashlights beamed into cars, officers leaned toward open windows, a stream of released drivers pensively accelerated north. In my rearview, I could see the fog moving in. Ten minutes later, it was my turn. I steered the car between the rows of orange pylons, greeted the officer with a nod, and waited. Behind him, I saw a familiar shape standing outside a prowl car, but just as I started to figure who it was, the flashlight beam ached into my eyes.

"How are you tonight, sir?"

"Fine."

"Drinking tonight, sir?"

"Couple of beers."

"That's all?"

"That's right."

"For a total of how many, sir?"

"A couple still means two, last time I checked."

He paused then, ran the flashlight across my backseat, the passenger seat, then into my face again. A voice came from behind him, but all I could see was white light. There was a moment of consultation—voices hidden by the brightness of the beam—then the officer stepped away, and Martin Parish leaned into my window. His eyes were bloodshot, his big, morally superior chin was unshaven, his knit necktie fell forward against the door. With the flashlight out of my eyes now, I could see the Sheriff's Department cars waiting up ahead—three of them.

"Well, I figured we'd run across you, Monroe," said Marty.

"Not hard, since this is the only road to my house."

"Shall I let 'em test you? This clever Chip is just sure you've had more than two."

"Up to you, Marty, but two is what I've had."

"That'll be the day."

Marty walked around the front of my car, the headlights throwing his shadow along the asphalt. He opened the passenger door, got in, and closed it. "I'll escort you home, Russell. These Chippies have your number."

"I sense an ulterior motive."

"I'm one big ulterior, Russ. Drive."

"Long walk back, Marty."

"I got it covered."

The officer waved me down a long corridor of pylons that angled into the road. My turnoff was less than a mile out. I stopped at the box, got my mail, then headed up the steep, winding drive that leads to the stilt house. When we made the top and leveled off, I could see the Sheriff's Department car parked outside my home. The idea came to me that it was more than just Marty's ride back to the checkpoint. I swung around it and down into my driveway. A deputy in uniform leaned against the car and watched us go by. I wondered whether Marty was about to return the beating I'd given him at the beach on the night of July the Fourth. Overkill, I thought. I parked in the garage.

We got out and walked back up the driveway to the departmental car. The deputy was a tall, wide man with short black hair, a strong nose, and high cheekbones. He looked Indian, and his badge said Keyes. Marty introduced us, but he neither spoke nor offered his hand. His eyes were black, small, and contained an unmistakable meanness.

"What's the deal?" I asked.

"There really is no deal," said Marty. "Not in the sense that you can negotiate anything."

"Sounds like you've got me cold."

"Everybody's cold tonight, Russ. Look, we're going to do something kind of unorthodox here, but the alternative is I take you downtown for the murder of Alice Fultz."

"Who in the hell is that?"

"Keyes," said Marty. "Roll 'em."

Keyes produced a video camera from the front seat of his car, Marty stepped away from me, and then the light went on and the lens aimed into my face.

"Come on, Marty," I said. "Get in here."

"I'll edit out what you fuck up, so never mind."

"Like the camera, Keyes? Like your job with the Sheriff's of Orange County?"

Keyes said nothing, but he looked away from the eyepiece and the light went out.

In the moment of bedazzlement that hits the eye when brightness goes to black, Marty swung a heavy fist into my sternum. I heard my breath heave out into the canyon air, felt the pressure shoot into my head, heard a siren whine shriek into my ears. Doubled over and still waiting for fresh air to get to my lungs, I tried to keep my balance. Marty grabbed my hair and belt and threw me straight down onto my face. The asphalt was warm; the gravel bit into my elbows and cheeks. But my breath came rushing back. I lay there, letting it in.

"This is what you're going to do, Russ. You're going to walk down the driveway to your garage, go in, turn on the light. Then you're going to stand in front of your game freezer and open it. Then we'll cut and I'll tell you what the next scene is. I'm the director; you're the star. Got it?"

"Yup," I said, but my voice was feeble and soprano-high.

"Repeat," he said.

I did.

Then he dragged me up by my hair, steadied me, and shoved me toward the garage.

"Action," he said.

I lumbered on reluctant legs down the steep driveway. The light of the video camera sprayed out on either side of me. I looked for a moment toward town, from which the fog continued to advance like a white blanket pulled by invisible hands. Where the slope of the driveway levels off at the garage, I stumbled and almost fell. My ears were still screaming.

The garage door was up and I went in. The video beam followed me, but I hit the light, as instructed. I turned to the right, away from my car and toward the freezer. I stopped in front of it, looked once at Marty, then reached out and lifted the heavy handle. The door followed, gaskets sucking, then releasing a brief cloud of frost into the air. When the frost cleared upward, I looked down and saw what I had been half-expecting ever since Marty had outlined his screenplay idea.

Twisted, stiff, blue-black and covered with blood, her hair a solid block against the far wall, her face beaten beyond recognition and frozen in a horror that seemed freshly, eternally preserved, lay the body of Alice Fultz. She still had on the blue satin robe. In her hair still lodged the white and pink particulars that had jumped forth from her bursting skull. Her legs had been crammed to fit the freezer, but her arms were still spread as they had been on Amber's floor—open, apart, frozen in midair now as if welcoming me: Come down, come down here, my love, take me, embrace me, own me. *I am yours.*

16

Keyes came up behind me and to my left, aiming the camera down into the freezer. I turned right, finding Marty, fixing him with a look that must have been half outrage and half revulsion. The idea crossed my mind that my expression could do more to establish my innocence than a thousand words, but by the time I turned to Keyes, his camera was down and he was studying me with his black unforgiving eyes.

"I guess we both know by now that you killed the wrong woman," said Parish.

"I didn't kill her."

"Right. *Grace* killed the wrong woman. It was a mistake even a daughter could make—a dark room, a bed that's usually got someone else in it, all those emotions boiling up inside. The way I've got it figured, Grace probably thought she'd done her mother until you got there later for the transfer and saw the, uh, mix-up. You cleaned it up anyway—that's what the fallback plan called for—but you couldn't dump Amber's body in *my* freezer because you didn't have Amber's body. So you put Grace's mistake on ice until you could figure out what to do with it. That thing in there used to be Amber's sister, Alice, if you haven't figured it out by now."

I searched Marty's face for a flicker of the madness I knew was in him, but all I saw was a gloomy, bovine conviction that he knew a terrible truth. It disturbed me almost as deeply as the woman lying in my freezer.

"Everything you believe is wrong," I said.

"Then enlighten me, Monroe."

"I can't. All I can say for sure is, I didn't kill her and Grace didn't kill her, and I don't know what's going on."

Marty nodded, a humoring, condescending thing. "That sure wouldn't play in court, friend, not with a body in your fridge. And it doesn't play with me."

"I'll take my chances," I said. I put my hands together in front of me—offering them for the cuffs.

"No."

"No? You're the head homicide dick for the whole county, you pinch me with a body in my garage, and you won't even make an arrest? What's the problem, Martin?"

"The problem is, I love two things that you don't—my wife and my job. If I take you down, both of those go with you. I'll be goddamned if I'm going to let JoAnn hear you testify that I was in Amber's house those nights. I'll be extra goddamned if I'm going to make Winters answer for what I did. He'd have to deliver my head on a plate, just to keep his own on. No. You're not worth it. Neither is Alice Fultz—God rest her soul. You surprise me, Monroe, in a weird way. I didn't think you'd be willing to drag Isabella through all that. Seems like the last thing she needs is you in jail on a murder rap. I guess anybody fucked-up enough to kill a lady for money is fucked-up enough to wreck his own wife, too. Or was trotting Isabella into court in her wheelchair one of your defense licks—if it came to that?"

I stared at Marty's smug, heavy face while the fury whirled around inside me. For a second, I was blind.

"Still want the cuffs, Russ?"

Martin Parish knew me well enough to know what I was feeling, and he was ready. He caught me coming in with a foot to my groin, then a fist to the back of my lowered neck, and I went down. I felt the cool steel of Keyes's revolver behind my ear as I gawked at the swirling pattern of the oil stains on the garage floor. For a long moment, I was lost in that aching, sucking pain that starts at a man's balls and makes him feel like shitting, pissing, vomiting, and crying all at once. For whatever reasons, I focused on the laces of Marty's scuffed brown wing tips.

Finally, Martin dragged me up by my shirt collar. The revolver rode up with me, adamant against the back of my skull.

"For Chrissakes, Russell, I'm offering you the opportunity of a lifetime."

I stood there, feeling the pain elongate through me. My ears were screaming from the blow and my neck ached.

"Pick her up and carry her up the hill," he said. "I'll toss a rock when I want you to turn."

"Why?"

"You don't ask why, Monroe. You do. You do, or I'll throw your ass in jail and you can watch the minutes tick by—all day long. You can think about your defense, and Isabella, and how you're going to make the payments for your lawyer and this stilt thing. Or, you can pick up Alice and march up the god-damned hill."

The revolver left my head. Marty motioned to the freezer. I looked down through the mist at Alice.

If epiphany is a moment of revelation and insight, what

came to me next was no epiphany at all. It was blinder than any kind of sight, it revealed nothing, and it came to me not through the brain but from a deeper, instinctual place inside me—a place of earth and stone, blood and birth, flesh and bones. It would have taken no dread of our criminal justice system to eschew the scenario Martin had just sketched for me. In fact, it would have taken a faith akin to religion to offer myself into the maw of society for the purpose of proving my innocence. No, I was a simpler being in that moment, honed by circumstance to something more essential. What I needed, what I desired more than anything else at that point in time, was a practical, workable method of saving my own trembling ass.

Judas's heart could not have been more heavy as he placed the final kiss than mine was at what happened—at what I *did* next!

A patch of Alice Fultz's frozen hair broke off with a click and stuck to the wall as I wrestled her out. I hefted her over my shoulder and put one foot in front of the other, heading up the driveway. Her waist rested against my left shoulder, and I had to spread my arms in order to grasp each of her icy, stiff ankles. I could see her right arm waving out in the darkness as I climbed. Her left arm knocked against the back of my head as if in some horrid reminder, and in the far-right periphery of my vision I could see her pale fingers jiggling tautly with each footstep.

I realized as I climbed, with every step I took, that few things in my life after this night would ever be the same. This terrible march was a simple, clear dividing line—a border—that would separate my future from everything that had gone before. The two might not be able to cohabitate within me; this much I knew. New rules would apply; alternate systems would be required; considerable adjustment would have to be made; bargains struck; concessions offered; treaties signed. My soul would never again belong only to me, but to this woman, these men, this night. I had never dreamed that I would be forced to tender it for so little.

What I prayed for as I struggled up the hillside (if grunting desperately can be called prayer) was that there be something left of my old life that I could recognize and remember—and maybe, in a moment of need, cling to—other than terror, fear, and shame. A rivulet of icy fluid ran from Alice's waist down my shoulder, the coldest thing this world has ever offered me.

The fog rolled in from the south and we vanished into the darkness of the canyon. I could hear three sets of footsteps as I labored higher, deeper into the thick, dry hillside brush. I ached and shivered as Alice's meltings ran down my body. The video light wobbled out in front of me. A pebble hit my back and I turned left into a deep ravine, an overgrown clot of oak and elderberry, sage and prickly pear. My legs burned. I penetrated the cover. I stumbled and fell. Alice rolled off and righted herself like some kind of weighted child's toy, faceup in a bed of cactus. The video light went out and I panted there on my hands and knees.

"Good enough, Monroe," I heard Martin say. "Now get up and we'll head back down to your garage. You can't dig a grave without a shovel."

■   ■   ■

I dug for two straight hours, and still wasn't deep enough. Marty had recommended a pair of gloves, which helped. I had to go back for a pick because the bedrock was so hard, the shovel just bounced. The fog hugged us. The moon disappeared. A dark circle formed on the earth around Alice. Keyes got most of it on video. I felt as if I'd been banished to hell, and spent probably twenty minutes trying to pinpoint—as I bent waist-deep and hurled the pick against the rock—the exact moment of my death. How could I have missed it? I half-believed, at times, that this was a severe nightmare from which I would surely soon awake. Fever, I thought: There must be fever involved.

But the deeper the hole got, the better I began to feel! I felt closer to being real, and I wondered as the sweat ran down into my gloves if maybe—just *maybe*—I would feel truly whole again when the last spadeful of canyon dirt sealed away Alice and Marty and Keyes and this hellish night forever. A surge of implausible optimism went through me. And it allowed me to concentrate on the particulars of this horror, on the madness that surely drove Martin Parish to put Alice's body in my freezer, on the dire aspects of his murderous obsession with Amber Mae, on the way—some way, *any* way—that I could salvage even one handful of redemption from this night. I vowed then and there that I would never let this touch Isabella, that if I had to I would lay down my life—and certainly most anyone else's— to keep the infection of this night from ever spreading to her. It seemed clear to me then that Isabella was the only good thing left in my world and that she must be spared this disease, this two-decade sickness of Amber and Martin and Grace and, most obviously, myself. I looked down at my dirt-covered shoes, half-expecting to see hooves. Never, I thought, never will I let you, Izzy, be tainted by this. If I die having accomplished nothing more than that, it will be a death greeted with a secret smile. I swear. I promise. I swear.

And with that silent vow, a clarity came to me, and I knew that there were questions I needed to answer. I was four feet down into the earth by then. I wiped the sweat from my face on the sleeve of my stinking shirt. Keyes was sitting on a rock, camcorder across his lap. I looked up at Martin.

"So," I asked, "how much money did I murder the wrong woman for?"

Marty's face, fog-brushed, regarded me from on high. "Well, as you know, she's worth about six million. I did some prying when I thought she was dead."

"Did you."

"*You* sure as hell didn't—you knew it all ahead of time. Grace came into the beginnings of her share when she turned eighteen. That's why you waited."

"What is Grace's share?"

"Five million," said Marty. "Come on, you know all this. I'm written in for half a million, and so is ex-flame, lover, friend, worshiper Russell Monroe. If you or I die before Grace does, or end up in prison, for instance, the winner gets a full million. If Grace goes first, the United Way ends up with the five. A little more prying finds you owe some pretty big bucks to the hospital. Tina Sharp, quite helpful when she thinks she's talking to an administrator. Motive, Russell. Lots of motive in the air around here."

I could hardly believe that Amber would include me in the dispensation of her fortune. But my belief was not important.

"Then there's the life-insurance policy she took out ten years ago, for Grace. Death benefit of another two million— payable over ten years. Were you and Grace going to split that?"

"I don't know," I mumbled.

"When did you figure out that you'd slaughtered the wrong beauty?"

I couldn't answer truthfully without admitting to Martin that Amber had defected into my camp. The fact that I knew where she was and had in my possession a boxful of evidence collected by Martin Parish—to save his own ass from the gas chamber, I could now assume—were my only two remaining hole cards. Why hadn't Martin figured she would come to me?

I thought long and hard about how best to play this. None of the obvious options seemed strong enough to bet on. I concluded that the best I could do while digging Alice's grave was to encourage Marty to dig one for himself.

"When I saw her," I said. "The body."

"I have to know, Russ, were you going to stick Amber in *my* freezer when you framed me, or somewhere else?"

I smiled up at him. My own boldness—or was it pure desperation?—frightened me, not only because it felt dangerous but because it felt good. "In your freezer, Marty, *naturally*."

Martin clapped his hands together, tilted his head back, and yipped into the darkness like a huge coyote. "I knew it! The first place I looked when I came up to your place two nights ago? The freezer! The freezer I gave you! Goddamn, I just feel so good about myself!"

He howled and yipped again, and I taxed my mind for a way—a plan—by which I could take my shovel to this lunatic homicide cop and bury him, too. Keyes was the problem, though, as Marty had foreseen. I wondered whether I could fatally spear Keyes by throwing the pick, but it was a faulty idea because it was a stupid one. His eyes gleamed at me in the darkness.

"Why don't you say something, shithead?" I asked him.

He aimed an index finger at my face and released the thumb hammer.

"I can see a lot of brains in this one," I said to Marty. "Where do you get these guys?"

"Wald sends us his cream."

Keyes looked at me steadily.

"Keep digging," said Martin. "You're almost there."

A wisp of fog blew past him; I turned back to my hole and dug.

"Russell, it was a good idea to make it look like the Midnight Eye, but why go to all that trouble if you were going to move the body?"

"You figure it," I said. "Earn your keep."

"Well, I've been trying to. What I figured was, you doctored up Amber's room to look like the Eye—*Grace* doctored it—before I got there on the third. Grace had bashed her earlier. It was easy enough to tell Alice was fresh. You had come back that night, when you saw me leaving, to check the work and realized it wasn't Amber at all—I suspect her message on the answering machine was one obvious indicator. So you figured, why leave the wrong woman there, done in by the Midnight Eye? It's too sloppy, too risky, and besides, you might have wanted to use the same trick on the right woman sometime. The best you could come up with was just to clean up the whole mess, which you did on the afternoon of the Fourth. You thought that I'd sit on the whole thing, especially with no body left. Another few days, you'd have buried Alice up here just like you're doing now, or dumped her in a trash can, or spilled her off a pier."

"What about that night—when I found you in Amber's bedroom with nothing on but your shorts?"

"You were making one last pass before Amber got home. Maybe figuring how to put on another coat of paint before she saw your Eye decor."

"You're good, Martin."

"You're damn right I'm good. Okay, friend—you're deep enough. Trade places with Alice and fill it back up. Double time, soldier."

I stood there, chest heaving, then climbed out. Both men were waiting for me when I righted myself on the lip of the grave. The sudden notion hit me that Keyes was going to shoot me through the heart and leave me with Alice, but it went away as quickly as it had come—nobody films a murder they're committing, do they?

Martin smiled and told me to put out both hands, palms

up. My gloves were still on. Keyes moved to my side and his revolver barrel pressed again into my neck.

"Just a little sting, Monroe, as the doctors like to say. Here—"

And with that, Marty's fist raked across my right palm, his knife leaving the glove leather split and a wash of blood oozing from the gash.

I yanked back my hand as the pain shot through it, but Keyes pulled hard on my shirt, my feet slipped, and I landed on my butt. Keyes, still behind me, took out a handful of my hair and sprinkled it into the open grave. I understood.

"For Dina," I said.

"For Dina," said Marty, folding up his pocketknife. "Give her something to remember you by."

I pulled off the cut right glove—the slice in my palm was long but not deep—and tossed it down to Alice. Plenty of blood for Dina to work with, if it ever came to that.

"Okay, Monroe," said Marty. "Put her in and pack it down hard. Chop-chop. Nighttime's a-wastin'."

Keyes taped the first few minutes of the burial. Alice Fultz sank one spadeful at a time into the sandy canyon earth. My palm tore and bled and burned. My balls throbbed; my stomach felt like it was trying to digest itself. My legs were weak and my arms ached as the middle finger of Alice's beckoning right hand finally vanished beneath the sand. Another half hour and I'd finished everything, right down to smoothing out the extra dirt and replacing—root balls and all—the three clumps of fuchsia gooseberry that Parish had ordered me to exhume before I started digging. I replaced the boulders and rocks properly so their damp undersides were against the soil, where they belonged. I hauled some beaten dry grass and strew it around. Marty used a flashlight to make sure my shovel smoothed out the last of the footprints as I backed out. A coyote might have been able to tell we'd been there—a deer, maybe, or Black Death and his buddies, for sure—but few men I knew would ever guess.

I led the way back down the hills, the video light bouncing on the path ahead of me, then leaving me in darkness. The fog clung around us. The pick and shovel were balanced over my shoulder. My adrenaline was spent and a deep weariness spread inside me as I labored down toward my house. "Just for the record, Marty," I said, "if someone sees this video, who took it?"

"Grace."

"Why?"

"Because you two are sickos? How would I know? People make movies of girls getting their throats cut in coitus. Back down to your garage, Monroe."

I stashed the tools in a corner, then Parish motioned me over to my car. He pointed to the trunk. "Open it," he said.

"What now?"

"I spent an hour in your house tonight, looking for something that belongs to me. I think it's in your trunk. Open it, or I'll pry it open."

I fished out the keys with a raw, blistered hand and lifted the trunk door. Marty smiled, flipped through the contents of his evidence box, then lifted it out and set it on the floor.

"Amber's a fool," he said, that placid, heavy-jawed expression coming back to his face. "A beautiful, crazy fool. She always adored the men who treated her like shit. I tried, but I actually wasn't good enough at it. She must be nuts about you again. Go figure. But you're a fool, too, Monroe. You and Amber are a perfect pair. You can spend the rest of your lives trying to mess each other up. You deserve each other. My money's on Amber, though—she's got stamina and lots of cunning. You? All you've got are brief moments of inspiration."

"Why the change, Martin? A few nights ago you were down to your skivvies in her bedroom, ready to get it on with your memory."

Marty leaned back against my car and let his bloodshot blue eyes wander my face, then the evidence box, then the window against which the fog moved like a snake. "Amber came to me when she saw your lousy cover-up—the new rug, the bloodstain, the fresh paint. She needed me. And I was willing to put it all on the line for her. My heart went out, like it always did. Wish I'd learned earlier to control that thing. I showed her how you and Grace had tried to kill her. I offered to leave JoAnn and try to make it work again. Us. Amber and me. She listened. She agreed. Of course, Amber agrees to everything, then does whatever she wants, right? So, in spite of all that, she ran off again. To *you*. To the son of a bitch who tried to kill her."

Martin's face was a momentary study in confusion and disbelief. But some inner strength—the sheer muscle of madness, I presumed—brought his confusion back under control and forced it to conform to something that could pass for reason.

"And somehow, when I realized she'd gone to you *again*, I saw myself from the outside. It was like a light went on. I saw myself standing there in my underwear, just like you saw me. I was ashamed. I was more than ashamed—I was nothing. Then I was floating above it, and suddenly I was free. It all just snapped."

Snapped. How many times had Art Crump used that dire verb? The idea hit me then that Martin had already traced Amber to my father's cabin and done to her what he had meant to do to her the night of July 3.

"And I realized, Russ, that when there's nothing left to fill the cup, just throw away the goddamned cup. I'm free, and I'm going to stay this way."

Free because he'd gotten to Amber? "What is it you want from me, Martin?"

Marty smiled, a vile, bitter thing. "If Amber winds up like Alice, I'll make sure my best dick gets a copy of this video. I might be free of her now, but I don't want you to bash her skull. I'd rather have her alive than have her money—I don't need it. If I hear any noises from you about Marty Parish and Amber Mae Wilson, I'll deliver the video. I'll have a copy of it and an explanation in a safe-deposit box, with instructions to my lawyer what to do if I come to any sudden, uh . . . reversal. If you bother me in any way, Monroe, if I even dream that you're brushing up against me in a way I don't like, I'll deliver the video. You exist to write articles that reflect well upon Dan and me. You do not exist in any other capacity. Fart in the same room with me, Monroe, and I'll deliver the tape. I own you. And I own your daughter, too. And remember, if I do hand it over, nobody on earth is going to believe one word you say about me being in Amber's house or me and some silent deputy forcing you to perform a low-budget funeral. And it's not just because you had a corpse in your freezer."

"Why else?"

Marty stepped forward and drove a finger into my chest. "Because, you, Monroe, are one crazy, desperate bastard. It's written all over your face. And I got it on *tape.*"

I thought for a moment, but Parish's insane logic seemed, in terms of practical application, not very insane at all. He might suffer, but he could make it work. He had the department behind him, a good reputation. Any dick could establish my motive and opportunity in about one day—to the tune of half a million dollars, an embittered heart, a vengeful, neglected daughter. Parish had my blood and hair mixed into the earth of Alice's grave. He had Keyes as an alibi, and the exact date and time of "my crime" indelibly tracked by the camcorder clock. Yes, Martin had built a good case.

"Where is she?" he asked.

"I don't know. She dumped the box and her story on me, then drove off."

"And didn't tell you where?"

"Sounds like her, doesn't it, Marty?"

"Sorta does."

"Well, there you have it," I said.

"Have *this*, Monroe."

His fist caught me low—just above the groin. All I could do was turn with it, trying not to take it full. But my reflexes were slow and I got most of it, and the next thing I knew I had landed on my side and rolled partway under my car. I stared up at the rusting muffler.

"That was for the other night at the beach," said Martin.

When I lifted my head to look, I could see two sets of legs climbing up my driveway toward the Sheriff's Department car.

I rolled onto my side and brought my knees to my stomach because that was what the pain told me to do. I looked at my right-rear shock. I closed my eyes. I lay there for a long while because things were coming clear to me. Oh, the clarity that can come with pain. One: Marty had killed Alice that night because he believed she was Amber. He had disposed of the club. Two: He'd mocked up the scene to look like the Midnight Eye, a serial killer that only Winters, Parish, Schultz, and possibly Chet Singer even knew was on the loose. Three: He'd changed his mind when he saw the opportunity to silence me—I, who had blundered into his plot—with Alice's body, which until tonight—I guessed—had occupied a similar space in Marty's own freezer. Four: He had done the cleanup. Five: He now had back

177

in his possession any self-incriminating evidence he might have left at Amber's and any planted evidence he had wished to add. Six: I now had a body buried not far from my house that I could—for all practical purposes—do little to explain.

I crawled out from under the car and went inside to the phone. My father answered on the fourth ring. He was okay. Amber was okay—though I made him get up and check her room.

"Are *you* okay?" he asked when he got back on.

"I'm in smithereens, Dad."

"I can be there in half an hour."

"No. There's nothing you can do."

"Izzy?"

"Worse. She was talking like a child yesterday. It . . . hurt me to see that."

All of my fear for Isabella came rushing in then, and all of the grisly horror that Marty Parish had visited upon my life. I felt the same frantic, gut-wrenching terror I'd felt once at the age of ten, hopelessly lost on a camping trip with my mother and father. But this fear was stronger by far. I wanted nothing more than to cry. But I would not, though not for the reasons given by pop psychologists who bemoan the male indoctrination that tears are for girls. No. I would not cry because I was truly afraid that it would take something out of me—some fury, some emotion—that I was going to need in the coming days. I was hoarding anything that could be used as a weapon.

"I think the knife is a bad idea," said my father.

"I know it's a bad idea. But nothing else is working."

A long silence followed. "I had a visit from your mother tonight. She still senses distress. You know, she had some wise words for me. She's fine. If you were real quiet for a while, she'd come to you, too."

"Ah hell, Dad, I know you miss her, but make some sense for a change."

Another silence ensued, during which I regretted my words, before he spoke again. "Don't let the storm take you with it, son. Somehow, you've got to get your head above it. I know I sound like a lunatic or some New Age fop, but when she comes, well, I just *feel* her."

"How is Amber?"

"Cooperative. Even gracious. She spends most of her time alone in the guest room—some of it on the phone. She's scared."

"It's important you be with her."

"The Remington is handy, but to tell you truth, I'd like a little better idea what I'm facing."

"One Sheriff's captain with a mean streak, and possibly a buddy or two of his."

"I'm plainly outgunned."

"Stay inside. If they come to you, it's your advantage. Don't be afraid to call the cops. I mean the local cops, not the Sheriff's Department. The one thing this guy doesn't want is a scene."

"We don't have any local cops. We're county out here."

"Shit, that's right." I felt my guts bunching up for another spasm of pain.

"Give me his name, son. It's the least you can do."

"Martin Parish."

"Marty?"

"That's right. He's lost it. He's in line for money if Amber dies, but I'm not even sure it's the money he's after. All I can tell for sure is, he's in a rage."

"He killed her sister, thinking it was her?"

"That's correct."

"Have you talked to Winters?"

"I don't have any proof. Yet."

"Oh boy."

My father was quiet for a long moment. "I like having her around."

"The second something seems wrong, call me."

"I love you, son. Pray to your mother. She'll be there for you."

I hung up. Guns and ghosts, I thought—two verities for my aging father.

I lay down on the sofa in my den and stared out for a while at the shifting fog. Sundry horrors passed through my mind, most of all, perhaps, the icy touch of Alice's body against my own. But even that feeling was soon surpassed by the image of the Midnight Eye staring out the window of his stolen Ford Taurus, the mute superiority in his face, the heft and power of his arm and hand. My body began to shake. Each recent blow from Martin established its own specific ache. I heard that howling up in the canyon, the one that Isabella had named the Man of the Dark. Isabella! How distant were her arms, her voice, the comforting proximity of her beating heart. Oh woman, do not leave me. I wept. I got up and closed all the windows and doors, setting the dead bolt twice to make sure it was right. I left on all the lights. I made sure my .357 was loaded and ready and set it under the pillow that for five years had been graced by nothing less beautiful than my wife's dreaming head.

17

If fear of the Lord is the beginning of knowledge, what is the beginning of fear? I have an answer, for myself at least. The beginning of fear is to understand that you are without power. It took me half a lifetime—40 years—to realize this. Oh, I can hear the protestant brayings of those who are "taking responsibility for their own lives," or "are God," but I'm not talking about the mundanities of happiness, success, self-fulfillment, weight loss, life without alcohol, or who is okay and who is not. I'm talking about powerlessness in the face of death, in the face of life, in the face of madness, love, disease, desire, in the face of all things beautiful and terrible that govern our every moment whether we know it or not. And I am talking about the fear of truly realizing that your best may not be good enough, that it may, in fact, be very little good at all. To understand this is to become fluent in the language of terror, to become intimate with the contours of the pit. It is the wisdom of the man before the firing squad. But fear—true fear—is not a reason for anyone to do something as simpleminded as to surrender. No. The acts of the powerless are among the lasting nobilities of the race. To advance with a stomach knotted in terror is more than courage. Fear is beauty.

All of which is to say that as I lay in bed on the Wednesday morning of July the seventh, bruised and still exhausted by the dismal events of the night before, I tried to separate my world into things over which I had no power and things over which I did. Against Martin Parish's bleak logic, I was temporarily helpless. There was no sense in divesting myself of Alice's body, when Parish had the tape. All an empty grave would prove is that I'd moved her! I had been crudely but effectively neutralized—exactly Parish's goal. Over the cancer cells that raged in Izzy's brain, I had no power. Over the actions of the Midnight Eye, I had perhaps even less. Dread began to work into me. But I knew that there were some things I could still accomplish. I could love Izzy, even if I couldn't save her. I could protect my daughter from the young woman's perils that had apparently befallen her. I could begin to outline my book about the Midnight Eye. I could shower, shave, eat.

"Coffee, Russell?"

Grace stood in the bedroom, a steaming cup in her hands. I had not heard her arrive, but that didn't surprise me: What little sleep I'd had had been the sleep of the dead.

"Russell, where's Isabella?"

I explained.

She set the cup on my nightstand and assayed me with her Monroe brown eyes. "I'm sorry I was gone," she said. "I could have helped."

"Where were you?"

"Does it really matter, Russ?"

"Yes, it does."

"Don't be silly. You look rather under the weather today.

A guy from the phone company installed something on the telephone pole about an hour ago. You slept right through it."

I groaned, sat up in bed, and hooked the coffee mug.

"Tell me if there's anything I can do for you," said my daughter.

"Thank you."

"Isabella didn't leave because of me, did she?"

"She likes you. I think she left because of me."

"Give yourself a little more credit than that," she said, then turned and went back down the stairs.

I called Corrine. Izzy was sleeping after a fitful night—the heat, bad dreams, many trips to the bedside commode.

"Thank you for your words last night," said Corrine. "It's important we not blame ourselves. I'm starting to understand what you've been going through this last year. She—we all owe you so much."

"Thank you. That's a difficult thing to believe."

"I hope you can use this time to enjoy yourself a little. Get some work done. Was yesterday relaxing for you?"

I thought back to Amber's astonishing reappearance. I thought back to last night, to Martin's palpable lunacy and the body I had buried in a grave not a hundred yards from my own front door. "Very relaxing," I told Corrine.

"I'm glad to hear that. Izzy should be awake in another hour."

"I'll be there."

"God bless you, Russell Monroe."

"I would like that."

My *Journal* piece on the Citizens' Task Force got front-page play and a large color photograph of Dan Winters and Erik Wald. The lead article focused on the Midnight Eye, a horrifying photograph of whom—culled by Documents from the home video—took up three columns above the fold. You could see his dark bearded face in the shadow of the stolen car, determine his girth from the size of the arm dangling from the window, sense his self-contained and predatory nature. Carla Dance had not changed a word of my article, though she did run an inset on Russell Monroe, the Task Force volunteer who was writing this special series for the *Journal*. I sensed Dan Winters's hand in this bit of minor manipulation—I had never told him I'd join his Force—and in the word *series,* which gave me a very specific idea of what my *Journal* employment was to entail. I had to smile at Erik's expression in the photo—so grim, so alert, so ... *indispensable.* God only knew how many phone lines were ringing at the Sheriff's Department, particularly on the desk of Erik Wald and the CTF. We had a hit on our hands; I could feel it.

I called surveillance tech John Carfax at County, and he confirmed that he'd installed the intercept device. It was a Positive Control Systems DNR (dial number recorder) that had CNI (call number identification) capacity built in. He told me he could get a trace number in thirty seconds. Under specific orders from Winters, he was to share his information with me.

I called my agent, Nell. I told her I had an inside track on the scariest, weirdest, most haunting serial killer to hit California in years and that I needed money to write the book.

"We won't get a lot," she said. "You haven't made the list since *Journey.*"

"I don't expect a million dollars," I said. "As much up front as you can arrange. I need it."

"I'll try."

"This will make *Helter Skelter* and *Fatal Vision* look like Hardy Boys stuff."

She was quiet for a moment, then sighed. "How come it seems like everybody in California is either writing a mystery or going on a killing spree?"

"Each has his own special gift," I offered.

"I'll try, Russ. That's all I can do."

With this bit of encouragement came the bravery to call my bank and check the balances of my three accounts—something I had not been able to do for nearly six months. They were down to a grand total of eight thousand dollars, about two months' worth. I had been subconsciously preparing myself to sell Izzy's car, my truck (rarely used), and liquidate our retirement money, which, after taxes and penalties, would have given us another year of living. There remained the specter of selling our home in the current bad market. Not to mention the eighty grand I owed the Medical Center.

I began to wonder how I could write anything close to the whole truth, with Martin's tape, with Alice Fultz buried within throwing distance of my typewriter, with my guilty fixation on Amber Mae so central to the story. No, I told myself. You will write the story of the Midnight Eye. The rest will stay consigned to the dark annals of your secret life. Maybe you can put it in a novel someday.

I asked Grace to come with me to see Izzy, but she declined.

"I'm not afraid to be alone up here," she said. "I don't think those men have any idea where I've gone. In fact, this is the *only* place I feel safe alone."

"I understand," I said. Besides, there was something I wanted to do in my car, and it wasn't something that I necessarily wanted my daughter to hear.

On my way to Joe and Corrine's, I listened to the tape that had come from Martin's box of "evidence." The voice of the Eye droned on, and I could still make little of it. I began to meditate on just how this tape had come into being and found its way into Amber's stereo. Was it faked? Dubbed from others? An original that Parish had failed to file as evidence in the case of the Midnight Eye? I finally tired of his slurred nonsense, removed the tape, and put it in my pocket. Surely, I thought, there's a safer place to keep this than in my car.

Isabella was sitting up in bed, propped up on pillows, her tape deck and a bag of cassettes resting on her lap, when I came in. From beneath her baseball cap extended the headphones, a little black cushion over each ear. She heard me come in, opened her eyes, and gave me a smile of such warmth and happiness that all I wanted to do was lie down beside her, take her in my arms, and tell her I loved her. I did that. She returned my hug as best she could—from her waist up—then pulled off her headset and put her cap back on.

"You look so bad," she said without a stutter. I must have looked at her strangely. "I mean," she said, "you . . . look . . . so . . . *good*. These days, everything c-c-comes out mix-mixed up. You look so bad, Russell. You h-h-have on my favorite red sidewalk."

She fingered my red windbreaker and smiled again. "Did you have a good day without me?"

"Well . . . " I said, but I wasn't sure how to finish. I could feel a pit opening inside me, a dark yawning thing into which two little dolls that looked like Isabella and Russ Monroe were falling, arms and legs spread, twisting slowly down into a cartoon abyss.

"Oh, baby, don't look at m-m-me like that," she said. "I know I'm not m-m-making any sense."

"No, no, you are," I said. "And I'm flattered that you like my red sidewalk."

She smiled again. Isabella's smile is everything good in this world. "You . . . are making f-f-fun of me."

"I know."

"I'll some e-e-even day get with you."

"You can't catch me."

"Not y-y-yet. After my o-o-operation, I'll catch you easy."

"After the operation, I better look out?"

"Gonna make you sucker, pay!"

"Typical hot-blooded Latina," I said. "Always thinking of revenge."

"I g-g-got my revenge when you mangled me."

"I did not *mangle* you. I married you."

"E-e-exactly."

I held her for a while, until she broke away and fixed her smile on me again. It was the same coy, near-guilty smile she always got before asking what she asked next.

"Guess what?"

"You're hungry," I said.

"W-w-would you see what breakfast is for?"

I climbed off the bed and went into the kitchen. Joe was sitting at the table in front of a fan, drinking iced tea. Corrine stood at the stove. I had the feeling that the silence between them had been going on a while. It had legs. I reported to Isabella that huevos rancheros was on the menu. She smiled and nodded.

Back in the kitchen, I understood the reason for their silence: Not only Isabella's speech but her moods were becoming strangely askew. I followed Corrine's stare out the window to the sky. A jet left a vapor trail high in the blue and I could see the twinkling wedge of silver out ahead of it. It seemed like a symbol for how high and perilous a life can be, but mostly it was just a jet in the sky. Far out to the west, a dark blanket of clouds eased toward us, unfolding over the horizon like a shroud for morning.

"Dr. Nesson says tomorrow," Corrine said, turning to face me. "They'll operate at six in the morning. It will take six hours. He doesn't want us to wait. He's worried, and so am I."

I thought it odd that Izzy hadn't mentioned it, and Corrine anticipated this thought.

"She can't keep anything straight," she said. "She forgot her own name earlier this morning."

I joined their silence. Images of the night before, of Alice's frozen arms embracing my chilled neck, mingled in my mind with those of my wife, not thirty feet away now. I would have loved a Bloody Mary.

"Russell," said Joe. "When Izzy was young, Corrine dropped her on her head. The doctors said she was fine. Do you think that maybe—"

"No," I snapped. "That's ridiculous."

I tried to tell Joe and Corrine that it wasn't their fault, that the tumor had simply happened. But I could almost see my words running off of them; I could feel them shouldering not only all the blame there was, but all the blame they could imagine. I recognized what they were doing because I had done it myself—for months—just after Isabella was diagnosed. We believe, in our helplessness, that the amount of blame we can carry somehow lightens the burden of the one we love. It is a heavy load to bear, but it is nothing compared to what the victims themselves are asked to carry.

Nothing is quite so terrible about cancer as the way its sufferers are encouraged to believe that they have caused their disease. Legions of pop thinkers, from psychologists to MDs (few of whom have had cancer, I might add), have adopted the stance that there is something deficient in the psyche of the ill, something that has allowed them to "create" their cancer. And as Isabella—and thousands like her—embarked on her battle for life, she read these books, listened to these lectures, watched these videos (all expensive, all packaged with advertisements for more product) promising her that, just as she had created her own disease, so she could also create her own cure. She meditated. She ate a macrobiotic diet. She imaged little cells eating up her tumor. She exercised. She was acupunctured, acupressured, energy-channeled; she had her medians unblocked, her colon flushed with enemas, her stomach filled with chlorella, ginseng, miso, royal jelly, astragalus, echinacea, amino acids, two-phase enzyme supplements, interaction supplements, vitamins in megadose, minerals by the ton—in short, enough fringe treatment and fraudulent "medicine" to render her, at one point, little more than a feverish, diarrheic mess who couldn't even stand the smell of her own body. As instructed, she told herself she was beautiful. When nothing worked, she did everything all over again. But still the cancer grew. And she knew by then whose fault *that* was: hers, of course, hers alone; it was a simple outgrowth of her imperfect mind. She had created it. She had encouraged it. She deserved it. She *wanted* it.

But then, something began to change.

Slowly, Isabella—always willing to blame herself first, as so many of us are—started getting mad. It started with a near silence that lasted for days. She eased off the potions, pills, and supplements. She ate something besides tofu and fake cheese made from soybeans. She stopped watching tapes of doctors exhorting her to imagine her tumor, change her defective character, take responsibility for creating her illness. She brooded; she wept; she screamed.

One evening, she said to me, "You know something, Russ? It's arrogance. Pure arrogance."

"What is?"

"The idea I did this to myself. I did not do this to myself. I was happy. My mother loved me. My father did not abuse me. No one did. I was a happy kid. I tried to be good. I smoked some cigarettes when I was fourteen, but that was all. I drank some. I smoked a joint when I was sixteen, but when I heard a tape of how I played piano stoned, I never tried it again. When I was twenty-three, I married the man I loved. I got up one morning, had a seizure, found out there was something growing in my brain. It was cancer. And I'll tell you something—I hate it. I even hate the word *cancer,* the way it hisses off our tongues, so eager to be said. I didn't create it, no matter what these . . . these . . . these *bliss ninnies* try to make me believe. They're selling snake oil in a New Age wrapper, that's all. They're in the cancer business, the phony-hope trade. I'll take the rap for almost anything—I'm a Mexican and a Catholic, right? But I refuse to take the blame anymore for this. I'm going to win; I'm going to beat this thing. *Damn* those people, those . . . parasites. Russ, what is it with this country? We think we control the whole world and everything on it—and beyond that, the moon, all the way from the heavens down to the metastatic level of the cells in our bodies. Where did we ever get so arrogant to believe that? Did it do any good? What did it get us but a place stripped of the people and animals who used to live here, a sky full of satellites and floating junk, a nation full of people who believe they can cure cancer by eating right? How can we be so arrogant to believe that cancer is our own fault? I *want* to live, Russ. I'm going to beat this thing. But I'm not going to *accept responsibility* for what's happened. I feel invaded. I feel cheated. I love you and I love life, but I *hate* what's happened to me. I'm going to fight with the tools I've got—love and hate. That's what I've got for weapons. You know what cancer is? Cancer is little cells growing where they shouldn't. Nobody knows why they start or how to stop them, but nobody can cure a cold, either. Cancer is not a symptom. Cancer is not a metaphor. It is not a theme. Mailer said that cancer is the growth of madness denied. Mailer is full of shit. The only thing cancer is for sure is bad luck. It's a vicious little bastard and I want it out of me. This is not a journey into myself to discover my secret desire to die."

And when Isabella said those words to me, I felt my own burden of blame begin to lift, because I had started to wonder, If a person can promote cancer in himself, why not in someone else? Was it *my* fault? I know a man—sixty years old—who has lost three wives to cancer. He believes himself to be carcinogenic, and if one does the arithmetic, he is. He stopped dating ten years ago, convinced that his love leads only to death. He golfs. He drinks. He lives alone. He has eight dogs.

I heard Izzy's words coming back to me as I watched Corrine preside with guilty intensity over the stove. I kissed her on the head and said, "It's plain old bad luck. It happened to her so it didn't have to happen to Joe, or you, or me."

She looked at me, then nodded slowly. Joe heaved himself up from the table to answer the phone. I looked out the window again to the clear, hot morning and wondered how all of this would end.

"For you," said Joe, handing me the cordless. "Erik Wald."

"Famous enough yet, Erik?"

"Sh-sh-sh-sh. Hello, Russ. I told a white lie."

I said nothing but walked outside to the porch and closed the front door behind me. The sunlight stunned me, but not as much as the fact that the Midnight Eye had traced me so easily to the home of Isabella's parents.

"What do you want?"

"I liked the articles. This Citizens' Task Force is an absolutely terrifying posse. I'm so afraid I can hardly show my face. Speaking of faces, that was quite a picture on the front page. I consider it a little unlucky to have driven by at that moment. I wondered if those neighbors had captured my image."

Something tried to dawn on me at that moment, but I was in no position to ponder it, trying my best to remember each word, as we talked. I tried to file it. . . .

"Everyone in the county knows who to look for."

"Sh-sh-sh-sh . . . I told you I was terrified. Has Wald completed his profile?"

"No."

"Because he's so busy becoming legendary."

"It's amazing what you pigs will do for a little ink," I said.

"Why no mention of our conversation? You didn't say anything about my racial cleansing. About the racial facial I'm giving our county."

"One thing at a time."

"You're making the mistake of thinking you have all the time in the world. Maybe I'll make my dramatic statement sooner. Or, there's another possibility...."

"What."

"I've made it already. Sh-sh-sh-sh."

I checked my watch. It was 9:36 A.M.

"Did Winters install the tracer on your home phone?"

"We decided against it. We'd rather talk to you."

"Oh, what a convincing, solid, just ... *believable* lie. I admire you, Russell."

"Believe what you want. The line's clear."

"I know this one is."

"Then what do you want?"

"*I want you to tell the county about my racial cleansing, you turd-sucking faggot. I've already told you that. What are you, even stupider than I thought? Do you think I call you for my own entertainment? Don't fuck with me, Monroe!*"

"Nobody wants to fuck with you. We want to give you what you want."

"I c-c-can hear Erik Wald's flimsy academic thought process behind you. Did Winters order him to coach you? Is it really you and Wald I'm dealing with?"

"Yes."

"Good. I assumed as much. The idea is to give me enough rope to hang myself. I'll bet that exact cliché was used by the nigger Winters. Now listen, Russell, I expect the following quote to be in your next piece. R-r-ready? 'The goal of the Midnight Eye is to inform all racial minorities that they are no longer welcome in the county.' Shall I repeat that?"

"I've just written it down."

"Read it back."

I did.

"Sh-sh-sh-sh. I feel better. Relieved. Overall, I'm in good spirits today. In fact, I gave some thought to your questions about the death of the model—Amber Mae? It's obvious that someone inside the department made a sophomoric attempt to blame that murder on me. Correct?"

"I believe so."

"Do you know who?"

"No," I lied. The idea of using the Eye to help me escape the clutches of Martin Parish seemed ludicrous, but then again, I didn't have many allies. Could the Eye realize something I had not?

"Have you defined the people who knew about my first two statements—the greaser and nigger couples?"

"I think so."

"Well, Russell . . . enumerate."

"Winters, Parish, Singer, Yee, Karen Schultz. Parish's top three or four people. Maybe the forensic crew put them together—that's half a dozen more. Wald suspected early, but he was out of the official loop—I talked to him about it."

"Um-hm."

I listened for background noise but heard none. I turned and looked through the front window to where Joe and Corrine both stared back at me, their faces mute and curious.

"And you, Russell? In or out of the loop?"

"Out."

"They were awfully slow to admit what was going on, weren't they?"

"Yes."

"That's one of the reasons I chose to talk to you, you know. Cops are so . . . bureaucratic, so . . . sluggish. Tell me, do any of the people you mentioned have a history with this Amber?"

"Parish and Wald."

"And, of course, you."

"Yes."

"Explain to me any monetary considerations. Her estate, to be specific."

I told the Eye of the basic dispensations of Amber Mae's fortunes, should an untimely death befall her. He listened without interrupting.

"Forget Winters, Singer, and Schultz for obvious reasons," he said finally. "Dismiss Wald, too. He's an academic, a dilettante, a coward. The Captain of Detectives, Martin Parish, would be a very interesting possibility. Sh-sh-sh-sh. It's so much *fun* to be a cop!"

"Maybe you should join the Task Force."

"Get a little cap and shirt! What self-aggrandizing silliness for Winters. Exactly what I'd expect from a nigger—always style over substance."

I said nothing.

"Tell me, Russell, are there maybe, just maybe . . . intimations from some quarters that you are a suspect?"

"Yes."

"Promoted by, let me guess, Martin Parish?"

"Yes."

"Oh, this *is* getting rich. You might have a hard time of it, because Parish could write, direct, and produce a convincing case against you—practically out of thin air."

The Eye's words eerily recalled those of Parish, spoken

not twelve hours previously, as he orchestrated the grim funeral rites of Alice Fultz.

"I've considered that."

"How's Isabella?"

"That's not your business."

"She is of . . . Mexican blood, isn't she?"

"If you touch her, I'll kill you. That is a promise."

"Testy, testy. Sh-sh-sh-sh. Look, Russell, get that statement into the paper tomorrow or I'll make your life so miserable, you won't be able to stand it. Quote me, *word for word*. Run my picture again if you think it will do any good. Winters will get a call today at noon. That's two hours from now. You might want to be there for it."

The Eye hung up. I listened to the clean disconnection, the ensuing loaded silence.

I felt invaded here, in what I had assumed was the safety of Joe and Corrine's home. The Eye had tracked me there as surely as if he'd been watching me from above. Was it luck, or did he have a surer way to following my movements? A hot wash of sweat broke over me. I stepped back inside to the cool of the house.

■　　　　　　■　　　　　　■

I helped Isabella into her wheelchair.

"Y-y-you're quiet," she said.

"Thinking."

"That's a t-t-terrible voice."

"What voice, Izzy?"

"On the t-t-tape that fell your pocket out."

I cursed myself for my carelessness. The last thing I wanted to add to the miseries in Isabella's mind were the words of the Midnight Eye.

"I'm so sorry, Izzy. I didn't want you to—"

"I think h-h-he's been to Laguna C-c-canyon. He's s-s-seen Our L-l-lady of the Canyon."

I settled her into the chair.

"What?"

"He's seen her, Russ."

"How can you tell that? What do you think he said?"

She grinned at me a little slyly now. "M-m-maybe I'll make you wait t-t-till after dinner."

My head had begun to feel light and my heart was speeding up. "No, girl. Please . . . I need to know how you know that."

"Kay-o! He says right there on the t-t-tape that he's s-s-seen the bright cunt woman."

I remembered the nonsense phrase: "C-c-cun seed brat cun wormin . . ."

"Can see the bright cunt woman?"

"R-r-russell. It's obvious. It takes someone s-s-screwed up as me to underplay someone as screwed up as h-h-him. Under*stand* him."

"He's been in the canyon," I said.

"You heard it first h-h-here. It's the Eye, isn't it?"

My mind was still reeling from Isabella's easy understanding of the Eye's speech.

"Yes, love. It's the Eye. And he's seen our Lady."

"You should put me in the c-c-case."

"You're hired, Lieutenant."

"*Chief.*"

"Okay, Chief."

I had breakfast with my wife and in-laws. I don't think I'd ever been so thankful just to have them around. My hands were shaking.

"Are y-y-you coming back tonight?"

"Of course, love."

"G-g-good. I have a farmhouse to ask you."

Our gently blank looks all closed in on Isabella. She glanced at each of us in turn, then down at her plate. A tear rolled off her cheek and her shoulders shook.

"You know what I m-m-*mean*!"

"A favor," I said. "I know exactly what you mean."

A few minutes later, I asked Joe to walk me to my car. I tried to explain to him, in the calmest way I could, that the Midnight Eye had just called his house. Joe nodded in his stoic fashion, always a man for whom no task of love can be too great.

"I'm the one he wants to talk to," I said. "I don't think he'll call here again. What I'm saying is, be very, very careful."

"I got two shotguns and two deer guns and two pistols."

"Keep them . . . available. Does Corrine know how to use them?"

"The pistols, okay."

"One of you stay up. Don't let everyone sleep at the same time."

"No. We been doing that for Izzy, anyway."

"You're a good man, Joe."

"She's my only girl."

18

The bedlam at the Sheriff's Department had gotten worse. The General Services people clogged the elevators, heading down into the bowels of the building to revive, allegedly, the dead air-conditioning system. Random sheets of drywall had been pried away to expose the ducting system, in front of which the orange-clad techs stood looking in with arms crossed, postures of stubborn defeat. Against the far wall of the Investigations section, the Citizens' Task Force phone bank was up and running, staffed by four volunteers in blue T-shirts with images of Kimmy Wynn on the front. The dicks came and went, giving wide berth to the phone-bank workers, as if they suffered something contagious. Reporters lingered, unable to restrict themselves to the press-room, clearly ignored by the dicks. Karen Schultz, gripping a bulky Records file against her body, tried to direct them back downstairs.

I proceeded down to the lab, where I found Chet Singer using an electron microscope on a piece of fiber left behind at the

Fernandez scene. I handed him the tape I'd taken from Martin's box of evidence, which Isabella had so beautifully decoded.

"Can you tell me what's wrong with this?"

Chet looked at me rather dolorously, taking the cassette in his large hand. "The Eye again?"

"Maybe," I said. "I think you should hear it. *Only* you."

"Then I shall. I will tell Karen to fetch you when I've had a chance. You certainly look bedraggled today, Russell."

"Long night."

"Ah, I can imagine."

Winters, Parish, and Wald were positioned around the desk in Dan's office when I walked in. Between Wald and Parish, directly across from Winters, sat a woman I'd never seen before. She was in her early sixties, with stiff strawberry blond waves of hair, bloodshot blue eyes, and a plain, not-quite-pretty face. She dabbed one eye with a tissue after looking up at me.

"Russell Monroe, meet Mary Ing. She's identified the photograph we ran in the papers. Our suspect is her son."

Wald grinned at me and nodded. Parish regarded me with a particularly hostile stare. Although Dan's voice was calm, I could see the satisfaction in his eyes.

Mary Ing offered her hand and I shook it. She sniffed into the tissue. "I'm still not positive."

"It's been eight years since you've seen him," said Winters. "We understand."

Erik leaned across the desk, picked up a small stack of snapshots, and handed them to me. They were all of the same man—in one shot, he was just a sullen boy. The last two pictures bore dates: 12–24–82 and 12–25–80. The subjects were identical, a male Caucasian of varying age, in the last three photographs wearing his red-brown hair quite long, with a full beard and mustache. He looked like the man in the video.

"Billy," said Mary quietly. "William Fredrick Ing."

"He's got a sheet," proclaimed Parish. "I've had a chance to study it. Interesting stuff. Schultz is burning copies right now."

Karen came through the door, lugging the bulky file. "Schultz is done burning copies," she said as she strode to Winters's desk and plopped the bundle down in front of him. "God, the media is a pain in the ass."

Wald introduced Karen Schultz to Mary Ing. A moment of silence covered the office, then Dan spoke. "Mrs. Ing, you might not want to be around for this. It's official business, and there's nothing in Billy's file you don't know about already. But if you'd like to, we want you to stay. Anything you can add to what we have might help. It's very possible, Mrs. Ing, that you may have already saved lives by what you've done."

Mary Ing stroked the wrinkles from the lap of her patterned cotton dress. "Of course." She glanced very briefly at me, then lowered her blue eyes. "I'll stay and do what I can."

Karen handed a file copy to each of us.

Winters nodded to Parish. "Martin, walk us through this— you had time to study it. Karen, keep Russell here on the straight and narrow."

I got out my microrecorder, rewound the tape, and turned it on. I got out my notepad and pen. Mary Ing looked at me with sorry curiosity.

"William Fredrick Ing," said Parish. "Male Caucasian, thirty-nine, six-two, two ten. LKA Dana Point, but it's four years old and patrol's already checked it. Nobody there has ever heard of him. History of epilepsy since childhood, alcoholism as an adult, some uh . . . family problems. The raps seem random until you get them together for a long view back. Stack up the fact that he's killed eight people in the last two weeks and you can read his sheet like a 'how to create a killer' manual."

"Don't quote him on *that*," said Karen.

I followed the sheet as Parish read. Ing made his debut

in the juvenile justice system on July 14, 1966, at the age of twelve, for "hunting" two girls with a BB gun at a junior high school campus. For reasons unfathomable, the girls had tried to hide in a glass phone booth. Ing had pinned them down with BB fire for an hour before some older boys caught him, broke the gun and Ing's nose. The riddled phone booth cost Ing's mother eighty-nine dollars to repair. Neither girl was hit or hurt. The girls' families didn't press. Billy was counseled at Juvenile Hall—six sessions—then the charges were dropped.

He was back a year later, when neighbors in his Santa Ana neighborhood told police that their pets were disappearing, and that "Crazy Billy" was their suspect. Billy denied knowing anything about the animals. The headless carcasses of three dogs and six cats were exhumed from shallow graves in a nearby orange grove a month later. Police found the heads— "crudely preserved with gasoline and newspaper stuffing"—in a makeshift lean-to beneath the bridge of a flood-control ditch. Also found in the lean-to were a vise clamped to a piece of scrap plywood, a blood-clotted coping saw, two containers of pet snacks—one for dogs and one for cats—and a bloodstained Nelson Foxx model Louisville Slugger baseball bat. The Santa Ana cops could find no evidence that the lair "belonged" to Billy, although the same flood-control channel ran directly behind his house, which was less than half a mile away. It also ran along the grove where the bodies were found. Following Ing's July 6 interview with the cops and the dismantling of the lean-to, no more pets disappeared from the neighborhood.

"He's active this time of year," I said. "Look at the dates."

"Like a rattlesnake," said Parish, making an embarrassed avoidance of Mary Ing's sad face.

"He always liked warm weather," she muttered.

And then it hit me that Ing might have been leaving us his name on the tapes he left at the scenes. "Coming," I said.

"Seeing . . . having . . . willing . . . they're all on the Wynn tape. Ing."

"Right, Russell," said Erik. "Gamesmanship. Mrs. Ing, was Billy fond of trickery, deceit?"

Mary looked at Erik with her blue, red-rimmed eyes. "I don't know if he was fond, Mr. Wald. But he . . . well . . . he was what I would call a born liar. He lied about almost everything, just as a matter of course. Did he enjoy it? I don't know. Billy's emotions were almost never . . . visible."

I stared for a moment at one of the glossy blowups of the photograph taken from the video. Ing's bearded, wild-haired face was a fear-inspiring thing to behold, precisely for the absolute lack of fear that it contained. Beneath the deep brow, his eyes had a look of determination, boldness, cunning. I saw something else there, too—superiority and arrogance. Here was the face of a man proud of the horror he could personify, a horror he had worked a lifetime to possess.

"He was in some kind of trouble with the police or juvenile authorities every summer until he turned eighteen," said Parish. "At which time he dropped out of continuation school and took a job as—get this—a live-in attendant at a veterinary hospital."

"Perfect," said Wald. "He was searching for integration."

"Integrating what?" said Parish.

"His hatred, which was directed at helpless animals. He was trying to find a way to live with that hatred, for the hatred to become manageable. If he could integrate the animals into his life, he could accomplish this, at least on a surface level. For Billy, it would have been a start."

"Either that or he was looking for more animals to kill," said Parish stubbornly.

"No," said Mary Ing. "He took that job against his own fear of dogs. Mr. Wald is right—Billy was trying to overcome his fear."

"Of course he was," said Erik. "I'll bet he didn't look forward to his first days on that job."

"He came down with the flu," said Mary.

"I'll rest my case," said Wald. Then, to Parish, with a smile: "Read on, Captain."

Ing had managed to keep the job for four years. He was fired after an argument with the doctor, who filed a police report in the summer—of course—of 1976, claiming that Ing had been stealing various drugs stored at the facility. The doctor had also claimed that Ing had "removed" bodies from the hospital freezer, though exactly what the night attendant had done with them he "couldn't imagine." Police interviewed Billy, who denied any wrongdoing. No charges filed.

With Parish's mention of the word *freezer*, I looked hard at him, while he stared dully back at me. It had been clear to me how Martin's work in Amber's bedroom was supposed to turn out: the bloody walls, the bludgeoned woman, even the tape left in the stereo would have been more than enough to aim investigators straight at the Midnight Eye. Parish had practically signed the Eye's name to the scene. Then, for reasons I still hadn't been able to decipher, he'd changed his plan and was trying instead to stage *my* and Grace's guilt by removing the body to my property and documenting its burial. Why the change of plan? What had Martin learned between the time he killed Alice on July 3 and the time on July the Fourth when he removed his victim and the "evidence" of the Midnight Eye? Why had he laid it on me? I remembered something that Chet Singer had told me once—that premeditated murder required audacity. Parish's just-spoken words rang in my mind—that the doctor "couldn't imagine" what Ing might have done with the carcasses stolen from the deep freeze. It was only the doctor's limited imagination that kept him from the truth. And that concept—the unimaginable—

was always applied to the serial killer, to the fact that Randy Kraft would drive around with his latest victim in the seat beside him; to the fact that Art Crump would return to the rental yard a chain saw still clogged with blood and hair; to the fact that Richard Ramirez would simply walk into quiet suburban homes late at night; to the fact that Jeffrey Dahmer would cut up his victims with an electric saw right there in his little apartment while the smell of rotting human flesh crept out from under his door and filled the hallway. The audacity! It was all, truly, beyond imagination. So as I returned Martin Parish's stare, I understood the secret he had kept—that behind his calm exterior and his badge lived a man capable—quite literally—of the unimaginable, a man intimately familiar with audacity.

He smiled at me and said, "What do *you* think Ing was doing with the bodies from the freezer, Russ? You writers are supposed to have imagination."

And that was when it occurred to me that the only way to bring Martin Parish to any kind of justice was to outimagine him, to meet him on his own audacious turf. But how?

"Maybe he had a friend bury them and taped it with a video camera," I said.

Martin retreated behind the blankness of his smile, while Wald, Winters, Schultz, and Mary Ing all looked at me and then at one another with a series of unconnecting glances that left all eyes on me again.

"Billy didn't have any friends," said Mary Ing in all seriousness. She was not fluent in the language of the unimaginable.

"They didn't have commercial video cameras in 1976," added Wald, clearly a man who did not understand audacity.

"Who in hell cares what he was doing with the dog bodies, Marty?" asked Winters. He looked at his watch. "Get on with this, Martin. Russell here has a story to file sometime this year."

Martin looked a little gray but forced a grin at me.

As an adult, Ing had been arrested three times, questioned on three other occasions, and had done a total of 123 days in lockup. At twenty-two, he'd been popped on a standard DUI and found to have a pocketful of peyote on him—no charges for the drug; no probable cause for the search. Two years later, while working as a groundskeeper for a private school, he was questioned on complaints from his employer that certain animals in the school's "zoo" were disappearing. No charges filed. Two years later, he was in on a complaint from his landlord, who said Billy had broken into three different apartments in the complex and stolen nothing but women's underwear. Nothing filed. In 1984, at the age of thirty, Billy Ing had been convicted of his first real crime—an indecent exposure to a woman on Laguna's Main Beach. The ninety-day sentence was suspended in favor of out-patient psychiatric counseling—seven sessions. A year later, Ing fell for grand theft auto, which earned him four months. The car was stolen from a side street in Laguna Beach and returned to a hilltop residential area of the same city two days later. He was questioned in 1987 regarding an attempted rape at Laguna's Thousand Steps beach, and again two years later for a series of dogs and cats that had washed up, beaten to death, near the Aliso Pier just south of Laguna. No charges filed.

"Russell," said Karen, "this personal history may be of interest to our readers. Most of it is taken from the psych evaluations done here at County—the rest from some phone interviews Probation did. You can't quote the evaluations—they're confidential—especially what Billy Ing said. You may quote Martin, Sheriff Winters, Wald, and me. You may quote Mrs. Ing if she will consent. Are we clear on this?"

"Clear."

Ing was born in Anaheim, Orange County, in 1954. His

father, Howard, was an aerospace draftsman at Rockwell; Mary worked in food service in the hospital in which Billy was born. He was an only child.

"Nothing could have been more 'normal,'" said Wald, looking up from the sheet. "But while Mr. and Mrs. Ing worked hard and young Billy was left in the care of a day-sitter, he was beginning to lead, I suspect, a very unhappy life. Is that true, Mary?"

"He was not a happy child," she answered, looking down at the page. "I can't believe how much you have on him. On . . . us."

"Mrs. Ing," said Erik, with a look of deep gravity, "you have absolutely nothing to be ashamed of. You have come here, and you are saving lives. You are a good person."

Karen shifted uneasily in her seat, as did Martin Parish. If Winters detected the massive condescension, he did not let on. Neither did Mary. She blushed deeply, looked down at the pages, and wiped her eye again with the wadded blue tissue.

Parish went back to reading.

Ing was a large child, plump and not athletic, shy and friendless. More aggressive boys hit him; girls derided or ignored him; teachers disliked him because he was slow and stubborn as a student. His epilepsy was a topic for chiding. Ing came in at 136 on the Stanford-Binet IQ test. He was often truant, for which he was beaten by his father. Howard, according to Billy, was "always drunk" and abusive, sometimes to the point of hitting Mary with his fists. Howard had told his son many times that Billy and Mary were "anchors" around his neck, that the long hours he worked to support them were hours he would have spent—without the curse of their presence—in a life devoted to, of all things, the study of law.

I looked at Mary, who continued staring down at the papers on her lap. She gave off a clear, if inaudible, wail of distress. Sensing my attention on her, she glanced quickly at me, held my gaze for a moment with her hopeless blue eyes, then directed them back toward her lap. Her fist clenched hard upon the tissue.

Parish flipped a page and continued.

According to Billy, Howard was a man "so stupid and fat" that he got along better with animals than people.

"I expected this," said Wald. "It fits perfectly."

"Then maybe you should let me read it," said Parish.

"Pardon me, Captain," said Erik.

Parish grunted and went on. According to Billy, the Ings always had three Staffordshire terriers (pit bulls) and three cats. One of Billy's jobs was to feed and clean up after them before his father came home from work. He hated the animals, the way they "slobbered and shit everywhere," the way they seemed, for reasons beyond his understanding, to receive more love and tender attention from his father than he did. He was attacked at age eight by all three of the dogs one night, receiving 135 stitches to close the wounds. As an adult, he grew facial hair to cover the scars.

Karen interrupted. "Sheriff, what's your call on the scars? We can publish it, or we can hold it."

"Why publish?" asked Wald, "He's wearing a beard."

"It can't hurt," said Parish. "What if he shaves? Which is a distinct possibility, after the picture we ran."

Winters contemplated this. "Drop the scars, Russ. Let's hope he keeps the beard. Mrs. Ing, any pictures of Billy with no beard and the scars visible?"

She shook her head. "He's worn a beard and mustache since he was in his early twenties. The scars embarrass him. I don't think he would shave."

Winters nodded. "Save the scars, Monroe. You got only so much space."

Parish shook his big head as if he were dealing with children, then continued.

According to Billy, the dog attack, although terrifying and deeply angering, was not nearly as painful to him as the incident that immediately preceded it.

At this point, Parish looked at Mary Ing and asked with a gentleness that surprised me, "Is it okay to read this, Mrs. Ing?"

She nodded but didn't look up.

Apparently, during one of his rages, Howard began beating Mary. Billy could hear them behind the closed door of the bedroom. His father was "grunting," something—or someone— was slamming against a wall, and his mother was sobbing. Billy threw open the door. Howard's back was to him, and he had his coat on, but his pants were down around his ankles. All Billy saw of his mother, blocked as she was by his father, were her two hands, fingers spread against the wall, and the profile of her face—"strangely angled"—also pressed to the wall, "like she was trying to hear something on the other side of it." Billy said that it looked "painful" for his mother. So he jumped onto his father's back. Howard easily shook him off, and when Billy rushed to his mother's aid, she slapped him so hard across his face that he stopped dead in his tracks. Billy said later that the feeling of Mary's hand on his flesh was "the single worst pain I ever felt." Billy had then run out the back door of his bedroom, across the darkened backyard toward the fence, behind which lay the flood-control channel, and made two unsuccessful leaps to get atop that fence before Howard's pit bulls—in a snarling fury of mistaken protection—dragged him down.

"Note the date," said Wald. "Fourth of July, 1962. The County shrink notes that the dogs might have been aroused by the neighborhood fireworks, which in '62 were legal and popular. Look, even Billy says, down at the bottom of the page, that he remembered hearing the scream of a 'Picolo Pete' going off as he tried to get over the fence. This is the answer to the question of why he took the vet hospital job. Not the answer, actually—but the question itself. Fear and its governance. Do you integrate it or isolate it?"

"Who cares?" asked Martin.

"If we understand him, we can help him," said Wald.

"I thought we were supposed to stop him," said Parish.

Wald, obviously trying to accommodate Mary's feelings—and to pave in advance a layer of trust, should we need her help—smiled at Parish and shook his head. "We help Billy, we help everybody in this county, Martin. *That's* what we're paid to do."

Karen looked at me. "This isn't the kind of stuff we expect to see in your next piece, Russ. It's background."

As Parish proceeded with his reading, I couldn't help but feel some pity for the Billy Ing who used to be. And I also couldn't help but wonder whether anyone—especially a county psychologist—could ever really locate the reason why a human turns into a hunter of other humans, a thrill killer, a living nightmare. True, Ing's story was horrible enough—a violent family, bad experiences at school, even the awful attack by his own dogs. But there were thousand of others with comparable—or worse—lives who had managed somehow not to break, not to turn, not to slip over that final edge and fall into the numb, self-pitying, remorseless rage that is the hallmark of the sociopathic murderer. Why Ing, if indeed Ing was the Midnight Eye? Why not someone who had suffered even more?

I have a theory, though perhaps it's less a theory than a simple point of view. I'm not a religious man, though faith has something to do with my theory, as does the cold truth of mathematical probability. (The idea has come to me that God and mathematics are one.) But I've always believed that there is a God somewhere, that certain people are closer to that God than others, that some are tied to a "purpose" that seems to come from outside of themselves, from "above." My list would include people as diverse as Solomon, Buddha, Gerard Manley Hopkins, Muhammad, Blake, and certainly Jesus Christ. Thus, statistically, one in every X million people are "chosen" or "choose" or simply end up being closer to God than the rest of us, and they function much as journalists, scurrying between above and below, reporting back, keeping us informed. It is their job to carry out the high-level diplomacy that people like me would only bungle— misquoting, missing deadlines, missing the point, losing the notes, erasing the tapes. Similarly, there are those "chosen" to do the darkest work of the world, to function as God's continuing curse upon us, or—for those amused by the concept of God— to fulfill the mathematical fact that for every X million men and women who walk the earth at a given time, one of them will be little more than a merciless predator of other men and women. Solomon was chosen for his gift of poetry; the Midnight Eye for his gift of rage. One celebrates his specific blessing; the other bears his unique curse. But both do their work so that *we don't have to.* The Eye was a serial killer for the simple purpose of allowing me to be a writer. In a sense, I owed him. I extend this sense of gratitude to all sufferers of disease, too. Especially to Isabella, who, I am convinced, received her sickness so that I would not. None of this is to say that the best place for the Midnight Eye is not the guillotine or some modern equivalent—it probably is. And if called upon to lower the blade, I certainly would, though less with a feeling of vengeance than a sense of duty. I would lower the blade so you wouldn't have to. Cancer is a serial killer; a serial killer is a cancer. No one chooses either.

Parish then briefly reviewed Ing's history of epilepsy, while I wondered whether his taped stutterings might have been influenced by seizures, or postseizure confusion. Had he taped them

210

during the "aura" experienced by some epileptics before a fit, those seconds of ecstasy, vision? Ing had admitted to being a heavy drinker from the age of eighteen, when he left his parents' home and took the job as hospital night clerk. After his four-year stint there, Ing began a life of localized vagrancy that took him further and further out of contact with his mother, and, oddly, further away from contact with law enforcement.

Something else I found fascinating, if pathetic: Ing had been questing for religious belief from an early age. He had tried it all. Lutheran, Methodist, and Baptist churches as a boy (his mother often moved the family's place of worship); as a young man on his own he'd tried Catholicism, the Four-square Church, Judaism, Buddhism, Islam, Confucianism, Rosicrucianism, Scientology. In his own words, Ing had been "looking for simple answers to complex questions. All religions, I discovered for myself, are based on the fraudulent assumption that there is a Father who cares. There is no greater lie."

An uneasy quiet settled over the office then, broken only by the distant sound of the General Services crew still yanking away at the sheetrock. Winters sat back, crossed his arms, and contemplated the desk in front of him. "Mrs. Ing," he said finally, "you have anything to add?"

She breathed deeply, squaring her burdened shoulders. "Well . . . I think . . . I suppose that most of what you just read is true. When Howard died, ten years ago, Billy seemed to take on a certain . . . courage? I can say that all through my life with Billy, there seemed to be two of him—one that was there and one that was somewhere else. Truly, deep down inside, he's a good boy. I know that sounds like I'm blind, but really, he was never, I mean he was always . . . I mean, I don't know what I mean."

"You mean he's your boy and you love him," I said.

"Thank you, yes."

"What were his interests, his hobbies?" asked Parish.

"He liked electric things, electronic things. He took apart our phone once and tried to put it back together."

"Did he succeed?" Wald asked.

"Yes. It took him a while, and Howard was furious. He was . . . is quite talented that way. He made radios and walkie-talkie devices. He was always a good listener."

"Did he like to dress up? In your clothes, or Howard's, or in any kind of costume or disguise?" Erik asked.

"Oh my, yes. All of that. Halloween was his favorite day all year."

"Who gives a shit?" asked Parish.

"I do," I said. "Wald is onto something."

"Like what?"

I thought of Chet finding the heavily sprayed hair. I then remembered—began to remember—my train of thought while I was talking to the Eye at Joe and Corrine's house: Why was he so smug about having his picture in the paper?

"Like the fact that the beard and ratty hair are fake," I said, looking at Erik. "He's wearing a costume. He sprays the hell out of the hairpiece to keep it looking . . . sharp."

Wald smiled. "I'll take credit for that jump. It makes perfect sense on a psychological level, too. Part of what this man is doing is performing a ritual. He's reversing the roles of childhood trauma so that he can come out the victor now, not the victim. The long hair and beard are part of the ritual. Mary, did Howard—"

"Yes! His hair was long—for the time, that is—and he was always bearded."

Wald shot a glance at Parish. "There's another reason for it. It lets him run a *normal* life. He's got a job. He's got an identity—undoubtedly a false one—but during the day, when he's not the Midnight Eye, he wears no beard and his hair is probably short."

"So we've got the whole county looking for the wrong face?" asked Winters.

"Exactly," said Wald. "His own opposite. If it's a face you want—get Graphics to take off the hair. It would be close enough."

I was once again impressed by Wald's understanding, if perhaps only because it aligned so closely with my own. "He's right," I said. "Over the phone, he's almost always clear and lucid. If he holds a job, he doesn't wear that blanket around himself. He leaves the garbled tapes to make us think we're after a moron having a fit. He's signing with his left hand."

Again the quiet prevailed. Finally, Winters stood and offered his hand to Mrs. Ing. "Thank you."

She rose and took it. "I wish I could identify that picture for sure," she said. "I believe it is Billy, but I can't be positive. Needless to say, I hope it . . . it . . . isn't."

"We will be in touch," said Winters.

I stood myself then, checking my watch. "Dan, I think Mrs. Ing should stay."

"What for?"

"I talked to the Midnight Eye an hour ago. He said he'll be calling here at noon."

A wry smile passed over Winters's face. "Here?"

"It's about the 'dramatic statement,'" I said.

"Oh God," said Mary Ing.

"Mrs. Ing, can you wait another forty minutes and listen to his voice?"

"Of course."

Then, to Parish: "Martin, get Carfax in here for a CNI intercept. He's got forty minutes to make the installation."

Parish grunted, glaring at me, then at Wald.

"*Now.*"

"Russ," said Karen Schultz, already heading for the door, "Chet wants to see you in the lab."

■   ■   ■

Chet sat, rumpled as usual, on his stool, his heavy mouth turned down as if not only gravity but years of acquaintance with the dark side of human nature were tugging his entire face earthward. His eyes behind the thick glasses were sharp as always. He glanced at Karen, and some unspoken signal sent her from the room.

"Sit," he said.

On the table in front of Chet was a tape player and a stack of cassettes. The tape I had given him sat beside them. He eyed them forlornly as I sat beside him. "I'm unhappy with what I have discovered," he said. "It makes no sense. And when I put it within the larger picture, it still makes no sense." He turned and stared at me over the tops of his glasses.

"Students of the incomplete?" I asked.

He looked at me again with his lugubrious and penetrating eyes. "Russell, what we have here is something far more disturbing than incompletion. I fear that we may be looking right into the heart of an evil. An evil very close to us."

"You listened to my tape."

"Yes, I want to know where you got it, and why it hasn't been properly booked into evidence here."

"I got it from the trunk of Martin Parish's car."

Singer studied me for a long while. I could almost see the thoughts racing behind his eyes, and I easily sensed in his deliberation the speed and economy with which Chester Fairfax Singer organized information.

He nodded finally. "Let us backtrack. I am employed, as you know, in the Hair and Fiber section of our forensic crime lab, although I spend much time in the other areas of the lab. By default, seniority, and perhaps experience, it has fallen upon me to run the day-to-day operations here. I have a hand in almost every piece of evidence that comes through here, from fingerprints to semen samples to trace soils to spent cartridges. And it has come to my attention, Russell, that there is forensic work being done in my lab on a crime for which we have no record, no file, no case number, no information at all. A certain . . . ranking official in this department has been doing this work on his own. He is inexpert in technique but patient enough to arrive at sound results. I have observed him both early and late, before and after hours. The evidence involves hair, latents belonging to a suspect, taken from the scene of what crime, I cannot fathom. Also, there are paint chips, fiber samples from the floorboard of the *suspect's* car, which match samples taken— again, I assume—from the scene of whatever 'crime' was committed. I have come to learn the name of the *suspect,* if that's the right term. I've said nothing of this to anyone yet except for you. Supply for me the name of this suspect, Russell."

"There are two, if I'm not mistaken."

He arched an eyebrow and smiled.

"Grace Wilson and Russ Monroe," I said.

"Your daughter, I believe."

"That's right. Did you solve the tape I gave you?"

Solemnly, he nodded, and looked down again at the offending cassette. "It's not an actual recording made by the Midnight Eye. It is his voice. They are his own words. But the tape you gave me is a composite, a collection of sentences from the tapes left at the Fernandez and Ellison homes. You knew this, I assume."

"I was pretty sure. I recognized the phrases from before."

"And Martin had this tape in his possession?"

"Yes."

"Russell, you will now be as forthcoming with me as I have been with you, and tell me what in the name of God is going on."

"It's simple," I said. "Martin Parish killed a woman on the third of July and tried to frame the Eye. But he changed his mind—I'm not sure why yet—and now he's using your lab to build a case against Grace and me."

Chester listened in a rapt, if not stunned, silence as I explained to him the drear events that unfolded on the nights of July 3 and 4. I told him everything—my desire to see Amber Mae, my witnessing of Martin leaving the house and wiping the gate, "Amber's" demolished body, and later, the sanitized crime scene, fresh paint and throw rug, the missing body, Martin's near-naked appearance in Amber's bedroom, and his claim that Grace had been there on July 3.

Chester listened like a man hearing the unspeakable name of Jehovah for the first time. When I was finished, he moaned quietly.

"What does Parish actually have?" I asked.

Singer's eyes took on a focused ferocity I had never seen in him. "No. You will not get that information from me. You will take that tape of yours and proceed out of this office now. I will not allow my lab, or this department, to be used by Martin Parish, or by you, or by anyone else. You have made me feel filthy, Russell, as has our captain. And I will tell you right now that I will give my last breath of effort to maintain the high standards this lab has always sought. We are not going to be caught between you men and your primitive obsessions. *We will not be used.*"

His chin was trembling.

I could not blame Chester for his fury or confusion. I could only admire his honesty.

"Russell," he said. "Exercise extreme caution. We have a grand jury. And I will ask you now not to betray me for what I've confided in you. At some point, I will protect only myself and the integrity of this department."

"I understand."

"And I understand nothing. Please, go."

■   ■   ■

The Midnight Eye called Sheriff Dan Winters at exactly noon. Winters, Parish, Wald, Karen, Mary Ing, and I all listened to his voice on the conference phone while John Carfax monitored the CNI intercept.

"Hello, fellas," he began. "Hello, nigger Dan. This is the Midnight Eye. Look for the pampered pets in the town that pampers perverts, too. I have a surprise there for you. Enjoy it in all its richness, and remember that I won't stop until every nigger, greaser, chink, slope, cocksucker, and kike starts to pack his bags and get out of my home. I'd print something like that, if I were you. See you in hell."

The Eye hung up.

"What in Christ's name does that mean?" asked Parish.

The canyon, I thought.

Carfax shook his head, bewildered. "He's bypassing the intercepts. All of them. I don't know how."

Winters glared at the conference speaker, then at Carfax, then at Mary Ing.

"Well, Mrs. Ing?" asked Wald.

"It's Billy," she said.

"He means the Pampered Pet Palace in Laguna Beach," I said. "It's in the canyon."

There are only seven small streets that intersect Laguna Canyon Road, most of which branch into still smaller tributaries that narrow and wind and finally disappear into the rough hills above. The people who live there are an admittedly oddball lot, and I can say this with no sense of denigration because I am one of them. There is a history of lawlessness in the canyon, going back to the days when bandits on horseback preyed on the travelers who used the road, which was then just a wandering dirt path that was the only inland route into the city. Much later, in the 1960s, Timothy Leary's Brotherhood was headquartered on Woodland, moving many thousand of tabs of LSD outward to the continent. (Leary was finally arrested by a Laguna Beach patrolman, which led to the discovery of his operation and a prison term. The patrolman went on to become a very fine chief of police here; Leary, of course, is now a counterculture gadfly popular on the college lecture circuit.)

In more recent years, the outlaw heritage of the canyon

evolved into a quiet suspicion of authority, a prickly tone of independence and pride at not living "in the city" at all. It was only four years ago that we canyon people allowed the city to annex us into its domain, a move not made without endless dickering for "concessions" and seemingly interminable meetings. The canyon is one of the few places in Laguna where artists can still afford to live, an irony in an upscale town that prides itself, profitably, on being an art colony. The canyon is a hodgepodge place, by Orange County standards: a cave house stands beside a Jehovah's Witness temple; trailers hide on flattened pads hidden by eucalyptus and near mansions; artists live next door to tax attorneys; there are families, gay couples, horse people, bird fanciers, bonsai growers, snake collectors—the friendly, the meddlesome, the isolated, and the bizarre. There are also littered along the narrow roads a number of ramshackle cottages no larger than rooms, really, that are rentable, cheap, and private.

All of which is to say that as we climbed the steep, winding road called Red Tail Lane, I saw the houses and people in them as neighbors; I felt a sense of kinship with the dwellers there; I believed that so far as the word *community* went, we had a fine one; and I was already wondering whether the Midnight Eye had chosen this place because of its proximity to my home, whether it was his way of showing how easily he could strike in this, my virtual backyard. No victim is faceless, but anyone of this canyon was of myself, too. I felt responsible. And I also felt in the pit of my stomach the soft, shifting reflection of dread as I pictured Elsie and Leonard Stein, proprietors of the Pampered Pet Palace. They were two very kindly people who ran the place, and they had taken fine care of Isabella's beloved dog one summer when we were away in Mexico. I remembered, very specifically, that Mrs. Stein wore a small Star of David on a chain around her neck.

■　　　　■　　　　■

Much can be said for the mercy of forgetfulness, although I have actually forgotten very little of what I saw inside the Pampered Pet Palace, 1871 Red Tail Lane, Laguna Beach, at 2:35 P.M. on Wednesday, July 7. Forgotten, no, but... well, edited. Organized. Arranged.

I still own every detail of that scene, but they are far from useful in everyday life, in fact they are counterproductive. Occasionally, one detail—for example, the wall calendar in the lobby, picturing the July dog (a papillon) with a piece of human brain matter stuck to its surface, obliterating the dates 17, 18, 24, and 25—slips from its appointed place and I have to guide it like an escaped mamba back into the box. Sometimes—rarely, so far—they all manage to get loose at once, and I have a situation best described as untenable.

So bear with me now, if you choose, some of the particulars—trapped but relentlessly active—that I will carry to my deathbed, such as the body of a woman (Elsie Stein, fifty-one) strewn raglike in the lobby corner behind the desk, face gone, head open and emptied, the gold Star of David necklace still attached and dangling in a red-black pond that rippled in the currents of a ceiling fan, all illuminated by the desk lamp, still on; such as the lobby calendar marred with her brains and the comet of fluids that struck the wall around it; such as the first room on the left down the hallway, the door to which said VIPOOCHES ONLY and contained in the very center of its floor an actual arrangement of small canine bodies stacked in opposing threes like firewood, the top row of poodle, miniature dachshund, and Pomeranian having slumped out of alignment and rolled off; such as the sweetish gag of urine and blood in that place; such as the room marked CAT HOUSE, in which all six guests

220

ended their six or fifty-four lives in one corner—two tabbies, a Siamese, two calicoes, a black, draped with such feline grace as to appear asleep if not for the heads; such as the outdoor row of kennels, six on one side of a cement walkway and six on the other, over the gates of which hung the larger dogs, like towels, drying on the chain link, shattered, leaking audibly— each drop distinct and resonant—into the narrow drains that ran along the front of each row and deposited by invisible slope their contents through circular screens at the end of the rows, each drain clogged red and black and stagnant; such as the guest house beyond the kennel run, squatting quaint and yellow beneath the eucalyptuses, potted pansies, and carnations on the steps, this small cottage, door open, housing sprawled and naked in the bedroom Leonard Stein (fifty-six) facedown and still clutching a long-barreled .38, a large, plump man with thin white legs bowed even at rest, the trail of black ants scintillant but orderly from his head to where they vanished cargo-laden through a corner crack in the floorboards; such as Dorsey, a mixed-breed toy that had dodged the slaughter and wailed alone from the narrow space between the wall and the refrigerator in the kitchen and had to be pried out, trembling, with a broom handle by none other than stoic Martin Parish, who announced in a voice almost a whisper that the sound was going to drive him crazy but that was understood by us others, given the context, as a brief escape from the helplessness of death to the terrified demands of the only thing left living there; such as, an hour later, the largely mute crowd that gathered at the crime-scene tape suspended across the road between a crepe myrtle and a cottonwood, these faces bereft of everything but fear, somehow fully understanding the scene behind the tape—an old gray couple dispirited and solemn, a boy of perhaps ten who sobbed and inquired repeatedly after the condition and whereabouts of "Tiger," his mother with one hand pressed lightly to her face in an extended signal of tragedy while the other rested on the corn-silk pale hair of her boy; such as, almost astonishingly, the group of youngish women and older men arriving en masse, each bearing a walkie-talkie, each wearing the blue T-shirt marked CITIZENS' TASK FORCE and sporting the silk-screened face of Kimmy Wynn, each conspicuously aware of and silently acknowledging how unsuitable he and she had been to the task, how superfluous and minor and absurd they were, what a great and unintended insult was their presence—you could see the profound shame on their faces mixed with the one faintly redeeming conviction they had left: to stick this one out, at least do what they could, even if nothing more than to bear witness to their own gross ineffectuality and confirm the terrible lopsided rout in a battle that their God was supposed to help them with because they believed He would; such as the ashen faces of Winters and Wald; such as Karen Schultz on the steps of the rear porch, her head resting on her arms resting on her knees and her back shaking; such as the chopper fiercely cutting the sky to little effect on the vultures who simply lowered their orbit so their shadows met the ground clearly and you could see the dark shapes of wings gliding across the road and angling without effort up the walls of the old house and finally into the trees, only to circle and pass again; such as the Labrador I nearly tripped over at the far end of the compound where the small yard met the canyon scrub, an animal beaten but still breathing, very rapidly, too damaged to do more, his smooth old dog's teeth red in his panting mouth and drops of blood still shining around the base of a staunch native oak; such as the fact that I sat down near that oak finally because my legs felt aching and old, sat there for a long while because it was the only thing I was absolutely positive I could do, and do well.

20

Later, my legs still shaking and a storm of disgust brewing in my heart, I walked into my house, to be greeted by Grace. She was wearing a kitchen apron belonging to Isabella, a T-shirt, and a pair of shorts.

"God, Russell, your face is gray," she said.

I don't think I answered her. I poured a large whiskey over ice, took it into my den, and shut the door. I stared out the window. I fanned through the mail Grace had left stacked on the desk: the usual assortment of bills and junk fliers—and a rather serious-looking envelope from case manager Tina Sharp. I filed it, unopened, with the unpaid medical bills. It was half an hour before I could lay eyes on another human being again. I felt as if my soul had been dragged through a sewer. Finally, I went back out.

Standing there with her legs exposed beneath the apron and a wooden spoon in her hand, she looked like either an advertisement for the spoon or an intro for some men's mag "sex in the kitchen" spread. Images of Elsie Stein flickered in my mind as I looked at my daughter, subliminal postcards from hell.

"What happened?" she asked.

"Some people and animals died."

"Is that why all the helicopters are out there?"

"Yes."

"It must have been horrible."

"It was truly horrible, girl."

I poured another large whiskey over ice and shut the door to my study behind me.

My father called to say that Amber had left without his permission. She claimed to have urgent private business. She was calm and apparently unafraid to be out alone.

"I'm sorry, Russ. I was on the pot when she drove off."

"It's okay for now. There's nothing you can do."

"I hear something wrong in your voice," he said.

"The Eye hit here in the canyon."

"People you know?"

"Kind of."

"Do you need me there?"

"Wait for Amber. Later, Dad."

I wrote the Ing piece first, based on Mary's partial identification of the picture and full conviction that the voice on the conference speaker was that of her son, William Fredrick.

My article on the latest killing spree by the Midnight Eye was finished an hour later. It simply projected out of me like vomit, and I felt the same sense of spent foulness that a good retching would have left. I faxed both pieces off to Carla Dance and Karen Schultz, then made another drink and sat out on the deck. The two Sheriff's Department choppers and one borrowed from the Newport Beach PD roared through the sky above, their blades popping dully against the canyon sides. Two network news birds hovered low, getting establishing shots for the seven o'clock segments. I talked briefly with Carla, who was checking facts—how many dogs, exactly, were hanging on the fence; did Ing graduate from high school in 1972 or 1973; was "Tiger" a cat or a dog? She told me the crime-scene report was the best she'd ever read and speculated that there might be an award in it for me. The ice in my whiskey had melted and I felt sick.

Grace joined me in the shade of the deck, a shade that still registered 102 degrees on the thermometer nailed to the side of the house. The choppers persevered overhead. Grace looked lovely and composed; I sensed in her a desire to ameliorate the apparent darkness of my mood. She noted that the ice in my glass was gone and took it into the house for more. Grace did not speak as I explained to her what had happened on Red Tail Lane. I cannot remember what I said. My gorge rose as I finished the outline, and my mouth went dry and my face got cold. Through the open screen doors, I could hear the television newspeople slurring out the latest on the Midnight Eye's deeds in Laguna Beach.

I closed my eyes, saw the sun burning orange against my eyelids, concentrated on the slow, even pounding of my heart. "Grace, you ever wish something big, like God, would pick you up by the heels with a pair of tongs and just like dip you into something wet, and when you came out, you'd be clean and fresh again?"

"Oh, yes. I've pictured it as something like mercury, something silver and smooth that goes into your body, then drains out through the pores, and all the ugliness goes out with it."

"Yeah."

Eyes still closed and my head resting against the rough redwood of the house, I found Grace's hand with mine and squeezed it gently. Contrary to the early morning of July 5, when

I had last taken her stiff and reluctant hand, now she remained gentle and confident within my own and I sensed no notion on her part to withdraw from me. Her hand seemed, at that moment, the single most valuable thing in my world. Then I felt it grow tense.

"Don't take that away," I said.

It relaxed slightly and remained firmly within my own.

"Grace, I like the sound of your voice. Tell me a pleasant story, one with meadows or lakes or something, tell me something happy that happened to you."

"Well...okay, Russell, but I don't know any happy stories."

"You must know one."

"But I don't."

"Then make one up."

"I can't."

The sun continued its hot touch upon my eyelids and the sounds of the canyon traffic diminished, no doubt a result of the roadblock set up by Winters in meager hope of intercepting the Midnight Eye, or perhaps a witness. The whiskey surged around in my blood, unable either to fuel me or soothe me. I thought of Isabella and her surgery the next morning. I thought of life without her. There seemed to be nothing on earth to look forward to.

"Then tell me about you and your mother," I said. "It doesn't have to be happy, just true."

Grace sighed and her hand tensed. I squeezed it harder.

"What do you want to know, Russ?"

"I don't understand why you're so afraid of her."

"There are lots of things you don't understand."

"Tell me why. Tell me *something*. Let me hear your voice."

"Well . . . Russell, you must know that Amber is a profoundly selfish person. She is also extremely insecure and self-doubting. With every year I became older and more mature, she became more competitive. It was a revelation to me, at the age of thirteen, that my own mother was jealous of me."

Her hand grew stiffer, but I made no move to let it go.

"Jealous?" I was imagining horrible things now from the Pampered Pet Palace, and it seemed that Grace's voice was the only antidote. "I wish you'd explain that."

"For example, Amber and I gained the attentions of a very handsome young sommelier in a Paris restaurant one fall. He was thrilled to have our table—you could sense his desire just in the way he worked a cork from a bottle. It was also clear that he was interested in me. Amber, of course, in all her fake Continental sophistication, invited him—Florent—to a party in her suite on a Friday night. Florent and I had a wonderful talk out on the balcony while the other guests were inside. He told me he was more affected by my beauty than he'd ever been by a woman before. I told him I understood and would accept his call the next evening. Don't I sound like Amber now—'would accept his call'? It was all so . . . obvious, so predictable. The next morning, I got from Amber a one-way ticket back to Orange County, via Los Angeles, and was met at the airport by Martin. The phrase that still sticks in my mind was, 'Never, *ever* try to come between me and one of my men again. I have not raised you to be a whore.' Amber said it from the back of the limo as I climbed out at De Gaulle. I'll never forget the . . . aggression in her eyes."

I heard the choppers thumping overhead.

"One might argue that Amber saw in you a thirteen-year-old girl getting in way over her head."

Grace's hand tightened with an unexpected strength.

"The first key to understanding other people, Russ, is to remember that they don't think like you do. If you aren't ready to respect my answer, you shouldn't have asked the question."

"I stand corrected. Please go on."

"She basically just dumped me on the plane, Russ. Without a word of explanation beyond the clucking about her men. That's an example, a typical event. There was a coldness about how she moved me around her world like a piece of jewelry. I tried just to understand her. I forgave Amber a lot—I rationalized her behavior, figuring that was just the way she was. I'm not an unforgiving person, Russ. But by the time I was taken on a . . . desert sight-seeing tour by the fat man and his crew-cut friend, I was finally broken. I was terrified. I felt . . . hated."

"I'm not tracking."

Grace studied me silently for a long while. I could tell by the shadow the hair of her turned head made across my sun-struck face.

"Well, Russell, the desert tour was quite simple. Fat man and crew cut—they called themselves Sam and Gary—met me as I was getting into my car one evening to leave work. Gary had a gun—a Glock Nineteen, I believe. This was about eight weeks ago. They stuffed me into the front seat of a red Bronco and squeezed me in between them. A bloodhound was on the backseat, huge and slobbering. Name of Tex. Funny. The ride down was two hours of silence and BO from Sam. No gropes or suggestive talk, so I was half-wondering if they might not rape me. We went out by Joshua Tree, off on a dirt road, into the desert. They brought me out, rather gently I remember, then knocked me on the ground and burned the bottoms of my feet with cigarettes. Gary allowed me to chew on his shoe, to quiet me. They didn't say anything. Well, they said one thing, which was the whole purpose of the exercise. Gary said, and I quote, 'Show some respect, or you're out of the money.' Amber's been threatening to write me out of the trusts. I'm supposed to get a really big piece of it when I turn twenty-one. She's holding the money over me like some kind of glue, like she can put us back together with it. The truth of it is, I don't want the money. I can work. I have some savings. It's just like that stupid netsuke she believes I stole from her. She makes up something, then reacts to her own illusion. She scares me to death. Which is exactly what she wants."

"To scare you into . . . what?"

"Submitting to her. Talking. Calling. Begging to be let back into her heart. God, I don't know, Russell. Ask *her*. I've given up trying."

She regarded me, and her face came into better focus, and I saw the look of near exasperation on it. Her pupils were small and I sensed depths behind their depths, layers beneath the layers—fear and courage, truth and falsehood, youth and maturity—all tapering back toward the point in her life, all those years ago, when she felt betrayed by her mother. And I saw for my Grace no place where she might fall and hope to land safely. She seemed to be balanced above the abyss, like a dancer on one flexed toe, the question not being if but *when* she would tire and fall. And I felt myself tracking her through the same gaping wound that Amber had opened in her all those years ago, her violation making possible my own.

If one can feel a fissure open in the heart, that is exactly what I felt. A helicopter roared past, straight overhead, low. The windows rattled.

"Let me see the bottoms of your feet."

"It's comforting, Russell, to see you trust me as much as Amber does."

"Then I withdraw the request. I believe you and I trust you."

"Good. You should."

229

Then she reached down and untied her tennis shoes, peeled off her socks, and exposed first the left, then the right foot. The circular pits of distorted skin, the chaotic healing of burned flesh, were a living fossil record of pain. There were seven burns on each.

"It hurt so bad, I broke three of my back teeth, gnashing. You may see the new crowns, if you'd like."

"I wish you had come to me."

"I thought I could handle this myself, Russell. I am not inexperienced in taking care of my own problems. I tried. I am still trying."

"May I hold you?"

"Yeah."

She melted against me, burying her sobbing face in the crook of my neck. She did not cry long, did not cry hard. She did not speak. A few minutes later, when her breathing had evened, she stood, went to the bathroom, blew her nose, then came back out to the deck.

"I'm looking forward to helping with Isabella tonight," she said. "It will be a chance for me to do something good."

"We'll do something good for Isabella," I said. "She's the most beautiful woman in the world."

"More beautiful than Amber?"

"It's not even close, girl."

"I love her too, Russ."

She gazed out at the canyon, tracking the flight of a chopper as it banked low over the hills.

"I didn't want to add to your miseries, Russell. I didn't want to burden you. But I am scared of Mother and what she might do next, or have her . . . friends do for her. I'm sorry to have complicated your life. And I wish I could have been a better daughter."

The phone rang. Grace was kind enough to answer and bring the cordless out to me. "Dan Winters," she said.

I took the phone.

"Dan."

"Sh-sh-sh-sh . . . fooled again. I can sound just like a nigger lawman when I want to. How's the tracer working?"

"I told you, we decided against it."

"I'll make this quick. I just wanted to know what you thought of my statement."

"I hope you hang for it."

"An erection and climax at the moment of death. Better than lethal injection."

"Nice job, Billy."

The silence that followed was long.

"*W-w-what?*"

"William Fredrick Ing. Billy. Crazy Billy."

"Explain yourself."

"You're dead in the water, Billy. We've got an ID on your photo and one on your voice. You left a clean right index print at the Wynns." This, of course, was a lie. "It took us about two days to make your ass. You're not the Midnight Eye. You're a selfish fat little kid who got chewed by his own dogs. You got slapped around for walking in on your parents doing it. You think you're a great racial cleanser, but you're a fraud. By this time tomorrow, everybody in the county will know who you are."

I could hear him breathing then, a shallow, rapid sound that hissed across the line. "Y-y-you cannot write that. I forb-b-bid you."

"What are you going to do? Kill someone?"

"Yes! Yes! I'll d-d-do something so bad, you won't be able to believe it. And it will be on *your* conscience, Monroe. If you p-p-publish that information, *you* will be directly responsible for what I do next. I absolutely forbid you. You talk to Winters. You talk to W-w-wald. You talk to Parish. You tell them they cannot publish that lie. I am the Midnight Eye! If you write anything other than that . . . I will act t-t-terribly."

"You're scaring the sh-sh-shit out of me."

"Then consult your soul when I do the unspeakable. *It is in your h-h-hands!*"

"Cool off, man. Maybe I could use a little help myself. Maybe if you help me, that article won't get written. Just maybe."

A long pause followed. I could hear his heavy breathing begin to slow.

"You're talking about Amber Mae again."

"That's right."

"Parish tried to k-k-kill her."

"I know that. First he wanted it to look like you. Now he's working up a frame that will fit me perfectly. But he can't use it without damaging himself—his reputation, his marriage, everything. Why is he risking all that?"

"He's not."

"Explain."

"He'll fit you, but he won't use his . . . evidence, unless you threaten him."

"A bluff?"

"Partly."

"And the other part?"

"*Sh-sh-sh.* Well, it's possible, Russ, that he may still ask you to perform some act for him, to do something he desperately needs doing, and will call on you to do it."

"Such as what?"

"It's obvious. You want to catch a pig, think like a pig. Run that article and I'll make you sorry."

232

He slammed down the phone. The crack echoed in my ear as I pressed the OFF button, then dialed Carfax.

"Still no numbered line," he said. "All we can get is area code, and it's here, it's our area code. I can't figure this out."

"He's using a scrambler," I said.

"We can override that with enough time. We had enough time. But we've still got no active number."

"He's not calling from goddamned nowhere, John."

"No. No, he's not. Shit, I just can't—"

"Patch me through to Dan."

Winters came on the line, told me that Parish and Wald were on conference with us.

"Ing says if we print the ID, he's going to be an extra-bad boy."

"We shouldn't let that happen," said Wald. "It's the wrong way to play this."

"You guys are out of your goddamned minds," said Parish.

Ten heated minutes later, we had our answer. Wald and I prevailed over Parish. Winters finally decided to pull the article identifying Ing, perhaps using it as leverage the next time the Midnight Eye called.

"We gotta stop coddling this asshole," said Martin. "We know what he looks like. We got a name. Christ in heaven, Dan, what else can we do?"

"We've got to stop him, period," said Wald. "You don't do that by infuriating him. Not now, at least. There might be a time for that."

"Yeah? How many more people have to die?"

21

The choppers were still in the air an hour later when we left to go get Izzy. Laguna Canyon Road was blocked off again north-bound. I could see the badges leaning keen-eyed toward the idling cars and T-shirted volunteers of the Citizens' Task Force with handfuls of fliers to give out—no pretense to a Sobriety Checkpoint tonight, just a flat-out blanket search for William Fredrick Ing.

There were news vans parked along the shoulder of the road, too, reporters getting man-on-the-street segments from canyon residents, police interviews, even a word with our mayor, whom I spotted squinting into the lights with an expression of shock and indignation on her face. Traffic was stopped all the way into town. Horns blared and radiators hissed and condensers dribbled and tape decks boomed and human limbs dangled from open windows and the heat gave no hint of abating as the sunset ended in a western sky so clear as to appear polished.

Grace said she felt sorry for Billy Ing. I said to spend her mercies where the exchange rate was a little better. And that was all we said, the rest of the way down to San Juan Capistrano.

Half an hour later, we were led into the Sandoval living room by Joe, who stood aside, revealing Isabella sitting in her wheelchair, looking up at me, smiling. Her overnight bag sat packed and ready beside the chair. Her cane stood next to that. She was wearing a new outfit, involving an oversized T-shirt studded with mock gemstones and glitter. Her wig had been brushed and styled, her face made up, and her lips reddened with a bold lipstick. She blushed deeply when she saw me, and said, "Hi, baby."

"*You*," I said, and knelt down and wrapped my arms around her.

"I'm coming h-h-home tonight!"

"You've been away too long."

Behind me, I could hear Grace and Corrine introducing themselves to each other. It felt strange that my daughter had never met my in-laws.

"What a beautiful blouse," Grace said.

There was an awkward silence, finally broken by Joe. "Tea, beer?"

"No," said Isabella. "No. We're . . . we're . . . we're gone!"

"She started getting ready three hours ago," said Corrine. "She was happy as a kid going to Disneyland."

Izzy shook her head and wheeled forward toward the door. "H-h-happier than Mom, that."

"She has a surprise for you tonight," said Joe, a little worriedly, I thought.

"Oh no," I said, a running joke from the days when Izzy would heap home-improvement projects on me almost as fast as I could dodge them. Surprises, she called them.

"Oh yes," said Isabella. "But h-h-home first." She hugged

235

Corrine and Joe long and dearly as a person saying good-bye forever. And with a chilling clarity, I saw in her face the fear that this was exactly what was happening. I looked away.

■   ■   ■

Home. She wheeled around the first floor, touching familiar objects, exclaiming in surprise, delight, satisfaction, wonder. She seemed bedazzled as one might have been at the Creation. She opened the refrigerator and itemized the contents.

"Who m-m-made the stew?"

"I did," said Grace. "Would you like some?"

"Maybe I-I-later."

Izzy rode the lift up to the bedroom. The contraption did its usual screech-and-groan, a rather startling sound that I suddenly realized I'd been missing these last few days. She continued her tour. She stared for a while at our wedding picture; ran her hands over the polished wood of her piano; touched the hanging crystal hummingbird so it swung slowly. I could hear Grace downstairs, talking quietly on the phone.

"So h-h-hot," said Izzy.

"Over a hundred today. Welcome home, love."

"I love this h-h-house. I'll never run away from home anymore."

She reached back into the pack she kept tied between the handles of her wheelchair and came out with a small wad of shiny black material, which she held out to me. I took it and let it unfurl. It was a swimsuit.

"My surprise is y-y-you are taking me swimming. Then, t-t-t-tomorrow, the alteration."

Her face held a world of hope, another of fear, both of which were echoed by the hard, deep beating in my chest.

She smiled, steadying her eyes at mine. "I think it will be

a good th-thing. B-b-but Russ, there's the ch-chance I could wake up being a s-s-spit-dribbling v-v-vegetarian. Even Dr. N-n-nesson said so, but in different worlds . . . *words*. So I want to go sw-sw-*swimming*."

"Swimming? Where?"

"Ocean, silly."

"Gosh, baby—kind of rough out there."

"I c-c-called surf report. No s-s-swell, seventy-three in the water. I'm s-s-swimming."

She looked at me then without speaking, but volumes of emotion came through to me from her face. I understood that Izzy was more terrified of the operation than she would let on, that if she awakened even more damaged tomorrow—or not at all—she would have had this final trip to her beloved ocean.

"Can Grace come?" I asked.

She smiled. "Suretainly."

"Here, let's put on your suit."

"No. I w-w-want Grace to."

Grace was standing at the top of the stairs. "*Never* let a man dress you if you can help it," she said. "Your husband would probably put your new suit on inside out."

We all laughed. I had, in fact, managed to do that once.

■   ■   ■

The water broke coolly around my legs as I carried Isabella through the shore break at Main Beach. But the night was still hot and by the time I leaned forward to set her in, the water felt warm and welcoming. Izzy groaned as I placed her down in the waist-deep sea, the same groan—I recalled—that was often evoked by our lovemaking. She jerked abruptly when her head neared the water, grabbing my arm hard. Her legs, almost powerless, sank, then rose to the surface. Grace steadied her from the other side. For a moment, all three of us waited to see what Izzy's body would do. With my left hand under her head and my right hand under her butt, I eased her toward deeper water. I felt her grip release on my arm. She drew one hand through the water, up past her head. Then the other. Then, with a gently affirmative "ahhh," she brought them down together to her sides and I felt her glide ahead, self-powered. "*Ohhh, yes!*"

We floated out past the waves, which were small and occasional, nothing more than brief levitating humps that lolled through us without adamance, rose minimally, wavered, then crumbled as if with old age into faint suds that spread and flattened on the shore. With my right hand under the small of Isabella's back and my left pulling us forward, I could kick in a wide, strong scissor that gave us a delayed and subtle surge. Grace floated on the other side, her head close enough to Izzy's that her spreading black hair seemed to be shared by both of them. We progressed, under stars, westward. Then Grace rolled away and slipped under the water with an astonishing beauty, no visible means of locomotion, not even her scarred feet, which simply followed her down unmoving, then vanished. She surfaced ahead of us, pale, subaqueous arms in motion; hair shining in the moonlight. I guided Izzy forward and let go of her with a slow push. I felt her arms quicken, deepening their pull. I sidestroked alongside her, close as I could get without interfering, synchronizing my stroke with hers, watching her upturned profile, her face of concentration, her eyes wide and starward, the parted lips through which she breathed, her white smooth head moving through the water like that of a creature designed for water, her arms sure and unhurried and capable, the dead lower half of her only a faint suggestion within the dark ocean through which it trailed like some devolving superfluity that would diminish and disappear in a short few million years.

"This is what I want it to be l-l-like."

"What to be like?"

"The dying."

"You're not going to die."

"You know I am, Russ."

"We all are."

"But I'll die sooner than you. And I w-w-want it to b-b-be like this. N-n-not an end, b-b-but a . . . change."

"A beginning."

"Yes. And I think it w-w-would best be done w-w-ith the eyes closed. Th-then you could see where you're going. L-l-like this."

She shut her eyes and continued on, arms opening, arms closing. Grace appeared in the mid-distance, then was gone. Beyond Izzy's profile, the cars on Coast Highway crept along beneath streetlamps, and the bottom-lighted palms of Heisler Park drooped green-black against a sky of specifically rendered stars.

"Russell, c-c-close your eyes and come with me."

I did. The world became immediately louder. The water lapped at my ears with a new sharpness; the cars echoed from town with a kind of muted urgency; Izzy's breathing rose to a forceful rhythm.

"K-k-keep them closed, like me. Let's see h-h-how far out we can go. Kay-o?"

"Kay-o."

Blind, we continued. I turned onto my back so I might feel her, intermittently, with my fingertips. I stopped kicking and allowed my legs to sink partially, like hers. I listened to her breathe.

And then, strangely, I began to do something I had not done in a long time, something I once practiced with conviction. I had lost that conviction as Izzy lost her legs, as I sat in her

239

hospital room asking for it to stop—imploring, begging—to no effect whatsoever upon the continuation of Isabella's relentless and irreversible (the doctors refused to use that word) damage.

I prayed.

Dear Father in heaven, I am small, corrupt, hateful, mean-spirited and too much a coward to sin importantly. I am a fool. Hear my prayer. I know how you value humility, so I confess to all this to assure you I know my place in your order of things. I deserve nothing. I expect nothing. I will ask for nothing. But you are absent here, you ceded this earth to us, and there are some things you should know. We suffer. We cry. We toil. Sickness comes to us. Death moves among us with arrogance. We die, trembling, bound for unspecified destinations. Christ died for our sins once; we die for them again. His agony is over, but ours continues. Our anguish is real. Do you remember how it feels? I know that your design is huge, so I have stopped trying to understand it. In your larger hands, we leave the larger motions. My concern is this life you have given us. I am too stupid to believe it is only a prelude. I am too weak to be happy that there may be a reward at the end of it. I am too literal to believe that the heart of the matter lies elsewhere. This is the heart of this matter. Do not think less of me for holding dear the life you've given. I lied when I said I would ask for nothing. This is what I want: I want you to treat Isabella with respect. I want you to give me the love that I want so badly to have for Isabella in these coming days. Give it to me so I can give it to her. I ask to be your representative. Do not leave us without love. Respectfully submitted to you in this hour of need, Amen.

■   ■   ■

Two hours later, I got into bed and lay down beside my wife. We whispered and kissed and embraced and we made love.

Whatever motion she lacked, I tried to offer for her; whatever feeling she missed, I tried to feel. The cry that came to my throat hurt, and my ears rang and my eyes burned and my daughter, whom I had quite frankly forgotten was downstairs, banged out of her room and threw on a light. Of all things at that moment, I was only dimly aware, except for the quaking of my body and Isabella's voice.

"It's kay-o, Grace. Russ just s-s-sort of... *well*."

■　　　　　■　　　　　■

My father was waiting on the steps of the UCI Medical Center when we admitted Isabella just after sunrise the next day. He nodded at me rather curtly, which, in the minimalist language of his body, meant that everything was okay. Obviously, Amber was not with him. He smiled and wrapped his weathered dark arms around Isabella and held her for a long while in a strong and gentle embrace.

The morning was already hot as I pushed her wheelchair up the ramp toward the tower. We were expected; all was in order. A medical student from China conducted the preop interview. He explained the procedure to us—debulking by resection—introduced our anaesthesiologist, and informed us that one of the possible side effects of this procedure, among others, was death. We signed the consent forms. Paul Nesson appeared an hour later. He was grave and gentle as always, and I sensed in him the focus and intensity of a soldier preparing for combat. He seemed reassuring, in an invisible way. He shaved Isabella's head again, though there wasn't much hair to take off. Then the six of us—Grace, Joe, Corrine, Izzy, Dad, and I—squeezed into the prep room when Nesson left. Isabella was given Demerol. Her smock was tied in only two places at the back, and she shivered in the rampant air conditioning of the medical tower. A few minutes later, she was helped onto a hospital bed and we wheeled her up to the swinging double doors of the OR. She held my hand fiercely. I kissed her, then two orderlies took the bed and disappeared into a territory of chrome and tile and tubing and sheets. A group of green nurses converged on my wife as the doors swung shut.

■   ■   ■

The minutes could have been hours; the hours seconds. I drank coffee, bought all the morning papers, glanced at my front-page article, noted the garishly big headlines the *Journal* reserves for garishly big stories. TWO PEOPLE, 27 PETS DIE IN CANYON SLAUGHTER— Special to the *Journal* by Russell Monroe.

Theodore informed me that—as I suspected—Amber had never returned. But she had called the night before, late, to tell him she was all right and not to worry. I shook my head, hardly able to factor worries about Amber into the larger concerns of the moment. If she didn't have enough sense to stay with Theo, then she could suffer the consequences.

I was heading outside to smoke a cigarette and passed the main desk, where I overheard this snippet of conversation between a small, somewhat disheveled-looking woman and the security guard.

"I would like you to page a Mr. Russell Monroe for me. It is very important."

"Your name?"

"Tina Sharp, with Equitable."

Without breaking stride, I made it outside and sucked down the comforting smoke. I had another. I walked the hospital grounds for half an hour and then went into the cafeteria the back way.

I ate breakfast, locked myself in a bathroom stall and threw up, rinsed my face in cold water, then found an empty seat in the waiting room and leaned my head back against the wall. I felt like the most vital and precious part of me had been removed and that it might not ever be returned. I wondered how forty years of life could suddenly boil down to a lesson in triage. I closed my eyes, said a prayer, lost my train of thought, and fell asleep. In the dream—short and vivid as a memory— I approached a table tucked under a *palapa* at the edge of an orange grove, at which sat Isabella, who, when she lifted her face to me and moved her lips, made no sound at all.

■　　　　　■　　　　　■

Six hours later, Paul Nesson eased across the waiting room and approached. He looked calm, composed, and, strangely, shorter. He still had on his pale green scrubs, and each shoe was wrapped in a green plastic moccasin that bunched at the top like a shower cap. He smiled wanly at Joe and Corrine and Grace.

"She's doing fine. Everything went very well."

"How much of it did you get?"

"All I could. There are viable brain cells on the perimeter of the mass, so I worked with the core—the necrosed tissue."

"How much tumor is left?"

"It's hard to say. These astrocytomas grow in fingers, very small. They're like the roots of weeds. In a day or two, we can talk about some new modalities of treatment."

There was a pause in the conversation then, during which I noted in Paul Nesson's eyes the dullness of exhaustion.

Corrine wiped her nose with a tissue, then cleared her throat. "How long does she have?"

"It would only be a guess, so I'd rather not make it. It's an unpredictable neoplasm—we see them accelerate, then stabilize, then accelerate again."

"Do you ever see them go away?" asked Joe.

"No. Look, Isabella will be in Recovery for an hour, then I'd like to move her to ICU for the night. She'll be ready for a quick hello in a couple of hours. After that, maybe you all should get some rest, too."

"Thank you," I said.

"You're welcome," said Nesson, then he padded back through the double doors and out of sight.

■   ■   ■

Her head was wrapped in bulky white gauze that formed a turban. Both eyes were swollen; the left was already turning purple underneath. She was still on oxygen, fed to her by a plastic tube in her nose.

She became aware of me as I stood beside the bed. Her vitals issued across the monitor elevated in the corner. I put my cheek against hers and listened to her breathe.

"You're not going to believe this," she said. Her voice was slow and remote. "But...I'm going to get better. I dreamed it when I was under...that they were taking all the bad...things...away. I'm going to be...okay."

No stutter, no mistakes.

"I love you," I said.

"I'm so glad...you're here."

"Are you still my baby?"

"I'll be your baby as...long...as...you...want me."

"How about forever?"

"Forever...sounds just right."

244

■   ●   ■

I was surprised, even through my exhaustion, to see Karen Schultz walking across the hospital lobby's floor late that afternoon. Her heels clicked officiously on the tile, and she had picked me out of the intensely quiet crowd before I realized who she was.

She smiled briefly at the others, shook hands as I introduced them, then directed her tired eyes at me. "Russell, can we talk?"

I followed her outside. The temperature was ninety degrees, according to a mall sign across the street. I watched a tiny woman pushing a wheelchair containing a large man up the ramp, zigzagging up toward the medical tower.

"How is she?"

"Fine. They got most of the tumor."

"Oh, Russell, I'm so happy to hear that." At this point, she wiped a tear from her cheek and stared off toward the freeway. "I just never know what to do about . . . in situations like this."

"It's good of you to come. You could leave some flowers maybe, or a note."

"No. That isn't why I'm here." Karen hugged herself and walked to the far edge of the outer patio, where a dysfunctional wheelchair lift waited, neglected and unrepaired.

I waited and lighted a cigarette.

"Look," she said, returning to face me. In the harsh afternoon light, Karen Schultz looked a hundred years old. "I've been . . . life is . . . full of compromises sometimes. I'm a single girl who needs her job and likes her job, and if I've given Winters occasional shit about his decisions, well, that's what he pays me for. What I'm saying is, I don't act out of spite against anyone in our department—I like our department and I think we do a good job. But . . ."

Karen's voice vanished as she looked out toward the mall. "Couldn't they find an uglier place for a hospital?"

"I guess not."

Karen's eyes looked pained but inscrutable. "Look, you talked to Chet, right, about the . . . irregularities?"

"That's right."

"Do you appreciate what they mean, or have come to mean?"

"They mean Martin's building a case against me and my daughter for a crime we didn't commit."

"Yes. But you're a step behind, Russ. In practical terms, do you know what this means?"

I couldn't help but wonder whether Karen had seen Martin's videotape of me and Alice Fultz. What earthly good could it have done Parish to reveal it now? "I'm not sure how to handle Martin," I said.

"Russell, I'll tell you. Do you know a good criminal attorney?"

"Yes."

"Hire him."

This bad and somehow inevitable news seemed to come at me from some blind spot in my mind. "Do you think Parish is going to take his case to the DA?"

"Russell, he already has."

22

I sat with Isabella three hours that evening while she slept.

As I gazed at her swollen, sleeping face, at her once-lovely head now bound by gauze, at the clear plastic oxygen mask banded across her nose and mouth, I could only wonder at how far this woman had come, how compromised and tortured was the flesh of her body, how betrayed she had been by life.

I heard one of the nurses steal in behind me, but when I turned to see her, I found myself looking into the doleful dark eyes of Tina Sharp, from Equitable.

"May we speak?"

"Outside," I said.

We stood in the hallway. Tina Sharp wore an unpleasant perfume. She carried a briefcase. Her eyes were on the verge of bulging, and they looked watery and weak.

"I'm sorry to have to track you down like this," she said. "You answered neither my calls nor my letter."

"I couldn't face you."

"I understand. I only wanted to inform you that the resection just performed on your wife is not covered under the plan."

"Yes, it *is* covered under the plan."

"No. Mr. Monroe, as you know, we could not cover the radiation-implant operation because it is not one of our approved procedures. Nor, according to our contract, can we cover any expenses incurred *as a result of an elective, cosmetic, or non-plan-approved surgery.* Today's operation, unfortunately, was just that."

"So now I'm another eighty grand in the hole."

"I believe it will run closer to one hundred, Mr. Monroe. I didn't think you should bear that cost without knowing in advance that you would have to. If you had simply contacted me earlier, this would not have to come as the shock I know it is. I tried."

I looked at Tina Sharp. She could have been, and probably was, somebody's mother. And daughter.

"Well," I said. "There have been plenty of shocks lately. Thanks for coming down here."

She offered her hand, which I shook. It was cold and dry.

"I'm very sorry, Mr. Monroe. I know the facility will work with you on a repayment plan that will suit both parties."

"Thank you, Ms. Sharp. You've been a wonderful balm in an hour of need."

"I wish Equitable could have been there for you," she said. "I'm sorry we had to let you down."

She turned and walked down the hallway toward the elevators.

Back in Izzy's room, I sat and stared at the framed picture of her that she always brought for hospital stays—she considered it good luck. It stood on the bedside stand, leaning against flowers brought by Theodore. The picture is just a snapshot by an amateur, but the color is good and Izzy is caught just as she sees the camera—half surprise and half composure—regarding the photographer from beneath the black curls of her hair and the scalloped brim of a wide black hat. Her neck and shoulders are visible, bared by a strapless dress. Her smile is demure, confident, restrained. She shows no teeth, but her lips are beginning a happy rise and her eyes—to anyone who knows Isabella—are, I swear, reflections of a contentment so deep, it could come only from the center of her heart. For most people, it is a picture of a woman in her prime. But for me, it is the image of one life we did not get to finish; it is a reminder of one future that will not take place as we had imagined; it is an ambassador from dreams that have passed. Thus, it is a thing of great beauty and great pain. We were newlyweds ourselves then, and the friend who took that picture understood the core of Isabella's happiness, because on the back is written the simple caption:

Mrs. Monroe!!

At that moment, sitting beside Izzy in the hospital room, would I have liked to go back to the time that picture was taken? Oh, truly. But I couldn't stay, because although perfection is a nice place to visit, no one lives there for long. I would rather have the chance to live that moment through, forward up to now, with all the standard disappointments and struggles, all the commonplace raptures that lovers can expect, with all the simplicity of hope that picture holds. But I chose the woman, not the dream, and her path I will try to make my own. This is the promise I made, and that I intend to keep.

But while I looked at Izzy and her picture, a deep and specific rage began to form inside me, at Martin Parish—for what he had begun that night of July 3 and was attempting to finish *at the expense of Isabella.* Never had I been more needed.

Never again would Isabella need more love and care and understanding than in the days to come. And what could I do from behind the bars of Orange County Jail? How could I possibly raise bail with no money in the bank and the modest equity in our home? What about the medical bills?

I thought of calling an attorney—I know plenty of lawyers. But if I was to admit myself to the great maw of the criminal-justice system, when might I be free again? And if I was to submit to the machinery of the courts, wouldn't it be, on some level at least, a confession that I was willing to play this deadly game on Martin Parish's terms?

No. I called no attorney that night. Instead, I began to conceive a counteroffensive, one that would take as its keynote the very one that Martin believed was his alone: audacity. If I was to deal with Martin Parish, it would not be through the achingly slow gears of the bureaucracy.

The ICU nurses eased me out around eight. I rose from Isabella's bedside with a sense of purpose in my desperation, and not a little meanness in my heart.

Joe and Corrine were still sitting in the waiting area, but Grace and Theo were gone. Instead, Amber sat across from Isabella's parents. An uneasy detente prevailed over them, grouped together as a family might be, but only a simpleton would not have noted the rigid set of Corrine's back; the contrite, hand-folded isolation of Amber; and the intense attention brought by Joe to a magazine about cars.

"Where have you been?" I said, boring straight into Amber's gray eyes as if I could differentiate truth from fiction in them.

"Taking care of business."

"Grace and your dad left," said Joe.

A pause in the conversation implied Amber's invasion.

"I wanted you all to know I care about Isabella," said Amber. "I'll go now."

"No. You're coming with me."

They all looked to me.

I looked at Corrine, then Joe. "This is necessary."

"I don't understand," said Corrine.

"What are you going to do, Russ?"

"I'm going to try to keep myself out of jail."

■   ■   ■

I took Amber by the arm and guided her out. The night was compressed and heated, and the air felt dirty. Across the street from the Medical Center, the bright red sign for the World Hotel had gone haywire, now proclaiming, WORLD HOT.

"You seem to have a purpose," said Amber.

"Martin Parish was in your room the night Alice died. He beat her to death. We need to prove it."

"You're goddamned right we do, and you *saw* him."

"I saw him leaving. I need hard evidence now. He's trying to frame Grace and me. But he was there, and he has to have left *something*. Whatever it is, I need it."

"You sound desperate."

"How I sound doesn't matter."

She took my arm and stopped us. "Russ? She's okay. She's *okay*."

"Yes, she's perfect." The image of Izzy's swollen, blackened face sat right behind my eyes. She looked as if she'd been beaten half to death, maybe closer. Her pain was everywhere now, even in the air around me.

"You don't have to lie to me about her."

"She's perfect."

"Are *you* okay?"

"Get in."

I opened the door for her, then slammed it shut on her dress. It protruded from the steel like a caught animal. I cracked the door and she gathered it in, looking at me from the interior. Her expression was of fear and pity, two emotions I've never been eager to provoke from a woman. A wave of shame broke over me—my face went hot and for just a second everything blurred. What I wanted at that moment more than anything in the world was for no one on earth to know me.

I drove fast.

Once I was on the freeway, I called Chet Singer's home number and pleaded my case to him. I told him I needed his official presence at the scene of an as-yet-unofficial crime, in order to gather evidence against Martin Parish for the murder of Alice Fultz. He said no.

I told him an innocent girl was being framed, along with an innocent—in this regard, anyway—father. I told him that Parish was abusing his power with a skill and depravity that challenged the imagination. Chester said no.

I told him, as I flew through the traffic on Interstate 5, that I was helpless against Parish and his official standing, that only an honest and genuine member of the law-enforcement community could provide true resistance to Parish's outlandish—but effective—machinations.

"I can't and won't," said Chester.

Amber yanked the phone from my hand and pleaded an eloquent case to Chet. It might have been the best acting in the world, but I knew that Amber was as serious now as I had ever seen her, that her desire to see Alice's murder redressed was tied intimately with her own desire to believe that she, Amber Mae Wilson, was capable of loving someone other than herself.

Chet must have said no.

Amber literally slumped against the door, her eyes searching my own in obstinate disbelief.

"I'm sorry," said Chet Singer. "I'm very, very sorry."

Then he hung up.

During the silence that followed, I could feel the engine beneath me, the tires on the asphalt, the wind outside the glass, and the continuing speechless scrutiny of Amber Mae Wilson. The suburbs crept by on either side of the freeway, and I noted that most of the lights in most of the houses were on, discouragement to the Midnight Eye, and wondered how many fingers rested inches from how many triggers, how many new dead bolts had been set and reset and reset again, how many nightmares were ending in abrupt and sweat-drenched lurchings, how many fatigued eyes were fixed drowsily on paperback books or scanning the relief of acoustic ceilings in lamplight, how many children were sleeping in the beds of their parents while mother and/or father wondered dimly just what had gone wrong in a county that had once promised prosperity, security, a nominally bright future.

"Where have you been?" I asked.

"That is not your business."

"Then here's something that is. It's time to cut the shit, Amber. You sent two thugs to scare Grace back into your power. You're holding money over her. You ought to see what they did to her. She's scared to death of you."

"I had no idea," she answered quietly, "that Grace's capacity for delusion had reached such heights."

"Well, now you know."

"Could you please tell me who these thugs are?"

"Cute. You hired them, so tell me."

"I hired a licensed private investigator to inform me of my own daughter's whereabouts and . . . habits. I hired him to see if he could find the netsuke Grace took from me. I hired

253

him to tell her in no uncertain terms that she was on the verge of being written out of her trust—*because she refused even to acknowledge me as a person, let alone as her own mother!*"

Another long silence, then Amber said, quite flatly, "May I tell you a story about when I was young?"

"It's a little late for stories."

Amber's fist smacked into my shoulder, then my thigh, then landed squarely on my jaw. I kept both hands on the wheel. She hit me on the ear, then the jaw again, then brought both her hands into play, tattooing the side of my face with sharp blows. I finally steadied the wheel with my left, then backhanded her with my right, a swat that landed squarely on the side of her face and sent a fleshy report through the car. She hesitated, slugged me hard on the shoulder again, then backed against the door, crying quietly.

"I will not be held responsible for Alice," she said. "I will not."

"Fine."

"You must realize, Russell, that Grace is lying about almost everything."

"She is most definitely not lying about the burns on her feet."

"Burns?"

"Continue, Amber."

For the next twenty minutes, Amber built her case against our daughter: Grace had learned to lie while learning to talk; she had never answered to anyone but herself; she was self-serving, evasive, and capable of small malice; she had increasingly lived in a "dream world" since the age of four or five; she talked to "characters" who were not visible; she invented tragic histories for nonexistent friends; she spun tales of classmates and neighbors engaged in preposterous behavior that Amber, upon investigation, had rarely found to be true; she seemed to derive almost as much enjoyment from being caught at a lie as from getting away with one.

"She can change the truth faster than I can change expressions, Russ."

"I wonder where she learned to do that."

"Go ahead. Believe her. It's a game where she forces a choice. But I've been down this road enough times to know where the curves are."

"And you will not be held responsible."

"You've become cruel, Russell."

"I go with my strengths."

I sped down the interstate, the suburbs still sprawling in every direction as far as the eye could see. As far as the Midnight Eye could see, I thought. What a hell this place had become.

"I'm not trying to exonerate myself, Russell. I'm just trying to tell you there are explanations for what I did in . . . another life."

"What did you do *in the other life*?"

"For one thing, I ignored my own conscience."

"And Alice was a place for you to start."

Amber was silent for a long moment. "Yes. Yes, she was. You know, I was always so ashamed of her. One of the reasons I left home at sixteen was so I would never have the time to become like her. And now, Russ, when I say those words, I feel small and foolish and terribly selfish again."

Her daughter's mother, I thought, but did not say it. "What was so bad about her?"

"Nothing that I can see now, but then, when I was a little girl, well . . ."

"Well what?"

Amber breathed deeply. "I don't know how it happened, but since I was very small, my family frightened me. They seemed like . . . like . . . imposters, or beings from another planet.

Fultz. What a crude and backwoods name. Alice was two years older than I. Daddy was a roofer, always covered with asphalt that stuck in the cracks of his fingers and never went away. Mom took in cleaning. She had this dress I remember, a cotton/poly shift kind of thing with vertical stripes of green and pink, and a little pink tie at the top, and gathered short sleeves that pinched her arms tight. It was always clean. She wore it all the time, it seemed. I hated its ugliness, its shapelessness, the way it made her look aged and hopeless and unattractive. Alice wanted to be like Mom. She'd help with the washing and ironing. She'd wear the same kind of dress. They both liked wearing those fake leather sandals that have a band over the toes and a sole that wears out and slaps against your heel when you walk. So, *slap-slap-slap*, Alice and Mom going from the washer to the drying line, *slap-slap-slap*, Mom and Alice going back to the porch when the wash was hung. And the way Mom held the clothespins in her teeth, fanned out like wooden cigarettes, and Alice, of course, chomping her own collection, *slap-slap-slap*, back to the ironing boards. One time I remember sitting in the shade of the porch and watching them. They were side by side at the clothesline, moving the pins from their mouths to the clothes. Mom was heavy by then, and Alice still very thin, but I swear I could see my sister's posture becoming old even then, and she couldn't have been much more than twelve. I had a magazine on my lap, a *Cosmopolitan,* I believe, and on the open page before me was a picture of a woman and her daughter running across a street in Paris, the mom holding down her hat, the daughter swinging a tiny shiny purse, both of them smiling and the men in the café looking most appreciatively after them. And I knew I would be that woman—one of those women—someday. This may sound like a vanity beyond vanities, Russ, but when I held a good heavy magazine in my lap as a girl and I smelled the smooth paper and looked at the

attractive print and saw those advertisements, I simply knew—
I *understood* that was where I belonged. I was positive. No *slap-slap-slap*. I remember I cried then because I was so far away
from Paris. And Russ, I'm crying now when I think about what
a rotten brat I was, and when I think about Alice. How could
anyone do that to her? She was an innocent, Russ. I flew her
out to try to begin again, to become the sister I never was, and
got her killed."

"What were you going to do with her?"

"Love her! Treat her well. See if she or Mom and Dad or
anybody needed anything. Start over! Jesus, Russell, is that so
hard to understand?"

"How many of her boyfriends did you steal?"

"Shit on you, Russell."

"I imagine one was enough. One, Amber? One special
guy of Alice's?"

She slapped me again, quite hard. "*He* tried. I wouldn't.
It doesn't matter."

"Is that why you couldn't trust your own daughter when
she got older? Because your sister didn't trust you?"

She looked out the window for a long time. "There may
be some truth in that."

"How much truth?"

"None of your business how much. What you need to
know is that I'd become proud of her. She turned out pretty,
by the pictures she sent me, although she was poor and never
found a good job. And you know something? In the last few
months, I'd begun to feel proud of all of us. Proud of our poverty,
proud of the ugly dresses, proud of the fact that we were what
we were. And what I wanted more than anything was to hug
Alice and tell her what a fool I'd been, and that I was proud to
be a Florida Fultz. The last job she had was in a bowling alley,
cocktailing out by Orlando. I was feeling damned proud to have

a sister who was humble enough to cocktail at a goddamned bowling alley. I believed there was a lot I could learn from her. I wanted her . . . forgiveness."

By then, Amber was sobbing again. "And you know what made the change begin? Grace did. I looked back on our lives and I looked at all the fancy schools I dragged her in and out of, all the expensive tutors, all the elaborate meals in European capitals, all the attention we got, all the travel and excitement and money, money, money, all the paparazzi and covers and suntans and rubdowns and mud baths, and I couldn't remember one moment when we did anything like stand by a clothesline with pins in our mouths, just doing something together because it had to be done and making the best of it. I actually asked her, at one point, not to call me Mother. To call me only Amber. I lost Grace, Russell, more than you did. There was a point when she leveled those brown eyes of yours on me and I saw that she had distanced herself, that she feared me the same way I feared my own mother, and she was gone for me. The only thing I could think to do was hold on harder, keep her closer. Didn't work. Do you know that for the last six months she's never once returned a call? I do not exist for her. It breaks my heart."

It was my turn then for silence. Her words seemed so alien, her voice so, well, genuine. "Thanks for the updated Fultz family bio," I said. "The last I was told, Daddy was a banker and Mommy a beauty queen."

"It . . . it was easier to believe an appearance."

"So what appearance was it that let you keep me away from my own daughter when she was a girl?"

"Oh, Russell, no."

"If you're coming clean, include me."

She sighed significantly, perhaps a tad histrionically. "The idea of my daughter being brought up sheltered and conservative in boring old Orange County. Surrounded by dull, conventional, materialistic people. Inexperienced, untraveled, unsophisticated. God, I sound bad. But I wanted her to be a true princess in this world."

"Unpolluted by a common sheriff's deputy hauling down twenty-six grand a year."

"Yes."

"But you married Martin Parish, who later in life thought highly enough of you to try to kill you."

"Marty was interim. A way to get you out of my life."

"Christ."

"I know."

I thought for a moment. "Well, thanks for saying so. I suspected it was that, but it clarifies the stupidity of the whole notion to hear you admit it."

"Pound away, Russell. This is your big moment."

"How come nothing real is ever good enough for you?"

"I've always considered it a fault of mine."

"You can make up only so much before your head hits the brick wall of what is."

"I know that now. And Russell, for what it's worth, my head hurts awful bad."

"You still haven't answered my first question. Where were you yesterday, last night, and today?"

Amber shook her head. "God, Russell. I met with my attorney to rewrite my will. Does that meet with your approval?"

"It didn't take a day and a half."

She lighted a cigarette and blew the smoke out the window. "I had a rather long meeting with State Attorney General Allen Boster. In Sacramento. I spent the night."

I felt my heart flutter and become light as I considered the possibilities of the *People* v. *Martin Parish*. "And?"

"There's a chance he'll open an investigation of Martin."

"What did you tell him?"

"Just about everything. He'll take my deposition soon. You will be called later."

"We'll still need the evidence."

"Then let's go get it, Russ."

I looked at her, unable to decide whether this new direction would lead to exoneration for myself or to even more pressure from Martin.

I could only assume she had written Martin Parish out of his five hundred grand. Perhaps she had written me out, too. I could blame her for neither. And she had gone to the top to get what she wanted. Very smart. Very Amber.

◾   ◾   ◾

In Amber's house, the heat was stale and suffocating, but the sense of dread raised in me was even worse. How clearly I remembered that night of July 3, my anticipation of a secret life, my innocence, my stupidity, my desire; how clearly I remembered the smell of human flesh so strong, the sight of Alice, the painted walls, the resounding echo of insanity.

Amber's room. I worked the carpet on my hands and knees, with a flashlight and a comb. It was unreasonably clean. I rolled the bed away to get under it, but it wasn't likely that a piece of Martin Parish would be under the bed, and there wasn't. I inspected the fresh coat of paint, under which the spray-painted red of AWAKEN OR DIE IN IGNORACE was still scarcely visible. I checked the trash cans in the side yard for some clue to this artist—a can of paint, a brush, a mixing stick, a spattered shirt or drop cloth—and discovered not one useful thing at all. I tried the garage and found more of nothing useful. He'd probably loaded it all into his car by the time I saw him that night—yes, he was wiping his final fingerprints from the gate knob!—then stopped behind a store on his way home to use the dumpster. Could I match a dried drop of paint from the lining of Parish's trunk to the paint on Amber's wall? I couldn't match shit to shinola, I reminded myself, but someone like Chet Singer could. But Chet Singer wouldn't. I thought of driving Parish's route home and trying the dumpsters, but they'd have been emptied by now. I began to feel just a little bit sick. I desired a large quantity of alcohol, and I was hungry. My face was sore. Amber hovered, wordless.

When the doorbell rang in the cavernous entryway, I could feel the length of its diminishing echo all the way down my back. We were standing in the master bedroom. I looked at my watch. It was 9:45 P.M. Amber searched my face with a worry that looked close to panic. I pointed to her purse, which she had hung over a bedpost. She retrieved a little .32 and handed it to me, and I nodded her downstairs, toward the door.

The doorbell rang again as we walked across the marble floor. Amber peered through the peephole, then looked at me with a quizzical expression. I looked myself. Narrowed to the point of caricature, seemingly yards away, stood the plump and forlorn figure of Chester Fairfax Singer. He was toting an ancient misshapen leather suitcase.

23

"How badly have you contaminated this scene?" he asked.

I stood back and let him in. "Nice to see you, too, Chet. Chester Singer—Amber Mae Wilson."

He regarded her momentarily. "You're somewhat larger than on the hair-conditioner bottle," he said without a trace of humor. "And lovelier, too."

Wearing fresh latex gloves, we used clean paper towels to check the drains for blood, and found none. Surely Parish had washed up here, but surely he was careful enough to run the water long and wipe the grills himself. The hand and bath towels looked fresh, but Chet took them down, laid them on the tile counter, and worked them over with a magnifier. They revealed nothing. I felt stupid.

"What about fingerprints?" Amber asked.

"He wiped the gate knob on his way out, so he probably wiped everything else, too."

"We'll spray and dust to our hearts' content," said Chet.

"Even a homicide captain can leave a mistake behind. In fact, I am reminded of Martin's earlier days as a detective—he was always just a little bit impatient and contemptuous of the crime-scene specialists. He was not a man who worshiped detail. I would not be surprised at all if Mr. Parish managed to leave us something . . . telling."

"What about the weapon?" Amber asked.

"He likely removed it when he removed the body," Chester said patiently.

"How did he get her into his car without the neighbors seeing?"

"I can attest to your privacy here, Ms. Wilson. Your nearest neighbors are two hundred yards away. It was dark. It was late. How big is this lot, by the way?"

"Three point five acres."

"Have you searched it, Russell?"

"No."

"Well, we may have to."

"What about tire prints in the driveway?" Amber asked.

"You used it when you came home on the fifth," I said. "Your manager used it when he came here, looking for you."

Chester glumly shook his big head. "Russell, review for me the night you found Martin here, in his . . . informal wear."

I told him everything I could remember about that bizarre encounter on July the Fourth.

"Why do you assume he was intending to enter Ms. Wilson's bed?"

"He told me he'd done it before. And the bed was still made."

"But maybe he was finished and had already made it back up."

"That's true."

I considered Amber's bed, the prolific pink pillows, the

scented silk and satin. Chet worked over the pillows and discovered two short gray-brown hairs worked into a sham, hairs almost certainly not belonging to Amber or Alice. He put them in evidence bags, carefully labeling each. A little ripple of hope wavered up through me. We got another one from the top sheet, up near the pillows. Down about halfway, Chet found a short curly hair that could have come from about any crotch in the world. Chester bagged and labeled it. We looked for semen on the sheets—few acts have made me feel lower on the evolutionary scale—and found none.

Amber watched us in minor horror. "He wouldn't really have done *that*, would he?"

"You tell us, Amber," I said. "You were married to him."

"Jesus, I'm really not so sure. But you know something? I lived with him for over a year, and he's the most fastidious anal-retentive I've ever known. He'd brush out the toilet with disinfectant after he peed."

Chet ran a clean tissue under the toilet bowl's lip, for exactly what purpose, I wasn't sure. Clean. I remembered the shaving cut on Martin's Adam's apple the afternoon of the fourth and examined the razors—plastic, disposable—in the bathroom drawer. Dumb, I thought: What would possess anyone to stop in the middle of a murder and cover-up, then shave?

"Do you have anything to drink?" I asked.

"Gin."

"Light, ice."

"Make mine a little more substantial," said Chester.

We wandered the house. The carpet near the entrance was spotless, as it was inside the sliding screen door on which the mesh had been cut open as a nod to the Midnight Eye. We studied the stereo setup, in which Parish—after piecing together phrases from the tapes left at the Fernandez and Ellison homes—had left his dub. He would certainly have left no prints to go along with it. I saw an image of him, grim with purpose, using some rinky-dink boom box in his office before the murder, recording bits of monologue from tapes he had surely copied days ago, before they were booked into evidence. Amber delivered the drink to me with a guarded stare.

In the study, I noted the lamp and magazines I'd knocked over. In the kitchen, we prowled around under the sink, in the broom closet, the trash compactor, the cabinets.

I began to feel tricked, anticipated, suckered. Marty had already done all this, I thought—cleaned up evidence of himself and replaced it with evidence of Grace. Probably ran the fucking vacuum cleaner, I thought, and it actually sounded like something that anally retentive Martin would do.

"Where's your vacuum?"

"Corner of the den. Behind the room divider."

Chester smiled mildly. "Sometimes the obvious is best."

He pulled it out from beside an ironing board, popped off the back panel, and felt the bag.

"Empty," he said.

"Then he didn't use it," said Amber.

"Please get me some clean paper towels."

Chet worked off the roller and flicked the brush over a clean chain of towels. I used my pen to fan the bristles. What speckled down onto the white paper looked an awful lot like dried blood.

"Is that what I think it is?" Amber asked.

"Yes," said Chester. "The bag is empty because he used the machine, then put in a new bag. We are closer."

"And took the old bag with him?"

"Probably. It would depend on how calm he was able to remain, on whether the bag might mean an extra trip back into the house for him. Show me where your trash cans are."

Of course I had already been through the trash, in search

of a painter's mess. But this time through, we removed each item individually, bringing to our labor an attention that an on-looker would have found comical. The task was made more difficult by the fact that most of Amber Mae's trash had been run through the compactor. Not only that, but the garbage was over a week old because Amber had failed, with her disappearance, to have it taken out to curbside. The smell was not good.

The bag was, of course, nowhere to be found.

"Well," said Chester. "Another roadblock."

We all looked at one another rather gloomily.

"It wouldn't hurt to check the filter," Chet said finally.

We used a clean white towel that Chester carried, neatly folded, in his case. We spread it in the middle of the living room floor. Chet unscrewed the vacuum cleaner's lid and worked out the filter, which is engineered to keep large debris from the motor compartment. He cradled out the screen and laid it down on the towel carefully, as if it were an infant. What we had before us was a dusty mulch that covered almost a square foot of terry cotton, a bounty of dirt, dust, hair, fiber, more dust, a broken rubber band, a paper clip, a penny, more dust, a length of string, a wad of green dental floss that had somehow missed the brush, a warped postage stamp, and a great deal more dust.

"What a job," Amber noted.

Chester removed a bundle of evidence bags from his case and we began. "Ms. Wilson, we could use two standard table-spoons, rinsed and wiped."

First, we separated and bagged anything that might be useful. Several hairs could have been Martin's. Nothing else seemed indicative, even suggestive. The idea crossed my mind that I was a fool. We bagged the broken rubber band, which seemed to confirm this. Amber sighed. Using a spoon, I made little S patterns through the silt, disgusted.

"One of the hairs may help," I said, fully aware that you can't establish 100 percent identification of a human being with hair samples—not in court, anyway.

"What's that?" asked Amber.

"I said, one—"

"No. What's *that*?"

Amber's hand hovered over the towel, forefinger extended. I followed the aim of that finger, thinking—yes, even at this hour, even after this day, even after everything my dear Isabella had suffered at least in part for me—that if the entire promise of the female form could be contained in one finger, here it was, a perfect digit, graceful, firm, strong, lovely in composition and utility, the skin slightly tanned, the flesh full within its slender contours, the nail bold and bright and domed imperiously, red as blood, pointing now at something in the dust.

"There," she said.

"I can't see it from here."

"Then give me the spoon, Russ."

She reached with it and dipped the outer lip as if for soup. She jiggled the utensil, worked it down through the gray matter. She lifted it, tilting off a wad of nonspecific material that floated slowly back down to the towel. She presented the spoon to me, handle first. I took it and spilled the contents onto a clean paper tissue.

What I saw at first, I still couldn't identify—it was a U-shaped concave shell the size, roughly, of a fingernail. One end was jagged and looked as if it had been torn away from something else. The other end was smoothly rounded. It was covered with dust, but under the dust I could see pink.

"Turn it over, Russell," said Chet.

I flipped it with my pen. It *was* a fingernail—pink, tapered, chipped noticeably at the round end. I looked at Amber, who looked back at me.

She shook her head. "Not one of my colors."

"Alice's?"

"How would I know? I don't suppose when you—"

"No."

Chester keyed in on this truncated exchange, his patient eyes searching first my face, then Amber's.

I returned his stare with what innocence I could fake, while trying in my mind to recreate that night, and I could see Alice's rigid outstretched arms inviting me into the freezer, could feel her icy-slick weight on my back as I bore her up the mountain, but I could not for my life see her fingernails.

I touched it with my pen. "Fake?"

"Yes," said Amber "It was torn off. Maybe in a struggle. There's probably some real nail on it. Does that help?"

"Definitely. Get Alice's makeup stuff and bring it in here."

Amber returned a moment later with her sister's overnight case. She dug through and found two bottles of nail polish in a shiny black plastic kit. One was red, the other an opalescent white.

"Amber, what does this suggest...in the cosmetic scheme of things?"

"Proves it's not her nail."

"Absolutely not?"

"Russ, nails aren't absolute. But you don't do them pink, then leave town for two weeks with red and white."

"Oh my, I can almost hear this in court," noted Chet.

"She might have forgotten it," I said.

"Might have."

"Or carried the pink in a handier place, like her purse."

"I already looked," said Amber. "She didn't."

Naturally, I had thought about another possibility. Amber looked at me, her eyes steady but rife with the same dire inklings that must have been visible in my own.

"Grace's color?"

"Women don't *have* just one color, Russ. Remember our bathroom?"

I did, a veritable makeup department, an entire warehouse of paints and polishes, shadows and liners in every hue and shade; solvents, removers, applicators, brushes, tissues, swabs, lighted mirrors, hand-held mirrors, magnifying mirrors, wall mirrors. (It was our favorite place in the world to make standing, carnal, untender, image-drunk love.)

I said that I had not forgotten our bathroom.

"Well," she said, "then you know."

"Bag the nail," said Chester. "Perhaps, at some point, it will match nine others that we find in Mr. Parish's possession. They are probably among his 'evidence' right now at County."

I bagged it and continued on through the dusty rubble in front of me. A few minutes later, we were done. We placed the filter and contents in one large evidence bag. Chet arranged the bag in his case with the others after labeling each.

"You didn't get what you wanted, did you?" asked Amber.

"Maybe. Hairs. I don't know. A lot of it depends on the good graces of Mr. Singer."

"Mr. Singer cannot analyze what he does not possess."

"Did Alice wear a watch, or eyeglasses?" I asked Amber. I had not forgotten the tiny screw I had removed from the nap of the carpet here just a few nights ago. It was still inside the cap of my pen, with my own spares.

"I hadn't seen her in twelve years, Russell. What now?"

"Grace's."

Amber studied me. "To find what?"

"If Parish has been there, doing the same thing he did here, we need something to prove it. If there's a 'police investigation' tape up, it's too late."

There was no tape, and Amber had a key supplied to her by the private detective she had hired to find Grace.

It was the first time I had been inside my daughter's home. I stood in the short entryway, holding the batch of mail I'd gotten from her slot in the lobby, wondering again how I had managed to miss her life. The condo was not only expensive to start with but the furnishings and accents were expensive, too—all financed by Amber, as she reminded me. The carpet was a thick cream Berber, the sofas and chairs heavy rattan with white cotton cushions, and two of the three living room walls were hung with original oils by Laguna artists whose styles I recognized. The east wall was mirrored to extend the depth of the room; the west was all glass, including a sliding door that opened to a long but narrow balcony overlooking the yacht basin and restaurants. The kitchen was done in Euro style, which means everything is the same shape and color (black) and you can't tell the oven from the dishwasher. The bedroom had a big four-poster and was done in pinks. The whole place was organized, clean, neat.

"I guess she got my housekeeping style instead of yours," I said.

"What she got was a maid I pay for."

"How come you keep reminding me who pays the bills?"

"I think you should know."

"If I remember correctly, my child-support checks came back."

Amber looked away from me, visibly perturbed. She glanced at Chester, whose presence had started to resemble that of some acute and silent conscience.

"Say what you need to say," he said. "You don't have much that will surprise these old and increasingly hairy ears."

"I *provided* everything I could, Russ. I still do. That's what I mean. And that's why this whole thing she's fantasized hurts me so deeply. I don't expect a medal, but it would be nice if my only child tried thanking me instead of recreating her life with me as some kind of hell."

"Amber," I said, "not everything is about you."

I considered Amber's misty eyes, her quivering chin. I was right, I thought—not everything was about Amber. Nor about myself. This was about Grace, and how we might keep her from Parish's tightening net.

Chester broke the silence. "Ms. Wilson, begin in the bathroom and research what you can on your daughter's nails. Russell and I will try to find some sign of Mr. Parish. Since you are more familiar with her home than we are, anything you notice that wasn't here before, anything that seems out of place, might be of help to us. Remember, Martin Parish's goal is to demonstrate that Grace was in your home the night of July the third. *Our* goal is to demonstrate that he was here."

Chester began in the cupboards of the kitchen, no doubt wondering whether Parish had had the audacity to plant something incriminating there—the club, perhaps.

I went into the bedroom. Grace's nightstand held a leather-bound Bible with her name embossed in gold on the cover. Midway through Leviticus was a color postcard of the Champs Elysées, with the words, "Our city welcomes Grace with an open heart." It was signed "Florent." It had not been mailed. Hand-delivered to her hotel, I figured, by Florent himself or perhaps a friend, just in time for Grace to take it back with her to Orange County.

Under the Bible was a notebook that was mostly empty.

Grace had made a few journal entries—May 2,4,10,21—then stopped. I read them, learned nothing except that her job was boring and she wanted to travel again.

There were two photograph albums at the bottom of the stand drawer. I took them out and looked through: London, Paris, Cannes, Rome, Florence, Rio, Mexico City, Puerta Vallarta, Hong Kong, Tokyo. Most of the shots were faces that appeared once, then never returned. Only a few were actually of Grace. A girl's record of travel, I thought—the sights, the strangers, the obvious. Not one picture was of Amber. Strange.

I closed the drawer and pressed the message button on the answering machine that sat atop the stand. I wrote down in my notebook the names, messages, and numbers. Three calls from Brent Sides. Two from work. Eight from people I didn't know. Three from me, four hang-ups. One from Reuben Saltz, asking after Amber.

I lifted the cordless phone and pushed REDIAL. A recorded voice told me that I had reached the home of Brent Sides. The last call Grace made from home, I thought. I wondered.

For a long moment, I stood there and studied the stuffed animals that crowded Grace's bed and bed stand, covered her two chests of drawers, rested on her windowsills and book-shelves, even the floor. There must have been a hundred of them. The idea struck me that I was more interested in getting to know my daughter—at this late date—than I was in finding some trace of Martin Parish's presence in her house. I tried to concentrate: *What could Parish have left behind? What did he transfer from this home to Amber's in order to find it as 'evidence' later?*

I dug into Grace's jewelry chest, wondering whether Parish could have had the cunning to remove the tiny screw and leave it at Amber's. If he had, I could not match the screw to any piece of jewelry or to any of the several watches in the chest. Everything seemed . . . natural.

Chester continued his more objective path: He checked the closets for incriminating clothing that Parish might have put there; I heard him throwing open all the kitchen cupboards and drawers, doing likewise in the laundry room.

I opened the window, sat in a chair, and lighted a cigarette. The clock said 11:35. I watched the smoke slide through the window screen, felt the nicotine surround my brain, and realized how exhausted I was. The sounds of Amber's bathroom search issued down the hallway from the bath. Chester had joined her, and I could hear their voices, muffled, through the walls. God knows what she was telling him. I heard them leave the place and assumed they were headed down to the dumpster. What a pleasant business. I looked across the street to the dark water of the harbor. A rage continued to build inside me, directed at Martin. Had Martin done what he did so that I didn't have to? Had he been chosen for darkness, just as Izzy was chosen for disease and Ing for madness? Did it matter?

I was in no mood for understanding or forgiveness. No, I was much more in the mood to line up all the Parishes and Ings and tumors and evils in the world and bash out their lives with my ax handle. I would bash until I could bash no more. I would loose an ocean of blood upon which I would tread—my head held high. My wife would rise and walk to me and we would embrace. We would begin our family. My daughter would smile, thrive. We would have a son. My first-person account of the Midnight Eye would be a best-seller, receive awards, become a major film. My stilt house would become a museum after I died. Izzy would live to be 103, remember me fondly in a blockbuster of her own, marry a rickety old man who wore bow ties and adored her.

"Are you going to be sick?"

The voice was Amber's.

"Oh." I focused my eyes, which revealed my ankles and

shoes, crossed before me on the carpet. My cigarette had burned out and dropped its ash. "No. I'm fine. Resting."

She was standing directly beneath a recessed ceiling bulb, the light from which lent her a specific radiance. "Look what we found downstairs."

24

Amber regarded me with an odd look of pity but also with an exaggerated expression of pain, behind which I sensed some kind of victory. She stopped in the doorway of the bedroom. For a moment, tired as I was—or maybe because of it—all I could do was behold her form before me, the shape of her in space, the hang of her dress, the slight tautness of the material at her stomach and chest, the straightness of shoulder, the droop of hair.

"Let's have it," I said.

"It's from the dumpster outside. We found a wastebasket liner like the one in the bathroom—tied up and stuffed down around other people's things. I pulled out about five handfuls of pink-stained tissue, and these were there."

Chet came forward and gave me the small white bag.

A little covey of fingernails scratched down into the corner, and when I tilted it back the other way, they slid to another. Some wobbled on convex backs. They were uniform, off-white,

275

nearly opaque. Fakes. Remnants of pink polish remained on a few of their edges, just shadings really, as if the paint had been removed with solvent. I counted them once, moved them around, counted them again, moved them some more, and counted them a third time.

"Nine," I said.

"Nine," echoed Chester. "There're a few others things in there you should see."

They led me to the bathroom. The door to the cabinet under the sink stood open. Amber knelt down and pointed to a package of new, blank acrylic fingernails.

A terrible weight settled on me. My heart was wooden, mechanical, huge. My legs felt shaky and my ears were ringing. "What about polish?" I asked, hardly recognizing my own voice.

"They're all in that basket on the counter," said Amber. "Take your pick."

I took up the basket and looked in. I shuffled the bottles around. There were six shades of pink. I removed the Baggies from my pocket, spilled the vacuum-cleaner nail onto the cobalt blue tile of Grace's counter, flipped it upright. A color called Rosebud looked close. I painted my left middle fingernail with it, blew it dry. If there was a difference between the pink on the fake and the pink on my finger, I couldn't see it. Neither could Amber, an expert on such matters, whose face had gone pale, almost cadaverous in the harsh bathroom light. Chet nodded along gloomily.

"Martin planted the one at Amber's," I said but the feebleness of my conviction clearly wavered in my voice.

"No," said Chester. "If so, he'd have kept these nine, not thrown them out."

"Then he planted all ten," I protested.

"Not logical, Russell. He needs either the one from the vacuum or else these, in his possession. If he did place the nail

276

at Amber's, he certainly would have absconded with these by now. It supports his case against Grace. The tenth nail establishes the match."

"My daughter was in my house," said Amber.

My own voice sounded to me as if it were traveling across continents. "There will be an explanation. This isn't what it looks like."

We spent the next hour searching Grace's apartment for more proof that she had been in her mother's room on the night of July the third. She had done an exemplary job of either hiding it, or taking it somewhere else.

"We've got one more stop to make," I said.

■   ■   ■

We let Amber do the knocking on the door of Brent Sides's apartment, identify herself, and ask to come in. Chet and I stood against the wall so he couldn't see us through the peephole. His lumpy briefcase sat at our feet.

When we followed Amber in, Sides's sleep-heavy eyes went wide. All he had on was a pair of boxer shorts. His hair was a mess. He had a carving knife in his hand.

"Mr. Monroe." He blushed and set the knife on the counter. "Sorry. I was just dreaming about the Midnight Eye getting in here."

"Just us, tonight."

"Mr. Sides. This is Mr. Singer, Orange County Sheriff's Department. We need to talk."

He gaped momentarily at Chester's badge, then at Amber, recognizing her face—as would nearly any man in the country—without being able to place it. He blinked.

"Wanna sit?"

"No. I want you to tell me which part was the lie."

"Which part of what?"

"Of what you told me about you and Grace. You told me a lot, Brent, but there was one thing you made up. You made it up because she asked you to, and because you love her."

"No, man. Everything I said was true."

I stared at him, not wanting to hurt him, although certainly I was willing.

"There's been a murder, Brent. Grace is in terrible trouble. You don't understand that trouble, but you love my daughter. So do I. You have ten seconds to tell me what your lie was. If you don't, I'll make you wish you had, then you will, anyway."

He looked to Amber, the softness of appeal in his eyes.

"You really should talk with Mr. Monroe," said Chet. "Unless you would feel more comfortable in an interrogation booth at County."

"Please, Brent," she said.

Sides glanced at me again, then sat in a director's chair in front of the TV. His back was to us. I could hardly hear his voice when he finally spoke.

"We weren't together on July the third," he said. "I worked and came home. I don't know where Grace was. I was afraid to ask."

"Why was that?" I demanded.

"Oh . . . you know."

"I don't know. Why were you afraid to ask where she'd been?"

"Because of the way she . . . looked."

Clarity came to me at that moment. Of course. It would account for everything we hadn't found in the last hour of searching Grace's home. It would account for her showing up at Brent's house late that night, after her deed was done.

"You weren't with her that night, but you saw her. Right?"

He nodded.

"How did she look, Brent?" Amber asked him gently.

"Uh . . . real scary, like. And she smelled."

"Like what?"

"Like she was terrified, like, or had just been close to something real bad."

Brent turned then to face us, adjusting the director's chair in our direction in disconsolate little jerks. He looked at each of us in turn, then down at the carpet. "I tried to help. I'm not a complete idiot, though. You all should know that I'd do anything for her. Almost anything. I don't know where she was. But I know she was scared."

Chester looked up at me with the same ambivalent expression that always came to him when he'd nailed someone. A moth spiraled out of the patio light and landed on the screen.

Sides excused himself to the bathroom.

I stepped outside and smoked. I was watching the smoke rise and vanish into the air. I was thinking back to a time some years ago, just after Isabella and I were married, when we talked about selling the house and moving out of the county for good. We'd talked about other places: northern California, Hawaii, Mexico, Texas. What had made us decide not to go? We told ourselves, finally, that family was most important—Joe and Corrine, my mother and father, even, in some indefinite way, the promise of proximity to Grace. We told ourselves that we had everything we wanted right here: a house and a little land, clean air coming off the ocean, and no need to get out in the hellish rat race that commenced each morning on the roads that ran just a few miles from our private, isolated stilt house of an Eden. We had told ourselves that we could take on the world from our perch, defend our citadel and live our lives with whatever happiness and purpose we could bring to bear. We braced ourselves for success. But what had made us wonder in the first place? What had made us doubt? We did not confess it then, but I am certain Isabella suspected—deep in her heart, as did I—that this life of ours was not to continue, that some dark actuality, far off in the future as it may have been, had already brushed us with the shadow of its terrible outstretched wings. Perhaps this was the moment when the first cell metastasized in Isabella's lovely and loving mind. We will never know. But I do know that all I could think of that night, leaning against the rough wall of Brent Sides's apartment, was that we'd somehow made the wrong move, that we'd have been so much better off somewhere else—somewhere without cancer and Midnight Eyes and Martin Parishes and daughters so battered by bad fortune that the very cores of their futures were uncertain as the smoke from my cigarette, which continued to rise into the darkness.

Chet joined me on the patio.

"Texas," I mumbled to myself.

Chester Fairfax Singer, an unhappy spirit whose last effort for the side of innocence had revealed nothing more, probably, than just another exercise in the brutal, the stupid, the desperate, the eternal, studied me from behind his thick glasses.

"They say San Antonio is very nice," he offered. "May I ask you, where is your daughter at this moment?"

"My house. With Dad. Give me a day with her, Chet."

"Yes. One day."

■   ■   ■

Amber and I drove back to Laguna without saying a word to each other. But I was aware of her, acutely so: I could locate the precise plane—just beyond my right shoulder—where the perimeters of our heartaches met. We shared a common border. It buzzed like a power line.

Amber said the first words of our trip just as I was about to turn off Laguna Canyon Road onto my street.

"No, Russ. Keep going. Drive fast."

"Why?"

"Because I asked you to."

I eased back into the fast lane of the deserted road and pressed down the accelerator. The power of the V-8 seemed to start behind, then pick us up and take us with it. We were guests of velocity. We rode it through the curves, eucalyptuses rushing past the windshield like fence pickets. We gorged ourselves on distance. Amber rested her head on my shoulder and wrapped both her hands around my arm. And what a surge of re-membrance shot through me: We had been here before, a hundred times, a thousand years ago. I had forgotten how much Amber loved this motion, how she melted into it, how it calmed her. We used to drive too fast together, just for fun. The speed relaxed her, released her. I could smell the sweet dank odor of her hair and the light perfume of her breath when she sighed. You may not forgive, but you will understand that my craving for Amber came rising with all the power of an incoming tide.

The city appeared, was gone. We hit Coast Highway at eighty, raced through four green lights and a final red before settling into the open four-mile stretch to the next town. The Pacific glittered to our left. The moon presided. A trailer park vanished behind us, quickly as a road sign. The center divider on the highway blurred. To our right, the hills moved by with steady precision.

"I have a confession to make," whispered Amber.

"Make it."

"First, can I tell you how I feel right now? I feel dead. I believe that Grace was in my house to kill me. I feel like she accomplished what she wanted. I feel tainted and stupid and black. I feel like I've wasted everything that's been set on my table. Every single thing that could have turned out good."

"I'm sorry. I do, too."

"What do you think it was, specifically, that we did wrong?"

"Everything. But I think we did the best we could, with the tools we had."

"Is there any consolation in there?"

"Not much that I can see."

"Is there consolation in anything else?"

"In tomorrow, maybe. At least we can tell ourselves that."

"God, Russ, tomorrow's here."

"There is that problem."

"Won't this thing go any faster?"

"Oh yes."

The digital speedometer pegged at ninety-nine, but the car sped crazily on. Horn blasts followed our passage, fading quickly. For a moment it seemed possible, and somehow imperative, that we overtake the pools of our high beams shooting steadily before us. Hope impossible is the purest hope.

"I confess that I dream of you often," she said. "It's not always your body or shape, but I know it's you. The first time I saw your car parked outside my house, you know what I did? I parked outside yours the next night, down the hill, where you wouldn't see me. I felt like a teenager. Did you?"

"Yes."

"Do I surprise you?"

"You don't sound like the Amber I used to know."

Her head was still on my shoulder and her hair blew against my face.

"Twenty years is a long time, Russ. I am changing. The reason I asked Alice to come out was to try to know my family, to offer some love in that direction. I tried to explain that to you.

I'm not going to stop until whoever killed her is in jail and paying for what they did—even if it's my own daughter."

"That's a tough way to turn a life around. Maybe you should start with something on a little smaller scale." I heard the sarcasm in my voice and wished it wasn't there.

"I've been studying my Bible, giving lots of money to charity. I'm trying to feel the pain of others, not to judge them. I'm thirty-nine years old, Russ. That's old enough to know when something's missing."

"I understand what you mean."

"I made a list of every regret I could think of, and what I could do about them. Until tonight, I thought there would be a way to find my daughter again. I guess that's one regret that won't ever be fixed, by me at least. I'll try, though, I'll try to reach her."

"There may be time," I said, and the thought came to me that Grace might be spending a lot of that—time—in lockup.

"I did not have her tortured, Russ. I don't know who could have put that in her mind. But I want you to believe me. I'll confess to anything and everything under the sun. I was a terrible mother. But I never hurt her on purpose. Never that."

I shot into the right lane, braked as we approached the first signal in Corona del Mar, fishtailed into a right turn through the green, brought the back end into line, then cranked a hard U-turn to my left. We idled at the signal.

"Was sitting outside my house a way of righting some regret?" I asked.

"No. I never regretted us. I regretted losing us. It was the highest cost of my ambition."

"I regretted losing us, too."

"I know that. But I do believe you did your part to ruin us. I left, Russ, but you told me to. I'd appreciate it if you'd cop to that. You've had the luxury of me taking the rap for a long time now. Remember the talk we had, sitting on the floor by the fake fireplace that night, after I'd gotten my first contract offer? All the travel I was going to be doing? Do you remember what you said when I asked you what you wanted me to do? You said, 'I want you to go, Amber.' The *go* was loud and clear. I did the dirty work for both of us—I went."

"I know. I helped us crash."

And had regretted it, even as the words were coming out that night. I could remember every second of that conversation, even now, as if it was a scene from a movie I'd watched a hundred times. To all the charges that have been brought against the male—pride, stubbornness, unwillingness to communicate, selfishness, cowardice, insularity, macho inanity—I will gladly confess. Did I love her then? Certainly. But love is a poor excuse for anything. My sole defense is that I never desired any woman but Amber—at least not enough to act on it—when we were together, and for a truly frightening amount of time afterward. I was hers. Even when I began to take other lovers, I was hers. Until, that is, I stumbled on Isabella Sandoval sitting under a *palapa* amidst the sweet Valencias of the SunBlesst Ranch and my heart, so long detained, fled straight away to her.

"How could you let me go without a fight, Russ?" Amber whispered quietly.

Only time had given me the answer. If she had asked me this during one of our parting frays, I'd have told her she wasn't worth it. And she would have believed, because at that time I retained the ability to hurt her—she had not grown beyond me, yet. But that would not have been the truth.

"I thought then," I said, "that it was dangerous to take what wasn't offered. That I couldn't coax a love out of you that wasn't there to begin with."

"Afraid it would vanish?"

"Yes, in the end. Afraid of the collateral damage, too."

"Meaning what?"

"Meaning the love I felt for you."

The light finally changed and I gunned the car back toward Laguna. I maintained a more prudent double-digit speed. To the west, the ocean was an endless plain of black.

"And what do you think now, Russ, about taking what isn't offered?"

"I haven't changed my position on that. Some things, if you fight too hard to get them, get ruined in the war."

"You never had to fight for Isabella, did you? She offered you everything you wanted. Handed it right over to you, all of it, all of herself."

"Yes, she did."

"How did you choose to deal with that? Wasn't she bargaining with a diluted currency?"

"I loved and honored her in every way I could."

"Oh, Russell, you were a lucky man to find her."

"I've always known that."

"I'm so sorry for what happened to her. Will she ever be okay . . . ever?"

"No."

"Russ, do you believe in miracles?"

"No."

"What is it you hold on to late at night, when the devil's grabbing at your soul?"

"His throat."

"Do you feel anything tender inside at all?"

"Tenderness would unravel me."

My agonies were storming their walls. Was I powerless to stop them, or just unwilling? I heard a wild ringing in my ears.

"Do you want to die?"

"Sometimes. Then I think, There has to be more to life than a desire to be taken out on a stretcher."

"Is it really that bad?"

"I may just be exhibiting some sorry-ass version of brinksmanship. I've never considered myself cut out for this task—kindness just doesn't come easily. I don't know how much longer I can take care of her. I dream of tumors growing in my balls and lungs."

"What do you want?"

"A job where I wear a shirt with my name on it. A straightforward life."

"Really, I mean. Strip away all your self-pitying horseshit, all your writerly loop-the-loops, and what is it you truly want?"

"For the people I love to stop dying."

"There, Russell. I can believe you now. Why does it take you so long sometimes to admit the truth?"

The air whipped through the windows.

"Pull over," she said.

I braked and signaled and crunched off onto the shoulder. When the car finally stopped, the dust blew forward and swirled in the headlights. We were between the towns, on a bluff that opened to the sea. Down on the beach, wavering white ribbons rushed and retreated. My heart was in my teeth.

Amber got out, shut her door, and walked over to the bluff edge. I followed. The smell of sage mixed with the salt air, each intensified by the heat. Amber waited until I caught up with her, then took my hand. We walked the perimeter of the bluff, stopping where a deep gash opened into the abyss. The face of the cliff was back-cut, too steep for me to actually see, and as my gaze followed its invisible plane, I continued to see nothing but darkness until the sand below focused in my view, pale acreage studded with sharp rocks exposed wholly now by the low tide. The sand at the waterline shone as if lacquered. The ringing in my ears was so loud, my eyes began to blur. I had never in my life—except for those three hellish days with Izzy in a Guadalajara hospital, where her tumor was diagnosed—felt so fragile, so ready to disassemble.

To my heartache was then added shock when Amber turned me toward her on the edge of this bluff high over the sea and offered her lips, wet and parted, to my own.

There was nothing exploratory in this act, nothing of negotiation or the art of the deal. No, this was a kiss as pure as sacrifice. It was an offer of everything. She blew the breath of her lungs deep into my own as, two decades ago, she had so often done, always to the wilding of my blood.

I have a clear and permanent memory of what happened next. First, a breeze came off the sea, oddly cool in the static heat, and it struck my face directly. (How it got around Amber's face—locked so close to mine—I cannot explain.) And as it pushed cooly against me, I felt what seemed like the total contents of my mind—thoughts, precepts, memory—being lifted out and carried away. The Zapruder film is no more graphic than the vision I had, eyes closed, of everything inside me departing to join this fresh and unlikely breeze. But there was no violence to it. Rather, what was inside me simply stepped out and, like a child hand in hand with a grandparent, walked away.

Second, I remember the pink cotton material of Amber's dress bunched up on the small of her back, clutched in one of my hands, and the pure soft heat of her legs pressing against my trembling own, the forward bend and toe-strained perch of her, the lift of her dark brown hair in that breeze, a black even darker than the ocean beyond us, the brace of my fingers on her belly. And I remember, too, that we hardly moved—no great histrionics here—because every tiny motion, every fractional inch of contact was an agony of pleasure I could barely stand. The tremors deep within Amber were all the movement we required.

Last, I remember where we ended up, though not how we got there. The logistics of the transition are not hard to imagine. I was lying in the dirt, amidst the fragrant sage, staring straight up through Amber's hair to the sky. Her back was still to me. My arms were wrapped around her, my left locked in her right armpit, my right still open against her stomach, holding tight. My legs were spread and her rump rested deep between them, where—I noted—we were still very much connected. Her heart beat hard against the bone of my left elbow. We were both breathing fast. My butt hurt. I was, for the moment, blessedly opinionless.

But as quickly as my thoughts had departed, so they came scampering back, like rabbits to the hole. There they huddled, frightened, buck-toothed, ashamed. They curled together, hid their faces. They confessed. I closed my eyes again and imagined a fig leaf the size of the heavens. But I did not loosen my grip on Amber; if I had traded everything for this, then I was not about to give it up. I was the monkey caught in a trap because he's unwilling to release the bait from his greedy fist. I was even ready for the electric chair, but I would clutch this treasure to my lap, lodged so high and deep inside her that I could feel the bottom of her heart, until the straps claimed me.

Or not. Because along with the searing reentry of my conscience came the cooling waters of reason—all that keep the soul from self-immolation. For a moment, a terrible storm of contradiction began to form inside me, but it passed. I was no longer fit to battle myself. I had won and I had lost. I released my grip on Amber Mae and worked my nose into the aromatic crook behind her ear. I gently drove myself into her, to lessening effect. Very deeply, I sighed.

"Don't speak," she said.

I did not.

"That was a gift," she whispered.

"It certainly was. Thank you."

"It wasn't from me. I just delivered it."

"Who do I send the thank-you note to?"

"Isabella. We talked."

25

Driving back down Coast Highway toward my home was a journey of silence and bad conscience. Yes, I owned my secret life now, the very one I was hoping to begin on that awful night of July 3. But what a price to pay. I felt as if I had overdrawn my emotional accounts, that there was no way to finance this latest, wildest of expenditures. It was a perfect correlative to my actual financial quandry, the thought of which sent me further into a dismal spiral. What would I do when the bills came due? I became sullen and remorseful. And surprisingly—perhaps not—I found myself longing for the bed I used to share with Isabella, for the proximity of even her absence, for the darkness of the room in which we had loved each other and would, with some helpful nudge from the fates, love each other again.

Worst of all was my knowledge that Grace had almost certainly been in Amber's room on that night. Martin Parish had not been lying, after all. A thought came to me: What if Martin and Grace had planned this together? What if Martin had cajoled and helped to terrify Grace, perhaps even hired the men to burn her, used all his considerable influence as Grace's former step-father to widen the already-gaping chasm between mother and daughter? He could certainly have done so. But to what end? Vengeance for Amber throwing him over? Doubtful. The money due him in Amber's will? Possible. A chill fingered through me as another scenario presented itself: What if Martin and Grace were secret lovers, planning to marry each other's fortunes when Amber was gone? Could this explain Grace's many absences, her frequent phone conversations, her evasiveness? Yes, but if so, then why had Martin sworn to seeing Grace on the July 3? Was it as simple as self-protection, having been surprised by an unforeseen factor—myself? A simpler explanation might have been this: Grace's arrival at Amber's was every bit as coincidental as my own, and Parish, latching onto an opportunity to throw my curiosities a monstrous curve ball, admitted Grace's untimely entrance to me for the sake of pure confusion. But the overriding question was this: *If* Martin and Grace had been there together, planned the murder together, and killed the wrong woman together, why was Parish building a case against his own ac-complice and turning it over to the DA? It made little sense. Had I heard Karen correctly?

I picked up the car phone and dialed Karen's home num-ber, even though it was close to 2:00 A.M. She answered groggily. I hit a low spot in the canyon and the line went fuzzy for a moment, then snapped back into clarity. I asked her simply whether Martin's complaint to DA Peter Haight named Russell Monroe as the killer of Alice Fultz, or Russell Monroe and Grace Wilson.

"You promised," she said.

"I know, and I'm sorry. My ass is very much on the line here, Karen."

"You know how easy these cellular things are to tap?"

"I'm looking at death row. Tell me, Karen—is Haight going to indict me, or Grace and me?"

A long silence ensued, then another patch of static as we dipped behind a hillside, then the voiceless clarity again.

"Grace won't be named," she said finally. "Just you. They're banking she'll work with them and testify."

Whatever will was driving my body at that moment seemed to diminish to almost nothing. I was floating, as if in the horse latitudes, bereft of power.

Amber took my hand. "Martin plans to have Grace testify against you?"

I nodded.

"She was in on it. It's pure Grace. God, Russell, if you could only see her as I have."

"We'll both be seeing her in about five minutes."

◾   ◾   ◾

She was asleep in the guest room when we walked in. My father sat beside her, shotgun across his lap, drinking coffee and reading a magazine. In the limited light, Grace looked more like a child than a woman; her wavy dark hair hid her face and, in spite of the heat, she lay bundled to the neck in the blanket. The ceiling fan whirred above. Theodore examined us, and I sensed his understanding of what had just happened, then realized I hadn't bothered to so much as dust off my clothes or run a brush through my hair.

"Looks like you three have some business here," he said, rising. "I'll get lost for a while."

With this, I turned on the light. Grace stirred, whimpered, then opened one dark eye on me.

"What?" she whispered without moving.

"Get up," I said. "We need to talk."

I took her robe from the foot of the bed and handed it to her, turned my back for a moment, and closed my eyes. Let me find her innocent, I thought. Let there be an explanation for this. I heard the rustling of terry cloth on skin, then Grace's perturbed sigh. When I turned, she was sitting up, wrapped in the robe, both eyes trained, rather malignantly, upon Amber. The color had fallen from her face and her mouth was slightly open—half astonishment, half anger.

"I'm in hell," she said.

"Wonderful to see you, too, Grace."

Grace's eyes seemed to lose their focus for a moment, and I sensed in her the desire to run. For a moment, I thought she would.

But when she sprang from the bed, it was not to escape, but to charge Amber. I intercepted her, caught her strong wrists in my hands, and threw her back onto the bed. I beat her to the pillow and removed the .32.

"You hateful thing," said Amber.

"Russell," Grace said, training her fearful eyes on me, "Can you please make her go away?"

"No. But you can listen."

I came right out with what we had discovered: the ripped nail at Amber's, the nine matching it in Grace's wastebasket. I saved Brent Sides's recanted testimony, should it be needed later.

"Explain," I said.

Grace moved her disdainful eyes from her mother to me. "Twin horrors," she said. "It's like being raised by wolves."

"We were talking about July the third," I said.

"If you're accusing me of murder because you think nails in my bathroom match one found at *her* house—you're even dumber than I thought, Russ."

"Funny," I said. "No one mentioned murder at all. I was just wondering what you were doing at Amber's that night."

"I was not *at* Amber's that night. I was with Brent."

"We just came from his apartment. He said you didn't show up until real late. You were frightened. You smelled bad. He was afraid to ask where you'd been. So, now I'm asking— where were you?"

Grace colored deeply but not with shame. It was anger that showed through her skin and fueled a tiny fire in each eye. "I hate you both."

"That's nice," I said. "Where were you? And if you weren't at Amber's, how did your fingernail manage to get there without you? Grace—I'm tired of your crap."

The anger in Grace's eyes looked, for a moment, almost flamelike. I had never seen this in her, and yet it didn't surprise me. My own temper was a fierce, though temporary, thing. Amber's was, too. And as I looked at my daughter then, I saw that she was, both literally and figuratively, up against a wall.

Amber, silent throughout until now, turned to look at me. "Welcome to your girl," she said.

"*You're* the thing from hell," said Grace.

"I know, dear," answered Amber. "I know. But I'm trying hard to be something else. What were you doing in my house that night, Grace? You may as well tell us, since we have proof that you were there. Let me guess—you came to apologize for not talking to me for six months, for acting like I was dead."

"To beg your forgiveness and take your money, as suggested by those big oafs you sent. Here, *Mother*, do you like their handiwork?" Grace lifted a foot bottom toward her mother.

I heard the slight intake of breath as Amber understood what she was seeing.

"It worked," said Grace. "That is exactly what I was doing at your house on July the third. I was there to surrender to you.

I had had enough. I was scared enough of you by then to carry that gun in my purse. I admit that the idea of shooting you came to mind, and it wasn't a totally unpleasant thought. But what I wanted that night was to tell you I'd given up. I was done. You had won. I didn't want any more burned body parts. I didn't want your money, either. All I wanted was to be able to sleep at night without worrying who might be outside my door."

Grace looked steadily at me, then at her mother. The fires of anger were gone. "What I saw in your bedroom terrified me. I thought it was you. I called Martin, but he wasn't home. I called Russell, but *you* weren't home. Then I went to Brent's and tried to sleep. I wasn't going to call the police and talk to some rookie patrolman about my own mother's murder. Why? Because when I looked down at you, *Mother,* the terror didn't come from what had happened to you; it came from how... fitting it seemed to be. Looking at your dead body made me a little bit happy. And I knew by the time all the news of our bad blood got out—Grace Wilson would be the number-one suspect. So I hid out, then came here to Russell."

I listened to the motor of the ceiling fan, the gentle whoosh of the blades. "The nail, Grace."

Grace looked down now, at her knees still covered by the blanket. Her voice was suddenly weaker. "And I'll tell you something I have never told another human being, Russell and Amber. It almost hurts me to say it, but I will because it explains why I was there, and why my nail stayed behind."

She looked up at Amber now with an expression so different from before, I could hardly believe it belonged to the same person. Tears welled in her lovely dark eyes and her lips, so capable of scorn and sarcasm, simply trembled.

"I... I have always... in a way... I have always loved you, Mother. And when I saw you lying there, after I felt the relief of knowing you were dead and I was safe, and after I felt that horrid . . . satisfaction at what had happened to you, I fell down to the floor on my knees and cried and prayed and cried and prayed and I dug my fingers so hard into your carpet, the nail broke off. I didn't notice it until I was leaving. I looked for it but couldn't find it. Back home, I took off the others and threw them away so that if the police came to me, they'd see I didn't wear nails. I was too upset and too afraid to realize they'd be as easy to find in the dumpster as they would have been on my fingers. I think I probably left a fresh pack around, anyway. I'd make a lousy criminal."

Amber took a step toward Grace, then stopped. "When Russell told you it was Alice, why didn't you call me, Grace? Why didn't you . . . weren't you at least relieved I was still alive?"

"Mother," said Grace, "I believed you would blame it on me, as you and Russell are trying to do right now. What I wanted, more than anything, was a few days' rest with Russell—or any-where, really—then a long vacation somewhere alone. You can't believe how horrible it was . . . seeing what I saw and feeling what I felt. I love you. I hate you, too, but not enough to kill you like that. Believe what you want."

Amber stared at Grace but said nothing. There was more damnation in her silence than in any words she might have said.

Grace looked back down at her knees, sighed deeply, and rested her head against them. "And you, Russell?" she asked quietly.

"I've always believed you, girl. How much of this have you told Martin?"

"All," she answered, still not looking up.

Of course, I thought, it explained Parish's initial fingering of Grace at the scene, and his final decision to frame me—not her.

"Did you know he's going to charge me with Alice's murder?"

She looked up then, with a look on her face as close to hopelessness as I had ever seen from her. "I had no idea that's what he was doing. He told me very little. I thought Martin was a decent man. He always was—to me, anyway. But you should know, Russell, I'll do whatever I can to help you."

"I'm going to need your help. *Parish killed Alice.* Do you understand that?"

She shook her head. "Why?"

"Because he was in line for money if Amber died. And because, quite frankly, Martin Parish hates your mother more than you ever did. He hates me, too. And he found a way to knock us all down with one shot. He thought he could pull off a perfect crime."

"I'm so sick of everything," Grace whispered. Tears rolled down her cheeks. "Amber, I love you, but I still hate you. Russell, I'll do whatever I can to help you with Martin. I'll testify. I'll talk to the police."

"You already have."

"Then what can I do?"

Audacity, I thought. Meet Martin on his own turf. "I'm not sure yet," I said.

Amber had already left the room.

I walked past my father in the living room, fully unconscious on a couch. I caught up with her on the deck outside. She was lighting a cigarette and her hand was shaking. I lighted it for her.

"She needs you," I said.

"It wasn't clear to me until now."

"You can go to her."

"You don't understand. She's in it with Martin. She's his

partner. I'm positive. Nothing on earth interested her more as a child than my men. It's her and Martin, working together. With me out of the way, it would have been millions for them both. And all the jolly good fun they could have bashing my brains all over my bedroom. I think I'm going to puke, Russell."

She ran up into the brush of the canyon and vomited.

A few minutes later, she came back down, her shape materializing from the darkness. "I'm going home with Theodore," she said. "And in the morning, I'll see the State Attorney General again. Now that I understand Grace's role, it makes all the more sense. I will not allow Martin Parish and my loving daughter to get away with this. Not at your expense, and most certainly not at mine."

26

I hardly slept that night—or rather, morning—but the dreamy wakefulness offered me the clarity of mind that one enjoys just before falling asleep and just before fully waking. I wondered about Izzy, then wondered some more. I called the IC Unit every hour for reports. When I could momentarily assuage my worries about Isabella, I did my best to consider other actualities. I wondered whether Amber's tack to the Attorney General might be a sound one. But again, I had no desire to meet Martin Parish on the playing field of the law—his advantage was too great.

Instead, I dreamed—or imagined—meeting Parish in Amber's house. The scene played like this: He had come to finish what he'd started on July 3. He would have the club. I would be there, a witness to his second attempt. There, I could make a citizen's arrest for burglary, which would lead to questioning, investigation, and an eventual unmasking of Parish.

I liked the directness of this action, but, at the same time, Grace and I clearly needed help. Would Amber participate, perhaps help us lure Martin back to her home? Maybe. But where could we find an ally with power outside of the system? Just as the first light brought forth the basic shapes in the room around me, I thought of Erik Wald. At first, the idea seemed ridiculous, Erik being so ensconced within the court of the department. But looked at another way, I could see that he might cooperate, because taking down Martin Parish would not only clear Wald's appointment to undersheriff but would also be the glitziest coup he might pull. Imagine the headlines when the homicide captain lay exposed by the cleverness of Professor Erik Wald and journalist Russell Monroe! And I thought, too, that Erik's natural boldness might suit him perfectly. The question was, Would he believe us, and, if so, would he help us trap Parish?

I called him at 6:00 A.M. and told him we'd be at his house in one hour. He was too mystified to protest.

Then I called the ICU nurses again.

No change.

■   ■   ■

Wald lived in a ranch-style home in the Tustin hills, a swanky area that boasted an equestrian flavor, smatterings of sweet-smelling orange groves, and $5 million Spanish-style mansions on large parcels of land. His modest house sat back from the road, at the end of a drive lined by eucalyptus trees. The gate was locked, and I announced myself through an intercom speaker. Wald said nothing, but the gate swung open and we drove in.

"Can he help us?" Grace asked.

"I think so. The question is, will he?"

"I remember him as being swashbuckling. In his own mind, that is."

"There is that side of Erik."

We parked. Wald was waiting at the door, dressed in corduroy pants and a thin T-shirt that accentuated his tanned, well-muscled arms. His golden mop of hair was still wet from a shower. He looked at me as I walked past him into the house, then he rather formally hugged Grace.

"Nice to see you," he said.

"Nice to see you, too, Erik," she replied. "Have any coffee on?"

In the smallish kitchen, Erik poured us three cups. I could see the living room, which was large and furnished in heavy Mexican-style ranch chairs and sofas. A large trunk that looked quite old served as a coffee table. The fireplace at the far end was of brick—dark and well used.

Wald led us through a sliding glass door, across a small backyard with a fountain and plantain trees and giant birds of paradise, then into his study, which was likely built as maid's quarters. He pushed open the door without unlocking it and followed us inside.

All the rustic charm of the house proper was lost upon Erik's study. The walls were white, the floor was gleaming hardwood, the furnishings looked more corporate than domestic. It was clearly a place of work. Two computers sat at two different gray metal desks, two printers beside them. There were fax and copy machines; file cabinets lining three walls; two telephones; a large video monitor; two video cameras, each mounted on a tripod; a film screen. It was also a place of pride and self-absorption, as I noted the big portrait of Wald that hung over the far wall, the dozens of plaques and trophies (marksmanship, tennis), the custom-made cabinets that displayed Wald's certificates, badges, awards, pins—every commendation he might have collected in fifteen years of academic and law-enforcement work. Even the larger newspaper stories were available for viewing, spread on foam, then shrink-wrapped and framed. A dozen copies of his much-lauded doctoral dissertation, "Aspiring to Evil: Transference Identification in the Violent Felon," which had been published by the university after Wald's and Winters's spectacular snaring of the rapist Cary Clough, took up an eye-level shelf in one of the cases.

"One of these days, I'll write a best-seller," Erik said with a boyish smile. "Then we'll be equals in the field of letters, too."

"Russell can write better than you," said Grace rather seriously.

"Which is exactly why I work so hard at it," answered Erik, still smiling. "If I remember correctly from five years ago, when I was seeing Amber, your grades in English hovered around the *C* mark."

"And you suggested I reread *Moby-Dick*."

Wald shrugged, set his coffee on one of the desks, and took a seat behind it. I brought up a chair to face him. Grace sat atop the other desk, to our left, dangling a leg.

"Russell," said Erik, slipping on a pair of glasses, "I've been racking my considerable mind for the last hour trying to figure out why in hell you were coming here. You have my curiosity up. So shoot."

And shoot I did. I walked him through the dire events of July 3 and 4; the burial of Alice Fultz; Amber's reappearance; Martin's secret lab work and dubbed tape; the impending indictment from Peter Haight's office. I explained what I could of the bad blood between Grace and Amber; the monies at stake should she die; and Grace's actual presence at the scene.

Wald listened carefully and took very spare notes. His attention went back and forth between Grace and myself. He groaned when I told him about Alice's hillside funeral. He nodded when I tried to account for the competition and dislike between mother and daughter, Wald being familiar enough with both to fill in the blanks himself. He looked at me with an expression that suggested exasperation at both women, then turned the same look upon Grace.

"Now that you feel superior, are you ready to help us?" Grace asked him.

Wald said nothing for a long while. He stared off through a window toward his backyard fountain. He took off his glasses, studied the lenses, then put them on again.

"Parish disgusts me," he said quietly. "He always has. I can't say I'm dumbfounded that he'd do this. I always believed there was something profoundly unbalanced in Martin. The trouble is, you've got no evidence. Martin's got the evidence, and it all points to you."

"That's exactly why I'm here," I said.

"That was hardly brilliant, Erik," noted Grace.

"But it's true," he answered, turning toward her. "And what's true is going to get you out of this. Not what's brilliant." Pivoting back to me, he said, "Now . . . I assume you have a plan."

"He didn't leave anything behind at Amber's. I saw him, but that doesn't prove anything. I don't think we can touch him for Alice without touching him for something else first."

"Such as?"

"Another attempt on Amber's life."

He looked at me skeptically.

I explained that if the situation was good—no, not good, but perfect—Martin could be tempted to finish what he had begun on July 3. Until now, Amber had been safe with my father and his diligent Remington, but *if* Amber would offer up herself as bait, we could set a trap into which Parish might possibly fall.

"Why would he try again? I assume Amber was bright enough to do a little adjusting of her will. Right?"

"That's right. It's not the money anymore, Erik. It's the

hate, the violence, and he needs her silent. He'll try it again if he's sure he can get away with it. I believe that. All we need to do is create the opportunity for him—and be there to stop him."

"That is to say, *I* could make the opportunity," said Wald. "We assume that any information coming from you to Martin— especially information on the . . . vulnerability of Amber at such and such a time and place—would be instantly suspect. I, on the other hand, could point him in the right direction in all . . . innocence."

"How can you be so smart and so dumb at the same time?" Grace said.

We both looked at her.

"Amber won't cooperate. She's a total coward."

"Let us handle Amber," I said.

Wald was studying me hard now. "You're asking me to set him up."

"Yes."

He continued to stare at me. Grace's dangling leg swung to and fro. The morning light came through an east window and lighted the trophy case. He slid off his glasses again, wobbled the temples in his hand as he looked down at them, the right temple swinging loosely on the frame, barely secured.

"Lost one of the screws," he muttered, hopelessly searching his drawer, desk, lap, and floor. "I hate these things."

Erik's mind was obviously not on his glasses.

And neither was mine, until the realization crashed down on me that I had a spare screw—found in Amber's bedroom— still inside the cap of my pen. Involuntarily, I blinked. And with equal involition, my mind began to race.

"Me, too," I said.

Wald looked at the frames. "I only wear these damned things when the world won't see me, image being everything, right? Anyway . . . back to Parish. Look, if he's done what you've

304

said he's done, then I agree—he'll try to finish her off *if the opportunity is there*. It seems to me that we need to get him a chance at Amber alone. Right?"

"I think Amber's house would be best—he's familiar with it; it's remote. But we need to move soon. He's about to throw me to Haight."

Grace sighed impetuously. "I still don't think she'll help."

Wald turned to look at Grace, who was now leaning back on her hands, legs still lolling off the edge of the desktop. "You think more like your mother every day."

"I'm sure that sits fine with you."

"You are both very bright women."

He turned to me.

"Russell," he finally said, slipping his glasses back into the drawer, "let's set up a little sling, then get Martin Parish's ass into it."

He offered me his hand. I shook it. "Thank you," I said absently, smiling with a similar absence. My mind, in fact, was reeling.

Wald stood. "I actually think this may go rather smoothly. I'll have that oaf after Amber like a trout on a fly. I look forward to seeing the look on his face when we take him down for . . . well . . . what shall we shoot for? Burglary? Attempted murder? Russell, one hour from now, you and I will both be sitting in the same room with him, trying to figure how to play the Midnight Eye right. My guess is that Martin Parish will do everything he can to keep the Eye on the street until he can do Amber once and for all. He'll use the Eye's MO, like he tried to originally."

"I think you're right," I said.

"Thanks, Waldie," said Grace. She lurched off the desk and came to Erik, planted a polite kiss on his cheek, then shook his hand. "It means a lot to have a friend."

305

"You can count on me for that, Grace."

He was smiling broadly at her now, his blue eyes lighted with something like fascination, and something like mischief.

I used his phone to call the Medical Center. Isabella was awake and feeling well. I asked them to tell her I'd be there as soon as I possibly could.

27

One hour later, we were, in fact, seated in Dan Winters's office, gathered to devise our strategy regarding the Midnight Eye. I found myself unable to look at either Wald or Parish without fearing that my suspicions were written on my face as clearly as a headline. It was no easier to focus on Winters, whose penetrating black eyes seemed, as always, to find their way straight into the weakness behind my own facade. Why did he bother to include me here, with an indictment from the DA on its way? Was he simply keeping his enemies close? Or— outlandish as it would have been—had Parish bypassed his own boss? Was it even possible that the indictment was nothing more than a terror tactic from Parish, that he had no intention of arresting me for a murder he himself had committed? Karen would hardly look at me, so compromised did she feel at having tipped me to Martin's plans. The thought crossed my mind that he may have used her. The thought also crossed my mind that she was willing to be used. Suspicions of betrayal and treachery piled so high inside me, I could hardly hear myself think. I concentrated on the notepad in front of me, on the pen in my hand, and on the question that had been bothering me as much as it had been bothering John Carfax. How had the Eye managed to bypass the intercepts? We knew he had electronic know-how, this from the testimony of Mary Ing. We knew that there were commercially available products for scrambling, encoding, and decoding, for testing whether a line was "transparent" or not. With some experimentation and a little brains, the Eye might have found the application he was looking for—namely, making calls on a line with no number. But how could he get access to the lines?

In contrast to my silent deliberations, both Parish and Wald argued heatedly about how to handle the Midnight Eye. Their voices seemed to cascade over me like the roar of a waterfall behind which I was standing. *How did the Eye get access to the lines?*

The key question for Parish and Wald was whether to reveal him as Ing or not. He had threatened massive violence if we did, but, as Parish pointed out, keeping Ing active was the key to finding him. Wald took the opposite view, that to enrage Ing was to endanger the county, and that any time we could purchase with mollification was time we badly needed. At one point, Wald and Parish were yelling and Winters had to shout them both down.

"What's your call, Russell?" he asked me.

"ID him," I said absently. "Make him feel the pressure. I'm with Martin. Smoke him out."

Wald looked at Winters, visibly aghast. "It's going to back-fire," he said.

"First decent idea Monroe's had in a week," said Parish.

"Thanks. Here's another one. Ing works around phone lines. He knows how to work them, like taking apart the phone when he was a kid. That's why he can place the calls around the intercepts."

"We've already talked to everyone we could think of," said Winters. "Right, Martin?"

"Right. The linemen at the phone company, the utilities people, the city maintenance crews. Everyone."

"What about the phone company? Not the field crews, but right there at the hub, in Laguna?"

"Wald covered it," said Parish.

"*You* covered it," said Wald.

An utter grayness descended over Martin's face. "I haven't screened the hub people—that was Wald's goddamned Citizens' Task Force's job. He asked for it."

"Bull*shit,*" said Wald. "You said your people were handling it."

"Oh no," said Winters. "I can't believe what I'm hearing. You mean *nobody's* been out there to the goddamned phone company with that picture?"

The silence that reigned again seemed, logically, to focus upon Martin Parish. "No."

"*Enough of this shit!*" bellowed Winters, hurtling up from his desk and backhanding a pile of files to the floor. "This is what we do! No more games. No more crap between you people. I'll fire all of you motherfuckers if I have to. Now you will listen and you will obey. One, Monroe, file the article about Mrs. Ing's identification. File the one on Ing's childhood. See if the *Journal* will run the graphic without the goddamned beard. Karen, give them one of Mrs. Ing's snapshots of this bastard. Parish, get out to the phone company right now. Wald, either get those citizens to come up with something or get them the hell out of this building. They're using up my air conditioning. Now get out of my sight and do it!"

I gathered my notebook and left the room. Behind me

came the sound of Wald and Parish yelling again, the same accusations and warnings.

In the pressroom, I used a fax machine to file my story suggesting that the Midnight Eye was William Fredrick Ing. I talked to Carla Dance about the photographs and she was only too willing to run another picture of the suspect. She thanked me again for the best series of scoops she could remember printing.

"God, I hope this doesn't come back to haunt us," she said.

"Carla, I don't know what else we can do. And, by the way, can you hurry along those checks? I'm broke."

"I'll talk with Accounting."

Then I went out to my car and drove back down the freeway toward Erik Wald's house in the Tustin hills. I wanted to have a conversation with the walls of his home, and then I wanted, very badly, to see my Isabella.

■   ■   ■

The same overpowering heat that was allowing the Midnight Eye into the homes of innocents also gave me easy entry into Wald's study. I pried off the screen of an opened window in the rear, slid up the the glass, and climbed in, well concealed beneath the towering eucalyptus and oak that ran down Wald's property line to the east.

I went to the desk, opened the drawer, and took out Wald's glasses. From the pen in my pocket, I removed the screw I'd found in Amber's room. Working under the light of Wald's desk lamp, I placed the screw into the empty temple hole and twisted it in. The fit was perfect. It had the same coppery finish that the metal of the frames did. I tilted the glasses over, wiggled them gently, and watched the screw fall to the blotter. Stripped,

I thought, exactly what had allowed it to fall out in the first place. I could feel my heart pounding in my fingertips as I gathered up the little part and replaced it in my pen.

I left the study and broke into the house with an old set of lock-picking tools I'd used during my deputy days.

I stood in the darkened hacienda-style living room and wondered what I was looking for and where to start. The very idea that Wald had been in Amber's room had opened an entirely fresh pathway in my thinking, and I was still trying to accommodate his presence there. Was he in this with Parish, *two* men with grudges against her and money to gain by her death, two men connected to the upper levels of law enforcement? Was he in this with Grace? I knew not what to make of the strange tension between them, of the flirtatious belligerence one often sees in couples married for years. Surely, Grace and Erik had a history, as did Grace and I, but was I sensing the all of it? Or imagining too much?

I began in the master bedroom. It was also done up in a masculine, heavy style, with the same rough dark wood of the sofas and chairs of the living room. I noted that the bedspread was of crimson satin and the sheets of black silk. It was unmade. The scent of some cologne—a musky incenselike aroma—was deep and cloying. The wardrobes were of purposefully crude design and construction, massive things with handles wrapped in leather. I looked at the clothes inside. There were not a lot of them. Most were still in the thin plastic sheaths used by professional cleaners—Wald, the bachelor who could afford such a service. I noted the name of the company. I also noted the labels, which bespoke Wald's expensive tastes and, in turn, accounted for his limited quantity. Piles of neckties were draped over pegs in the right-hand side. Likewise, belts and suspenders hung on the opposite. A stack of underwear—silk, by appearance—caught my eye. I felt a little ridiculous. I looked inside a matching wardrobe on the other side of the room and found mostly winter and sportswear. Hanging on the far right side was a woman's satin robe, with matching pajama top and short-short bottoms. They were red, size ten. Next to them hung a rather skimpy black dress. I recognized the store's name on the tag, Ice Blue—the same one in which Grace had worked until being hounded underground by two men hired to torture her. My heart fluttered and wouldn't settle. I closed the door.

I looked through the personal items on and inside both bed stands. Wald's bedside reading was eclectic: forensic and psychiatric periodicals; Ian Fleming; Joe McGinniss; James Hillman. Three videotapes of National Geographic specials were stacked in the corner of the top drawer. He kept a journal, which I browsed. A bottle of Xanax prescribed to him sat beneath the lamp. It was not hard to imagine Erik, with his ceaseless energy, having trouble falling asleep. A remote control lay upon the stand, though I saw neither television nor stereo anywhere in the room.

The other bed stand belonged, quite obviously, to a wholly different personality. Two books sat upon it—my own *Journey Up River: The Story of a Serial Killer,* and Ellis's *American Psycho.* I had not inscribed the copy of *Journey.* A small but very plump panda bear with a pink ribbon around its neck leaned against the lamp. The top drawer contained copies of *Elle, Interview,* and *Vanity Fair.* Amidst the generalized disorder of the second drawer, I found a small bottle of perfume, a box of condoms—a brand different from the ones I'd noted in Grace's car—and an assortment of body lotions and creams.

I closed the drawer, thought, and leaned for a moment on the large wooden console that sat at the foot of the bed.

Strictly on instinct—or maybe because of the loomings I felt inside me—I left the bedroom and went again into Erik's study.

First, perhaps because I am at least in part a literary man, I went to the bookshelf. Wald's collection of forensic/psychiatric literature was extensive, ranging from copies of Diller's early studies with fingerprints, to pilfered syllabi from FBI lectures that Wald had both attended and delivered, to Ressler's tome on profiling, *Whoever Fights Monsters*. I removed a copy of Wald's own dissertation, "Aspiring to Evil," and opened it midway.

> Thus, the violent psychotic mind is an ever-shifting laby-rinth inside a constantly careening ego. No combination of pathology and consciousness is more potentially danger-ous, nor more difficult to predict. But when these conditions are coupled in an individual of high intelligence, profiling methods can easily yield faulty results, as the subject is— by his very purpose—fluent in the behavioral disguises which lead so many profilers to make wrong assumptions, erroneous connections, and, inevitably, false conclusions.

Exactly what he was propounding with regard to William Fredrick Ing, I thought. So far, he had been right.

I replaced the book and stood in the middle of the room, gazing at the sundry video equipment, the computers and print-ers, the endless file cabinets, and the ubiquitous testimonies to Wald himself. The room seemed to ring with his presence. I could sense his personality there, the way one hears a dimin-ishing echo. But still, it was only an echo I could hear, not the sound itself. I thought of something Izzy had told me about composing music: You hear the echo first.

Yes, but how do you follow it backward in time and trace it to the original sound?

I took a videotape of one of Erik's lectures—his entire collection of tapes seemed at first glance to be of himself doing something—put it in a VCR, and hit the PLAY button. It was dated

February of last year and featured Erik behind a podium, delivering a rather dry account on the basic principles used in DNA typing. He droned on about probes and probabilities. The tape itself was shot, apparently, from a fixed position at the back of the lecture hall, and the cameraman—a student, no doubt—had made only occasional attempts to close in, scan the attentive crowd, establish the larger context of the hall.

I tried another, dated some five years ago, with the cryptic title, "Motivation, Opportunity, and the Leap of Faith."

The hall was different, Erik was more youthful then, and his delivery was more enthused. Even the cameraman had had more spirit—he'd zoomed in and out, trying to anticipate Erik's tonic notes; he'd panned the students (actually, the backs of their heads and an occasional profile were about all he'd been able to capture); and he'd used, as some kind of symbolism, I supposed, several shots of the wall clock ticking away.

Something caught my eye, a head and partial profile in the front row. I could have sworn I recognized the face. I pressed REWIND, then watched again. I hit FREEZE FRAME. Yes, without doubt it was my daughter, Grace. She was looking up at Wald in a respectful way, her pen poised over her notebook. I hit PLAY again. As Erik made a crack about religious fanatics making good murderers, Grace smiled and shook back her dark wavy hair. She was approximately thirteen then—that would have been the time that Amber was involved romantically with Wald. I removed the tape and played several others, all dated within weeks of the first, all part of a course. And in each sat Grace in the same seat of the first row—precocious, poised, beautiful.

Like first daylight illuminating the rudimentary outlines of a room, an understanding began to form in my mind.

I locked the study, replaced the key in the kitchen, and went back into the master bedroom. It was here I felt Wald's personality most intensely—his discipline and hedonism, his mixture of the rough and the sensual, of the mundane and the fantastic. And it seemed to me that if I was to believe Erik had been in Amber's room that night—*with Grace*—I needed to locate the very core of his character in order to understand with my mind what my heart was telling me was true.

So I looked at everything again. Then I went through the guest rooms, the kitchen, the living and dining rooms, both baths. There is no end to what objects can suggest.

I found myself back in the bedroom again, drawn by one last desire to locate Wald's character through the reverberations of his absence. *Erik and Grace. Grace and Erik.* I again searched the bed stand belonging to Erik's female partner, again wondered at the contradictory powers emanating from the cute panda bear and the dreary books on her stand. Grace, I thought, is this you I am looking at?

I stood beside the nightstand—Grace's nightstand?—and considered the large wooden console at the foot of the bed. I found the switch, hit it, and watched the large TV monitor rise from its base. What manner of program could someone watch, this hugely displayed, from so short a distance?

I confess some shame at how easily I answered this question. Perhaps my quick understanding was prompted in part by the shrine to himself that Erik had erected in his study. But I understood the power of image. Why would Narcissus choose the pond when he could capture himself on tape?

As I removed "Polar Alert"—a National Geographic special on polar bears—from the bottom drawer of Erik's nightstand, I was convinced that nothing of bears would appear on the screen in front of me. I inserted the cassette into the built-in player and pressed PLAY.

All I can say now is that I found what I was looking for and hoping not to find, that the image of a girl sitting up in this very bed brought with it all the excitement and all the sorrow of revelation. Grace looked about sixteen. She was smiling sweetly, shyly, seductively. Then the screen flickered and the first frames of the documentary overtook the image of my daughter. I replaced the cassette in the box and slipped it into my coat pocket.

The last thing I did before leaving was to put the window screen back in place.

I was not five miles toward the Medical Center when my car phone rang. It was Erik.

"Foolish move back there, Russ." My heart sank. "We won't help this county by infuriating a madman."

I managed some semblance of composure. "I think it beats the alternative. Between you and Parish *forgetting* to check the phone company people, I'd say that was pretty lame police work. Especially for a professor of criminology."

"Parish dropped the ball. Maybe he had a little extra on his mind—like framing you and Grace."

"He's done a pretty damned good job of it, too. Where do we stand, Erik?"

"I've laid the groundwork to get Parish believing that Amber will be home alone. Tonight. I managed this with some creative thinking in the voice-mail department. Basically, it sounds like Amber left a message for me, but at the wrong extension. All Martin has to do is call in for messages, recognize her voice, and he's hooked."

"What time?"

"Eleven. We should meet there at ten."

"Amber was willing?"

"*Eager.*"

28

At three that afternoon, I helped the nurses of UCI Medical Center transfer Isabella from intensive care to a room on the neuro floor. That is to say, I walked alongside the wheeled hospital bed, holding a vase of roses in one hand and pushing the IV unit with the other, looking down at her swollen face. She seemed lost to gauze and puffiness. But from the center of those, her eyes focused on me with a calm clarity, and I could see—yes, even then—the shine of Isabella's lovely spirit twinkling through at me.

"How is my man?"

"Holding up, and proud to be yours. Do you hurt?"

"My head doesn't. Just my throat, where the tube was, and my wrist, where the IV is."

"Do you realize what you're doing?"

She smiled slowly, a smile limited by swelling and drugs. "I'm talking without stuttering. Dr. Nesson is proud of me."

"You've made him look good."

"I'm already lobbying heavily to go home. He said tomorrow maybe, or the next day."

"Baby, that would be great."

The room was a dreary affair with a view of Interstate 5, Anaheim Stadium, and a six-plex movie dome. But it was ours, and it was private. The nurses arranged Izzy, took vitals, got the IV pump working right, gave her a dinner menu to order from, and were gone.

"Isabella, I'm so happy to see you."

"I'm so glad you're here. How was your night?"

"Interesting."

She gazed at me from beneath the gauze turban, with eyes that I am sure—for a moment at least—were assessing the impact of her gift, offered through Amber Mae Wilson.

"I hope it was interesting in a good way, love."

"The nights I look forward to are ones with you."

"I'm so lucky."

"No, you're not. But I am."

"You look tired, Russ. Everyone here is talking about the Midnight Eye. The nurses are scared to go home, so they're w-w-working overtime."

"They're getting closer to him, Izzy. I think they'll have him soon. The whole county seems paralyzed."

I told her a little about the last two days, but what could I really say that wouldn't depress and frighten her even more? I avoided the essentials of Grace, Martin, and Wald and told her instead about the manhunt for the Midnight Eye, and as much as I thought she wanted to hear about our plan to bait him with the article. The article itself, I read in the afternoon edition of the *Journal* while the nurses helped Izzy to the bathroom. Beside it was the computer-aided picture of beardless Billy.

Already, I could see Izzy's concentration waning, the deep exhaustion showing forth from her lovely eyes.

She smiled dreamily, closed her eyes, and squeezed my hand. "Nap time."

As I released her hand and set it on her chest, I saw the blue bruising that the IV needle made, the tape that kept it in, the little loop of clear tubing that would fill with blood if the directional flow was interrupted. How vicious and factual, the way the steel of the needle disappeared into her living flesh— pure insult, pure affront, pure invasion.

Soon she was snoring, her face retreating into the turban, her chubby cheeks relaxed and pink, her mouth just slightly open, revealing the whiteness of her teeth.

I closed my eyes and felt my heart beating in my chest. *Remain*, I thought: *Isabella, remain.* My head dipped, then righted itself. I got up from my chair, shut the door to her room, then removed the seizure pads and lowered the railing on the left side of her bed.

I climbed in and worked my way up next to her. She did not stir. I reached back and raised the railing to give me some-thing to rest against—hospital beds are made for only one. I placed my head beside hers, my nose up close to the clinical gauze. I worked my hand under her hand, not disturbing the tubing and needle. I slept.

■   ■   ■

Later, from the lobby, I made three phone calls. The first was to Wald, who confirmed that Parish would be at Amber's some-time after eleven. The second was to Amber, who confirmed her willingness to participate in this trap. The anger in her voice was palpable. Last, I called Martin Parish—my second call to him since the disastrous meeting.

"You were right," he said. "He's been working at the phone company under the name of Stuart Bland. Mr. Bland apparently did not show up for work after his break. The son of a bitch saw us. And I'll swear on my mother's grave that Wald told me he'd covered them."

"I believe you. Now it's your turn to believe me."

"What I'll believe, Monroe, is the truth," he said. "You need to deliver."

"I'll do that."

I hung up, then I drove down to Mission San Juan Capistrano, where Isabella and I were married those few short years ago. I yearned for the proximity of the old adobe, the talismanic power of the crucifix and candles, the ancient whiff of miracle. I yearned for a joyful memory.

But the mission was closed for repair. I stood outside the tall adobe wall and read the sign. I walked around to the north end of the grounds and sat against that wall in the shade of a pepper tree. The noise I heard coming from the other side could have been Father Serra's Juaneños building the original structure, if not for the occasional buzz of an electric saw. As I sat there, I tried to imagine what might happen at Amber's house in just a few hours, if Martin stayed true to his own nature, and Wald to his. I felt possessed of a certain clarity of intention, however. I felt possessed, too, of a certain violence.

■   ■   ■

Grace was not at home when I arrived, as I suspected she would not be. She had left a note saying she was going to visit a friend tonight and would be back late. Some friend, I thought, and saw again in my mind's eye her image on the TV monitor in the home of Erik Wald.

At eight that night, the Midnight Eye called.

"You've made a terrible mistake," he said. "I am not William Fredrick Ing."

"Then there's no problem."

"Oh, there will be quite a problem, R-r-russell. And it will belong to you and those pigs at the department."

I said nothing.

"The flatfoots finally caught up with me. Brilliant, don't you think, to be creating my own phone lines?"

"It was brilliant. Where are you now?"

"Sh-sh-sh-sh. Out of a job, obviously. But I'm not worried. I have savings. I'm prepared. It was funny, watching Parish and his men pour into the phone company building at break time. I was outside eating a sandwich. Maybe I'll have my last pay-check mailed to me. You lied, Russell, about the intercept. I truly thought I could trust you."

"I was overridden."

"By Winters and Parish, right? They're the law-and-order types. You and Wald held out for the more . . . subtle idea of keeping me talking longer."

"We're talking now."

"Well, time is short. Just know that the next time you hear from me, you can take full responsibility for the lives that will have been crushed out. To call me an overweight epileptic is something you will regret. I am not Ing. I am the Midnight Eye."

He hung up abruptly. I dialed the intercept number at the department and got Carfax. "It was an L.A. County number— the airport. Winters is pleading our case right now."

Los Angeles International Airport, I thought. Had we run him off?

Just before I left to pick up Amber, I went into my study and opened the right-bottom drawer of my desk to get the Gold Cup Colt .45 I consider my finest sidearm. It was gone.

After a moment's surprise, I realized why, and smiled to myself.

I packed the Smith instead, a .357 with a four-inch barrel,

which I fitted into a regulation shoulder holster. It was heavy, bulky, and obvious, but I didn't care. Then I slipped a speed loader into the pocket of my coat and the videotape I'd taken from Wald's bedroom in the other. Armed with a gun and a snippet of the truth, I turned on the porch lights, locked the door behind me, and got into my car.

■   ■   ■

At nine o'clock, I picked up Amber at a posh hotel on the Laguna coast. She was wearing a white cotton dress, with a wide red belt and red pumps. She looked like the sacrificial lamb that we intended her to play. In the lobby, she took my arm and we proceeded across the marble floor like lovers going out for a night on the town. All eyes followed us—or rather, Amber—and even under so strained a circumstance, I could feel emanating from her the enjoyment, the sense of entitlement, that she derived from the position she had earned at center stage.

"You look nice," I said, content with understatement.

"You look like a tired writer with a gun under his coat."

"Some things don't change."

"I have to tell you, Russ, I am afraid of this."

"You should be."

"I am furious at Erik."

"Hide it for a while. There will be a time for that."

We arrived at Amber's at 9:30, after parking well away from the house.

Wald came exactly at ten, as planned. He had dressed for the occasion in a baggy cream-colored linen suit. The coat was perfect for concealing a gun, which, if I was correct in my surmise, would be my own .45, pilfered by Grace earlier in the day and delivered to Wald forthwith. He shook my hand and kissed Amber on both cheeks.

"I feel good," he said. "Charged to the max by the adrenaline of law enforcement. I love this kind of stuff. Out of the lecture hall and into real life."

"Do you think he's convinced?" asked Amber, never better at playing a role.

"I'm almost sure of it."

"And if he's not?"

"Then, my dearest, most beautiful Amber Mae, we try again." He smiled at her, in his boyish blue eyes the same shine of desire and conspiracy that I had seen him level at my daughter that very morning. He had known them both! I could hardly contain my desire to beat his face to meat with my fists.

"I think we should set up in Amber's bedroom," I said quietly. "That's where Marty will expect to find you."

"I'm guessing he'll come around midnight," said Erik. "He'll figure she'll be asleep by then, like Alice was. Make his whole op a lot easier."

"Erik," I said, smiling at him, "that's good thinking."

We climbed the stairs. In Amber's room, we made ourselves comfortable for the wait. I dimmed the lights. Amber reclined on the bed with a book. Erik claimed a divan to the side of one window and I sat in a rather punishing chair on the other side. I made a show of checking the angle, of assuring myself that an alert Martin Parish would not be able to see me through the glass.

Erik nodded approvingly. "Well," he said, "we've got at least an hour to kill. Shall we talk about our feelings, share personal experiences, come to terms with inner conflicts?"

Amber said nothing.

"Maybe you should start, Erik. Tell us, for instance, what you were doing here in Amber's bedroom on July the third and fourth."

He chuckled, but his eyes moved from me to Amber and

back again in a reflexive action he could not control. "Let's see, I was . . . getting ready to strip down and have a wank like Marty used to. Yes, that's it. Dream of Amber and shake hands with the unemployed."

I laughed quietly. "When, exactly, did your glasses lose that screw because it was stripped? Before wank or after? My guess is after."

"You've lost me already, Russ. Although you genuine law-enforcement types often do."

"On your cleanup detail the next night, a bad screw worked loose from your glasses. That left one to hold the temple on, but barely. You didn't know it was gone until this morning, when you put them on in your study. There were other things on your mind. I found it right here on this carpet on the Fourth of July. This afternoon I went back to your place after the meeting. And guess what? It fits perfectly."

Erik smiled a little uneasily. "Lots of screws fit lots of things, Russ. Maybe you should have tried a pair of Martin's glasses."

"He's got twenty/fifteen vision. And you only wear your glasses when the *world won't see you*, or you think it shouldn't. It didn't on the Fourth. Because you were painting over these walls, trying to cover up the spray-paint you'd used twenty-four hours earlier."

Erik glanced casually across at Amber, then turned back to me. "I get the distinct feeling you two are having a laugh on Professor Wald."

"I haven't really laughed in almost two years, Erik."

"Then maybe you could be a mensch and tell me what the hell you're talking about."

I removed the videotape from one pocket and held it out. Wald's face turned blank, and even in the diminished light I could see the color fade from it. I brought out the .357 and set the butt of it on the arm of my chair, positioning the barrel in line with Wald's heart.

Amber gasped.

Wald looked quickly to her, then back. For a moment, his entire body seemed spring-loaded, poised to explode. Then he leaned back more comfortably into the cushions of the divan and crossed his legs. He managed a smile. "Fire away, Russ."

"Not yet," I said. "I'd like you to hold very still while Amber comes up behind you and takes the pistol from the holster under your coat." At this point, I lifted my magnum and married its sights to the center of Erik Wald's chest. "If you touch her, I'll blow your heart out. And I'd like to make a small prediction right now that the sidearm she'll take away from you, Wald, will be my own Gold Cup forty-five. Let's run the experiment now, just to see."

His face, partially in shadow, took on the appearance of pale marble. A layer of sweat had come to his skin and the dim light turned it to an otherworldly shine. Even in his posture of repose, I clearly sensed that Wald's entire being was capable at any second of quick and decisive motion.

Amber approached behind him.

"Spread your arms," I said.

Wald did.

Amber's hand glided beneath the left lapel of the linen coat and reappeared with the bright shape of my stainless automatic positioned between her long and perfect fingers. Erik did not move. Amber retreated to the bed, dropped the gun on the cover, then stood looking at me.

"Shall we watch the preamble to your polar-bear tape?" I asked.

"Sure," said Wald.

"*You bastard, Erik,*" Amber hissed. "I wish Russell could shoot you right now. You're not good enough for a prison."

"I'm not going to any prison. You can be sure of that."

"Naw, Erik couldn't cut it in stir," I said. "Why don't you tell us how you and Grace planned to kill Amber but killed her sister instead? How you planted her body in my freezer and played Martin into it? How you started screwing Grace when she was just a girl, and scared her enough to believe her own mother was having her tortured? When you've explained all that, we'll just break up the party here and go our separate ways. You'll be back in time to watch all the home movies you want. See, Wald, you were right about one thing—I'm not willing to take down my daughter just to get to you."

Something of Wald's coiled energy seemed to relax just a little. "Jesus," he said, finally. "And here I thought you'd want to know something closer to the truth, such as how I managed to save Grace's butt from Parish for this long. Yours, too, buddy Russ."

I set the gun on the armchair and folded my hands in my lap. "Okay. That's what I want to know."

"Then I'm happy to tell you, though it breaks my promise to Grace. She dreaded the thought of . . . falling in your eyes, Russ. I knew Grace was scared enough to make an attempt on Amber. I'd seen those scars on her feet. I'd seen everything she'd gone through with loving mom here. She left my house late on the third, half drunk, with a thirty-two. I followed her. What I found was one dead woman in Amber's room, right here, and Grace standing there puking on herself. I took her to my place. Parish did it, absolutely. He wanted to frame the Eye, but when he realized he'd gotten Alice instead of Amber, it made more sense to come back and sanitize the scene and hope no one would have anything to report. If someone did, they'd report to *him,* anyway."

I smiled inwardly, though I don't know what was showing on my face then. Amber's look of hatred was unabated.

"That's a good story, but it doesn't match Grace's. She told me everything. And she's told Martin Parish, too."

I knew I was on my most tenuous ground here, lying absolutely that Grace had confided in me. If the bond between them was as strong as I feared it might be, Wald would dig in his heels and hold fast. If not, he might begin to weaken and contradict himself.

He shrugged. "Whatever Grace told you is from the mouth of one crazy babe. I've done what I can to protect her. I've done what I can do to help. Yes, I've made love to her, and she to me. I admit my pure unadulterated desire for her and proudly cop to the fact that I was screwing her while you, Amber, were trying to make me grovel at your royal feet. Boy, did that feel good. I'll also admit that I taught her to be the most sensual, tender woman in the world. But I give up. If she wants me to take the rap for this one, then all I can say is, it's time to get a good lawyer."

He stood. I took the gun. "You're saying we'll see you in court, Erik?"

"Last place I plan to end up. You know, that would ruin my whole career. You can't live down a scandal like this, even when the DA throws up his hands and realizes he doesn't have a case. But Parish and Haight? An unbeatable combination with regard to nailing *your* butt, Russ. You'll be in court long before my sorry ass gets there. That bastard Parish gets hold of something, he's tougher to shake than a pit bull, and he's got hold of you. He's a moron, but he's a determined one. You're holding the bag, Russell. You're the one who buried Alice Fultz in your own backyard. By the time you get Martin's fangs off your balls, you'll forget what it even felt like to have a pair."

He smiled and looked at Amber. "You? Look at yourself. The world's prettiest cunt."

Amber stepped forward, then slapped Wald across the face.

He leaned with the blow, refusing to surrender his smile. "You people are below me. You can't touch me. A money-grubbing whore and a dumb ex-cop who thinks he can write. It's a wonder anything as . . . beautiful as Grace could have come out of you."

Amber's voice shook as she spoke. For once in my life, I sensed not one bit of acting in her. "You won't get away with any of this, Erik. For what you did to Grace. And what you did to Alice."

"You dumb bitch—I've already gotten away with it. My only real regret is that I never quite had the pleasure of smearing your brains over this carpet."

With this, Martin Parish stepped from one of the two walk-in closets that house Amber's considerable wardrobe. In one hand, he held the tape recorder, its red light still blinking, and in the other his monstrosity of a revolver, the .44 Magnum.

"Woof, woof," he said.

Wald looked at him, then at Amber, then at me. "We all know that tape's inadmissible. That's the last thing I'll say without my lawyers. Well, second to the last. The last is, fuck all you dullards. I'm just plain better than you and I proved it. I'll marry your daughter while you rot in jail, Monroe. Parish—don't even think you can touch me. I'll grind you up like the dog meat you are. Stick with your case against Russell here. You and I can go on fighting crime together."

Parish shook his head. "Sure, Erik. We know. Until you manage all that, though, put out your hands so I can cuff you. You're about to be questioned in the death of Alice Fultz and the statutory rape of Grace Wilson. We'll make that call to your lawyer from the county building."

"Don't forget possession of stolen goods," I said.

"Namely, my automatic. If all had gone according to Erik's new plan, some beat cops would be discovering a murder-suicide here in this room, sometime tomorrow morning.."

When Parish had locked Wald's hands behind his back, he turned Erik around to face him and slugged him in the stomach so hard, I could hear the wind whistle from Wald's throat. Wald staggered but somehow remained erect, his martial-arts training no doubt putting him in good stead. So Parish hit him again, and Erik, gasping for air, went down like a dynamited building.

"What a beautiful sight," said Amber. "Not that I could *ever* recall it happening."

■   ■   ■

Parish called Dispatch, summoned the two units that were waiting down the street, and gave the go-ahead for the arrest of Grace Wilson, who, as we had predicted, was waiting in Wald's home for his triumphant return. Parish reported that the Eye had not been apprehended at LAX, in spite of massive, if somewhat belated, efforts on the part of the Sheriff's Department and Airport Authority.

Five minutes later, four large deputies took Erik away. The three of us—Amber, Parish, and I—then stood there in Amber's bedroom, where all this madness had begun. I cannot vouch for what the others were thinking, but for myself, I felt as if I was on one side of a shaky and dangerous pyramid that had nearly toppled over and killed us all. And there was still little stability to it, because what remained as fact were Marty's and my twin obsessions with this woman, our partaking in her past, our invasion of her present, and a terrible truth about Grace that we had finally begun to understand. Of lesser importance, but still very much in my thoughts, was the fact that Martin and

I had been so completely convinced of the other's guilt, so subtly pitted against each other by Wald. I felt that I had betrayed an honest man who was once a friend. The puzzled and uncomfortable expression that hung upon Martin's face suggested he felt the same.

About my daughter, I could only feel sickness, guilt, and remorse.

■　　　　　■　　　　　■

Later that night, as I lay alone in my bed, exhausted but unable to sleep, my thoughts began to drift toward Isabella, sleeping alone in her contraption-heavy bed at the hospital. I began to make a mental list of all I could do to prepare the house for her arrival. I was thankful that we had had the wheelchair lift installed when we did—loud and obnoxious as it was—because she would be needing it all the more in the coming days. I resolved to get fresh flowers for every room in the house and to wash all the windows inside and out, because sunlight was a constant delight to Isabella Monroe.

When the phone rang at 3:00 A.M., I was sure of the caller.

"You made it," I said.

"I boarded three minutes after talking to you. I was sorry to have missed all the activity. But maybe the good Los Angeles police found another nigger to beat up and the night wasn't a total waste for them."

"Where are you?"

"Sh-sh-sh-sh. Your intercept will tell you that. In a land far away. I'm done in Orange County for now. Tell your r-r-readers that. Then tell them I'll come back whenever I'm ready. It was a terrible thing you did, making them believe I am William Ing. And to have forced that pathetic Mary Ing to identify m-m-my voice. If the people had understood my mission, they would have supported me."

"I doubt it."

"You underestimate the intelligence and power of the white man and woman."

There was static on the line and a background sound suggesting hollowness and human activity. I wondered whether he was calling from an airport.

"We know who you really are," I said.

"You don't even know what I used to be," he said. "You are like street sweepers. You find the garbage only when it falls."

"What do you want?"

"How is Isabella?"

"We don't talk about Isabella. Parish took down Wald and Grace for Alice Fultz."

After a moment of silence, the Eye laughed again, that serpentine escape of breath. "I'll miss Orange County. In your article about our farewell conversation, tell all our friends and readers that the Midnight Eye will return when he is most needed. The cleansing will continue."

"I've got a message for you, too. I'm not writing any more about you. You want to talk, call someone else. You're not news here anymore, Ing. Have a nice life, and die soon."

With this, I hung up. I called Carfax.

"New York City," he said with a hint of annoyance in his voice. "JFK airport."

29

I brought Isabella home two days later, on Monday, the twelfth of July. Through a home-health-care network, I arranged—at an affordable rate—for a live-in nurse to be with us for one week. Her name was Dee. She was a very tall, big-boned woman with the round, smooth face of an infant and huge, gentle hands. It was difficult to tell how old she was, and I did not ask. Her hair was straight and honey-colored and she wore it back in a ponytail. She must have weighed well over 180 pounds.

Isabella slept most of the time. Our conversations were short; the trauma of what had happened overtook her often and without warning. We sat on the deck and looked at the canyon. Isabella was happy to see Our Lady—the formation of the supine woman with the lights of the city showing up from her middle—and even laughed when Black Death perched on a power pole and turned his unbecoming pink head our way.

Izzy ate heartily the meals prepared by Dee, who turned out to be a very good cook. Dee would never join us at the table, however; she took her meals in the guest room and left Izzy and me all the privacy we needed. But when it was time for Izzy's bath or nap or medication, Dee took over with a quietly proprietary air and dismissed me with a shy smile. It was obvious that Dee was investing more in Isabella than the simple reality of X hours for Y dollars. Isabella was hers, if only for a week, and Dee was not about to let one bit of her concern go unapplied.

During the first day following the arrests of Wald and Grace, Martin Parish kept me informed by phone of the status of the questioning. After nearly a full day of separate, high-pressure, relentless interrogation, Martin's entire team of detectives had gotten nothing from Grace or Wald except slightly elaborated versions of what Wald had told me that night at Amber's: that he had followed Grace there and together they had found Alice's body. They were both professing innocence and extreme outrage at what was being done to them.

With almost twenty-four hours having passed since their detention, only twenty-four more remained before either charges were brought or Grace and Erik were released. I was astonished to find Parish actually considering that possibility. An unsteadiness had crept into his voice as that first day lingered on without results, and by late that night he was openly doubtful that either Grace or Wald would contradict each other, much less confess. I asked him for the tenth time to let me see her.

"No. We need to do more than just place them there," he said. "They've rehearsed the story well. No chinks, yet. I'm trying to pry Grace away, let her believe he's selling her out. No go. They anticipated that. I managed two search warrants for the weapon, but we both know they won't find it. I got the judge to give us the porno stuff and any clothing that will match up with the fibers Chet has in the lab."

"Those fibers could just as well be from our clothes, Martin."

"Yeah. I may have a trump card in that box of evidence I collected myself. Chain of custody is going to be a problem. Winters is uh . . . fairly furious with some of my . . . activities. I'll keep you posted."

"Let me see Grace."

"Not while this is going on. It just wouldn't be a good idea."

"She might talk to me."

"For the first time in her life? She's acting more like she'd spit in your face."

"Time is short, Martin."

He considered for a moment. "Tomorrow afternoon, if we haven't made any progress."

"What did the airlines tell you on the Eye?"

"He traveled Continental under the name of Mike Eis. Tall guy, smooth-shaven, scars on his face. Cash only."

"And?"

"The trail went stone-cold at JFK."

∎   ∎   ∎

By noon the next day, Parish had made no progress at all with Grace and Wald. Peter Haight was feverishly trying to build charges against Wald for statutory rape, and one against Grace for breaking and entering, but these were thin shadows of the actual events that had occurred at their hands, and we all knew that shortly after midnight we would either have to spring them or charge them on shaky evidence. Chet Singer was doing legitimate workups on Martin's bootlegged evidence.

Parish let me into the interrogation room at slightly after 3:00 P.M. Grace was dressed in her street clothes still, and she was not handcuffed. Parish and two lumpish deputies waited outside the closed door, watching, I knew, through the window that to us inside was nothing more than a mirror.

Grace looked exhausted and offered me little more than an expression of tired recognition.

"Russell."

"Hi, Grace."

"Have you come to ask about my last meal?"

"It's not that bad."

She said nothing. She remained seated, hands on her lap and her long legs crossed beneath the table. She looked at the mirror, gave whoever was watching a little wave, then sighed deeply and rested her arms on the table in front of her.

"I'm tired."

"They working you over pretty good?"

She nodded. "It's just the hours. They can sleep and work in shifts. I have to sit here and look at my ex-stepfather's cowlike face. Sorry, Marty," she called toward the mirror. "It's a cute face, too. I mean, I always liked cows. I got some cow napkin holders at home. Somewhere."

"How long were you and Wald together?"

"I was thirteen when he was seeing Mom. It started then. You know, I've told *them* all about that. I might not have been a consenting adult, but I was consenting. I grew up fast. So what?" She yawned.

"Did it start as a way to get back at Amber?"

Grace nodded.

"Who hatched the idea of getting rid of her?"

"We never *had* that idea, Russell. That's what I've been saying for a day and a half now."

I sighed myself then, partly out of frustration, partly out

of knowledge of the pain that I was certainly causing my girl. "Is there anything I can do for you?"

"Make them let me go."

"They think you killed Alice. They're not going to let you go until you tell them what really went down."

"In that case, Russell, what on earth *could* you do for me?"

"I've been thinking about that."

"And?"

"Could I just offer some thoughts?"

"Offer away."

"It seems to me that the hatred you felt for your mother was . . . well founded. There were bad times, lots of misunderstanding, jealousy, competition. Amber admits as much."

"Large of her."

"And what I think happened was that Erik manipulated you with that. Did you know they found the netsuke you and Amber fought over so long, in Erik's house? They also found some phone records that establish communication with the two men who burned your feet. Amber didn't hire them. Wald did. It took him years to feed your fears but only a few months to twist your mind to the point where you were scared enough to commit a murder. He used you, girl."

She looked at me rather blankly then, and I fully realized the despair of her heart and the fatigue of her body. "I actually loved him."

"I understand that. Some things about Erik can be loved."

"You're not so dumb, after all."

"It doesn't take a genius to see a girl can fall in love with a guy. Handsome. Smart. Mommy's castoff."

"God," she said quietly. "Love."

"Yeah."

She breathed deeply and leveled her beautiful eyes on

me. I wanted only one thing more than to put my arms around her, and that one thing was to hear her acknowledge the truth.

"You know, the first time we talked about it . . . it was kind of a joke. A perfect-crime fantasy. It was fun to . . . speculate. But then when Mom started getting the men after me and threatening me, it all of a sudden started sounding reasonable. It kind of takes you over. Like, if you talk about something enough, or plan it enough, you pretty much have to go through with it at some point. It . . . gets real. And I was so afraid."

Oh, how I understood the insane logic of that statement! Had I passed it down to Grace through my genes, this compulsion to make the imagination real, to act upon thoughts so that thoughts *became* acts? Was there perhaps in Grace, as in myself, some weakness of the faculties dividing impulse from action?

"I know. Can I tell you a true story?"

"Sure, Russ."

"About three weeks after Izzy was diagnosed, I got real drunk and went out to the hillside with my revolver. I wasn't sure why. I sat down and looked down at the house, the lights of the city. I prayed to God that He'd make the nightmare stop, that He'd cradle Isabella in His healing arms. I offered Him my soul instead. Then I emptied all the cartridges but one from the cylinder, closed it and spun it and put it to my head. If He let me live, it was my sign that He was with us. If not, it was a simple trading of one life for another. A stupid idea, right? But the more I thought about it, the more sense it made, and the more actual that gun became. I had gone that far, and I *had* to follow through. At the last second, I lowered the gun, pointed it at the hillside, and pulled the trigger. My hand jerked and the sound blasted into my ears. I had my answer then, at least to my own satisfaction: Go home, get sober, take care of your wife, and don't fuck with the Lord anymore. That's as deep as my faith ever got. I didn't even think another prayer until that night we went out swimming in the ocean."

Grace betrayed no emotion to me, but something about her exhaustion seemed to deepen even more. Then, a wry smile came to her lips. "I'm sorry for all that's happened to you and Isabella. I wish there was something I could do to make it better."

"There is."

She waited.

"Tell these men what happened. And understand that Erik will do everything he can to make you take this fall alone."

Grace drew a deep breath.

I could only imagine the silence behind our one-way mirror. Grace eyed the thing, then returned her gaze to me. Her eyes were moist.

"Would you do one more thing?" I asked.

"Why not?"

"Call me Dad, or Pop, or anything but Russell."

She smiled very weakly. "I would accept a hug now, Pops."

■   ■   ■

That Tuesday evening, I picked up my mail and headed directly into town to do the grocery shopping. In the market parking lot, I fanned through the letters, bills, and catalogs—you might imagine how Izzy, confined to a wheelchair, loved those catalogs—and found to my great dismay a postcard canceled in New York City, July 10. The picture on the front was of the Flatiron building, New York's first "skyscraper," and where my editor works. On the back was the following, in an almost illegible scrawl:

Dear Russell—New York a lovely city with so many . . . possibilities! Aren't your publishers in this building? Am flossing regularly and considering minor cleansing action, but it would take an army of crusaders such as myself to dent this cesspool of humanity. Miss OC. Cuddles, ME.

My scalp actually crawling in the heat, I set the card carefully in the glove compartment of the car, knowing that the Eye had wiped it clear of fingerprints. But it would never hurt to try. The people in Documents—Handwriting Analysis, to be specific— would be more than happy to have it.

As I walked the familiar aisles of our grocery store, a deep, if fragile, sense of contentment began to come over me. I shopped with Isabella in mind, picking out all the things she loved to eat. Few things can soothe a troubled soul like the simple act of loving another person. Every bag of produce, can, or jar, I touched with the knowledge that it was for Isabella, and that if I could not stem the sickness in her head, I might at least comfort her body with the fruits of my labor. There were other blessings to be counted: the *Journal* checks had begun to come in; Nell, my agent, had gotten a modest offer for the Midnight Eye book and I accepted it—while both my publishers and I realized that the end of that book was far from being written; I had witnessed the beginnings of surrender in my daughter. I stopped by the health-food store for some tea that Isabella especially liked.

Then I loaded the groceries into the car and walked down to the beach to watch the sunset. It was an odd hour, because the dry, searing heat of the last week was getting ready to break. Far out over the horizon, a bank of moist dark clouds hovered, and as the sun dipped into them, its bottom flattened and the cloud tops seemed to ignite. When the sun had fallen fully behind the bank, it glowed there, softly, like an orange wrapped in tissue, and sent angled bars of light down onto the ocean. A few minutes later, it emerged beneath the cloud bank and touched the water. As it sank, the clouds caught fire from below and soon the whole western sky was a blanket of black and orange patchwork settling over a flame-touched sea. I took a deep drink from my flask.

I began to see more clearly the tasks that lay ahead. Isabella would require more and more care, and there would be victories as well as defeats. I hoped that what joys we could find together would mitigate the agonies; I prayed that through it all we would keep our love alive; that if it was the desire of the heavens to kill her here on earth, we could still manage a laugh, a smile, a touch. My feelings of just a few weeks ago, of wanting so badly to escape, had diminished. The tug of the whiskey was still there, but it was a tug—not an irresistible yank. I felt slower as I sat there on the board-walk bench, more able to occupy the moment. Amber had given me something in her desperately sweet surrender: She had broken the bonds of my own making, allowing me to grasp the heart of an obsession and understand that once possessed so fully, an object of desire can no longer hold such a tidal sway. Did I want Amber again? Oh, yes. One cannot eradicate genetic imperatives. But I no longer believed that she, or the secret life that went with her, was an anti-dote to the actual one I would now begin to live. As I looked out over the darkening water, it occurred to me that the core of a life is not what one will lose but what one will fight to keep.

And I realized one more thing as I sat there, which was this: I would never truly lose Isabella. Because some people never shine, no matter how much they are given; and others will shine forever, no matter how much from them is taken away. Isabella was a light. Shine on, my dearest wife!

The car phone rang as I was heading out Laguna Canyon Road.

"Hello, Russell."

I felt my scalp tighten and a cool sweat moving from my palms to the steering wheel.

"I told you not to call."

"That was rude. I just wanted to ask you one more thing. In your article about my departure, will you remark that queers of either sex will not be safe when I come back? I didn't mean to discriminate against them, but I couldn't remember if I'd been specific."

"You can't come back. Everyone knows your face. Everyone knows your name. It's just a matter of time before the New York cops come to your door. Then it's back to California for a long trial, a couple of appeals, plenty of prison time, and the gas chamber. Winters offered me a front-row seat for that. I'll be there."

"*Sh-sh-sh.* You cutups! I wish there was a way for me to show you how important this last article is. Just because I've left the county doesn't mean I don't care. I want to be remembered accurately. Remember to be accurate, Russell. You have professional codes to live up to."

With this, he hung up. I dialed the Sheriff's Department immediately and got Carfax.

"It was a Brooklyn number," he said, the excitement clear in his voice. "We've got the address. He's meat."

Back home, arms loaded with grocery bags, I managed to let myself in the front door. I had just kicked it shut behind me when I turned and saw Dee lying on the stairway with a bullet hole in the middle of her back and a streamlet of blood dripping down the steps.

In front of me, through dim light, something moved. A light went on. The Midnight Eye loomed not ten feet from me, bearded, bewigged, wrapped in a rotting green blanket, pointing a small automatic with a large silencer directly at the bags still clutched to my gut.

"Hi, Russ."

My first reflex was to look up the stairway, past Dee's body, to the bedroom where I had last seen my wife alive. The bags dropped to the floor. I leaned in the direction of the stairs, then held myself.

"She's s-s-sleeping," said the Eye. "I looked in on her. Don't worry. *Sh-sh-sh.* Now, step toward me slowly, with your hands away from your body."

I did so. I stopped to look upstairs again, to perhaps see a shadow cast by her breathing body, perhaps hear some tiny sound that would indicate life. The rage that rang from my stomach, up my backbone, and into my ears nearly deafened me. My breath was short.

"Yes, like that," he said. "Here . . . sit at your table."

I saw that my typewriter and a fresh stack of paper had been placed on the dining room table. I walked toward it, still straining, even through the dreadful ringing in my ears, for some sound from the bedroom above.

"Sit."

"I need to see Izzy," I said.

"I told you, she's sound asleep. Deeply asleep."

"May I see for myself?"

"You may not, you shit-sucking liar! You cheat. You coward. You *sit!*"

I pulled back the heavy dining room chair and sat before the typewriter.

"I took the seven o'clock out this morning."

"How did you make that last call register in Brooklyn?"

"I have call forwarding in my little cage in Brooklyn. Your CNI intercept tells you that the call originated there. Actually, I made it from your study and routed it through New York."

"Clever."

"All of these gadgets and tricks are in the public realm now. It's part of the peace dividend. Most people don't know that. Most people are idiots. All I used was some very basic electronic know-how. Of course, two years at the central phone office in Laguna didn't hurt me."

As I sat there, I got my first truly good look at the Midnight Eye. He was as tall as we suspected—six three perhaps—and heavily, though softly, built. Even from this distance, it was easy to see that the beard and disheveled red-brown hair were false. But aside from his size and the piecemeal manner of his disguise, little about the man himself commanded the kind of dread we had all felt looking at the things he had done. His eyes were a very dark brown. They had a brightness to them, a luminosity that was intensified by the ceiling lamp. They were slow eyes, deliberate and calm. His skin was pale, and I noted that his fingers, wrapped around the handle of the gun, were plump, with longish nails. His legs were heavy and large, and his feet quite big, which gave him a bottom-heavy, weighted appearance. Magnifying this effect was his slight pigeon-toed stance. A flicker of anger charged his eyes when mine met them again.

"It's not polite to stare."

From what I could judge from Mary Ing's earlier pictures, I was now looking at a disguised version of William Fredrick Ing. Rather, reverse-disguised, to mimic an earlier manifestation of himself. What did he really look like now, beneath the fake hair and beard? Wald and I had been right—the Midnight Eye had been impersonating an "other" all along, playing a part in his own ritual. As we had suspected, Ing had been able to work, move about in public, and continue his murderous nights because in real life, he looked little like the beast he could become. Now I knew why he had been so nonchalant about our presenting his picture to the public, precisely because it was an image that no one would recognize. Except, of course, his own mother.

"You have one m-m-more article to write," he said. "I'll tell you what to say. Put in the paper."

I scrolled in a sheet and threw back the carriage return. Again I trained my ears for some sound of life in the room above. Nothing. Not so much as a rustle of sheets, a breath.

"Now," he said. "The first two sentences should read, The 'Midnight Eye' is not William Ing, as earlier stories have c-c-claimed. I met him personally just last night and he assured me of this."

I typed the sentences.

"Do you like the lead?" he asked.

"I'd change it a little."

"How?"

"I think I'd say . . . William Fredrick Ing, the notorious Midnight Eye, visited me last night in my home. First, he killed my wife's nurse, then my wife, and by the time you read this, he will have killed me, too."

"No. Don't get ahead of things. You have some of it right, and some of it wrong. You don't have to worry about Isabella. *Sh-sh-sh.* And I have only one name—the Midnight Eye. Ing is a person who used to be and is no more. You must remain accurate as a reporter, right?"

"That's right."

"Next sentence: He is a tall and powerful man, who commands respect even with a glance of his dark eyes."

I typed it. "He's a tall and powerful man," I said, "who was picked on when he was a kid and didn't have any friends. He didn't have much of a family life, either. Very early, he began a secret life of his own."

"No! If you write one word of that, I'll kill you and finish it myself. I can t-t-type!" He extended the gun toward me, its dark barrel a condensed version of the black eternity into which he would certainly blow me.

"I'm just saying it," I said. "I didn't write it. I'm saying you were a kid who got torn up by his own dogs on the Fourth of July. You walked in on your parents and got slapped for your concern. You were a miserable kid. You weren't always the Midnight Eye. Why not include that?"

"Because it isn't relevant."

"Can you explain?"

"The Midnight Eye *was* born. He did not develop. He was chosen. Your next paragraph goes like this: According to the Eye himself, he has had murderous impulses for almost all his life. He began by killing animals. As a young man, he saw the rape of the county by foreigners, people who came to Orange County only to make money. The Midnight Eye then realized his calling."

I typed out the graph and waited, staring into his dark, bright eyes.

He continued. "And as the Midnight Eye's body grew lean and strong, his urges became tied to a greater good."

"The good of killing people not like him?"

"The good of killing the parasites and leeches. The good of clean sand and skies. Of earth in balance, and all people in their places."

"I'd change that."

"How?"

"I'd say, He looked for God and when he didn't find him, he began to think he was God himself."

"Not true. I am merely a servant. Write that! The Midnight Eye claims he is only a servant."

"Of what?"

"Of . . . history. Of progress toward the future. Of . . . redreaming our way out of what has gone wrong here."

I wrote this down.

Ing stood for a long moment, apparently lost for words.

"Can I see your face?" I asked.

"Gaze."

"The one under all the stage stuff."

"You see my face as it is meant to be seen."

"You're going to kill me, right?"

"Yes, of course."

"Then let me see your face. Let me see the Midnight Eye that no one else can see. Give me this . . . exclusive."

Ing seemed to ponder this. He looked at me, then at his gun, then back to me. "When I saw your wife upstairs, I realized she would suffer more if I left her alive. How could you marry a filthy Mexican?"

"I loved her. I still do."

"You would compromise your sperm with her egg?"

"That won't happen for us."

"Good. Good for the place we call home. Now . . . next sentences: The Eye told me that the county must be cleansed, and cleansed thoroughly. After a brief sabbatical on the East Coast, the Eye returned here yesterday to continue his work. If possible, the Eye is just as impressive in person as he is through his generous and self-effacing acts."

Generous and self-effacing acts, I thought, like the Fernandez couple. Like the Ellisons and Wynns and Steins. Like all the animals. Like Dee, and probably Izzy, and—shortly—myself.

Something then dawned on me. "You hate couples, don't you? Married people."

"I loathe you."

"Why?"

"The dependence, the way you cling to one another, the way you are . . . exclusive and out only for material gain."

"You detest our happiness. Is it because you've never had it? Are you jealous?"

"Man was meant to be alone. Marriage is a necessary aberration for continuing the race. Priests are celibate for good reason."

"You ever had a woman?"

Ing's gaze hardened and I could see his hand stiffen on the gun. "Next," he said. "The Eye says that any and all minorities are welcome to leave the county, but this must be done soon. No one offering a home for sale will be harmed; no one packing to leave will be stopped. All who stay will live in fear of violent death."

I wrote out the paragraph. The terrible ringing in my ears still had not abated. I was having trouble getting my fingertips to the keys of the typewriter.

Ing was behind me. I could see his reflection in the mirrored wall. He was reading, from a distance, over my shoulder. As he leaned forward, I could see the club hanging over his left shoulder, exactly where Chet Singer had predicted it would be. The Eye had not cleaned it. It was clotted with hair and blood, a patina of gore now dried and blackened by time. The combined smells of the club and the Midnight Eye were almost overpowering.

"Next, Russell. The Eye stated he had to kill me because

I had been dishonest with him. The Eye values honesty above all other traits in human beings. I had been led to believe that the Eye was William Ing, which he is clearly not. But because of that untruth, I must go the way of the others, whose cleansing makes the air of this place clearer and cleaner with each passing day."

I wrote nothing. "Are you going to sign this?" I asked.

"My signature will be left all over this house."

In fact, I thought, it mattered not at all. But I was grasping for time, and for some idea—no matter how desperate—of how to keep him from shooting me in the back.

"A signature would help . . . dramatize it," I said.

"In your blood?"

"Very good," I said. "And I think you should say something about what people can do to save themselves."

"They can go away."

"Can your offer a time? A kind of grace period while they make arrangements to leave?"

I could see the Eye pondering this. His reflection was clear. He lifted the gun hand to rub the side of his face and came a step closer to my chair.

"Offer them one month," I continued.

"No! Too long!"

"Two weeks?"

"Shut up! Shut up while I th-th-think."

Into the silence that surrounded Ing's thought came a shrill mechanical screech from upstairs, followed by the groan of a motor. The lift!

I watched Ing look up, startled. And in that moment, I used all of the strength I could summon to lock my hands on the typewriter, pivot, and hurl the heavy machine into the chest of the Midnight Eye. Then I was on him. My forward charge caught him low and I drove him clear across the kitchen, slamming him ferociously against the refrigerator. I heard his gun thud against the hardwood floor. I found his throat with my hands, but as I had feared—and as I had experienced as a deputy on the beat—the strength of the furious and insane can be prodigious. His hands closed over mine and pulled them from his throat in one grunting motion that left me spread-armed and looking helplessly into Ing's wide dark eyes. It can only have been luck that allowed me to act first. I brought my knee up hard and felt it penetrate the softness of his groin. He screamed and went momentarily limp as I pulled free one arm and landed a chopping right-hand blow that struck him exactly where I had hoped—on his temple. He shuddered and I felt his body sag. I threw a wide left hook, harnessing all of my momentum from the first blow and aiming for his jaw. What happened next seemed to take place in one second at the most: I saw his right hand reach up and intercept my fist in midair. His body hardened with a fresh fury and his left arm clamped around my neck and drew me—like a combine gathering a shaft of wheat—snugly against his stinking body. I pushed off from the floor with a throttled groan and ran us both back against the table, into which we crashed, rolled, and landed on the carpet—both of Ing's powerful arms now locked around my neck and my breathing all but choked off. With my fingers, I found his hair, which I yanked—only to feel the wig slide off in my hands! Then I found his eyes and dug my thumbs in with what diminishing energy I could find. I could hear his labored piglike breathing just above my head, and I could hear, too, the groaning descent of Isabella's wheelchair lift as it landed in its platform on the floor. My thumbs sank in! Ing bellowed with pain, and in the instant he reflexively reached for his face, I broke free of his clench, brought both of my hands from his eyes to his throat, and tightened my fingers as if over the last tree branch between me and the abyss.

I turned him over and squeezed harder, trying to bring

my inferior weight to bear. But just as the air rushed into my lungs and fresh blood surged into my head, I saw Ing's hand extend and close over the gun. I yelled and called upon my last reserve of muscle to choke the life out of him before that gun could be turned at me. It was not enough. His hand closed over the grip and his finger slipped inside the trigger guard. At that instant, when I would have to release his neck in order to defend myself against the gun, I saw in the far-right side of my vision a figure standing over us. Suddenly, Isabella's quad cane smashed down over the gun, pinning wrist and weapon against the carpet. I could look up at her for only an instant, but I will never forget what I saw there: Isabella in her blue pajamas, her turbaned head and swollen face, her weakened legs unsteady as she did her best to balance her weight over the handle of that thin cane, concentrating with all her considerable might upon the task of remaining upright. She swayed like a cotton-wood in a high wind. But, charged by her courage, I drew a new strength and applied myself to nothing at all on earth except wringing the life out of the monster in my hands. I glared into his fierce eyes and bellowed myself, a roar that echoed through the room around us and seemed to settle in William Fredrick Ing's very eyes, which bulged, quivered, then focused on me a look of penetrating hatred that froze in place as I roared again, felt the bones in his throat popping beneath my fingers, and began slamming his lifeless head against the floor, again and again and again. Izzy's cane stood fast! When, breathless and emptied of all power, I rose upon my knees and released the throat, I looked up at Isabella, still wholly focused on maintaining balance on her damaged legs. Her eyes were closed and her gauze-wrapped head lifted as if to heaven. She swayed, righted herself, then swayed again. She began to fall. I caught her, still on my knees, and managed to settle her descending head into my left arm and guide her down gently to the floor. With my other hand, I took Ing's gun and planted the barrel of it against his head, should there be any life at all left in him. And with that gun in my right hand, extended, and Isabella's frail head crooked into the elbow of my left arm, I lay there, crucified to the carpet and unable to do anything but listen to the gasping of my own lungs and to the deeper, slower workings of Isabella's.

Slowly, our breathing became one rhythm. The ceiling lights shone down upon us. Sweat burned my eyes. I turned and looked at my wife. The wheelchair stood behind her, locked in place. Isabella's eyes were open now and she blinked slowly. I could see the quick pulse of cotton where her heart was beating. Her legs trembled from their effort.

"Is it over?" she whispered.

"It's over. It's over. It's over."

■   ■   ■

Martin Parish was the first to arrive. I welcomed him wordlessly, pointed to the body of Dee lying on the stairway, then led him into the living room, where Isabella sat again in her wheelchair and the Midnight Eye lay sprawled between kitchen and dining room.

"Hello, Isabella," he said softly.

"Hi, Marty."

"You okay?"

"I think I am."

Martin stood for a long moment over the body of the Eye. I stood beside Izzy. As I watched, Martin pulled off the false beard and set it down beside the Eye's head. What was revealed to us was quietly shocking: a rather plain but still handsome face marred by the scars of long ago; a straight, intelligent nose; high forehead giving way to thinning brown hair that now stood up in errant wisps; a pair of deep-set, very dark eyes, still open, that seemed more than anything else to be reflective of pain.

Martin shook his head and looked at us.

I stood above Isabella, my hands upon her still-trembling shoulders, and stared down at the lifeless man now occupying my kitchen floor.

Martin walked toward us and pointed at the couch. "Mind?"

"Go ahead," I said.

He sat heavily. "Eleven human lives. And his own miserable excuse for one."

"A cancer," said Isabella.

"We cured it a little late," said Martin.

"B-b-better than never," said Izzy.

After a long silence, through which the whine of distant sirens intensified, Martin cleared his throat and looked at me. "Grace cracked about an hour after you left. She and Wald did Alice and the cover-up—the whole show. We don't have to talk about this now if you don't want."

Isabella gasped quietly.

"Who actually did it?"

"Wald did the clubbing. They were going to get rich and married. She planted the body here, on Wald's instructions. Covered it with the trash bags, so it wouldn't stain her car. According to Grace, the club went off the end of the Aliso Pier, so we'll get our scuba team out at daylight."

"That's good."

"Dan's thinking about firing me for my hillside antics that night. It'll depend on any complaint you might or might not bring. I'm not going to ask any favors at all, but you should know, Russ, I was really convinced you'd done it. All I knew for sure was that I hadn't."

I could think of not one appropriate thing to say.

"Wald trailed some things past me a couple of times," he continued. "Bits of information about your finances, questions about your past relationship with Amber. I thought I was clever, making some solid conclusions. If I'd been smarter, I'd have smelled *him*, not you."

"Well, I believed it was you. We all got taken pretty good."

Martin looked down at Ing again. "Jesus. Maybe you two could take a vacation or something. Get away. Get clean."

"We will."

"Go after some birds this fall?"

"Let's think about that one, Marty."

30

Now it is winter and we can begin to forget. The wind blows, the rain steadies down, the old withers and the new awaits birth.

Mary Ing identified the body of her only son. The county seemed to breathe a collective sigh of relief at the death of the Midnight Eye—there were candlelight vigils in three cities to mourn his victims, endless editorials in the papers and on TV, and an intangible lightening of the human spirit that prevails over a place as surely as the weather.

But even with these, in the wake of the Eye's slaughter, the county looked at itself as it never had before. As psychologists and sociologists looked for patterns and causes for his behavior, they could find nothing in Ing's past truly to account for his character. There was the usual talk of biochemical imbalances and sociopathic personality disorder, but the Ing who surfaced in continuing interviews with his mother and people who knew him revealed little more than a typical Orange County kid, raised middle-class, publicly schooled, introduced to religion, who found himself with a job at the phone company and a rage he could not—or would not—control. His hatred of minorities remained largely inexplicable, though a small incident from his high school days—shy Billy Ing had developed affections for a Mexican girl who eventually jilted him—might have shed some tiny bit of light upon his development. The girl had kept his love poems, which were reprinted in the *Journal.* They were simple, touching, dear.

Moreover, the county's stark realization that Billy Ing was their native son coincided with a lingering economic recession that found property values falling, housing starts down, and a general feeling that the "Orange County Dream" had gone bad. For the first time in my memory—and I have lived here all my life—the easy optimism that had prevailed here for decades was suddenly shattered, and in its place arose a sense of self-doubt and questioning that the people here had heretofore done without. We were like a seemingly robust woman, just told by her physician that she has cancer. We were, in our souls, aghast. And though we could sleep with our screen doors open and our guns locked safely away, there was always the chance that the Midnight Eye would enter through our dreams, or that some new evil might arise from us and begin it all again.

Alice Fultz was exhumed, examined, returned to Florida by Amber for a more proper burial near her parents.

Grace, within the jail, is timid and withdrawn with everyone except for Isabella and me. We visit every day that Izzy feels strong enough, which is three or four times a week. Grace seems like a creature just born; she is curious about the world outside and seems to assume nothing.

In late fall, the preliminary hearing established sufficient evidence to try Grace and Wald on charges of murder. During that proceeding, the basics of what happened on the nights of

July 3 and 4—and in the days following—were outlined in Grace's deposition. She and Wald had entered the house together, though Wald had parked on a side street below Amber's home. (This accounted for Parish seeing Grace leave but not Erik.) Wald had carried the club in a tennis bag slung over his shoulder—not an altogether-odd accoutrement for Amber's neighborhood. They had found "Amber" sleeping, and Wald had killed her while Grace waited downstairs in the living room. It was only while they were setting out the evidence to direct authorities toward the Midnight Eye that the answering machine betrayed Amber's real location—she was calling from Santa Barbara to tell Alice she'd be late. It had been Wald's decision to try to cover up the whole thing—hoping to conceal fully one crime and save his framing of William Ing for another attempt on Amber. Together, they had returned to Amber's house the next afternoon and done their best to erase all evidence of what they had done. Grace was tasked with delivering Alice's body to my game freezer, which she had just accomplished late on the night of July the Fourth, when I found her waiting for me in my driveway.

Grace has been cooperative with Haight's attorneys, as well as her own, and from what Haight has told me, they will try to use Grace's testimony to convict Wald of first-degree murder, offering a more lenient prosecution of my daughter. This means he must be willing to drop the conspiracy charge against Grace, which, if proven in court, would qualify both Erik and her for the gas chamber. The DA seems more intent on nailing Wald well than on trying to prove the always-difficult conspiracy to commit murder. A second-degree rap against Grace will land her a sentence of about fifteen years. It appears that Wald's lawyers will argue that their client was seduced by a vengeful daughter, blinded by love, and eventually tricked into being in

Amber's house on July the Fourth. They have been predictably mum with regard to details.

Some portion of her inner life seems to have left Grace, and she is more tender now and sweet, resigned to the truth and its consequences.

It took me almost a month to muster the courage to ask her the question that had been torturing me most since I'd learned of her liaison with Erik Wald: Did Grace know that the .45 Wald ordered her to steal from my study would be used to kill both me and her mother? It was the first time since her arrest that Grace truly broke down, and the rush of her tears convinced me that Wald had convinced *her* that only Amber would be there the night that we had sprung the trap on him. I believe her, and it is what I want to believe.

She told me just the other day that she is almost ready to see her mother.

Amber has visited us twice at home. Needless to say, the undercurrents prevailing during a visit from Amber Mae do not encourage comfort or intimacy between husband and wife. Amber knows this, and her second visit—at our invitation—was, I believe, probably her last. She is off to New York next week. I walked her down the road to her car when she left that second time, an uneasy silence between us.

"Stay my friend, Russ. We're not getting any younger, you know."

"I know. I will. I am."

"Am I as bad a person as I seem, given certain standards of measure?"

"No. You made yourself and I love you for that."

"Made myself, like a science project. Crude, bubbly, but to no particular effect."

"You had a disadvantage."

"What was that?"

"You were alone."

She considered this. "You know something? I was always happiest that way."

"I know."

"Do you think that somehow, in a different time or place, it might really have been good for us, together?"

"Yes."

"That's a nice sentiment. Thank you."

"Does it matter?"

"If we think it does, then it does. Take care in Mexico, Russ."

"Thank you, Amber."

"Please know the offer is there, if you need money."

"We'll make it. That wasn't what I meant."

She smiled, actually blushing a little. I kissed her on the cheek, then held the car door open for her. The car is a red Maserati. It roared and echoed down the steep street. I could hear it all the way to Laguna Canyon Road. Amber Mae Wilson— surrounded by herself, and alone as always—guided her fast car around the bend of Our Lady of the Canyon and disappeared toward town.

■　　　　■　　　　■

Isabella greeted me back to the porch with a knowing look on her face. She had always been able to carry on a conversation without the words, and I wondered if, in the future, this subtle capacity might serve us well.

She was sitting in her wheelchair, with a cap on her head. I guided her over beside the patio bench, then sat next to her. Fall was approaching. A warm breeze filtered in from the desert and the shadows had begun to change.

We looked out at the canyon, my hand in hers. She squeezed it.

"This is what we have, Russ."

"Yes."

"It isn't what we wanted, but it's what we have."

"I'll take it, Izzy."

"No matter what happens, remember how I loved you. Please don't ever forget that."

∎   ∎   ∎

Next month, Isabella and I will leave for Mexico. Our destination is the unglamorous hamlet of Los Mochis, where Isabella's relations—a great many of whom she has never seen—live. She yearns to know the people from whom she came. They have prepared a home for us, cleaned and painted and furnished. It is reputed to have a nice view of a small valley. Joe and Corrine will arrive ahead of us.

There has been some assumption on the part of friends—unvoiced but nonetheless apparent—that we are going to Mexico for Isabella to die. When viewed from the outside, this idea is understandable. Three days ago, I received in the mail a condolence card from a distant friend, comforting me in my great loss. I had the notion that Izzy would get a laugh out of this ill-timed gesture but then decided she might not. I chucked it, sent the friend a photograph of Izzy holding a current newspaper (date visible!) and a brief note of correction. Isabella pressed me for an explanation of the newspaper ploy, but I refused, good-naturedly, to give one. She has since lost interest in the incident. We are not a man and woman who live in terror of secrets. The known is terror enough.

Our secret, if we have one, is this: We are going away next month not for death, but for life.